I USED TO BE A MOUSE

Mouse's eyes still glowed from beneath the chaise.

Aelliana sighed and sat down on the floor, her shoulder against the chaise and her legs curled under her.

"I had used to be a mous   know," she murmured. "Utterly craven.   own reflection and would scarcely   saving that I had students a   h. I thought that my   in the long term, it   om my existence threatened   re mouse-like behavior. Willingly, I   ngth away, but I was never safe, and I w   ays—*always* afraid.

"My fear almost killed me, though by then I had been growing bolder. But I had given so much of my strength away . . . it was a near thing, and I take no credit for my own survival. What I have learned is—mark me now!—life is not safe. Random action threatens us all. The choices we have are between fear and boldness, between joy and terror.

"If at all possible, I believe it is necessary to choose joy. One may survive no longer, nor ever be safe, but one's life will be worth living."

She sighed, and rested her head against the side of the chaise.

"I don't presume to make your choices for you," she told the cat, her eyelids drooping. "I merely offer the fruit of my own experience."

MOUSE & DRAGON

A New Liaden Universe® Novel

SHARON LEE & STEVE MILLER

BAEN

MOUSE & DRAGON

This is a work of fiction. All the characters and events portrayed in this book are fictional, and any resemblance to real people or incidents is purely coincidental.

A Baen Books Original

Baen Publishing Enterprises
P.O. Box 1403
Riverdale, NY 10471
www.baen.com

ISBN: 978-1-4516-3759-5

Cover art by David Mattingly

First Baen paperback printing, November 2011
Third Baen paperback printing, January 2013

Library of Congress Control Number: 2010009563

Distributed by Simon & Schuster
1230 Avenue of the Americas
New York, NY 10020

Pages by Joy Freeman (www.pagesbyjoy.com)
Printed in the United States of America

MOUSE & DRAGON

ONE

. . . .

The delm is the face and the voice of the clan, representing the interests of the clan to the world and solving those problems presented by the members of the clan. The clan's whole honor and *melant'i* reside with the delm.

—Excerpted from the Liaden
Code of Proper Conduct

ON BALANCE, DAAV YOS'PHELIUM THOUGHT AS HE strode down the hall toward his office, it had not been one of his better solvings.

Oh, it had produced the desired result—he was free of a marriage that could only have ended in tragedy, and had preserved the sanity of a fine pilot in the bargain. Surely, on first glance, it were done well enough.

On second glance, however, it was a shambles of a solving, unworthy of one who had stood as delm of Clan Korval for five heartbeats, let alone very nearly five Standard Years.

Clan Bindan held out to society's gossip, and himself to ridicule—those outcomes concerned him not

1

at all. He did regret that he had not been able to entirely protect Samiv tel'Izak, who had until scant hours ago been his affianced wife. But his failure to shield Aelliana—his pilot!—from the eyes of the curious and the tongues of the malicious was clumsy beyond excuse.

"Really, Daav," he told himself, his voice muted by the wooden walls, "you might have had a better result from Shan."

Alas, that his small nephew had been abed just when his advice had most been needed.

He opened the door to his office with rather more force than was necessary and was nearly at his desk before he registered the presence of another person in the room.

Stride unchecked, he glanced over his shoulder, where Master Trader Er Thom yos'Galan sat before a card table fetched from the game closet, his portcomm open, and a neat stack of papers resting on the rug at his side.

"Good morning, brother," Daav said, his voice brittle in his own ears. He moved 'round the desk and slapped the computer up. "Has your lifemate barred you from your own office?"

"My own office," Er Thom replied crisply, "would not inform me immediately you had arrived home."

Daav dropped into his chair, fingers flashing across the keys. "You might have left a message," he noted, his attention more than half on his screen. "I would have called."

"Would you? Is it ill-tempered to note that last evening you failed of calling—and this morning, as well."

Oh, Daav thought, hearing the thread of anger beneath the precise words.

"You will think it a poor enough excuse, but last evening there was no time to call. A life hung upon speed."

"Were you speedy enough?" Er Thom inquired.

"In fact, I was not," Daav answered, splitting his screen into quarters and assigning a task to each.

Er Thom was heard to sigh.

"Delm Guayar came to me this morning," he said.

Daav closed his eyes. Guayar had been his weapon of choice, whom he had primed with news of scandal, and aimed at Bindan. The other delm had done his work thoroughly, and had doubtless enjoyed the doing of it. It was not, however, to be expected that he would keep such a fine story in his vest pocket. Most especially not when Bindan could be expected to very soon shout the whole of it to the stars. *Of course*, he would next impart his news to Er Thom, who was, after all, Thodelm yos'Galan, heir to Delm Korval, *and* Daav's *cha'leket*. Not only would Guayar enjoy retelling the tale, but it would seem to him a kindness.

"All honor to him," he said, opening his eyes. Guessing his pilot's size, he ordered the jacket, and directed it to Chonselta Healer Hall, priority.

"All honor to him," Er Thom echoed, dryly. "Indeed, he did much to prepare me for *The Gazette*."

Daav's fingers stilled; he looked down at the keyboard. *The Gazette*. Yes, certainly. "Brother, I confess all: I am an idiot."

There was the sound of a chair being set back and a rustle of clothing as Er Thom stood.

"I would hardly say that," he commented, his steps soft as he came behind Daav's chair. "Surely it takes a certain genius to create quite so...*comprehensive* a muddle?"

Despite the fear roiling in his gut, Daav shouted a laugh. "Wretch." He returned his attention to the screen, fingers moving once more.

"What do you?" Er Thom asked, the chair shifting as he crossed his arms on the back. He leaned forward, his cheek next to Daav's, his attention likewise on the screen.

Terror wrenched Daav, so potent that his fingers stumbled.

"My pilot requires proper clothing," he said, voice tight. "Her own could not have survived the night."

"Ah."

There was silence while Daav ordered ready-mades: a robe, shirt, sweater, trousers, undergarments. As with the jacket, he must needs guess her size, but he could hardly do worse than the clothes her own House had seen fit to give her. After a moment's hesitation, he admitted that the boots were beyond him. Well, he thought, and if he must carry her to the nearest cobbler, she was no great weight.

"Tell me, brother." Er Thom's breath was warm against his cheek. "Does Korval now speak for this pilot? Aelliana Caylon, I should mean."

"I am her copilot," Daav grated. "It is nothing less than my duty to see her properly clad." He closed his eyes. "At least that."

"Yet," his brother persisted, "the pilot has kin on-planet. Surely—"

"She will take nothing else from that House!" He gasped against the jolt of anger, and bowed his head, staring at his fist resting on the keyboard, and the shine of Korval's Ring on the third finger of his left hand.

"Daav?"

"I am her copilot," he said harshly, "in a hostile port. Her kin—her brother!—did his utmost to murder her, and nothing to his credit, that he failed." He took a breath. "If he failed."

"Surely, he had done so," Er Thom said after a moment. "Else the lady would have no need of new clothes."

"He—she was brain-burned. The Healers ... were with her, when—finally!—we found her. It is possible that Aelliana as she had been has not, after all, survived."

"I see." The chair moved as Er Thom stood away. Daav heard his steps, approaching the card table. He spun, watching as his *cha'leket* plucked a sheaf of hard copy from the pile on the rug and came back to the desk.

"There is something else in *The Gazette* that will interest you, I think," he said, placing the paper into Daav's hand. He hitched a hip onto the edge of the desk and used his chin to point. "Page eight."

Clan news, that would be; listings of marriage contracts signed and contracts fulfilled; deaths; adoptions—

Deaths.

Daav riffled the pages, scanning the lists. Near the bottom of the third column, he found it:

Mizel grieves for the death of its son, Ran Eld Caylon.

There were no kin names listed, no indication of Ran Eld Caylon's standing within Clan Mizel at the moment of his sad passing, nothing to identify the instrument of his will, or the crime for which he had died. Merely that stern, sad statement, letting all the world know that Ran Eld Caylon had been cast out from clan and kin and was a dead man, metaphorically, if he had, indeed, Daav thought, managed to live out the night.

Daav raised his head and met his brother's serious gaze. "At least, they had enough honor to do what was needful," he said, schooling his voice to something approaching temperance.

"Just so," Er Thom agreed. He tipped his bright head. "It was well done to rid yourself of the marriage contract with Bindan," he continued after a moment. "Shall I expect dea'Gauss?"

"I have already forewarned him of Bindan's interest." Daav tossed *The Gazette* onto the desk top and leaned back in his chair, suddenly weary beyond words.

"We are not out of it intact, you know," he said. "Doubtless, there will be penalties to pay. I have instructed Mr. dea'Gauss to scrutinize Bindan's every claim for the clan. For those things represented as being toward Samiv's good—there we shall be generous."

"Shall we?" Er Thom asked interestedly.

"We shall, indeed. She took harm from us twice, through no fault of hers and all of mine. I owe her much—more, perhaps, than I can hope to Balance, yet the attempt must be made."

"Indeed it must, but that, surely, is for later."

"Yes, it is for later," Daav agreed. "For the near term, I return immediately to Chonselta Healer Hall. Having seen me safe and scolded me well, you may now seek the comforts of your own office. I swear to you that I will call, when I am again in house."

"Is it wise, I wonder, to go *immediately* to Chonselta?"

Daav blinked. "Master Ethilen had said I might come today, after Aelliana had rested. I—they denied me last evening, and she is of such a mind—It would not be wonderful to her, that she had been abandoned, and I will not have her doubt me!"

"Indeed, indeed." Er Thom leaned forward, cupping Daav's cheek in a warm hand. "I only ask you to consider, *denubia*. You claim copilot's duty. I honor that—how can I not? But the copilot must also be competent in his service, must he not—and even more so in a case where his pilot may not be able?"

Warily, Daav nodded.

"Yes. Might Pilot Caylon's copilot then ask himself how best he might serve her: by returning immediately, exhausted and scarcely in command of himself, to Chonselta? Or by sleeping for an hour or two, knowing the pilot well guarded in Healer Hall, so that he returns to her fit and able to see to her safety?"

Daav smiled, feeling it waver on his lips.

"You argue like a trader, beloved," he said.

Er Thom laughed.

"Do I take that for a promise?" he asked.

Daav sighed. "A promise, yes."

"Good. Will you wish to have me with you, at Chonselta?"

"I think not. Best for you to stay and play nadelm. I fear there may be some calls today."

It was Er Thom who sighed then. "I was afraid of that," he said.

· · · · ❖ · · · ·

Inviolate, she floated, at ease among pinpoints of memory. Her course was meandering, though some way in her control. If she focused on that point, *there*, why then, she would draw close enough to observe something like a playlet, save she knew the characters intimately.

Here was Ran Eld, his face twisted in anger, blood from the blow she had dealt him marring his cheek.

There were Frad and Clonak, urging her to accept an escort, rather than go home, to her delm, alone.

There again was the noisy table, the comfort of familiar faces, the weight of the first class license in her hand.

Here was Daav, his slim body warm as they danced— and Daav again, shoulders slumped, walking away from her in the dawnlight.

Each playlet she observed lent her weight, so that by the time she had reacquainted herself with the events of the past day, she was aware that she lay upon a mattress, blankets pinning her gently.

Aelliana opened her eyes.

The woman seated next to her bed was neither expected nor unexpected. Short, hull-grey hair waved back from a face softened by wrinkles. Her eyes were also grey, and not soft at all.

"Good morning," she said ironically, as if the commonplace were a joke. "How do you find yourself this day?"

Another commonplace, yet it seemed that this woman actually wished to hear the answer to her question. Aelliana considered. Doubtless, she had been bruised in the tussle with Ran Eld. She also remembered, as if it had happened some very long time ago, and to someone else, that she had been... ill. There had been—she had been too unsteady to walk, had fallen... several times. Then the taxi and the pilots at the Guild Hall...

"I find myself...at peace," Aelliana said slowly, "and less wounded than I believe I had been."

"Excellent on both counts. Peace is a gift of the House. I urge you to treasure it, for it will, I fear, too soon fade. As for the hurts that you recall—the autodoc made quick work of them."

Another memory rose, distant still, but with the power to alarm.

"My brother—the Learning Module..."

"Yes, exactly so," the woman interrupted briskly. She extended a hand and touched Aelliana's forehead. Warmth flowed from her fingertips, dissolving distress, introducing a pleasant languor...

"Of your kindness, I would keep you thus a short while longer. No harm will come to you—I, Kestra, Master of the Healing Art, attest this. It is merely that the examination I must now perform is best done in...peace."

"I...am at Healer Hall?" The warmth filled her head, flowed down her neck, her back, her arms.

"Healer Hall. Just so."

"But..." Aelliana snatched at her flagging will, and focused on the other woman's face. "Am I—damaged?"

"That is what I wish to determine, child. Now, rest, and let me in."

· · · ✦ · · ·

Aided by a Scout meditation technique, he slept for precisely two hours: dreamless, revitalizing sleep, from which he rose as fresh as if from a long and comfortable night. He showered, dressing in simple white shirt and tough trousers, with his pilot's jacket over all—a compromise between protocol and necessity.

Aelliana knew him best in leathers, which simply would not do for this; nor would he discomfort her by appearing in delm's finery.

"Though she must straightaway know you for Korval," he scolded himself as he snatched his hair into a tail and snapped a ring 'round the thick, dark stuff to hold it tame. He looked at himself in the mirror, seeing sober eyes and a face tight with dread. "If she is able."

Brain-burn was a serious matter. To be subjected to the direct attention of a Learning Module at full intensity for five hours—she could not have escaped injury. How dire were her wounds, and in what manner they altered the Aelliana he knew...

His reflection blurred into a smear of black and gold and silver.

"Take your Jumps in order, Pilot," he whispered, blinking his vision clear. "First, to Chonselta, and the gathering of such facts as the Healers may feel inclined to impart."

He touched his pockets, making certain of such necessities as license, key, and cantra, before leaving the room.

In the lower hall, his cloak was still over the chair where he had thrown it, and where orange-and-white Relchin had found it and made it into a nest. The cat looked up and yawned as the man approached.

Daav sighed. "It's rare one beholds a creature so comfortable," he said resignedly. "However, there is a thing which belongs to Pilot Caylon in the pocket. Believe me, I would disturb you for nothing less."

So saying, he scooped the cat to the floor and plucked the cloak up. In a moment, he had the ring out and stowed safely away. The cloak, he dropped once again across the chair.

"Your forbearance is noted," he said, inclining his head. Relchin yawned again, and jumped up to the chair, where he began kneading, eyes slitted in pleasure.

Daav winced at the sound of claws piercing silk. "Perhaps the news has not yet reached you. The clan's fortunes are by no means assured. I may need to wear that cloak for some while."

Relchin continued to knead.

TWO

· · · · · · · ·

IMPORTANT INFORMATION: The Learning Module utilizes intense, direct-brain stimulation to impart preprogrammed information. Direct-brain stimulation is painful, even dangerous, to some individuals. Always run a compatibility test before logging into a full Learning session.

In no case should a Learner undertake more than one six-hour session of moderate intensity within one twenty-eight-hour period. Cerebral vesication may result from overuse of a Learning Module.

—From the manual for
Learning Module No. X5783

WHEN AELLIANA WOKE AGAIN, SHE WAS ALONE. CONTENT within the comforting embrace of the blankets, she lay, considering the sense of *absolute wellness* that infused her. She could scarcely recall a time when she had not been frightened upon waking, heart pounding and mouth dry before ever she opened her eyes. When her grandmother was delm, perhaps then she had woken knowing herself well—but failing to understand what a gift that knowledge was.

She stretched, luxuriating in the sweet working of limb and muscle. Truly, she was well, strong, and whole. Now, it lay with her to remain so.

Another stretch, and a lazy smile. Surely, she had her whole life to plan, but first—she wanted a shower.

Tossing the blankets aside, she slipped out of bed, finding a rug, warm beneath bare feet. She never dared to sleep naked at home, not when Ran Eld might come into her room at any hour. Not quite incurious, she glanced down at herself. Her skin was smooth and golden, free, as the Healer had promised, of any bruise or contusion, but—she frowned slightly at prominent ribs and hip bones. Was she truly so thin? No wonder Scouts felt compelled to feed her!

She smiled at that, and glanced about her. The room was furnished in pinks, yellows, and blues. Light washed in through tall, open windows, which also admitted a small, sweet-smelling breeze. This, Aelliana thought, must be what it was like to stand inside a flower.

Her bed sat next to the wall, a low table at its foot. Thrown over the table, as if she had negligently dropped it there just before retiring, was a leaf-green robe. Aelliana stepped forward and picked it up, sighing in pleasure as it silked over her skin. She owned nothing so fine; surely it had been provided by the kindness of the Healers, and she was glad of it. Later, after her shower, she would try to find what had happened to her own clothes.

*   *   *

Her own clothes, what remained of them, lay next to a box atop the new-made bed when she emerged from the 'fresher. It was plain that the House had attempted to do its duty to the guest, and no blame to the Healers if her orange shirt—already frail—had come apart in the washer. Or, she thought, raising what was left of that venerable garment and frowning at the pattern of tears, perhaps it had not been the wash, but its treatment beforehand that had destroyed it. Her overlarge trousers were scarcely in better shape, stained and ragged as they were. Even her bold blue jacket showed the worse for its recent adventures, though she ought, Aelliana thought, to be able to wear it out into the street.

Her boots, sitting neatly on the floor next to the bed, gleamed, entirely without blemish.

Aelliana laughed. "Only see the pilot, clad in boots and jacket, desiring the House to call a cab!"

Abruptly, her laughter stopped, and she turned away from the bed, to the window. Below her stretched a pleasant prospect: rows of flowers tumbling in the breeze, birds darting among the shrubberies, and the play of a fountain, somewhere out of sight.

That cab...

"Where, precisely," she asked herself, staring down into the gentle riot of color, "will you go?"

Certainly, *not* to Mizel's clanhouse. Her clan had failed to protect her for the last time. It was the pilot's duty to protect her ship—a duty she could not carry out if she were injured or captive.

So, then, she thought decisively, she would go to her ship, which would protect her as much as she protected it. As it was urgently necessary to put herself beyond the reach of her nadelm, and therefore, the clan, she would need to lift—

"Immediately," she whispered, distress nibbling at her peace.

To leave Liad immediately—that had not been the plan. The plan had given her a full Standard Year to prepare. She was ignorant of Outworld customs, had scarcely begun her study of Terran. Despite her first class card, she had the most glancing acquaintance with the protocols of her own ship. Such deficiencies might easily kill her.

And, to leave immediately, with Daav in ignorance, and her comrades in danger of Ran Eld's despite—*that* she would not do.

She bit her lip.

Now that Ran Eld knew she owned a ship, he would not rest until he had wrested it from her. She had already refused once to sign it over to him, which had been the cause of their coming to blows.

"He will steal nothing else from me!" she told the garden fiercely—and gasped, raising her hands.

The antique silver puzzle ring that was her death-gift from her grandmother was still on her finger. But the other—her gift from Jon dea'Cort, the Jump pilot's ring that had for generations been in the care of a *binjali* pilot—

Aelliana spun back to the bed. She shook her tattered clothing, turning out every pocket. She found a cantra piece in an outside jacket pocket, and the precious piloting license tucked into an inner. But of the ring, there was no sign. Snatching the lid off the box—she froze, assaulted by the scent of leather, and stared down at the jacket folded neatly within.

A Jump pilot's jacket, its supple black finish as yet unmarred by such small adventures as might befall a pilot on a strange port.

It looked as if it might fit her.

Hands shaking, she set it aside, for there were other things in the box: a plain white shirt; a high-necked black sweater; a pair of tough trousers in dark blue, and another, in dusky green; underthings—everything, to look at it, near or at her size. She put it all aside, lifted the pretty paper lining the bottom of the box—but Jon's ring was not there.

Ran Eld! she thought. It had caught his eye, and easy enough to have it off her hand, once she was unconscious.

"He will not have it!" she snapped, and turned back to the window.

Overlooking the flowers, she tried to make a plan.

It seemed she would be returning to Mizel's clanhouse again, after all.

· · · ✳ · · ·

The doorkeeper showed him to a private parlor, served him wine and left him alone, murmuring that the Master would be with him soon.

The wine was sweet and sat ill on a stomach roiled with fear. He put it aside after a single sip and paced the length of the room, unable to sit decently and await his host.

Behind him, the door opened, and he spun, too quickly. Master Healer Kestra paused on the threshold and showed her hands, palms up and empty, eyebrows lifted ironically.

Ignoring irony, Daav bowed greeting, counting time

as he had not done since he was a halfling, throttling pilot speed down to normality, though his nerves screamed for haste.

The Healer returned his bow with an inclination of her head and walked over to the clustered chairs. She arranged herself comfortably in one and looked up at him, face neutral.

"Well, Korval."

He drifted a few paces forward. "Truly, Master Kestra?"

She waved impatiently at the chair opposite her. "I will not be stalked, sir! Sit, sit! And be *still*, for love of the gods! You're loud enough to give an old woman a headache—and to no purpose. She's fine."

His knees gave way and, perforce, he sat. "Fine."

"Oh, a little burn—nothing worrisome, I assure you! For the most part, the Learner never touched her. She knew her danger quickly and crafted her protection well. She created herself an obsession: an entire star system, which required her constant and total concentration—I should say, calculation!—to remain viable."

She smiled, fondly, so it seemed to Daav. "Brilliant! The Learning Module will not disturb rational cognition."

She moved her shoulders. "Tom Sen and I removed the obsession, and placed the sleep upon her. We did not consider, under the circumstances, that it was wise to entirely erase painful memory, though we did put— say, we caused those memories to feel *distant* to her. Thus she remains wary, yet unimpeded by immediate fear." Another ripple of her shoulders. "For the rest, she passed a few moments in the 'doc for the cuts and bruises. I spoke with her not an hour ago and I am well satisfied with our work."

Daav closed his eyes. She was *well*. He was trembling, he noted distantly, and his chest burned.

"Korval?"

He cleared his throat, opened his eyes and inclined his head. "Accept my thanks," he said, voice steady in the formal phrasing.

"Certainly," Kestra murmured, and paused, the line of a frown between her brows.

"You should be informed," she said, abruptly, and Daav felt a chill run his spine.

"Informed?" he repeated, when several seconds had passed and the Healer had said no more. "Is she then not—entirely—well, Master Kestra?"

She moved a hand—half-negation. "Of this most recent injury, you need have no further concern. However, there was another matter—a trauma left untended. Scar tissue, you would say."

"Yes," he murmured, recalling. "She had said she thought it—too late—to seek a Healer."

"In some ways, she was correct," Kestra admitted. "Much of the damage has been integrated into the personality grid. On the whole, good use has been made of a bad start—she's strong, never doubt it. I did what I could, where the scars hindered growth." She sighed lightly and sat back in her chair.

"The reason I mention the matter to you is that I find—an anomaly—within Scholar Caylon's pattern."

Daav frowned. "Anomaly?"

The Healer sighed. "Call it a—seed pattern. It's set off in a—oh, a *cul-de-sac*—by itself and it bears no resemblance whatsoever to the remainder of her pattern. Although I have seen a pattern remarkably like it, elsewhere."

"Have you?" Daav looked at her. "Where?"

Master Healer Kestra smiled wearily, raised a finger and pointed at the vacant air just above his head.

"There."

It took a moment to assimilate, wracked as he was. "You say," he said slowly, "that Aelliana and I are—true lifemates."

Kestra sighed. "Now, of that, there is some doubt. The seed pattern was found in the area of densest scarring." She looked at him closely, her eyes grave.

"You understand, the damage in that area of her pattern was—enormous. Had a Healer been summoned at the time of trauma—however, we shall not weep over spilt wine! I have . . . pruned away what I could of the scar tissue. At the least, she will be easier for it, more open to joy. That the seed will grow now, after these years without nurture—I cannot say that it will happen."

He stared at her, seeing pity in her eyes. His mind would not quite hold the information—Aelliana. She *was* his destined lifemate—the other half of a wizard's match. He was to have shared with Aelliana what Er Thom shared with his Anne . . . She had been hurt—several times hurt—grievously hurt and no one called to tend her, may Clan Mizel dwindle to dust in his lifetime!

He drew a deep breath, closed his eyes, reached through the anger and the anguish, found the method he required and spun it into place.

He was standing in a circle of pure and utter peace, safe within that secret soul-place where anger never came, and sorrow shifted away like sand.

"And who," Kestra demanded, "taught you that?"

He opened his eyes, hand rising to touch his earring. "The grandmother of a tribe of hunter-gatherers, on a world whose name I may not give you." He peered through the bright still peace; located another scrap of information: "She said that I was always busy—and so she taught me to—be still."

"All honor to her," Kestra murmured.

"All honor to her," Daav agreed and rose on legs that trembled very little, really. "May I see Aelliana now?"

THREE

· · · · · · · · · · ·

On average, contract marriages last eighteen Standard Months, and are negotiated between clan officials who decide, after painstaking perusal of gene maps, personality charts and intelligence grids, which of several possible nuptial arrangements are most advantageous to both clans.

In contrast, lifemating is a far more serious matter, encompassing the length of the partners' lives, even if one should die. One of the pair must leave his or her clan of origin and join the clan of the lifemate. At that time the adoptive clan pays a "life-price" based on the individual's profession, age and internal value to the former clan.

Tradition has it that lifemates share a "bond of heart and mind." In view of Liaden cultural acceptance of "wizards," some scholars have interpreted this to mean that lifemates are "psychically" connected. Or, alternatively, that the only true lifematings occur between wizards.

There is little to support this theory. True, lifematings among Liadens are rare. But so are lifelong marriages among Terrans.

—From "Marriage Customs of Liad"

HE PAUSED ON THE LANDING TO COMPOSE HIMSELF. It would not do for Aelliana to see his anger at her clan, nor yet his most ardent desires. Whatever choices resided within the circumstances they shared, those choices belonged wholly to her. That she was drawn to him was plain. That he was likewise drawn to her . . . might not be so apparent to Aelliana as it was to himself, who had some hours past shouted his desire to stand as her lifemate into the branches of Korval's meddlesome damned Tree.

That she and he were the two halves of a wizard's match—but, no. Master Kestra had been careful to say only that *they had been intended* to be thus. Before Aelliana's clan chose to see her come to harm, and having done so, denied her even the courtesy extended to any stranger that might have fallen, in need, among them.

He shook his head, baffled anew at how little her kin cared for her whom Scout and pilotkind revered: Honored Scholar of Sub-rational Mathematics Aelliana Caylon, reviser of the ven'Tura Tables, who had therefore saved, and would save, hundreds of pilot lives.

It was seldom enough that he willingly took up the *melant'i* of Delm Korval; at this moment, however, he could scarce restrain himself. Korval Himself would make short work indeed of Mizel—but that choice, too, was Aelliana's.

For all he knew, she was fond of her mother, her sisters. It had seemed to him that at least one sister—the halfling with the speaking brown eyes—held Aelliana in genuine regard.

There on the landing, Daav closed his eyes and ran the Scout's Rainbow, stabilizing thought and emotion.

Much calmed, he sighed, opened his eyes, and went up the last flight to the third floor, and the second door on the left. Her room.

He put his palm against the plate, expecting a chime to announce his presence. Instead, the door swung soundlessly open under his hand. Startled, he went one silent step into a fragrant and sun-filled room.

She stood in the open window, looking out on the rows of flowers—a slender woman in a long green robe, her tawny hair caught back with a plain-silver hair ring.

Silent though he was, she turned of a sudden, as if she had heard, a smile on her thin face, and her eyes gloriously green.

"Daav," she said, and walked into his arms.

He held her lightly—*lightly*, so he told himself, and so he did, despite his more urgent wishes. Her cheek lay against his shoulder, her arms about his waist; her body was sweet and pliant against his.

Lightly, he told himself again, though his blood was warming rapidly. Aelliana moved against him, her arms tightening. Carefully, he lay his cheek against her hair and closed his eyes, breathing in the scent of her, and, gods pity him, he was on fire and *she was his*!

Aelliana stiffened slightly, certainly less so than he. And it was not meet—it was far from meet, and if anything like what he wished for went forth in the Hall, be sure that the Hall Master would see to it that he could not function for a *relumma*—or longer. So, say, it was desperation—or self preservation—that made him reach again for the old Scout trick and spin the Rainbow, reaping calm from the flow of its colors...

"That was pretty," Aelliana murmured against his shoulder. She stirred slightly. "Daav?"

"Yes, *van'chela*."

"I wonder—how long will you be wed? Because, you know, I—I don't quite understand why it hadn't occurred to me—I can come back for you..."

Gods. He took a breath, deliberately calming.

"I—shall not be wed," he told her.

Unexpectedly, she laughed, straightening away from him. He let her go and stood staring down into brilliant green eyes.

"Certainly, you shall not wed," she said, freely ironic. "I suppose you have informed your delm of this circumstance?"

"The delm requires—" he began, and stopped. She was his natural lifemate, whether she ever knew it or not, and his pilot. In either face she deserved nothing other from him than the truth. And it was, he thought bitterly, long past time for her to have *this* truth.

"Aelliana—*I* am my delm," he said, and raised his hand to show her the ring.

She stared at the Tree-and-Dragon for a long moment, then sighed, very softly.

"Korval." She looked up into his face. "You might have said."

"*Ought* to have said, certainly," he answered, bitterness tinging his voice. He spun away from her, stalking over to the window to glare down at the blameless and pretty little garden.

"Why did you not call me?" he asked, which was badly done of him, but he had to know...if she did not trust him, after all, to hold her interests before his...

"Because I would not place my friend and my copilot in harm's way," she said with more sharpness than he was accustomed to hearing from Aelliana. "My brother is—capable of extremes of mischief. Even now, he may be designing a Balance against Jon and Binjali's—" Her voice was rising, horror evident. Daav spun away from the window and caught her arms.

"Aelliana—" A third time, he invoked the Rainbow, seeking his own balance—felt her relax in his hands; saw her face smooth and her eyes calm.

"That is—useful," she murmured. "What is it?"

For a moment, he simply stared, remembering Kestra's warnings of damage and dreams dead before they were known . . .

"Daav?"

"It is—" he cleared his throat. "It is called the Rainbow, Aelliana—a Scout thing. We use it to reestablish center, and, sometimes, to—rest." He tipped his head. "Of course, one should not depend overmuch . . ."

"Of course not," she murmured. "But useful, all the same. My thanks, *van'chela*."

"No thanks needed," he replied. He hesitated . . . and did *not* quiz her about what she had seen, or demand to hear how she might explain having seen it. Time for such things later, after this current topic was retired.

"Your brother," he said, and her gaze leapt to his, eyes wide and green, yet not—entirely—panicked.

"He—"

Daav lay light fingertips on her lips.

"Peace, child. Allow me to give you news of your clan."

Beneath his fingers, her mouth curved, very slightly.

"So," he stepped back, breaking physical contact, and bowed formally, as one imparting news of kin.

"In this morning's *Gazette*, it is reported that Ran Eld Caylon Clan Mizel has died. He will endanger you no more."

"Died?" Aelliana repeated. "Ran Eld? He was in the best of health!" Her hand flew to her mouth. "Clonak—Jon—they did not..."

"Not so far as I know," Daav said, carefully. "Though Jon would certainly be within his rights, should your brother be so foolish as to seek Binjali's. But, no—your delm has cast him out."

For a heartbeat, he thought she hadn't heard him; her face and eyes had gone perfectly blank. Then, she moved, two steps forward, and took his hand.

"Mizel has cast Ran Eld out," she said, and it seemed to him that it was in some way a—test, though what she should be testing he could not have said. "Ran Eld Caylon, Nadelm Mizel, is made clanless."

"That is so," he said, watching her with Scout's eyes. She sighed, sharply and suddenly, and closed her eyes, as if she had received...information—and of a sudden jumped, her eyes snapping open.

"But this is terrible!" she cried. "Where will he have gone? I must find him—at once!"

Daav stared. That she was in genuine distress was apparent, yet this same Ran Eld had in the not-distant past done his utmost to destroy her.

"He will likely have gone to Low Port," he said, keeping his voice calm. "All of the clanless do, soon or late. It is the only place on Liad where their voice is heard and their coin is good."

"Then I must—go to Low Port," Aelliana stated, and bit her lip. "Will you come with me?"

"If it transpires that the errand must be run, I challenge you to hold me from your side," he answered. "However, if I may...what is this urgency to seek a man you describe as spiteful and dangerous—and who has in the last day lost everything—because of you."

"He has stolen the ring that Jon gave to me!"

Ah. Here, then, was not madness, but sensible outrage.

Daav bowed slightly. "Indeed," he said gently, "he did so. However, it was recovered, through the good offices and sharp eyes of Pilot tel'Izak. Your delm requested that I hold it for you and return it to your hand, when you were found." He reached into the inner pocket of his jacket and produced it. "I regret. I should have given it to you immediately."

It sparkled against his palm, seeming at first glance the most garish and gaudy bit of trumpery in the galaxy, formed all of glass and gypsy silver. Second glance saw that the rubies, emeralds, diamonds and sapphires were every one of the first cut, and the metal too heavy for anything but platinum. Daav dared not hazard a guess as to how long the ring had been in Jon's family; dea'Cort was an old piloting line. Say it was an antique, precious beyond its worth, and leave the matter there.

"I am in the pilot's debt," Aelliana breathed. "Pray, how do I find Pilot tel'Izak?"

"I will tell you—later," Daav said carefully. "Just at this present, she stands beneath her delm's displeasure."

Aelliana stared up at him. "On my account?" she asked, and he could see that she meant to sally forth immediately and do battle on Samiv's behalf, if it were so.

"On mine, if you will have it. I used her shamefully."

She frowned. "If it were done in service of protecting your pilot, then the debt is mine, as well," she said.

Daav straightened his face with an effort, but she shot him a sharp glance, as if she had heard the laugh he had swallowed.

"Is there a joke?" she asked sternly, reminding him all at once that she was a teacher.

"Only that you had never used to lecture me on Code, Aelliana," he said meekly, and smiled when *she* laughed.

"As to that," she said, taking the ring from his hand and slipping it onto her finger. "I have just completed an intense study of the Code."

It was humor—and Scoutlike of its kind—yet too close, far too close. Daav shivered.

"Oh, no!" She stepped forward, bold as she had never been, and put her arms around him. "It is well, *van'chela*! The Master Healer has said it—and, truly! I feel—I cannot recall when last I felt so well!"

He returned her embrace—how could he not?—his blood heating with unruly passions. Dazzled, he reached once more for the Rainbow...yet, here was Aelliana stretching high on her toes, her arms around his neck now, and her face turned up to his, eyes wide, lips barely parted. He bent his head...

Pounding roused him, and a voice shouting, "Korval!"

He stirred, breaking the kiss tenderly, and raised his head, as fuddled as if he had been woken from deep sleep. Aelliana moaned, her arms tightening, her body taut against his.

"Korval!" The call came again, and he had wit

enough now to recognize Master Kestra's voice. "I remind you that there are children in this House!"

"What does she mean?" Aelliana whispered.

Daav laughed, breathless, and found the strength to step back from her and put his hands down at his sides.

"Why, she only means that the Healers find me very—*loud*—as they have it, and rightly fear the impact of our—passion—upon the tender empathies of the students of the House." He raised his voice to address the door.

"We are reminded, Master Kestra."

"Bah," the door returned comprehensively, followed by the sound of footsteps moving, much too heavily, away.

"Daav."

He looked to where she stood, her eyes vividly green, her robe more than a little awry.

He managed a shamefaced grin. "Your pardon, Pilot. It will not happen again."

"Now, *that* was not the proper answer." Aelliana tucked her hands into her sleeves and shook her hair away from her face. "Daav—I—do not wish to—lift without you. Yet, to preserve myself, I must go. Even with Ran Eld . . . dead . . . *Ride the Luck* is not safe. The delm—Mizel is by no means wealthy. The sale of a starship would go some distance toward reasserting the clan's fortunes."

"You still intend to work the ship?" Daav asked her.

"Yes! But—circumstances are come upon me so quickly, that . . ." She closed her eyes. "I must think, and not call Mizel's attention to myself until I have thought myself through." She bit her lip, though her gaze never wavered. "I am different from who I was. I need time to understand this."

He inclined his head gravely.

"I offer assistance," he said, carefully.

"Assistance?"

"It may be no better—you must be the judge of that, Pilot. But, I offer, if it will serve you, to place you under Korval's protection."

She blinked. "Can— Is that by Code?"

His lips twitched. "Oddly enough, it is. Korval's interest in pilots is well-known. It falls well within my honor to offer Korval's protection to an endangered pilot." He tipped his head. "Such an action will, perhaps, not please your delm, but it *will* freeze all of the pieces on the board, for however long you choose. You will have your peace, you and your ship will be safe, and you will have however much time to think as you need."

She closed her eyes, and it seemed to him that he could hear her thinking. A dozen heartbeats passed, and she opened her eyes with a slight smile.

"I believe it will answer," she said. "Did you send those clothes?" She tipped her head toward the bed.

"Yes."

"Thank you for your care," she said softly. "I will be a moment, dressing, and then we may leave the Healers to their peace."

"Well enough." He tipped his head. "When did you last eat?"

Aelliana hesitated ... sighed.

"I don't recall."

Of course she didn't recall. Food was never among Aelliana's priorities.

While you dress, I will petition the chef."

"But, to linger—"

"We have time for you to drink a cup of tea and eat a biscuit," he interrupted. "As I'm perfectly certain that I'll be able to impose upon you to eat very little more." *And*, he added to himself, *since you seem to have less control than a halfling, it would be best if you were not present to watch her dress.*

Aelliana sighed. "I know better than to argue with a Scout," she said, and gave him a measuring glance. "When did *you* eat last?"

He raised an eyebrow. "Lunch, yesterday."

"Then you will," she commanded, turning toward the bed, "ask the House for the kindness of two cups and two biscuits."

He grinned and inclined his head. "Yes, Pilot."

FOUR

· · · · · · · · ·

In the absence of clan, a partner, comrade or copilot may be permitted the burdens and joys of kin-duty. In the presence of kin, duty to partner, comrade or copilot must stand an honorable second.

— From the Liaden Code of Proper Conduct

AELLIANA DRESSED QUICKLY, HARDLY ATTENDING WHAT she did, her thoughts dashing in all directions, rather like a gaggle of particularly rambunctious puppies.

Daav was dear to her, and yet that she had dared— her marriage had taught her to be wary of intimacy, to dread even a touch! The joy that had infused her, on beholding him—it had seemed the most natural thing, and then to all but demand that he...kiss...

"It was sweet," she whispered defiantly, carefully folding the white shirt and blue pants into the box with the other unused clothes.

Oh, it had been sweet, and she aching for more, ready to—well, and she hardly knew what she had been ready to do, had the Healer not interrupted them. Certainly, Daav, with his clever fingers, had

35

seemed to entertain some notions of a direction they might travel.

She put the lid on the box, and reached behind her head, pulling the ring free. Holding it in her teeth, she finger-combed her hair away from her face, and clipped it once more into a tail. To show her face before the world, after so many years in hiding...with the aid of her comrades, she had begun to learn again how to hold herself in pride, as a person of honor...

Hands shaking, she lifted the space leather jacket. She had earned the jacket, as she had earned her license—and Jon's ring—and the cantra piece. If nothing else, she must strive to be worthy of her accomplishments. *Melant'i* demanded no less.

The jacket settled firmly onto her shoulders. She slipped her license into one inner pocket and the cantra piece into another, sealed both—and turned, prompted by some new and entirely appropriate sense, as the door opened to admit her wayward copilot.

Tall and graceful, he came across the room to the windows, bearing a tray on which reposed a teapot, cups, and a plate piled high with shaped sandwiches.

"Will it please my pilot to sit by the window and break her fast?"

His deep voice was grave, though she knew him well enough to hear it for irony.

She tipped her head. "What if it does not please me?"

He settled the tray on the cushion and looked over his shoulder at her, one strong dark brow quirking.

"Why then, I will only say that there are messages here requiring your attention."

"Messages..." She came forward to sit on the edge

of the other cushion, her eyes on the tray. A message pad leaned against the teapot, its surface opaque. With her hand half extended, she hesitated. Who, after all, would send her a message? What if Ran Eld—

"Pilot?" His voice was entirely serious.

Aelliana cleared her throat and looked up into his black eyes.

"Sky nerves," she said, gratified that her voice was firm. "Nothing more."

Resolutely, she picked up the message pad and put her thumb against the plate.

The surface lightened, revealing a list of names: Jon dea'Cort, Clonak ter'Meulen, Sinit Caylon, Trilla sen'Elba, Qiarta tel'Ozan.

Sinit Caylon. Aelliana touched her sister's name and put the screen on her knee.

"Pilot."

So soft it might have been her own thought. She barely glanced up, taking the cup from his hand with a murmured, "My thanks."

"Aelliana," Sinit's voice was quivering and high with strain, entirely unlike her usual brash and sunny mode. "Sister, I hope—with all my heart I hope—that this message finds you well. If I'd known, please believe that I would have let you out—I would! Don't think badly of me, Aelliana. I—you can come home, whenever you like. Ran Eld has been cast out, and he won't strike you anymore. I think—I think it's—wonderful—exciting that you fly with Daav yos'Phelium. He has your ring, the one that Ran Eld took—Delm Korval, I mean. He told Mother that he'd give it to you . . ." There was a pause, and the suggestion of a sniffle, then, "I love you, Aelliana."

She tapped the screen again, pausing it, and swallowed hard in a throat gone tight. For Sinit to think of stopping Ran Eld—it horrified one who knew all too intimately what pain their brother took pleasure in inflicting upon those who thwarted him. Aelliana shivered, raised her cup and sipped tea.

Ran Eld is cast out, and beyond harming Sinit. She formed the thought with care. It scarce seemed believable, yet surely Daav was not mistaken.

Somewhat less unsettled, she looked again to the device in her hand and tapped the first name on the list—Jon dea'Cort.

"Good day to you, math teacher, and hoping this finds you well. I have your ship keys safe, and will hold them, per your instructions, until you or your rogue of a copilot claim them. Rest easy on that score, and come back to us, when you're able."

She bit into her sandwich, tasting mint and *vehna* fish, while the message pad cycled down to the next name.

"Goddess, you will not again refuse my escort, if I must follow three steps behind you the whole way into peril." Clonak's voice was almost stern. "I'm quite aware that I am ridiculous, but believe me sincere in my regard for yourself. If you have *any* need, call on me."

There was muted chatter while the pad sorted over Sinit's message, and found the next unread message—from Trilla. Aelliana sipped tea and had another bite...

"The master will have called and told you; just thought I'd add my well-wishes—and Patch's. Come back when you're able, Pilot, and we'll dance in earnest."

Another sip emptied the cup. She sat holding it while the last message played out.

"Scholar Caylon, it is Qiarta tel'Ozan, the least of

your students." Unlike the others, Qiarta spoke in the High Tongue, in the mode between student and honored instructor. "I have seen the news, Scholar. I would be honored to serve you, in whatever fashion that you may require. Please do not hesitate to call upon me, at any hour."

Tears pricked. Aelliana closed her eyes.

"Tea, Pilot?" a respectful voice inquired.

She opened her eyes and looked down slightly, into Daav's lean, clever face, a novel view. Her fingers twitched as though she would reach out and touch his cheek, which would, she told herself, take wrongful advantage of him—and perhaps dismay the Healers, her kind hosts.

Even seated as he was, cross-legged on the pale blue rug, Daav was tall enough to reach the tray. As if to prove it, he hefted the teapot, quirked an eyebrow and glanced down. Following his glance, she saw the cup cradled in her hands, and held it up, whereupon he poured.

"There are sandwiches left, if you'd like another one or two," he commented, pouring for himself before setting the pot back onto the tray.

"Another!" she exclaimed, looking once more to the tea tray. In fact, the sandwich plate was empty, save for precisely two, cut into the shapes of a crescent moon and a star.

"Did I—I never ate all of those!" she exclaimed, remembering the pleasant tastes of mint and *vehna*. "Did I?"

"I accounted for three or four," Daav said calmly, raising his cup to sip. "Yesterday's lunch *was* quite some time gone."

She sipped her tea and considered the remaining sandwiches.

"The stars are mint and *vehna*," Daav murmured. "The crescents are cress and cheese."

She was, Aelliana thought, hungry. Not ravenous, surely, but—another sandwich would taste...*good*.

"I'll have the star if you'll have the crescent," she said, giving Daav a sidelong glance from beneath her lashes.

"Done!" he said merrily, and swooped the plate up, offering it first to her.

She took the star, and bit into it, sighing in pleasure. It was a dainty thing, gone in two bites, which was, she supposed, how she had managed to eat *several* while listening to her messages.

That, and a vigilant Scout, who had no doubt made sure that a new sandwich came into her hand as soon as it was empty.

"I can see," she said, "that I will have to be on my mettle."

"You were...a bit...distracted," Daav admitted. "Which is rarely the case." He stretched to put his cup on the tray, and looked back to her, black eyes serious.

"What do you require of me, Aelliana?"

There it was, she thought. Daav had the gift of asking the question she hesitated to ask of herself. In this instance, what was required of Aelliana Caylon?

"It would seem," she said slowly, "that I have amends to make, and reassurances to present. My sister—she is only a halfling, the youngest of us. To thwart Ran Eld—was not in her power. I must show her that I find her blameless. Clonak—I could put him in danger no more than you. I thought he had understood..."

She finished her tea and put the cup on the tray.

"For the rest—people are far too good—*far* too good to me."

"In the case of your comrades at Binjali's," Daav said slowly. "They offer what a comrade will. You have not stinted them; they do not stint you. Clonak, if one who loves him may say it, is not so ridiculous as he makes himself seem. That he blames himself for not insisting that you take his escort—I think you are correct in thinking so. That he blames you—"

"But it is not his blame to take!" she cried. "The burden of blame rests entirely upon me, for ignoring the best advice of my comrades, and for believing that my right to see the delm would shield me from harm. Ran Eld—I do not know how Ran Eld came to be... as he is. Was. However, I *knew* what that was, and yet I took no precautions, nor arranged for backup. Such foolishness would surely find me robbed, if not dead, on an out-port. It is scarcely wonderful that I very nearly had the same result here."

"Ah," Daav said.

Aelliana smiled, and leaned forward to place her hand over his, where it rested on his knee.

A sense of carefulness touched her senses; and a fierce yearning. Startled, she drew back. The sensations faded, leaving her as she had been: grateful and reluctant.

"I think, if you will bear with..." she said slowly, and paused.

Daav tipped his head in an attitude of courteous listening.

"I think that I must go to my sister. At the same time, I will inform Mizel that I—that I will reside for this present under your care."

Daav took a deep breath, and leaned slightly forward, his eyes hard upon her face.

"Is that your wish, Aelliana?" he asked, and once again she tasted that attitude of wrenching carefulness. "This must be as *you* wish it to be—not as I wish it, nor Clonak, nor anyone else, save yourself."

"Yes," she said, feeling suddenly very small. "But, Daav I trust you . . . more than Mizel."

His mouth tightened, and he bowed his head. "I will try to be worthy of your trust, Aelliana."

"You already have been," she said, reaching out to touch his hair. It was warm beneath her fingers, coarse and resilient. "Many times over."

FIVE

· · · · · · ·

It must be the ambition of every person of *melant'i*
to mold individual character to the clan's necessity.
The person of impeccable *melant'i* will have no
goal, nor undertake any task, upon which the clan
might have reason to frown.

—Excerpted from the Liaden
Code of Proper Conduct

THE SHABBY ROUND CHAIR IN THE LIBRARY WAS SINIT'S
favorite seat in all the house, big enough to curl
around in with feet tucked up, bound book braced
comfortably against a shapeless pillow. It was also a
refuge of sorts; neither her brother nor her eldest
sister were at all bookish, so most times Sinit could
be certain of having the room to herself.

This afternoon, however, the chair had no comfort
to offer. Sinit had retired to it directly after lunch,
taken with only Voni for company—and poor company
at that. Apparently, Ran Eld's . . . Ran Eld's death had
struck her hard, so that she could scarcely be troubled
to correct Sinit's manner at table, much less prose on
about the soup being watery—which Sinit, usually the

43

most forgiving of diners, allowed that it had been—or the salad being wilted—which was inarguable—or the tea being tepid.

After one half-hearted snap at Sinit to keep her elbows off the tabletop, Voni had drunk her soup, pushed the salad aside, and wordlessly handed Sinit her cheese roll. Then, she had risen, teacup in hand, and quit the dining room. Sinit heard her climb the stairs slowly, and the door to her room close with a *snick*.

They were, so Mother had told them at breakfast, a House in mourning. That meant that all appointments were canceled, and no unseemly racket was permitted. She had given Sinit an especially stern look when she had said that, which was, Sinit thought now, curled uneasily into her chair, hardly just. It wasn't as if she were a *baby*. She had fourteen Standards—*quite* grown up, even if Voni chose to treat her as—

Chimes sounded.

Sinit blinked, slid out of the chair—and paused with one foot resting on the capacious seat.

They were a House in mourning, and therefore ought to be closed to the world for the twelve-day of grief specified in the Code.

On the other hand, if the chime sounded again, her mother would surely come out from her office, and that—might be very bad.

Sock-footed, Sinit padded out of the library and down the main hall. She pressed her hand against the plate, waited for the tiny click that signaled the lock had cycled, and pulled the door open.

Two pilots stood on Mizel's ramshackle porch: To the fore was a lady, trim and upright in her leather,

her thin face dominated by a pair of vivid green eyes. A much taller pilot stood at her back, and Sinit knew his face all too well.

"Delm Korval!" she gasped. Recovering her wits, she bowed, doorkeeper-to-honored-guests. "The House is in mourning, sir. Come again in a twelve-day and Mizel will receive you, gladly."

"Sinit?" The lady's voice was fine—and familiar. "Have I changed so much overnight?"

"Aelliana!" Sinit stared, finding her sister along the edges of this stranger's face. "I—you've done something with your hair!"

Aelliana smiled. "Why, so I have. May we come in? I would have a word with you, if I might."

"Of course you may come in!" Sinit cried, stepping back—and hesitated, looking up into Aelliana's escort's sharp, clever face. "Although—"

"No, I will *not* have Daav await me on the porch!" Aelliana interrupted, stepping into the hall, Korval but a bare step behind her. "He is my copilot, and stands as close as kin, according to the Pilots Guild, so we had best let him in."

"Good-day, Sinit Caylon," Korval said, his deep, grainy voice unexpectedly gentle. "I welcome the opportunity to thank you for the aid you gave to me—and to my pilot. I am in your debt."

Sinit's cheeks heated. "Oh, no, please, sir! We are— we are perfectly in Balance. Pray regard it no more."

"She thinks I'm going to eat her," the man said, perhaps to Aelliana. He bowed, easily. "You must really allow me to judge the magnitude of my own indebtedness. Your assistance was timely and to the point. I do not forget."

Sinit swallowed and bowed acceptance—she could hardly brangle with him here in the entry hall, after all.

"That's been settled, then." Aelliana said. "Truly, Sinit, we are *both* in your debt." She glanced about the hall. "Where is Mother?"

"In her office," Sinit said. "She—Ran Eld . . ."

"Yes, it must have struck her hard," Aelliana murmured. She took Sinit's hand and tugged her down the hall. "Let us go into the library. We must talk."

Ran Eld had once kicked the library door in a fit of pique; it had never closed right after that. However, Korval pulled it as tight as it would go, then took his long self down to the farthest corner of the room, where he immediately began an earnest perusal of the shelves.

Biting her lip, Sinit stared at his leathered back. The last time she had let this man into Mizel's House, her brother had died of it. Of course, if she had refused him, Aelliana might well have died of *that*. And what would Mother say, if she found him in-House *now* . . .

"Sinit?"

She gasped and spun 'round, staring into a face so familiar, and yet made so strange. It was the eyes, Sinit thought, so bright—or, no. It was that Aelliana had always used to wear her hair close around her face, as if she were in hiding. And she had stood with shoulders rounded in submission, Sinit remembered suddenly, while this lady—this pilot—stood straight, shoulders level.

"Aelliana, I—" Tears rose, as they had when she had called Healer Hall. "I didn't know! You might have died in the Learner and I was sitting right here and I didn't know!" she wailed.

Aelliana caught her, and gathered her close. Sinit began to sob in earnest, her forehead pressed into her sister's shoulder, the leather of her jacket slick and cool beneath heated skin.

"Sinit, Sinit. All's well. More than well." Aelliana rocked her, and Sinit put her arms around her sister's waist in a fierce hug as the tears subsided somewhat.

"If there is any one thing that I am grateful for," Aelliana went on, her voice soft and warm, "beyond my own happy outcome, is that you *did not* know I had been locked inside the Learner."

"Why?" Sinit sniffled, smelling mint and leather.

"Because you would have felt compelled to *do something*. To go against Ran Eld would have—" Her sister paused, arms tightening briefly. "It could have been very bad for you." Sinit raised her head, looking into a face suddenly gone gaunt, brilliant eyes fogged.

"Ignorance spared you," Aelliana said, suddenly brisk. She smiled, too thin over her apparent pain. "And I am grateful."

She put her hands on Sinit's shoulders and set her back, looking seriously into her face.

"You must not blame yourself," she said. "Sinit— *promise* me that you will not. All has ended very well. Daav has said your assistance was invaluable and he does not, you know, simply say such things, unprovoked. I think you did just as you ought, and wisely. I thank you, and—and honor you."

Sinit sniffled again, and lifted her chin, feeling a... warmth in the center of her chest, where the knot of frightened misery had lodged.

"That will do!" Aelliana said approvingly. "Now—"

"Sinit, who was at the door?"

Aelliana's eyes widened. Sinit felt her own heart
stutter.

The door went crookedly back on its track and
Birin Caylon stepped into the room.

Mother had been weeping, Aelliana thought; which
surely she would, having only recently lost a favored
child. Perhaps it was her air of weary disarray only,
but she seemed . . . smaller, in some way: a woman
edging beyond her middle years with trepidation.

She froze for a moment in the doorway, arrested
between one step and another, staring. It seemed that
she, too, had failed of recognizing the House's third
and least regarded child—then the moment was passed.
Mizel completed her step, and inclined her head.

"Aelliana!" she said, perhaps a little too loudly;
perhaps with an unintended edge. "It is well that you
are home, daughter. Sinit, why did you not bring your
sister to me at once?"

"Sinit and I had an urgent matter to discuss," Aelliana said, drawing their mother's attention to herself.
"I insisted that we speak immediately."

She felt a subtle shifting in the air to the rear and
right, and put her hand behind her back. Warm fingers
met hers, squeezing gently. She was aware of a sense
of heightened determination, absent only a heartbeat
before, and a thrill of space-cold anger, gone before
she could shiver.

Mother frowned slightly, then looked up and over
Aelliana's shoulder, directly, so she judged, into Daav's
face. Her mouth thinned, but she bowed with courtesy, delm-to-delm.

"Korval. Mizel is in your debt; do not doubt that

we shall see ourselves Balanced, and that soon. At this moment, however, our House is in mourning, and I ask that you honor our grief. Sinit, pray show Delm Korval to the door."

"No!" Aelliana said sharply, which was not how one spoke to one's delm.

Mizel's stare was equal parts disbelief and anger.

"I beg your pardon, daughter?"

"Daav is my copilot," she said, arguing Guild rule as if it had meaning here, in the heart of her own clanhouse. "He has a right to be here."

"Having delivered you to your kin, his protection—which Mizel honors—bows to mine. Korval is aware of these things, daughter, if you are not." She looked to Daav once more.

"Korval, I do not ask by-your-leave within my own walls, but I will plead your indulgence. There has been a death in this House. Further, it would seem that the child you return to us is . . . beyond herself, and perhaps yet burdened with the effects of her misadventure. Pray, withdraw."

"Ma'am," Daav said gravely, "I cannot. My pilot requires that I stand with her, and here is where she stands." He paused, and Aelliana had a sense of weighing, as of two courses of action, and then—

"If my pilot has fulfilled her commission here, then certainly, I shall leave with her."

"Leave *with* her?" Mizel's voice expressed disbelief. "She is only just arrived, and in a state quite unlike her usual self. Where would she go?"

Aelliana cleared her throat. "In fact," she said, her voice sounding much steadier than she felt, "I had only intended to stop for a moment, ma'am, to speak to Sinit. I have . . ." She took a breath, squeezing Daav's hand so hard her fingers ached, felt a rush of certainty, and met her delm's eyes.

"I have placed myself under Korval's protection."

For three heartbeats, Mizel stared into Aelliana's face, her own devoid of expression.

"I see," she said at last, and again addressed herself to Daav.

"With Korval's permission," she said, in the mode of delm-to-delm, "Mizel will speak with the clan's daughter Aelliana in private."

Once again, that thrill of frigidly intense, short-lived anger.

"That decision of course rests with Pilot Caylon," Daav said, also in delm-to-delm.

Mizel sniffed. "Indeed." She gave Aelliana a hard look.

"Step into my office, if you please, Aelliana."

For a moment, she thought she would not; that she would declare that anything Mizel had for her could be heard by her copilot as well.

The weight of culture, however, is not always so easy to shrug aside.

Aelliana inclined her head, licking lips gone suddenly dry.

"Daav," she said, and her voice quavered, now. "Pray wait for me. I will be—I will be no longer than a quarter-glass."

There was a sense of weighing, and of worry. Then he slipped his fingers away from hers and there remained only—worry.

"Pilot's choice," he said, in the mode between comrades. "I will wait for you, Aelliana; never doubt it."

"Very good," Mizel said, acidly. "Pray accept the hospitality of our House. Sinit, fetch refreshments—and call your sister down to entertain our—guest."

"Now, Aelliana, you will tell me truthfully: This placing of yourself into Korval's hands—was that coercion?"

The door to the delm's office shut very firmly indeed, and no sooner had it done so than Aelliana's throat closed, all the old fear clawing in her belly. Mizel walked behind her desk and stood, hands gripping the back of her chair, waiting with visible impatience.

"Well? Or am I to take silence for assent?"

"No!" The word tore her throat, as if it were edged. "Daav would not coerce me!"

Mizel sniffed. "Korval did not arrive at their reputation by accident, daughter. I learn—from news reports, and . . . other sources . . . rather than from your own lips—that you have some skill as a pilot, and are also the owner of a spaceship. Korval cannot help but to covet you for those reasons. Pilots and ships are at his clan's core; and it is well-known that dragons are acquisitive of treasure."

Daav only desired her ship? For the blink of an eye, she believed it, as the herself of only a day past would have done. Surely, he would need some reason, other than the dubious pleasure of her company . . . But no. She knew him better than that.

Aelliana took a breath and looked into her delm's eyes.

"Clan Korval owns dozens of ships of all classes, ma'am. There is nothing about a Class A Jump to tempt them. As for Daav—he is my copilot. He offered his best care, as he is bound to do, and I accepted the course he proposed, after consideration. You do not know him, and cannot speculate upon his reasons."

"I have no need to *speculate* upon his reasons; they are quite apparent." Mizel pulled her chair back. "He must look to the best good and profit of his clan. As must we all."

She sat down behind her desk and pointed peremptorily at the stiff wooden chair to Aelliana's right.

"Sit."

Unwillingly, she obeyed, placing her feet carefully, so that she might rise quickly, and balanced, should there be need. The back of her neck prickled as if in anticipation of the door opening behind her.

"You may not yet have received the news," Mizel said slowly, giving Aelliana a hard stare. "Your brother will—no longer disturb your peace."

Disturb her peace? A dozen memories rose: Ran Eld striking her across the face; twisting her hair; slamming into her room in the dark of night, dragging her out of her bed to huddle, impotent, in the corner while he hurled the contents of drawers and shelves randomly about. Ran Eld, gloating at the course her marriage had taken, and lovingly telling over each bruise; smiling when she flinched from the shadow of his raised hand...

"Disturb my peace?" she repeated. "Say rather that he sought to destroy me by every means at his hand!" She took a breath, meaning to stop there, for surely she had already given a grieving parent pain enough—but her traitor voice continued, in a tone so cold she shivered, hearing it: "Though not too early, nor too easily. There would hardly have been any *pleasure* in that."

Mizel inclined her head. "He has paid the final

price," she said, her voice stringently steady in the mode between delm and clan member. "Your safety and your peace is now assured in our House." She took a breath, and continued more briskly.

"Ran Eld's ... departure leaves Mizel thin. Your resources and your intelligence are needed in the service of your clan. Your grandmother had thought highly of you, and considered that you might best stand as nadelm. We had, as you know, disagreed upon the point—where two are worthy, it is often the case, and no dishonor to any. Now it is come time for you to take up duty, and learn what must be done to husband Mizel's interests. I do not hide from you that we are in ... unfortunate straits. I believe that we may make a recovery, if we are diligent and wise, and if all the clan accepts their duty, and, in the case of those more able, beyond their duty."

Aelliana swallowed, her stomach tight, breath short. She could feel the bars snapping in place around her, shutting her away from Daav, *The Luck*, her comrades ...

"To absent yourself in these times of turmoil is less than even the simplest duty to the House demands. Korval will accept this, when you tell him that your clan has need of you. As I have said, and as I do swear to you, on the honor of our clan, you are safe here among us."

Safe. In this house where she had been tortured, while the delm preferred not to see. Where she and her *resources*—her ship!—were suddenly seen as precious. In this clan where both her delm and her mother knew her for the murderer of her brother. And neither would forgive her.

"So!" Mizel said, placing her hands flat atop the desk. "It is decided. You will inform Korval of your obligations, thank him—graciously, mind you, Aelliana!—for his many kindnesses to yourself, and release him to his own affairs. You will be able to rest easy here, and recuperate further—"

Aelliana stood. She *must* stand, she thought, her heart pounding, or the weight of Mizel's words, the weight of duty, would bind her where she sat and she would never, *never* free herself; never fully realize this new self, who was not entirely ruled by fear...

"Why?" she gasped.

Her delm glared. "Because there is no one else, if you will have it," she said coldly.

Aelliana inclined her head. "No, ma'am, forgive me. I am well aware of the logic that would have you heap duty upon me. My question is: Why did Mizel send no one to me at Healer Hall? Sinit knew where I was, and yet—it was not kin who sent clothes to replace mine that were torn, or to offer companionship on the way home. It was Daav who came, not you."

Mizel drew herself up. "This is a House in mourning," she said. "Surely, the Healers would have called a taxi for you."

Yes, even in death, Ran Eld came first in their mother's heart—it was no surprise; but the chains of duty were made lighter for the confirmation.

"Aelliana?"

"I—" She took a hard breath. Even lightened, duty was no inconsiderable weight. Nor would it do to offend Mizel—any more than was necessary. "The clan has done without my input, my intelligence, and my resources for many years. I cannot remain here. Forgive me."

Mizel frowned. "Aelliana, have you not been attending me? Your brother is made clanless by reason of his attack upon your person. I have sworn that you are *safe* here. Do you question your delm?"

Aelliana shook her head, her hair snapping with the force of the gesture, and raised a hand, fingers splayed, in the sign for *stop*.

"I cannot calculate a point in the future when I will feel *safe* here, ma'am. There may be a time when I will be able to abide these walls for more than an hour. That, I cannot know, until—until I have gone away from here, taken thought, and allowed what the Healers have begun to . . . bear what fruit it may."

"You can *think* here!"

"No, ma'am, I cannot. Doubtless, this is my own deficiency." She bowed, forcing herself to the courtesy: clan-member-to-delm. "I have abused my copilot's patience long enough. Good-day to you, Mother."

"Aelliana."

There was cold anger in Mizel's voice, but that could not be allowed to matter, not now. Now, what mattered was Daav, and gaining the untainted air of the day on the far side of Mizel's front door. She forced herself to turn, and to walk on legs shamefully unsteady—across the room, and out the door.

• • • ❊ • • •

"More tea, Delm Korval?" The elder sister leaned forward with what she had doubtless been taught was grace, and placed a soft hand on the teapot.

"Thank you," he said gravely, "my cup is but half-empty."

And not likely, he thought, to become full-empty.

The quarter-glass that Aelliana had specified was almost done. While he did not doubt his ability to extricate her from her delm's office if it became necessary, he was at a loss as to how to perform such an outrage with even a modicum of subtlety. It would be better—far better—if Aelliana found a way to end the interview and return to him. *Then*, they might continue the airy fantasy of pilot and dutiful copilot that she had spun for them, and with a fair semblance of courtesy, slip away.

"Do you make a long stay in Chonselta?" Voni Caylon asked him.

He sighed to himself and inclined his head. "Only so long as is necessary, ma'am," he answered, and thought he heard the winsome Sinit sneeze softly.

"Perhaps your plans might extend to an informal dinner," she persisted. "Mizel would be pleased to—"

From down the hall came the sound of a door opening, and light uneven steps, moving not quite at a run.

Daav put his cup aside and rose, turning to face the parlor door.

Aelliana hesitated on the threshold, eyes wide and shoulders stiff, distress informing every muscle.

"Pilot?" he asked, voice deliberately soft; all of his attention on her.

"We—leave now," she said. Her voice was firmer than he had supposed it would be, from her countenance.

"Aelliana!" the elder sister exclaimed from her seat across the tea-table. "Leave? When the clan needs every adult? How can this be?"

"Necessity," Aelliana whispered, and he saw that the resolve she clung to was barely more than a thread. Now, was her copilot needed, and truly.

"Necessity," he affirmed, giving the word what weight he might, in Comrade. "Is there anything you require from this house, before we go? Books, clothes—" *Your daughter*, he added silently, but that would surely cross the line into kin-stealing. Yet, ought she not at least give her child farewell?

She shook her head. "No. I—it is time for us to leave. Please."

"At once," he said.

Turning to the younger sister, he bowed as one acknowledging a debt-partner. "Sinit Caylon, it has been a pleasure to renew our acquaintance. You have my particulars."

Her face flushed, and he turned to the elder sister, awarding her a bow for the courtesy of the House.

"Ma'am." He did not stop to see what her response might be, but stepped to Aelliana's side, and offered her his arm.

"Pilot."

SIX

......

The number of High Houses is precisely fifty. And
then there is Korval.

—From the Annual Census of Clans

"I HAD BECOME ACCUSTOMED TO KEEPING SUCH THINGS
as—as mattered, in my office at the Technical College,"
Aelliana said, as he guided the ground car through
Chonselta's thin afternoon traffic.

Almost, he asked if she wished to go there—to her
office—but it seemed to him that she had something
more to say on her topic, and held his tongue.

"My brother," she continued, after a moment. "Ran
Eld had used to . . . find pleasure . . . in coming into my
room after the house was asleep, and, and emptying
my drawers and shelves. Of course, fragile things
broke, and books were sometimes . . . damaged. Those
things that remain are clothes, and—easily replaced,"
she finished resolutely.

Anger tightened his fingers on the stick, and a sad
pity it was that Ran Eld Caylon's throat did not rest
beneath his hand. He took a breath, calming himself,
and glanced aside, seeing wide green eyes watching

his face carefully.

"If a copilot may be so bold," he said, keeping his tone cool in consideration of her concern, "your brother was a monster."

There was a pause, as if she weighed this judgment. He waited, wondering what the outcome of her thought would be.

"Yes," she said eventually, turning her head to study the passenger's viewscreen. "Yes, I fear that he was."

"Do you wish to go to your office?" Daav asked, eying the readout on the driver's screens. The deciding turn was two blocks distant—right for Chonselta Technical College, left for the spaceport.

"Not today, I thank you; it is the long break, and what is there is safe enough for now."

He nodded. "We to the spaceport, then, Pilot."

"That sounds—excellent," she replied and fell silent once more.

Daav did not press her, having thoughts of his own to pursue. The more he heard of Aelliana's life, clanbound, the more he wondered that she had managed to survive at all. All very well for Master Kestra to praise her strength, but the horrors under which she had struggled to thrive—surely, he thought, she might have been given some small comfort?

Instead, she had been given a kinsman bent on doing her what damage he might, and who reveled in her pain. She could count on no moment of privacy; hold in fondness no fragile geegaw; be certain that a walk down the main hallway of her very clanhouse would not result in bruises—or worse.

His anger was building again. Grimly, he brought his heartbeat down, smoothed his breathing.

Small wonder she had spoken so distantly of her daughter, he thought, remembering how cold she had seemed, entirely unlike the woman he knew. With her brother on the lookout always to harm her, how could she regard her child? The best she might do for the girl was disdain her, and hope that Ran Eld Caylon never looked in her direction.

"Daav?" Soft as it was, Aelliana's voice jolted him. He turned his head briefly and offered her a smile. "Aelliana?"

She extended a hand, rested it on his arm; withdrew with a sigh.

"You—I feel that you are distressed. I regret it. If it had been possible, I would have gone alone, but—" She gave him a smile, well-intended, but wavering visibly at the edges. "Truly, *van'chela*, it was only the knowledge that you were in-house that gave me the courage to resist Mizel."

He blinked and glanced over to her, meeting eyes in which worry was plain. And yet—*she felt*? Had she informed herself of the state of his unruly emotions through that fleeting touch? Hope rose, twined with confusion, and a measure of disquiet. Perhaps Master Kestra's estimation of her results had been pessimistic? Perhaps Aelliana would, after all, know him as her lifemate? Yet, to subject her—or anyone!—to an intimate knowledge of *his* thoughts and feelings . . .

"Daav?"

"Forgive me," he said. "I am stupid today. Notwithstanding, I think we came away from Mizel as gracefully as possible. It was well done of you to invoke Guild law."

"It was all I could think to do, though it cannot,

you know, stand against kin." she said, sounding rueful. "Cat-ice, I thought it, even for Sinit."

"Thin as it was, it bore us up, and no one's *melant'i*
has taken harm."

"Excepting Mizel's." Aelliana sighed. "She offered
me nadelm's duty."

"You should have been nadelm all along!" he said,
more sharply than he had intended.

"Yes, my grandmother thought so, as well. But
you misunderstand, *van'chela*. She offered the duty;
I did not hear that she offered the rank." Abruptly,
she pointed at her screen.

"Daav—the turn for the ferry station!"

"Ah, but *we* have no need to depend upon public
ferries."

She turned to him, lips parted. "*You* have a ship
here?"

"Korval has a yard here," he said, shifting for the
turn.

"It keeps slipping away from me," she said, slowly,
"that you are Korval."

"Yes, but just at the moment, I am your copilot,"
he answered, guiding the car through the gate and
gliding to a stop before the yard office. He powered
the vehicle down, and pressed his thumb against the
ID screen. "Master Fis Lyr was kind enough to lend
me the use of the yard's car. Now, if you are game
for a small walk?"

"Even a long one," she said, suddenly gay. "So long
as we need not walk to Solcintra."

"Now, *that* is too long a walk," he said, popping
his door.

Aelliana laughed, working the mechanism on the

passenger's door. By the time he had gotten 'round the car, having paused to retrieve her box from the boot, she was looking around her with frank curiosity.

"Ought we to tell the master that his car is back?" She asked, using her chin to point at the office door.

"It will already have done so, I fear," Daav said. "Aelliana."

She looked up at him, surprise edging the pleasure in her face.

He raised a hand, reached inside the collar of his shirt and slowly drew out a silver chain. Depending from it was a set of ship's keys.

Aelliana's eyes blazed. "You brought *The Luck*!"

"Of course I did. How else?" He slipped the chain over his head and offered it to her. "How could I know my pilot's plans? It could have been that she wished to lift immediately. In which case her ship should be nearer to her hand than Solcintra."

She grasped the keys tightly, her face tilted up, but not, he considered, seeing anything other than her thoughts. He held himself as still as he might.

I will not, he told himself, *influence her by so much as the twitch of a muscle. If she decides after all that lift is less chancy than Liad, even under Korval's wing...*

"It was very good of you, Daav," Aelliana said.

"Nonsense, you know that I like a lift as well as you do! And what pilot worth his leather would sit on the ferry by choice?" He leaned forward, conspiratorially. "Besides, you know, the ferry takes too long."

She laughed, and waved her free hand, capturing the yard, the car, and the office in one fey movement.

"If it will please my copilot to produce our ship?"

Our ship. The words thrilled him. It was what she had offered, before—and she had almost died of his refusal. Had he been with her the next morning, when her brother had come to Binjali's in search of her...

"Has my copilot," Aelliana asked teasingly, *"forgotten* where he left our ship?"

"Indeed no!" he assured her, rallying. "See? I have a map drawn right here on my palm."

He made a show of turning his free hand up, subjected it to a moment of frowning study and strode off, deliberately long-legged, but not so much that she had any trouble keeping up.

· · · ❖ · · ·

"A hotpad!" Aelliana threw a hand out and caught Daav's arm, calculating the expense between one breath and the next. *Ride the Luck* had money in her account, of course, but she was no wealthy merchanter.

"Forgive me, Pilot," Daav said seriously, looking down into her face. "I should have said—this is where I bring my own ship down, when I fly to Chonselta. A courtesy of the yard, and no expense attached."

Korval Himself, she reminded herself, yet again. Of course there would be a hotpad available for the delm's use at a Korval yard.

She sighed and looked up at him. "I am...somewhat unused...to such courtesies."

"Perhaps you should try to accommodate yourself," Daav said, still in that tone of utter seriousness. "Aelliana Caylon will doubtless be extended like courtesies."

"For a few days, perhaps," she said, frowning. "But it will soon be forgot, you know—our lift."

"If you insist. However, I would point out that

the ven'Tura Revisions are not so easy for pilots to overlook." He nodded at the ship, sitting proud and beautiful on her hotpad.

"Shall we?"

"Yes!" she said decisively. "We shall!"

She went up the ramp first—her right as pilot and owner. Her hands were steady as she slotted the key. The hatch opened and she stepped inside, aware of Daav's presence at her back, but more than that—aware of the presence, the *actuality* of her ship.

Before the tragedies of yesterday, she had loved *Ride the Luck* as well and as truly as she had been able. Though it had given her the courage to defy Ran Eld, she now knew that emotion for a weak and impotent thing. What filled her now was heat and light; awe and pride—there was no power of which she could conceive that would wrest this ship from her care.

Half-dazed, she entered the piloting chamber, putting a hand on the back of the pilot's chair to steady herself. Her hand showed stark against the white leather, the Jump pilot's ring flashing in the test lights from the waking instruments.

"We could lift now, this minute," she whispered. "Set a course for up and away..."

"Aye," Daav answered softly, "so you could. Nothing holds you here but gravity."

Stricken, she turned, one hand rising toward him.

"No," she breathed, "More than that, *van'chela*."

He came forward one short step, and took her hand between both of his. His skin was warm, the band of Korval's Ring cool. She felt longing, and a hesitant sadness.

"Aelliana, if you must lift—"

She raised her free hand and set her fingers across his lips, stopping the words. He grew very still, as if he had turned off his very thoughts.

"In fact," she said, voice shaking, "I must lift. To Binjali's Yard at Solcintra Port. Pray, do me the honor of sitting my second."

Her heartbeat was overloud in her ears: one, two, three, fo—

Daav pressed her hand and released it, moving slightly to one side, so that her fingers fell away from his lips.

"The honor will be mine, Pilot," he said, with careful gentleness. "However, we should settle a thing, before proceeding further."

He leaned over and placed her box on the copilot's chair. Straightening, he considered her out of serious black eyes, then bowed, with deliberation.

She was not much accustomed to moving in the polite world, and for an instant the mode confused. All at once, she had it: delm-to-one-not-of-the-clan. She bit her lip, and took a breath as Delm Korval looked down at her.

"It is possible that Korval has presumed," he said, the High Tongue striking her ears like so many crystalline pebbles. "Pilot Caylon, speak your truth without fear of offense. Is it your wish—and yours alone—to be taken into Korval's protection?"

Aelliana took another breath and met his eyes. The shift in *melant'i* had been unexpected, and momentarily shocking, but she found herself much more at ease than she had supposed she ever would be, come face to face with the most powerful delm on all of Liad.

"If it must be said before Korval to be true," she

said slowly, "then I say that I wish—very much—to come under Korval's care. That I share this desire with Daav only warms me; it does not compel me."

Korval inclined his sleek head and reached into his jacket. A moment later, he held out to her a pin in the shape of Korval's sigil, the Tree-and-Dragon.

"Wear this whenever you venture beyond Korval's grounds. It will mark you out as one who rests beneath the Dragon's wing."

"I thank you," Aelliana said, formally, and took the token from his hand. By the time she had affixed it to the collar of her jacket and looked up, Daav had her box stowed in the net between the pilot and copilot stations, and was webbing into his chair.

"Lift for Solcintra, Pilot?" he asked, looking up at her with a half-smile that made her chest tighten.

"Lift for Solcintra it is," she said, with as much composure as she was able, and took her place in the pilot's chair.

SEVEN

· · · · · · · · · · ·

Home is where the heart is.

—Terran proverb

THE LUCK SETTLED SWEETLY ONTO ITS COLDPAD.
Aelliana gave the board one last, comprehensive
sweep—all lights green—looked over to her lanky
copilot and smiled.

"Please tell Tower that we are berthed and will be
taking systems down."

He nodded and touched the comm key. *"Ride the
Luck* down, Binjali's Yard. Pilot Caylon's putting her
to sleep."

"Affirmative, *Ride the Luck*. Welcome home, Pilot
Caylon."

She took a breath and, when Daav did not immediately close the line, another.

"Thank you," she said, pitching her voice as if to
be heard at the back of a crowded classroom. "I am
pleased to be home."

Daav nodded, flicked the key off, and began to
shut down the copilot's station.

"Accustom myself?" she asked him, her fingers

69

moving effortlessly along the controls, as if they knew what to do of themselves.

"Tower did seem sincere," he answered, his tone so bland that it could only mean mischief. "You will notice that they did not welcome *me* home."

"That was very wrong of them," she said, matching his intonation as nearly as possible. "Open the line and I shall have them make amends."

He laughed, and gave his board one last flick before leaning back in the chair, grinning.

"In truth, it is . . . a relief to be ignored. And I would not have Tower abused."

"Abused!" Her hands had finished shutting down the pilot's board. She spun her chair to look at him. "As if I could abuse anyone!"

"Could you not?" he asked, and there was a thread of seriousness beneath the mischief that gave her pause.

"It is true that I . . . struck Ran Eld," she said slowly, "but my object—as Trilla has taught me—was to run away."

He appeared to consider that, his gaze straying over the dark board.

"The difficulty with running away," he said slowly, "as with most solutions, is that one must judge when it will answer—and when it will not."

He focused on her. "I do not say, in the case, that running away would not have served you, and well. But, sometimes, we must stand and fight, Aelliana, and be deliberate in the mayhem we choose to inflict."

She bit her lip, feeling again the blaze of her anger, the smooth swing of her arm, the jolt, when the back of her hand, weighted with the Jump pilot's ring, connected with her brother's cheek.

"I fear that I was not . . . thoughtful in the inflicting of mayhem."

His lips twitched. "Happily, the knack may be acquired."

"Through practice?"

"Alas."

"And yet, I don't know that I could . . . coldly . . . harm someone. Without anger as an impetus . . ."

"Anger is a chancy copilot," he said, suddenly rising, arms over his head. When his stretch was done, he looked down at her, his expression almost sleepy. "As I have cause to know. Does it please you to exit, Pilot? The hull is cool."

Jon dea'Cort was leaning over the workbench, eyeshields on, using what seemed to Aelliana to be one of Patch's whiskers to tweak the internals of a device no larger than her palm. A few steps out, she hesitated, not wishing to disturb his concentration, but he spoke without raising his head.

"Back already, are you?" he asked, his tone distinctly grumpy.

"Indeed, we are, Master," Daav answered, and Aelliana saw Jon's shoulders stiffen.

Carefully, he withdrew the probe and placed it on the bench, straightened and pulled the eyeshields up and off.

For a heartbeat, he said nothing. Indeed, he seemed to Aelliana to be cataloging her face, her person. She stirred, stilled—and Jon smiled.

"Pilot Caylon. You're a bold sight, child."

Her eyes filled. "Jon—" She swallowed, unable to find words adequate to the riot of emotion that enveloped her.

"Jon—I thank you, for . . . for all of your care."

"There's no need to thank me for that, math teacher," he said, turning away with a sudden briskness and peeling off his gloves.

"And yet," Daav murmured, "one might be grateful for the sunlight at the end of a bitter night, and thank it, most sincerely, for its warmth."

"Lecturing your elders again, Young Captain?"

"It's this standing at the head of my clan, you see," Daav explained earnestly. "It puts the most absurd notions into one's head."

Jon considered them both. "Finally got 'round to telling her, did you?"

"Too late, as you'll make your point, but yes."

"It is not Daav's fault that my brother is—was—an aberration," Aelliana stated firmly.

"That's said fair enough," Jon said. "But you would never have had to endure last evening's adventure, if you'd known your copilot for a Dragon."

Aelliana tipped her head. "Possibly that is true, but it hardly matters now. And, if I had not been the target of Ran Eld's anger one more time, then I would not have had the Healers, and I—I think that having the Healers was a very good thing, indeed."

"There are less risky roads to a Healer, math teacher," Jon said, and threw up his hands. "I bide by your judgment, and not another word from me."

"For now," Daav added, sotto voce.

The elder pilot snorted. "So, the past being past, have you taken thought for the present, or the future?"

"For the present," Aelliana said, "I have accepted Da—Korval's protection."

Jon's eyebrows rose. He looked to Daav. "Protection, is it?"

"Is there a problem, Master Jon?"

"Why ask me?" He looked back to Aelliana. "All right, that's a reasonable course. And the future?"

"The future . . . must still be determined." Her chest was once again tight with conflicting emotions. "I need time to think, Jon. So *much* has happened since yesterday . . ."

"No need to make excuses for taking thought," he told her. "Just remember your comrades, eh?"

"Of course I shall! You will doubtless grow tired of seeing me, and answering my questions, for you know, Jon, I am still quite desperately ignorant about—so many things!"

"Well, we can't have that," he said comfortably. "Recall that you and I have a meeting with the Scout Commander and a tour of the World Room before us."

"On Trilsday," she said. "I remember. Jon?"

"What's on your mind, math teacher?"

"When is Clonak's next shift? I—I must speak to him."

Jon's gaze slid to one side—to Daav, Aelliana thought, and wondered what information passed from old Scout to younger in that rapid glance.

"Clonak's off these next few days," Jon said, carefully, to Aelliana's ear. "He said he had some business to lay before his father."

"Oh." Aelliana bit her lip. "I had hoped to speak with him—soon."

"As it happens," Daav murmured, "I have Clonak's comm number. I might, if you wish, and after you are settled, call him and ask if he will speak with you—or when you might meet him."

"Thank you," she said, much relieved. "That will answer. I don't wish to leave him in distress..."

"'Course not," Jon said, gruffly. "'Course not."

· · · ✴ · · ·

Aelliana had been silent for some time, her head turned slightly away from Daav, paying attention, so he thought, to the spectacle of Solcintra Port. The vehicle they traveled in was smaller than the car loaned for his use in Chonselta, and far more nimble. Had he been driving only himself, he would have made use of several of the smaller ways known to him and so put the port behind him sooner. With his passenger so rapt, he drove along the main thoroughfares, at a mostly decorous speed, and kept his tongue between his teeth.

They had cleared the gate and were into Solcintra proper, when she stirred and looked over to him.

"Is Clonak High House?"

She knew Clonak's surname, which ought to have given her the answer, but Aelliana appeared to have never learned the teaching songs matching Lines to Clan. Or, he thought, she had forgotten them, as less important than mathematics, or, perhaps, survival.

"ter'Meulen belongs to Guayar, certainly," he said gently. "And Guayar holds place among the Fifty."

She nodded as if she had suspected as much, and her face grew more serious.

"In that case, I feel that I must speak with Clonak— very soon, indeed. I do not wish to count myself too high, but the tenor of his message leaves me to fear that these matters he intends to put before his father might have to do with a, a strike against Mizel."

"Mizel has offered Clonak no insult," Daav pointed out, wondering at this new political sensibility.

The corners of her mouth tightened.

"Clonak sat my copilot, too," she said.

"Ah. I understand." He maneuvered the little car down the Boulevard of Flowers—not the most direct route out of the city, but a pretty, winding way that he thought might please her.

"Clonak's father is not likely to allow him to act precipitously. I fear that an account of my actions on your behalf last evening has found its way into *The Gazette*, of which he is an avid auditor. I am certain he will not endorse any plans Clonak proposes for Balance with Mizel until he has spoken to me and, now that you are able, to yourself." He glanced over, reading tension in the tilt of her chin.

"You are very right that you must speak with Clonak soon, and give him what ease you may. But I believe that we may depend upon his father to keep him in hand for a few hours more."

Aelliana inclined her head. "You have knowledge which I lack," she said. "Doubtless you are correct, that Clonak's father will not allow him to do anything . . . foolish."

She glanced out at the street, and her smile flickered, which was the usual response to the Afternoon Garden. It was a small plot, scarcely larger than a patio, planted with blooming things in all shades of orange and yellow, with a few benches artfully adrift in flowers.

"That's lovely," she said, and cast a quick look to him. "And perhaps not the straightest route out of the city."

"Discovered! No, not the most direct route—nor the least. I thought a casual survey of the gardens might do us both some good."

"Chonselta Public Garden is very grand," she said, her attention focused out the windows. "But these are—pocket plantings! And the houses, with *their* flowers! It's like being in the middle of a wildwood!"

Daav, who had spent some considerable time in wildwoods of one sort or another in his capacity as a Scout captain, did not correct her.

"The yellow is the Afternoon Garden," he said, instead. "There is also an Evening Garden, a Dawn Garden, and a Midnight Garden. Groups are made up to visit each at its proper moment; in between, there are tours of the house gardens and refreshments alfresco."

"It sounds a marvelous way to while away a day," Aelliana said, and laughed slightly. "I don't think I've ever taken such a tour."

No, very likely she had not, Daav thought darkly. Though the elder brother had doubtless taken as many pleasant excursions as he might have wished.

"We leave the flowers here, alas," he said, turning onto North Street. "If you like it, we may come back and take more time with them, another day."

"I would like that," she said, and shifted in her seat.

He glanced over and met wise green eyes.

"Now that our diversion is done, if you please, Daav: *an* account of your actions last evening? Is there more than one?"

Discovered, indeed! He sighed lightly.

"In fact, there are. Mind you, both accounts detail

the same actions; it is the *meaning* of those actions which is appropriated ... rather differently."

"And *The Gazette* tells the misappropriated tale?"

"It does—which was my intention. It was necessary to shield Pilot tel'Izak as much as possible from her delm's anger. Unfortunately, in taking what I might to myself, I fear that I have exposed you to the eyes of the curious."

He met her eyes, soberly.

"It was a clumsy solving, Aelliana. I beg your pardon."

She considered him for a long moment, then put her hand on his knee.

"There is no need to beg my pardon, *van'chela*. Indeed, I was well on my way to making a spectacle in my own right. Had I not arranged to have my name appear in the news sheets, Ran Eld should never have known that I owned a ship." She gave him a smile.

"You needn't hold your speed down for my sake, Pilot," she said.

Daav laughed, surprised and delighted.

"Transparent, am I?"

Aelliana frowned slightly. "I would not say *transparent*, only ... strangely obvious. It is odd, but not unpleasant." She looked over to him. "Do you find it so?"

"Unpleasant? No. Surprising, I would say."

"And not precisely what you anticipated," Aelliana murmured, her fingers warm on his knee. "What did you anticipate, Daav?"

He hesitated. "Any number of things, since last evening, and been joyously proved wrong in most." He took a breath. "May I ask that we pursue this topic ...

later, after we have made you known to my *cha'leket*, gained his smile, and seen you comfortably settled? It may be that a few hours more will illuminate that which is presently obscure."

After a moment, she nodded. "That may be wisest. Tell me about your brother."

Encapsulate Er Thom? Almost, he laughed again, but—no. Aelliana was tentative among strangers. Her manner was—or had been, he corrected himself—self-effacing, and her *manners*, while not boorish, were... unpolished. Well she might be shy of meeting a High Clan lordling in his own house. Especially with the example of her own brother before her.

"Er Thom is... very dear to me. And you must forgive me for miring you immediately in another of Korval's muddles."

"Is he not your brother, then?" Aelliana teased.

"Ah, you think it a simple question! We are the children of identical twins, near enough to the brothers our hearts believe us to be. However, Er Thom was born to Petrella yos'Galan, and I to Chi yos'Phelium. More! The delm ordered our births, and thereafter took both of us into her care and training. We were two seeds in one pod, you understand, neither one greater nor lesser than the other, until we came halfling. At that point, the delm decreed that I be sent to the Scouts, as the children of yos'Phelium often are, and that Er Thom join his mother aboard *Dutiful Passage*, there to learn all he might of the mysteries of trade."

"It must have been very hard," Aelliana said softly. "To have grown so near, then parted so sternly."

Daav sighed. "Certainly, it seemed so at the time. But, Delm's Wisdom will out, you know, and in the end we both saw that it had been no random cruelty. Er Thom now stands as Korval's master trader, thodelm of Line yos'Galan, and heir to the delm. I trust him with my life—indeed, I trust him with Korval! And that was wisdom—to weave us together, so that either might become what the other is, at need, for the profit and the strength of the clan."

"Your delm was . . . farseeing," Aelliana murmured.

"She did her best, which is all any of us may do. Even those of us doomed as delm." He gave her a swift smile. "But of Er Thom! He is lifemated to Honored Scholar of Linguistics Anne Davis, and his heir, young Shan, is a joy and a terror to all."

"Scholar Davis?" Aelliana sat up straighter. "I have not yet read her book!"

He gave her an amused glance. "She would scarcely have expected it."

"Truly? I have read reviews in the journals, and seen discussions among the scholarly forums—indeed, the scholar's work seems to me to be at least as weighty as you would have me believe the Revisions to be. Perhaps more! Jon had said he would lend me his copy, when he was done."

"I am certain Anne will be happy to give you a copy of her book, if you truly wish to read it, though I warn you, she may seem bemused. She had expected, you see, that the work would be of interest to perhaps another dozen scholars in her immediate field. The excitement that it has caused among—shall we say, among those who are not scholars?—has quite taken her by surprise."

"Shall I not mention her work?" Aelliana asked worriedly. "I would not wish to offend—and it is true that a mathematician is not a linguist."

"As you have an interest in the work—and an opinion!—I believe you will not offend. And, you know—Anne is a native speaker of Terran."

Her eyes widened. "Of course she is! Would she care, do you think, if I were to practice my Terran against her?"

"I think she would be delighted," Daav said truthfully. "And now, Pilot—are your straps secure?"

She touched the shoulder harness and the lap strap.

"They are. May I know why the pilot asks this question?"

"Because now that we are out of the city, I intend—very much—to give over holding down my speed."

Aelliana smiled, and settled back into her seat, moving her hand from his knee to her own.

"Good," she said.

EIGHT

· · · · · · · · · ·

Each clan is independent and each delm law within
his House. Thus, one goes gently into the House
of another clan. One speaks soft and bows low.
It is not amiss to bear a gift.

—Excerpted from the Liaden
Code of Proper Conduct

THE WIND ROARED, YANKING HER HAIR HARD ENOUGH
to bring tears. Aelliana recalled that she had used to be
frightened of speed; certainly the blurred countryside
through which they pelted—houses, trees, flowers, and
fields smeared into the abstract—ought to sent her
curling into the corner of the seat, face hidden behind
her arms.

Instead, she laughed, and sat forward, giddy with
sensation. Drunk with speed. Drunk, indeed, with
Daav's joy and a sort of feral alertness, so potent that
there was no need to touch him in order to clarify
what he felt.

The car swooped to the top of a hill, spun into a
thin lane and dashed downward. Stomach in free fall,
Aelliana laughed again, and heard Daav laugh, too.

At the base of the hill, he downshifted, and followed the lane to the left, through a series of twists and turns, slowing almost imperceptibly as they negotiated each until, by the time they passed beneath an archway thick with flowers, the car was proceeding very nearly at a stately pace.

Colmeno bushes lined the lane on both sides, their lemony scent cleansing away the sweet breath of the flowers. At the end of the line of bushes, the lane intersected another. Aelliana caught a glimpse of a stairway, a glitter that was perhaps a window, then Daav turned the little car left, then right, going quite slowly now, and pulled into a 'crete apron between a building that might have been a garage, and a pleasant lawn.

"And so we arrive," Daav said, shutting the car down. He raised his hands and smoothed them over his head, utterly failing to tame his wind-snarled hair.

"That did no good whatsoever, if you were trying for decorum," she told him, her voice effervescent in her own ears.

"Now, have I ever tried for decorum?" Daav said musingly, looking down at her from snapping black eyes. "I must have done, mustn't I? Once or twice?"

"Surely, Korval must be decorous!" she returned.

He moved his shoulders. "Korval of course must be decorous, lest society fail. Daav rarely has such calls upon him. However, you are correct! One's brother has endured an unsettling morning, and very likely a less-than-amusing afternoon. He deserves better than to be treated to the spectacle of the two of us, with the dust of the port—and half the valley!—on us and our hair in matching mares' nests." He raised an eyebrow.

"There ought to be a comb or three in the drawer under your seat."

There were, she found, exactly three—disposables, each sealed into a transparent envelope. She handed him one and took another for herself, reaching behind her head to open the silver clasp.

"Ouch!" Biting her lip, she worked the comb carefully through the knotted mass of her hair, and after a time was able to once again snap the hair clasp into place.

"Behold us," Daav said gaily as she slipped the comb into the pocket of her jacket, "respectable!"

"If your brother's day has been distressing," Aelliana said, frowning up at him, "ought we to disturb him with a stranger's affairs?"

"We ought by all means make him aware of the clan's obligations, and immediately. He stands as nadelm, recall. If aught were to happen to me, it is Er Thom who will continue those arrangements guaranteed by Korval. You may be sure he would ring a peal over me the like of which you have never heard if I failed to acquaint him with one who stands within Korval's protection."

Aelliana shivered, suddenly cold in the warm afternoon. *If aught were to happen to me . . .* So blithely said, and yet—

"Aelliana?"

Nothing, she told herself firmly, *is going to happen to Daav.* She took a deep breath and looked up at him. "I beg your pardon," she said.

He frowned slightly. "I'm a brute," he said comprehensively. "Pulling you from here to there with no time to rest. It will be quickly done here, I swear it, and gently, too. Er Thom at least has address."

He opened his door. After a moment, Aelliana opened hers, and stood out onto the 'crete apron.

Before her, the grass stretched like blue-green velvet from apron's edge to a pleasant patio agreeably populated with chairs and small tables. Behind them, tall glass doors stood open to the day, the house stretching above and beyond...

She stared, suddenly understanding the scope of the building before her. This was no humble thing such as Mizel's house on Raingleam Street. This was *house* writ large, bold, and proud—and if she had not been told "house" she might instead have supposed it to be a—a mercantile center, or a building attached to an university, or—

"Aelliana?" His hand came lightly to rest upon her shoulder; she felt concern, and a tang of self-anger.

"Your brother lives *here*?" she demanded. "It is— how many? In your clan?"

"Ah. You must understand that Trealla Fantrol is Korval's showpiece. Our mother taught that, in the past, it was also a fortress, guarding the mouth of our valley, and denying those with...unfriendly intent... access to Jelaza Kazone—yos'Phelium's house, you know—which is much less grand, and quite a bit older.

"As to how many we are—very few, in these days. We have never been a large clan, even at our most fulsome."

"I see." She took a breath, recalling the calming spin of color Daav had named the Rainbow. Carefully, she called a prism to mind, one hue after the other—but the exercise failed to calm her.

"I suggest that we press on, Pilot," Daav said softly. "I engage that Er Thom will not eat you. He will make his bow, fix your face in his memory, and doubtless say something pretty and pleasant. We need not even stop for a cup of tea, if you would rather."

He was, Aelliana realized with a start, soothing the woman she had been yesterday. The woman she was today—she was startled, and uneasily aware that her manners were not High, but she was not *afraid*.

"I am not frightened," she said, firmly. "I agree that it is best to continue—and even to drink a cup of tea. It would be very bad of me, as one who has accepted Korval's protection, to disdain the nadelm's hospitality."

A flicker of brightness, gone before she could identify it, as Daav took his hand from her shoulder and moved across the lawn with his long, noiseless stride.

I am not, Aelliana told herself, following, *frightened*.

The room beyond the patio was small—perhaps a family parlor, with comfortably shabby chairs and a litter of books and projects in process adorning various side tables. Near the open doors, a smaller chair sat next to a larger, both angled away from the garage. A fleece throw was draped, haphazard, across the back of the larger chair. In the smaller sat a stuffed animal with large round ears and rounder blue eyes, apparently left to enjoy the view.

Daav moved quickly through the room to the hallway beyond, unhesitatingly turning left, as silent on the polished wooden floor as he had been across carpet and grass.

Aelliana sighed. Every Scout she knew had the

knack of silent movement; perhaps she would ask one of them to teach her. For this afternoon, however, she contented herself with walking as lightly as she might, and taking care not to bump into the occasional artfully placed flower table or art piece.

Ahead of her, Daav paused at the intersection of halls, head tipped as if he were listening to the house.

"Perhaps if we called out?" Aelliana said, coming up to stand just a step behind his shoulder.

"No need—he will be in his office. I left a bit of a tangle in his lap, I fear."

"Then perhaps I should lead," she suggested, and heard him chuckle.

"Perhaps you should! Only a step more and we are arrived." She felt his glance settle on her and looked up to meet his eyes.

"How do you fare, Pilot?"

"It has been a full day, but I believe that I fare well enough," she said, truthfully. "The sleep that the Healers put on me was—most amazingly restorative."

"Good." He smiled. "We play on?"

"We play on."

Down the hall they went. Daav put his hand on the knob of the first door on the left and pushed it wide.

For a heartbeat, she thought that he had guided them to the wrong room. Surely, the bright-haired man with the stern, beautiful face could not be Daav's brother!

Then he smiled and rose from behind the desk, his hands held out in welcome.

"So, you are returned at last!" he exclaimed in the Low Tongue. "I had begun to fear that you had left me to solve all, forevermore!"

Daav laughed and swept forward, catching Aelliana's hand and bringing her with him.

"I am twelve times a wretch, but even I must pause at such perfidy! Has it been dreadful for you, darling?"

"Not unremittingly," the other said, coming around the desk. He was slim, and studied, and moved with a pilot's effortless grace. "I have entertained several people on the delm's behalf, though not everyone I had expected, and learned some things which will perhaps be useful. At the moment, we are in a lull. Anne has gone to her office at university, and I had thought to catch up on some matters of use to yos'Galan."

"And now I interrupt you yet again! It will be as quick as can be, then I to home, and duty!"

"There's no need to rush away," Er Thom said. His tones were soft and sweet, entirely unlike Daav's deep, rough voice. "Make me known to your guest, do."

"Not only a wretch, but a unmannered wretch!"

Daav brought her forward, and she felt affection warming her. "Aelliana, here is my brother Er Thom, Thodelm of yos'Galan and heir to Korval. Brother—I show you Aelliana Caylon, scholar and pilot, reviser of the ven'Tura Tables. As of this day, she stands enclosed by Korval's protection, until such time as she shall call enough."

Aelliana bowed, choosing the mode of adult-to-adult upon finding herself uncertain of the hand-motion for the proper forming of greeting-a-thodelm-not-one's-own.

"Er Thom yos'Galan, I am pleased to meet you," she said, and even though she was not afraid, her voice trembled, just a little.

Violet eyes considered her gravely, and it seemed to her that he was indeed committing her face to memory. He answered her bow precisely.

"Aelliana Caylon, I am very pleased to meet you. You may rest easy in our care."

"Thank you," she whispered.

"No," he answered surprisingly. "It is I who thanks you, Pilot, from the bottom of my heart."

Before she could react to this, he turned again to Daav.

"If you and the pilot are at liberty, I would like to share some of what I have—"

There was a sudden clatter in the hall beyond, footsteps—a quiet pair and a noisier. Daav exchanged a wild look with his brother, caught Aelliana's hand and brought her to the right just as a regal-looking gentleman in green-and-gold livery appeared in the doorway.

"The Right Noble Lady Kareen yos'Phelium," he announced, too loudly for the circumstances, and stepped nimbly to the left.

Er Thom yos'Galan inclined his head. "Thank you, Mr. pak'Ora," he said, as serene as if he did not hear that second pair of footsteps, stamping angrily down his fine wooden hall.

The regal gentleman bowed slightly, turned, and paused to allow the owner of the footsteps by.

Into the office she came, her steps only somewhat muffled by the rug. That she was neither a pilot nor a Scout was immediately obvious. Despite this, Aelliana owned, she was a handsome woman, her dark hair a silky cap adorning a shapely head, and bright stones glittering in pretty ears. Her face was at the moment marred by a monumental frown, well-marked brows pulled tight, and lips thin in anger.

"Good afternoon, cousin," Er Thom yos'Galan said, gentle-voiced, and speaking the Low Tongue, as one did with kin. "I had expected you earlier in the day."

"Had you, indeed? I am desolate that the demands of my duty to Liad put me in a closed meeting all of yesterday and half of today." The lady's voice was sharp, her choice of mode High—elder-kin-to-junior. "It was only after lunch that I was at leisure to catch up the world, and then what should I do but first call upon the delm."

Her frown increased, and she turned her head suddenly, sharp gaze going past Aelliana and resting—on Daav.

"You!" she snapped, and *that* was a mode Aelliana knew well—superior-to-inferior.

"Indeed, I." Daav agreed, also in the Low Tongue.

"I suppose that it should not surprise me to find you here, sheltering behind your *cha'leket*, as you have always done! Of course it is nothing to you, that the clan dances on the brink of ruin, as long as you have had your diversion! And such a grand diversion it was, with your hand all over it, leaving no doubt in the minds of the vulgar. I say nothing of the shattered contract with Bindan—you have made it plain in the past that you intend to steer Korval into ruin, and will hear no advice from your elders! But one would think that you—*even* you!—would understand the impropriety, to say nothing of the cost, of ransacking a clanhouse, holding the nadelm at gunpoint, subverting the youth—"

Aelliana flushed hot. "You will *not* hold Daav to account for that!" she snapped, and there was the High Tongue come to her, after all: pilot-to-passenger.

Wondering dark eyes turned her way.

"I beg your pardon?" The lady's words fair glittered with ice.

"I said," Aelliana repeated, somewhat more temperately, "that you will not hold Daav to account for insisting upon entry into Mizel's House, nor his employment of those willing to aid him. The muddle was of my making, and it is my shame that it fell to him to put all right for me! If you will cast blame, Balance and doom, then I am your proper target, ma'am! Daav did only as he ought!"

The room was utterly silent. The dark-haired lady did not go so far as to gape, though she was certainly taken aback. As who would not be, Aelliana thought, her hands suddenly cold, addressed thus heatedly by a stranger in the house of a kinsman? From the side of her eye, she saw Er Thom yos'Galan, lips parted; an expression of startled delight illuminating his face.

"Who," the lady asked, in the mode between strangers, "are you?"

Aelliana swallowed, and brought her chin up.

"Forgive me, cousin, I am remiss!" Daav's brother moved forward, slipping his hand gently under Aelliana's elbow. "Allow me, please, to present to you Aelliana Caylon Clan Mizel, the foremost practitioner of mathematics on the planet today! She and my brother have only just returned from Chonselta. Scholar Caylon honors us by resting in our care." He pressed her elbow gently, as if, Aelliana thought, encouraging her to be of good heart.

"Scholar Caylon, I make you known to my cousin, Daav's sister, Kareen yos'Phelium Clan Korval. You will of course know of her ongoing work with the Code.

Now, please," he said to Aelliana, "allow me to make amends for my dreadful manners, and offer you a cup of tea. I hear from my brother that you have endured much these last hours..." He turned her away from Lady Kareen, who stood with her glare in place, and led her to the tea table by the cold hearth.

"Daav, ring for Mr. pak'Ora, will you?" Er Thom called over his shoulder. "We'll want fresh tea." He saw Aelliana situated in a chair and smiled down at her. "Will you have something to eat?"

"I thank you, but—no. However, tea would be most welcome."

"Of that, I have no doubt," he murmured, his smile widening. "Well played, Pilot," he added, for her ears alone.

Mr. pak'Ora, arrived at the door, received his orders and departed, promising tea on the instant. Er Thom yos'Galan turned to address the other lady.

"Kareen? Will you take tea?"

There was a small hesitation before she moved forward. "Certainly, cousin. Why should we not take tea while the clan crumbles about us? Already, I apprehend, we are a laughingstock, our credit fallen on the Exchange. Tea will be pleasant, as we watch all that we once were fall and burn." She seated herself across the table from Aelliana and inclined her head. "Don't you agree, Pilot-Scholar Caylon?"

"Certainly," Aelliana said, warily, "tea is often pleasant. It is very good of Thodelm yos'Galan to offer such kindness to a stranger."

"No, you must acquit him," the lady said. "It is not kindness, but yet another diversion."

"Diversion is also welcome," Aelliana answered,

meeting the other's eyes firmly, "and so a further kindness."

"Own yourself bested, sister," Daav said, folding his lanky self into the chair at Aelliana's right hand.

She turned slightly, the better to see him, and barely restrained herself from snatching his hand as she put her question.

"*Van'chela*, is this true? Has your clan taken so much harm?"

"No, nothing so dire," he assured her, smiling. "It's merely Kareen's humor."

"My *humor*?" the lady inquired, raising shapely eyebrows.

Daav tipped his head, as if considering her question. "It is either your humor or your distemper, sister," he said at last, and with less goodwill than Aelliana had expected. "Choose wisely."

"Ah, the tea." Er Thom yos'Galan slipped into the chair at Aelliana's left. "Thank you, Mr. pak'Ora."

"Will there be anything else, sir?"

"Not at the moment, I think."

"*Thank* you, sir," the butler said, and departed, closing the door softly behind him.

Er Thom yos'Galan poured, handing the first cup to Aelliana, the second to Daav, the third to Kareen yos'Phelium, keeping the fourth for himself.

"Speaking to your point, cousin," he said, after he had sipped his tea, "I had the felicity of a visit from the Master of the Accountants Guild today. He had gone first to Jelaza Kazone, and on discovering the delm away, came to me." He looked to Aelliana and inclined his head gravely. "Forgive me if I touch upon a painful subject, Scholar. In sum, it would appear that the departure of your former kinsman has uncovered a mystery that has for several years puzzled the master accountants. They wish me to convey to Korval their gratitude."

"Pray, what mystery is this?" inquired Daav's sister, her tone almost civil.

Er Thom turned to face her.

"It would seem that certain small- to mid-sized endeavors held by clans of modest means have come on the market unexpectedly over the last while, to be sold for absurdly low cash amounts. It was thought at first that these sales were to ameliorate cash-flow difficulties, but it rarely seemed to benefit the clans in question at all. Indeed, if anything, they came to be less robust than before the sale."

"Bad business sense is hardly a mystery," Lady Kareen pointed out.

"True. However, today, in the new hour of the morning, a man approached the Mid Port office of the Accountants Guild, demanding payment of a note, signed by one Ran Eld Caylon, ceding a half-share in Sood'ae Leather Works, or cash equivalent, to the bearer, one San bel'Fasin. The master at the desk placed Master bel'Fasin into a waiting room while she called Mizel, and the port proctors. Mizel reported that Ran Eld Caylon was clanless; his signature without worth. The Six Masters then questioned San bel'Fasin, closely, and with the assistance of the proctors. In short, it appears that this person is the key to an entire enterprise of fraud." He inclined his head.

"Once again, Korval is shown to be a champion of Liad."

Aelliana sipped her tea, her brain racing. Ran Eld

had signed a note—signed a note *after* he had been made clanless, ceding half the worth of Mizel's most profitable venture to a—port tough? It made no sense. Unless . . .

She put the teacup back into its saucer with an unsteady clatter. Unless he had been at peril of his life and snatched at any straw, in order to preserve himself?

"Well, younger brother!" Lady Kareen said, not sounding pleased at all, "Your luck holds firm."

"So it would seem," Daav answered cordially. "Who could have looked for such good fortune?"

"And the contract with Bindan? Has your luck stretched to that?"

"Bindan expresses dismay that the clan's daughter Samiv tel'Izak has been exposed to—unsavory elements—while in the company of her affianced husband. It is Bindan's pleasure to suppose that it would tarnish the luster of the clan's jewel to continue the contract, thus it has been rendered null. I expect that Mr. dea'Gauss will be hearing from Bindan's man of business, if he has not already done so."

Lady Kareen was seen to take a deep breath.

Daav held up a hand. "Peace, sister. It is done."

"I see that it is. Has the delm in his wisdom decided to allow yos'Phelium to wither?"

"Perhaps," Daav said, matching her tone for acid. "Certainly it must come under consideration, given the disappointing recent yields."

"Now, that, I cannot allow," Er Thom yos'Galan said, softly. "Pat Rin is growing quite accomplished."

Daav inclined his head gravely. "So he is. Thank you, brother, for reminding me."

"I see." Lady Kareen placed her cup on the table and stood. "I have done my duty, futile as it is. Good-day to you, Pilot-Scholar Caylon. Cousin. Young brother." She bowed to the table in general, and moved across the room, waving Thodelm yos'Galan back to his seat.

"I can find the door, Cousin. Do not trouble yourself."

He followed her, however, leaving Aelliana alone with Daav.

"I—" Unable to restrain herself any longer, she reached out and grasped his hand, immediately receiving a potent stew of irritation and relief, spiced with too many lesser emotions to identify.

"Daav, tell me true—is your clan in danger on my account?"

His fingers tightened on hers and he looked seriously into her face.

"Korval is in no danger on your account. It is true that there will be penalties to pay, though it was Bindan who resigned the contract. I trust that Mr. dea'Gauss will hold us from utter ruin. In any case, that outcome was mine and mine alone."

"Part of your clumsy solving?"

"The greater part, if you will have it."

"Does she mind," Aelliana asked, carefully. "Pilot tel'Izak?"

Puzzlement reached her, followed by a bolt of understanding, and a flitter of amusement.

"Pilot tel'Izak herself said to me that she felt we would not suit. I believe we parted on terms, as we should have, for she is a fine pilot and holds copilot's duty close.

"Now,"—he slipped his hand free, and leaned

forward slightly—"do you wish to go to Jelaza Kazone? You may, you know, guest here, with Er Thom and Anne and young Shan, if you think it will suit you better."

"No!" she cried, and bit her lip. "If you please, Daav, I would prefer to stay with you."

He closed his eyes briefly, and inclined his head. "That is what you shall do, then. Come, let us find my brother and make our excuses."

NINE

· · · · · · · ·

The heart keeps its own Code.

—Anonymous

DAAV'S HOUSE NESTLED AT THE FAR END OF THE VALLEY, a hollow square, glimpsed briefly as they crested the hill, with a tree soaring out of the center. Perhaps, Aelliana thought, there was also a garden in that inner court. Korval's Tree was—somewhat taller than she had expected, its arms reaching high and wide across the pale sky.

"I thought you said that your house was less grand than Trealla Fantrol."

"And so it is! Jelaza Kazone is quite old, and while I do not say that the roof leaks, it fails to approach the first level of elegance. Historically, Korval has preferred its comfort, indolent breed that we are."

Aelliana smiled, and hesitated slightly before asking a question that had just lately come to concern her. "Will I meet your sister again at Prime Meal?"

Daav turned his head, both eyebrows up and an expression of nearly comic horror on his face. "Good gods, whyever would you?"

"It is yos'Phelium's house that I am to guest in," she pointed out.

"Ah, I see! Never fear that you will meet Kareen between kitchen and small parlor! She lives in the house at Grand Lake, and ventures out to the country but rarely. I fear that it is only myself, and a few staff, and of course Relchin and Lady Dignity to bear you company. You may find us a bit thin—how could you not? Immediately we are to house we will ask Mr. pel'Kana to assign a car to your exclusive use, so that you are not wingless."

"You must not stint yourself," Aelliana protested. "I—surely there are taxicabs."

"Surely there are," Daav said dryly, "and not the least need for you to summon one. yos'Phelium owns... several cars, Aelliana. You need only indicate which one will suit you best. In truth, you will be performing a service for the House. I have my favorite, you see, and do not give the others the attention they deserve."

She considered him. "And if I choose this one?"

"Why, then, I would be obliged to point out that— while it is a satisfactory car in many respects—there's scarcely sufficient room to carry oneself, a passenger, and a very small box. For one who may be expected to visit the city in pursuit of shopping, it may prove to be less than ideal. There is in the garage an extremely nice vehicle, with a larger cargo space, very light and responsive to the stick, which I think you may find more suited to your needs. Though the choice is, of course, entirely your own."

Aelliana bit her lip until the urge to laugh aloud had somewhat subsided.

"That was very well done," she said, when she was

certain of her voice.

"Thank you," he answered gravely.

"But I would not dream of depriving you of your favorite car," she said, as he slowed to make the turn into a hedge-lined lane.

"Thank you," he said again, and this time she did laugh.

She had been made known to Mr. pel'Kana, who bowed grandly, and solemnly agreed with Daav's suggestion that the "blue car" be assigned to her use. That detail retired, her hand- and voice-prints were filed with the house, then she followed Daav upstairs and down a hallway to the midpoint, where he paused and stepped back, gesturing that she should precede him.

"I hope that this apartment will win your approval. However! If it does not, please speak out immediately. There are others available."

There was *some*thing in his voice, or in the air between them. She felt her fingers twitch toward him and folded them into her palm, placing the other hand against the plate. The Jump pilot's ring sparkled on her finger in the soft light, then the door opened and she stepped inside.

Her first instinct was to cry out that it was too precious a place to house her. The worth of the rugs alone!—not to say the couches, or the clutter of knickknacks on the mantle. Well into the room and to the left was a closed door, doubtless leading to the bedchamber itself; next to it, a compact kitchen nestled inside an alcove. So much she saw in her first glance.

It was the second glance that taught her that the furniture was, if not precisely shabby as Clan Mizel knew *shabby*, then at least well-used and even worn. The wooden walls were dark, perhaps with age.

The third glance caught the window, and she was lost. Scarcely attending to herself, she crossed the room, light-footed as Daav on the thick carpet, past the desk with its computer and comm unit, and put her nose against the glass, looking out and down into as wild and glorious a tangle of growing things as ever she had seen.

"Do you like it?" Daav's voice breathed into her ear.

"Like it?" she repeated. "*Van'chela*, the little gardens of the city pale."

He laughed softly.

"Tame and civilized has its place," he murmured. "So I am told. We have the front gardens under somewhat more control, for the house's dignity. This..." He rapped his knuckles lightly against the glass. "This is *our* garden."

"I like it very much," she said, "and the room—" She turned her head to look into patient black eyes, suddenly and achingly aware of how near he stood, and recalling a slow, growing heat, the feel of his body against hers...

"The room—" she said again, turning away from the garden, and coincidentally putting several steps between Daav and herself, "—is...very large, *van'chela*. I daresay I will not do it justice, but the view—that I will not willingly surrender."

He smiled at her from his lean against the window frame.

"It is yours, then, too-large as it is. Though I fear you have not seen the whole of it yet."

Shifting out of his lean, he crossed the room to

the closed door, slid it open with a touch and stepped back, bowing her through ahead of him.

The bed alone was larger than her room in Mizel's clanhouse. Heaped with pillows, it sat beneath a ceiling port through which she could see the paling blue-green sky of a fading afternoon. Chest of drawers, wardrobe, and another door, which she opened, revealing a 'fresher big enough to accommodate most of Binjali's regular crew, all at once.

"What are the rescue protocols, should I become lost?" she asked, stepping back into the bedroom. Daav, she noticed, had not followed her within, but stood in the doorway, his hands tucked into his pockets of his jacket, watching her with an intensity that made her shiver.

"Merely call out," he said, and his voice was calm as always. "The house keeps its ear open for certain words—*help* and *thief* among them. There is a complete list in your computer, in the House file."

He tipped his head. "Speaking of which—do you still wish to speak with Clonak? I can make the call from your comm."

"Yes!" she said decisively. "That I must do."

"Very well, then." He disappeared from the doorway. Aelliana took one more look around the room, touched the pale blue coverlet over the bed, and went out into the parlor.

"She is here now, if you have a moment," Daav was saying into the comm. He paused, then nodded, as if to himself. "The next voice you hear," he said, and held the earpiece out to Aelliana.

She stepped forward and took it from his fingers, looking at the blank screen questioningly.

"He asks for voice only," Daav said.

That was peculiar, but perhaps he was in disarray. "My thanks," she said to Daav.

"It is no trouble at all. If you have need of anything, only call." He bowed slightly and left her, moving swift and silent across the rugs and out, the door closing gently behind him.

Aelliana bit her lip and brought the earpiece up. "Clonak?"

"Aelliana, are you well?" His voice was so earnest that she scarcely recognized it.

"I am most wonderfully well," she assured him, walking over to the window and looking down at the magnificent tangle of greenery and color. "The Healers' care was beyond anything I could have imagined, and you have no least cause for concern, or to—to rebuke yourself."

"That I have no cause for concern is welcome news," Clonak said, carefully. "But I do rebuke myself, Goddess. More than you may know."

"That is quite ridiculous," she said sternly, watching a large orange-and-white cat stalk, tigerlike, through a bank of pink-and-white roses. "You could scarcely force your escort on me. If there was error, Clonak, it was mine, in ignoring your very good advice. I should have not, I see now, leaned all of my weight upon custom."

There was an . . . odd . . . silence from Clonak's side, though Aelliana could not have precisely said *how* it was odd.

"Why did you refuse me, Aelliana?" he asked then, his voice low and intent. "Didn't you believe that I would stand between you and danger?"

"I believed it all too well—and that was my reason for denying you! My brother—Clonak, you must understand that, yesterday, all I knew of the world had taught me that my brother would gladly ruin anything I held dear—and that he had the power to do so! I see...now that the Healers have someway opened my eyes—now I see that fear had bound and blinded me. It was beyond foolish, to have refused your escort—today, I would have known to do so. Yesterday...I acted as best I might, to preserve my friend's honor and his life." She closed her eyes against the garden, and wished that she could see his face. "Please forgive me, Clonak."

There came a sigh, very soft.

"How can I refuse you anything, Goddess? If it is forgiveness you require of me, then of course it is yours." He cleared his throat. "Daav has you under wing, does he?"

"Indeed. I am a guest of Korval for the moment. I need...some time to think."

"As who does not?" he returned, with a flicker of his more usual manner. "Well, then. *All's well that ends well.*" That was in Terran—a Terran proverb, so he himself had taught her, meaning that, despite the methods, a fortunate outcome was to be celebrated.

"I think that it has ended very well," she told him seriously.

"Then I shall endeavor to think likewise," Clonak said. "Now, of your kindness, Goddess, I must leave you and attend to other matters. If you have any use for me, only tell me so."

"Yes, of course," she said, frowning after a particular note in his voice. It seemed to her, but surely not—

"Clonak, are you well?"

"As well as may be," he answered. "Fair evening to you, Goddess. Until soon."

"Until soon," she whispered, but Clonak had already closed the connection.

· · · ✳ · · ·

"Bindan asks high," Daav murmured, scanning the document to which Korval's man of business had directed his attention. Indeed, the amount demanded was ... bracing. They would need to sell stocks, or perhaps one of the lesser houses, though not so much as a ship.

"Too high," Mr. dea'Gauss said dryly. "The next document more accurately illuminates Korval's final accounting in the matter, as adjudicated. It was Bindan, after all, who called the contract void. While there is some recourse under Clause Eighteen, they failed of proving that Samiv tel'Izak has been materially harmed by the event Bindan points to as the breach point. Pilot tel'Izak herself gives as her firm opinion that she stood in less danger from the relevant incident than a pilot may find on any strange port, and further states that your care was in all ways respectful of her *melant'i*."

Daav glanced from the screen to his accountant's face. "She said so? That will not have pleased her delm."

He looked back to the screen, flicked to the next document, and blinked. Mr. dea'Gauss had worked wonders on Korval's behalf, he allowed. Again.

"Perhaps Bindan would not have been pleased," Mr. dea'Gauss murmured. "However, Ms. tel'Brieri, who sat as the impartial *qe'andra* required by Guild law, ruled that we should hear the pilot's testimony in confidence. It is very true that Bindan was not best pleased with this ruling; however, the pilot was then at leave to speak her own truth, which she did, most eloquently." Mr. dea'Gauss paused to glance down at his notepad, as if verifying a point.

"It may be, your lordship, that Korval ought to undertake an entirely separate Balance with Pilot tel'Izak. If I understand her tale correctly, it would seem that she suffered some abuse from . . . an agent of the clan."

"Indeed, the Tree used her terribly, and Balance is surely owing. Do you advise a separate accounting? I had thought merely to attach a rider to the breach payment, marked for Samiv tel'Izak's personal account."

"In this case, I believe that a separate accounting would . . . avoid confusion on the part of Pilot tel'Izak's delm," Mr. dea'Gauss said imperturbably.

Daav sighed. "As acquisitive as that, is she? Well, then. It is Korval's natural desire to see Balance appropriately placed. Of your kindness, Mr. dea'Gauss, please draw up the document. I wish it to be—generous, but not so much as to seem overabundant. Those monies will be withdrawn from my private accounts."

"As your lordship wishes." Mr. dea'Gauss made a note on his pad. "The final documents will be on your desk tomorrow morning."

"Say rather on your desk," Daav said. "I have business in the city tomorrow and will come by your office—by midmorning?"

"They will be ready for your signature," Mr. dea'Gauss assured him, making another note. "Is there any other service that I may be honored to perform for your lordship?"

"In fact, there is. Please create the usual accounts for Aelliana Caylon, seeded by precisely half of my

personal fortune, prior to deducting the Balance owed
Pilot tel'Izak."

The older man looked up from his notepad. "That
is," he said carefully, "a lifemate's portion."

"So it is," Daav said with more composure than he
felt. He inclined his head. "The situation is delicate,
Mr. dea'Gauss. The Healers at Chonselta Hall believe
me to be Pilot Caylon's natural lifemate. Unfortunately,
the pilot has suffered . . . an injury in the past, which
may prevent the bond from ripening. It is my wish,
however, to honor it—and her—as . . . fully as possible."

Mr. dea'Gauss looked rather quickly down at his pad.
"Of course, your lordship. One can readily apprehend
your *melant'i* in the matter. Those papers, too, will
be awaiting your signature tomorrow."

"Thank you," Daav said softly. "Is there anything
else which requires my attention, sir?"

"We are to the end of my list, your lordship. I
thank you for seeing me so quickly."

"No, it is I who thank you, for your skill in hus-
banding Korval's resources. You should know, however,
that Lady Kareen will be most disappointed."

Mr. dea'Gauss paused in the act of slipping his
notepad into its case. "I am of course desolate to have
disappointed Lady Kareen. In what way have I erred?"

"In no way that I can perceive," Daav said, already
regretting his joke. Mr. dea'Gauss was not known for
his sense of humor. "It only seemed that my sister
was quite eager for the clan to be turned out onto
the port, and the delm reduced to taking up employment as a pilot for hire."

"Ah." Mr. dea'Gauss finished sealing the case and
rose to his feet. "Your honored sister was not, of

course, familiar with all of the particulars of the case. Korval's danger was . . . very small and, as your lordship sees, extremely easy to contain. Shall I call upon Lady Kareen and reassure her?"

"That won't be necessary, Mr. dea'Gauss. You have done quite enough for us this day." He touched the pad on the edge of his desk. "Allow Mr. pel'Kana to show you out," he concluded.

"Thank you, your lordship."

. . . . ❖ . . . .

She unpacked her box, hanging her jacket, the white shirt, and blue trousers in the wardrobe, folding the new small clothes into a drawer, and draping the green robe over the foot of the bed. The remains of her old clothes, she left in the box, and tucked it into the bottom of the closet. The room swallowed her possessions without noticing them, and the rest of the apartment would do the same to her.

She shook herself, and pushed the encroaching grimness away.

Work was what she needed, she thought determinedly, and returned to the parlor.

Sitting down at the desk, she woke the computer, and was very shortly engaged in bringing her working files over from Chonselta Tech.

Having achieved that, she opened the most recent: a proof for pseudorandom tridimensional subspaces. But for once, mathematics—the elixir that had healed the damage her husband had inflicted; the magic that cast Ran Eld's constant cruelties momentarily into another time and place—mathematics failed her. Instead of the pure forms suggested by her equations, she heard Clonak's voice, so subdued. Surely, she thought, surely he *had* been weeping, and Aelliana Caylon, his student, his pilot, and his comrade, had been too dim-witted to ease him.

"He wouldn't show me his face," she muttered, as for the dozenth time her eyes wandered from the screen to the window and the garden beyond.

Her failure gnawed at her, and yet she could think of nothing that she might have done—might now do—that would mend matters. She was at a loss even to know how to discover what trouble afflicted him.

Finally, with the setting sun casting deep shadows in the corners of the garden, she put her work away and rose from behind the desk.

She would, she thought, find Daav and put the question to him. He and Clonak had been friends for—since Scout Academy! Daav had been the captain of Clonak's team. Surely, he would know what was to be done to ease their comrade's dismay. Indeed, hadn't she seen that glance between Jon and Daav, when she had asked after Clonak's shift?

Scouts, she reminded herself, opening the door and stepping out into the hallway; one must always take care to ask the right question of Scouts...

She went down the stairs and paused, suddenly aware of her folly. Where in this enormous house could she hope to find Daav? She ought to have called him, or—

To her left, a door closed. She turned her head and here came Mr. pel'Kana, followed by a very upright man in sober business dress, with brown hair going grey, and a case tucked under one arm. Upon seeing her, he checked, murmured a word to the butler and stepped forward.

"Do I have the honor of addressing Aelliana Caylon?" He spoke in the mode of servant-to-lord, which was surely an error; his voice was precise and pleasant.

"I am Aelliana Caylon," she said, offering adult-to-adult as a more realistic approximation of their relative *melant'i*. "You have the advantage of me, sir."

"I am dea'Gauss," he said, and bowed profoundly. "Your servant, ma'am."

"I— That is very kind of you, Mr. dea'Gauss. However, you mustn't let me delay you, sir! I am only looking for Daav..."

"Certainly," he said promptly. "Allow me."

With that he slipped his arm through hers and guided her down the hall to the second door. He knocked, one sharp rap of knuckles against wood, and paused, head tipped.

"Come!" Daav called from within.

Mr. dea'Gauss turned the knob and pushed the door open.

· · · · ❊ · · · ·

The door closed behind Mr. dea'Gauss. Daav did not so much rise as spring to his feet, spinning toward the window as if the view of the inner garden would answer his need for action. He felt every nerve a-quiver— some part of which might, after all, be attributed to relief. While he had never truly supposed that he had been the agent of the clan's ruin, he *had* considered it possible that his misstep had cast Korval into stern economy. Which might well have been the case, had Korval employed a *qe'andra* any less able than the very able dea'Gauss.

For the rest—

A knock at the door shattered his thought. Doubtless, Mr. pel'Kana come to inquire about his preference for Prime.

"Come!"

The door opened.

"My thanks," Aelliana said.

Mr. dea'Gauss answered with a grave, "My pleasure."

Daav turned in time to see the accountant's shadow fade away from the door, as Aelliana stepped within.

His heart rose to see her, walking assured and firm—sharp and telling contrast to the tentative, near-invisible woman who had slunk into Binjali's so short a time ago, and whispered the name of her ship.

"Aelliana," he said, smiling. "Bored to distraction already?"

"Indeed, no," she said, pausing at the far side of the desk. "Only bedeviled by my own stupidity and wondering if I might ask you, yet again, to help me!"

"Of course I will help in any way I can. What has happened?"

She hesitated, and it seemed to him that the glance she leveled at him was more sightful than previously, as if she saw past face and eyes and someway into his heart.

"Perhaps I should not plague you, just now," she said slowly, and stepped 'round the desk, her hand darting out to grasp his.

He stiffened, then relaxed as cool fingers wove between his.

"Aelliana," he said softly, "what do you see?"

"See? Nothing save a weary face and some sadness about your eyes," she answered, her own face troubled. "However, I feel—*Van'chela*, what a stew!"

"Your pardon," he said, stiffly. "I fear I'm all at

dozens and daggers." He slipped his hand away from hers and tucked it into his pocket.

"Daav—tell me true. Is your clan in peril?"

"It is not."

She tipped her head, as if she considered whether that bald statement might yet harbor some ambiguity.

"Your sister—"

"My sister," he interrupted, his voice sharper than he had intended, "sees a hundred-year scandal—"

Aelliana's eyes widened, and he made haste to finish.

". . . in a teacup misaligned within a formal setting. You must not, as much as she does herself, take Kareen too seriously, Aelliana. In this instance, you may discount her fears entirely, as Mr. dea'Gauss has just shown me the outcome of today's negotiations." He produced a smile for her earnestness and had the satisfaction of seeing her face lose some of its tension.

"Now," he said, "you are troubled. What may I do to assist you?"

She sighed and walked to the open window, leaning one hand against the frame as she looked out into the early evening.

"I—as you know, I spoke with Clonak—it was the strangest thing, Daav, but I feel . . . I feel that assuring him of my safety failed to ease him, and that I left him more distraught than I had found him. He was . . . very subdued—not at all in his usual mode, and—the entire purpose of speaking with him was to give him heart's ease . . ."

"Ah." He stepped up to the window, too, and looked out over the riot of gladoli blooms. That Clonak's case was bad—he feared it. He had known that his friend had formed an attachment to Aelliana, as had all of the crew at Binjali's. If his heart was truly engaged—and it seemed now that it must be . . .

He took a breath. "Perhaps Clonak still needs some time," he said carefully. "We were all of us—anxious for you, and recall it has only been a day since it seemed likely that you were . . ." he paused, wondering if he should bring such things to a mind newly Healed.

"Brain-burned and unlikely to recover," Aelliana said crisply, which seemed to answer that question.

"That—yes. Sometimes, it is relief which plunges us into terror, once we are certain that danger is beyond us. Certainly, Clonak has been of that persuasion. Scouts are taught to act first and panic later, when one is safe from the worst effects of stupidity."

"I . . . see." She was silent for a long time, her attention seemingly on the darkling garden.

He took a deep breath of flower-scented air, and sighed. She was right, he thought; he was weary, and trained as a Scout as much or more as Clonak had been.

"Daav?" she asked softly.

"Aelliana?"

"Do you know—what it was that the Healers did to me?"

Now, *there* was a question he had hoped not to hear for some days. And yet, she had asked it, and it was his to tell her.

"I know . . . what Master Kestra told me," he admitted. "Which I will tell you, if you like, but I wonder, Aelliana . . ."

She turned to look at him.

"Yes?"

"Would you care to go for a walk in the garden? It's far too fine an evening to languish indoors."

TEN

· · · · · ·

The Guild Halls of so-called "Healers"—interactive empaths—can be found in every Liaden city.

Healers are charged with tending ills such as depression, addiction and other psychological difficulties and they are undoubtedly skilled therapists, with a high rate of success to their credit.

Healers are credited with the ability to wipe a memory from all layers of a client's consciousness. They are said to be able to directly—utilizing psychic ability—influence another's behavior; however, this activity is specifically banned by Guild regulations.

—From "The Case Against Telepathy"

THE GARDEN SMELLED OF GREENLEAF, DAMP SOIL, AND a hundred other subtle perfumes. Walking beside Daav along the overgrown path, Aelliana's hand brushed against a tall lavender spike, releasing a burst of mint scent.

"To address what the Healers have ... done to you, Aelliana, we must first allow you to know the state in which you were received into the Hall. The report I had from the pilots at Chonselta Hall was that you were raving, clearly assigning meaning to words which were...inappropriate to the case..."

The taxi driver, and her own voice, quavering in and out of audibility, the words tumbling in a meaningless chatter of sound. "I remember," she said, and that was true, though the memory was distant and without emotional charge, as if it had all happened a very long time ago.

"Ah. Then you will not find it surprising that two Master Healers were immediately called to your side—Kestra and Tom Sen. It was Master Kestra I spoke with today when I arrived at the Hall.

"Of the most recent trauma, you have been healed. There was, so Master Kestra tells me, some small bit of burn, which she pronounces insignificant. She is, by the way, all admiration for you and the solution you employed to preserve yourself."

"Solution?" Aelliana frowned, trying to recapture *that* memory, but it eluded her, lost inside a sound like shouting and the image of a solar system entirely unknown to her.

"You had created yourself a piloting problem," Daav said softly. "A model star system, the balancing of which kept your mind focused and the...more inimical effects of the Learning Module at bay."

"Oh, but that's standard protocol," she said. "The Learner will not disturb a brain at work."

"Thus did you save yourself, when those of us who would have, could not." There was something in that which reminded her too nearly of Clonak, but when she turned to look into his face, all she saw was weariness.

"The Healer who was with me when I woke, the

first time today," she said, the memory suddenly upon her. "I had asked her if I were brain-burned. She said she was trying to determine just that, and then—I fell asleep. How odd, that I hadn't recalled that until just now! When I woke again, I had no question but that I was perfectly well."

"Healers are bright, and terrible, and wise," Daav murmured, with the air of one quoting . . . poetry, perhaps.

"I've had so little experience of Healers—none, in fact." She bit her lip and glanced at the side of his face, waiting for him to continue, but he merely strolled on, a man communing with his garden. The impulse to touch him was very strong. She curled her hands into fists, counted to twelve, and then asked another question.

"They—the Healers did something else, didn't they, Daav?"

"The gloan-roses are doing well, don't you think?" he said, pausing to call her attention to a mound of glossy green leaves and flowers the color of heart's blood.

"They're very pretty," she said, but he was gone, angling across the short plush grass, to a wooden bench set within the embrace of the rosebushes.

Daav sat, one knee folded on the seat, his arm on the back of the bench, chin on his arm as he regarded the roses. The perfect study, Aelliana thought, of a man who very much did not want to answer the question that had just been put to him.

A step out from the bench, she paused, and asked herself, very earnestly, if she *truly wished* to know what the Healers had wrought. If it were enough to give *Daav* pause, perhaps she did not. And yet—

"I scarcely know myself." The words rose to her lips unbidden, a whisper no louder than the soft brush of the breeze over rose petals.

"Daav." She sat on the bench, folding her hands tightly onto her lap. "What *else* have the Healers done?"

He closed his eyes. "Aelliana, have mercy."

Mercy? Her stomach knotted painfully, familiarly.

"Have I escaped brain-burn only so the Healers might discover a greater flaw?" And yet, what? What might be so terrible that he wished to hide it from her, when copilot's care—

And if the copilot's best care of his pilot was to conceal an unpleasant truth?

"I am an oaf." His voice was cold.

He straightened and turned 'round on the bench, his feet flat on the ground. Leaning forward, he put his hand over hers where it was fisted on her knee.

"Aelliana, it is nothing dire—I had only wished you to have some days to become accustomed, and to know yourself again before hearing the rest of what confronts you."

Anguish swept through her, and self-loathing, tenderness, avarice, and pain.

"I think," she said unsteadily, "you had better tell me."

"Yes, I suppose I had better." He sighed, and took his hand away, settling back into the corner of the bench. It took a ridiculous amount of willpower, not to snatch his hand back to her, but she managed to sit seemly, fingers folded tightly together.

"The other thing that the Healers did is that they *pruned away*, as Master Kestra styles it, a layer of scar tissue—again, an approximation—from the old trauma. She felt that you might be ... 'easier,' *van'chela*, though there was no healing it entirely."

"It had happened too long ago," Aelliana said.

"And compensations had been built. Yes, exactly so." He took a breath, and exhaled, carefully, she thought.

"What they found, when the thing had been done, was—a hint, Aelliana—that you and I are the two halves of a natural lifemating." He raised his hand, as if to forestall the question she could not think to ask.

"Master Kestra warned me, most plainly, that the seed which ought to have blossomed into a full joining, had been ... stunted; oppressed by the scarring. She did not—she *would not*—say that we should ever become what we were intended to be."

Ran Eld, Aelliana thought bitterly, had been a genius, indeed. Always, it had been given him, to know precisely how best to harm her. Yet, she had loved Daav, now that she was not too craven to call it by its proper name—had loved him perhaps from the first ...

"You understand that my brother whom you met, is linked to his lady, heart and mind. He—they—speak of their bonding as ... the greatest joy of their lives." Daav cleared his throat. "In our circumstance, with the link stunted, or dead—"

"It may not have had room to grow, but it is not dead!" she cried, and stood up, one knee braced on the bench as she put her hands on his shoulders.

"Can you *not* feel it?" she demanded.

Silence was her answer; or perhaps the shiver of wonder, leavened with fear, was her answer.

She looked down into his face, angular and beloved,

his lips just parted, black eyes watching her with such care. Her blood heated, and a longing so fierce that her eyes teared tore at her, even as she bent and put her lips against his.

Deeply, she kissed him, feeling his answer in every cell of her body.

· · · · ❀ · · · ·

Her mouth was sweet, and unexpectedly cunning. Desire stiffened him all in an instant, and he ran his hands into her hair, sweeping it free of the silver ring, returning her kiss wholly, as her fingers stroked deliciously down his throat. With him wedged into the corner of the bench, it was she who had the upper hand, and it seemed she wished to exploit her advantage, as she explored him, each touch an agony of pleasure, as if her desires and his were one. Never had a lover known him so well; nor played him with such surety. He was molten, all but beyond thought.

But not quite.

"Aelliana—" Her name was scarcely more than a moan; the question: "How do you know these things?" incinerated as her mouth found him.

Too fast, too fast. A laborious thought, but thought nonetheless. He reached for her, but she eluded his hands, focused entirely upon his pleasure, and in such manner... Aelliana did *not* know these things.

He moved, not in passion now, but in horror, his blood going from molten to ice. Loud as he was, he had overtaken her, who could access his inmost feelings through a touch! She started back with a strangled cry, lost her balance, and crumpled to the grass.

"Aelliana!" He threw himself after her—and froze as

her hands came up, warding him, green eyes dazzled, panting with mingled horror and lust.

"Help me," she gasped, and closed her eyes.

Help her, when her danger was all from him? And, yet, who better then her copilot—her lifemate?

He took a deep breath, reached through the turmoil of emotion and spun himself into a circle of quiet peacefulness. For the space of three heartbeats, he only breathed, letting calmness inform his mind. When he was certain of his control, he opened his eyes, and settled himself comfortably on the grass beside her.

She was panting yet, and shivering where she lay, her hands fisted at her side, muscles hard with anguish.

"Aelliana," he said, softly. "Look at me."

She whimpered, her brows drawing together, but she did not open her eyes.

"Look at me!" The command mode, flicked with precision against abused nerves.

Her eyes snapped wide, and met his.

"Copilot's duty, Aelliana," he murmured, willing the sense of his words to reach beyond her disorientation and fear. "I will help you. Can you trust me so much? And do exactly as I say?"

"Ye-e-s . . ."

"Good. I am going to teach you the Scout's Rainbow. You saw it, this morning, and thought it useful, eh? And so it is, useful. It is the first tool we learn, and the one we reach for most often. There is nothing to fear in the Rainbow. However, if at any step you should begin to feel anxious or afraid, only open your eyes. Do you understand?"

"Yes."

"Good. Close your eyes, now, and visualize the

color red. Let it fill your head to the exclusion of all else. Tell me, when you have it firm."

Three heartbeats, no more, which was better than most hopeful Scoutlings achieved.

"Now," she whispered.

"Good. Allow your thoughts to flutter away, unconsidered. Focus on the color red, warm, comforting red. Let it flow through your body, beginning at the top of your head, warm and relaxing—down your face, your throat, your shoulders..." His voice was soft, softer, the rhythm of the words timed precisely to aid the student in achieving trance.

Watching, he saw her muscles lose some tension and felt a flutter of relief.

"Visualize the color orange. Let it fill your head, to the exclusion of all else. Tell me, when you have it firm."

There was a pause, and a whisper of velvet along silk. He glanced away from Aelliana's face, just as orange-and-white Relchin settled himself at her opposite side, chicken fashion, his eyes slitted in approval.

Distantly, Daav felt relief. Relchin had an...affinity for the Rainbow. That he appeared to oversee Aelliana's inaugural journey could only be a good omen.

"Now," Aelliana whispered.

"Good," he answered, drawn back into his role as her guide.

Color by color, he took her through the Rainbow, watching her relax more deeply at every level.

Once, at yellow, and again at purple, he reminded her that she might exit the exercise simply by opening her eyes, which was the protocol. She chose to continue, which everyone did.

In the choreography of the Scout's Rainbow, the ultimate safe place lay beyond violet. Each person who traversed the colors found a different door at the end of the Rainbow, uniquely theirs, the room behind it always a refuge.

At the far side of violet, with Aelliana breathing as sweetly as a child asleep, he asked the question, softly as her own thought: "What do you see?"

"Hatch," she murmured. "*Ride the Luck*'s hatch."

Oh, indeed? And what shape had her safety taken before she acquired her ship, he wondered, and shuddered to think that there might have been none.

"Will you enter?" he suggested.

She did so, and he guided her into a deeper trance— not as rich as the Healers might provide, but restorative beyond mere sleep.

Copilot's duty done, he stood, ordered himself, and took stock. Reviewing the Rainbow had lent him an extra level of lucidity beyond even what the grandmother's art had given him. Which was well. For now, he must take up lifemate's duty, which was stern. Stern, indeed.

He dropped to one knee and gathered her into his arms, his lifemate, his love. Rising, he turned toward the path, and the house, Relchin his high-tailed escort.

One-handed, he flicked the blue coverlet back, and laid her gently down among the pillows. Relchin leapt up to the bed and was already curled next to her head by the time Daav had dealt with her boots and straightened again.

He drew the cover over her, smoothed his hand along her hair, lying in a tangled fan across the pillow—and dropped to his knees, his face buried in the cover by her side.

His lifemate, for whom he had ached, whom he had waited for, and despaired ever of finding. Against all odds, she was discovered, willing—no, eager!—to stand with him—

And he was a deadly danger to her.

That Aelliana could sense his emotions—*that* was abundantly plain. As plain as the fact that his will had overruled hers and influenced her to knowledge and actions beyond her—and perhaps repellent. Daav shuddered, and pushed his face deeper into the coverlet.

Despite the gift that Aelliana had received of the Healers' meddling, he knew no more of her now than a Scout with a high empathy rating had ever known. And how they two might remain together, when he could overpower her with a thought—

That was not a lifemating. Lifemates stood equal upon all things. This . . . *aberration* that the Healers had wrought—

"It will not do," he said, raising his head, and looking down at her sleeping face. So precious—and his, to treasure as she deserved, and to protect from any who might do her harm.

Even from himself.

"We are a broken set, *van'chela*," he told her, tranced though she was. "And I could wish your brother not already dead so that I might thank him fitly for his care of you."

Which was perhaps, he thought, something that he might not wish Aelliana to feel from him.

He stood, staggered and caught himself with a hand against the wall. Looking down, he saw her face through a fog of tears, and shook his head.

"Good night, beloved. Sleep deeply. Dream well."

He bent, and kissed her, chastely, on the cheek. On the neighboring pillow, Relchin yawned.

"Mock me, do. It's no more than I've earned." He extended a hand and rubbed the cat's broad head. "Guard her well," he murmured.

At the door, he paused to turn on the night dims, so that she would not be frightened to find herself in a strange room, should she, after all, wake.

Then he went away, eventually to his own apartment, stopping first at the central control board, where he removed himself from the list of those whom the house would admit to her rooms.

ELEVEN

. . . .

A scholar is illuminated by the brilliance of her students.

—Liaden proverb

AELLIANA STIRRED TOWARD WAKEFULNESS, NOT KNOWING what roused her, nor with any memory of having gone to sleep. They had returned late to *The Luck*, tipsy with wine and drunk on the good wishes of their comrades. She had gone up the ramp, Daav a warm shadow at her back, opened the hatch, and stepped within. They had talked; though she failed of recalling their topic. The sound of his voice—*that* she recalled, serious and comforting; his arms when he embraced her warm and certain.

Someone tickled bristles across her nose. Aelliana sneezed, and opened her eyes.

A large orange cat looked curiously into her face from its nest on the pillow beside her. Its whiskers had precipitated the sneeze and, very likely had been what had set her on the path to wakefulness.

"What have you done with Daav?" she demanded, and pointed an accusing finger at its nose. "I know you—you were prowling in the garden last night!"

Which meant, she thought with a start, that she wasn't on *The Luck*, after all.

The cat bumped a damp nose companionably against her finger and purred gently. She rubbed its ears absently while she looked about her at the sun-filled room, the blue coverlet, the wooden wardrobe with its fanciful carvings of winged lizards lounging among fruit-heavy vines.

"This," she told herself, or perhaps the cat, "is the apartment Daav has given me in Jelaza Kazone."

The cat pushed his head into her fingers, demanding more robust attention.

"Brute," she said, which was how one addressed Patch, the resident cat and co-owner of Binjali Repair Shop, when he made demands upon one's affections.

To judge from the increased level of purrs, the orange cat likewise found this to be an acceptable mode.

She had been so certain that she—that *they*—had come home to *The Luck*! Aelliana sighed.

"All very well for the Healers to give one the capacity for amusing dreams," she told the cat, "but I believe I would prefer the reality."

And that quickly, memory arose, as if all she needed to do was wish for it.

The tangled skeins of desire and need, the heat in her blood, Daav's flesh under her hands . . .

Aelliana gasped and sat up, clutching the coverlet to her, abandoning the cat utterly.

"I—repelled him," she whispered, shivering with the memory of cold horror. "How—it was everything he desired; I—I *felt* it . . ."

The cat yawned, stomped across her thighs and jumped to the floor.

Aelliana swallowed.

The Healers' gift was plainly a double-edged blade, new to her hand and risky to wield. That she had in some way misused it—and Daav! Would he even see her, after he had thrust her from him so coldly?

She closed her eyes, visualizing a gradation of color, and felt the panic growing in her stomach subside. Daav had done copilot's duty; he had succored her when she had asked for his aid. Someone must have brought her—and the cat!—here to her rooms, and she thought it had not been Mr. pel'Kana.

"I must speak with him," she said firmly, as she would to a row of attentive students. "Surely, we can sort this out."

She pushed the cover back and followed the cat's example. Once on the floor, however, she hesitated, looking down at herself. The olive trousers were rumpled and grass-stained, the black sweater flecked with stems and small bits of fluff.

"First a shower," she told her invisible class. "This is not something to be discussed in less than a clean face."

The cat was sitting in the window, gazing down into the garden, the tip of his striped tail flicking—one . . . two-three!—when Aelliana came into the parlor, her hair damp and loose along her shoulders.

In the shower, she had decided that the best course would be to send him a note through the house base, asking when they might speak together. She would be careful not to touch him, or in any other way offend him. In the time between, she would study the problem as she knew it to exist. She would, she vowed, do better for Daav than she had for Clonak.

She loved him, she thought, coming 'round the desk. Ought she to tell him so? She glanced at the computer; the message light was glowing a steady blue. Slipping into the chair, she touched the proper key.

Words bloomed on the screen; his name was the first she saw.

> *Good morning, Aelliana. I trust and hope that you slept well in our house. Korval's business rules me today, and so I am early away. That being so, I have asked my sister Anne to come to you and take you to the city to acquire clothing and whatever else you may need or desire. Please do me the honor of placing yourself entirely in Anne's care, and be guided in all things by her judgment.*
>
> *Daav*

She blinked and slumped back in her chair. Shopping? But—she needed nothing! Moreover—shopping with a strange lady—a *Terran* lady, whose book she *still* had not read? Was he mad?

"No," she said, leaning forward abruptly. This was, after all, Daav, who did nothing for one reason if it could be done for six.

So, then, reason number one: Perhaps a wardrobe consisting entirely of two pairs of trousers, a sweater, a shirt, and a pilot's jacket was, just a bit, thin.

Reason number two: She had wanted to practice her Terran against a native speaker.

Reason number three: The lady was lifemated to Daav's sunny-haired brother, and counted the bonding as the greatest joy of her life.

"This is," she told the orange cat, "a person I will wish to see."

He had asked the lady to come to her, he said, but made no mention of an hour, nor left her any means of contact.

"Well, let us find Mr. pel'Kana," she said to the cat. "Doubtless, he knows everything."

As it happened, Mr. pel'Kana had been well-informed on her topic. He engaged to call Trealla Fantrol's butler with a message for Lady yos'Galan while Pilot Caylon chose her breakfast from among the foodstuffs on offer in the morning room.

Pilot Caylon had submitted to the morning room, seeing Daav's hand once again, and discovered herself most wonderfully hungry. By the time Mr. pel'Kana had come with the news that Lady yos'Galan would be pleased to wait upon her at the turn of the hour, Aelliana had consumed two cheese rolls, a cup of curried vegetables and drunk two glasses of tea.

"Thank you," she said to the butler.

"Certainly, Pilot. Will there be anything else?"

"No, I—yes! I wonder, what is the name of the cat?"

Mr. pel'Kana leaned forward gravely. "Which cat, Pilot? There are several."

"Oh! The orange one."

"That would be Relchin. Quite the outdoors enthusiast. You'll find him more often in the gardens than the house, though he does enjoy his little luxuries. Lady Dignity prefers to observe the wilderness from the comfort of a window seat or an adjacent shelf."

"I will watch for her," Aelliana said solemnly, and

Mr. pel'Kana bowed as if were perfectly natural that she do so.

"If I may, Pilot, you will not wish to forget your jacket, for your trip into the city."

Her jacket. She looked at him doubtfully. "Is that... proper wear for—shopping?" Her cheeks warmed; she ought, she told herself, to know these things.

"A pilot's jacket is proper attire everywhere," Mr. pel'Kana answered her gravely, and not as if her question had been absurd at all.

"Then I will fetch it immediately," she said. "Thank you."

"You are quite welcome, Pilot. Will there be anything else?"

"No—not at the moment."

"Very good, Pilot." He bowed again, gently, and wafted out the door.

Aelliana finished her tea, cast a speculative eye on the remaining cheese rolls, and regretfully decided against. Lady yos'Galan was due in a very few minutes, and she still had to fetch her jacket.

She had just gained the second floor hallway when the bell rang.

Mr. pel'Kana met her at the bottom of the stairway, guided her to the threshold of the small parlor, and left her to enter alone.

A very tall lady stood by the mantle, her chestnut hair brushed back from a face that was both interesting and intelligent, but in no way beautiful. The jacket she wore open over her dull-gold shirt was good, serviceable twill. She smiled when Aelliana came into the room, as if the sight delighted her as few things had, and bowed in the mode of adult-to-adult.

"You must," she said, as she straightened to her full, improbable height, "be Aelliana Caylon. I am Anne Davis."

Aelliana returned the bow. "Lady yos'Galan," she said, glad of adult-to-adult. "Thank you for your consideration."

"Please, call me Anne," the tall lady said. "I am very happy to meet you at last."

At last? Aelliana inclined her head. "If you will be Anne, then I will be Aelliana," she said, her words freighted with more formality than adult-to-adult easily carried. "It— It is very good of you to take me to the shops. I hope that I have not disrupted your whole day."

"Not at all! If I had stayed home, I would only be reading student papers."

Aelliana smiled. "I would rather go shopping myself," she said. "But is the university not at recess?"

"The university is on recess, but I have six graduate students who do not know the meaning of the word 'rest.' Their enthusiasm does them credit, of course." This was accompanied by a knowing look from well-opened brown eyes, and Aelliana smiled again.

"Of course. I hope, however, that they will grant their mentor the gift of a few days."

"Oh, I have a plan," Anne said airily, and plucked up a package from the mantle.

"Daav said that you were interested in reading my distillation of Professor yo'Kera's theory of the common root-tongue. Please, accept this as a gift."

Aelliana received the book, and bowed. "My thanks to you for your kindness."

"Please, think nothing of it," Anne Davis told her. "If you are at liberty, we might go up to Solcintra now."

"I lack any students as enthusiastic as yours," Aelliana assured her, "and so am perfectly at liberty. I wonder... I wonder if I might ask a boon."

Anne Davis tipped her head to one side. "Certainly."

"I have... very small Terran," Aelliana told her, in that tongue. "It would oblige me, if we might speak so." She paused and said, more rapidly in Liaden. "It is for selfish purposes alone; I would very much like to improve my command. If it will be tiresome for you—already burdened with six eager students—then I thank you for your consideration of my request."

"Has Clonak been teaching you Aus dialect?" Anne asked her, in the brisk modelessness of Terran.

Aelliana blinked up at her. "Trying, he has," she admitted. "An apt pupil, I am not."

"I think you're very apt, indeed. And I will be perfectly happy to let you sharpen your Terran against me. After all, I practiced my Liaden against Er Thom and Daav. Still do," she added thoughtfully.

She moved toward the hall, and Aelliana perforce went with her, finding to her dismay as they approached the house's entrance hall that she was still carrying the lady's book.

A shadow moved to the the right of the door: Mr. pel'Kana, coming to unlock for them.

"Lady. Pilot. A pleasant day to you both."

"Thank you, Mr. pel'Kana," said Anne Davis, sweeping out the door with a stride even longer than Daav's.

Aelliana paused, and pressed the book into the old man's hands.

"Please," she said, "if it is not too much trouble—would you put this on the stair? I'll carry it up with me when I return."

"I'll take care of it, Pilot," he said solemnly. "Never fear."

TWELVE

· · · · · · · · · · · · · ·

If honor be your clothing, the suit will last a lifetime.
—William Arnot

"HERE WE ARE," ANNE DAVIS SAID, PAUSING ON THE
walk before a crystal-laced gate.

Beyond the gate was a tapestry of tiny flowers,
shy among glossy green leaves and interwoven with
pinpoint lights. At the garden's foot was a door and a
large window, half-hidden by an artful rain of crystal
and leaf. To Aelliana's eye it looked—expensive. In
fact, the *whole street* looked expensive, hardly a shopping district at all, and certainly not a street where a
daughter of Mizel ought to be looking for a few shirts
and some serviceable pants. Why, even Voni's most
expensive marriage-clothes had been bought ready-
made, and adjusted by the in-shop tailor!

"Your pardon," she said to her guide, distress plunging
her into Liaden, when they had been happily conversing
this last hour in Terran.

Anne looked down at her. It seemed to Aelliana,
feeling her cheeks warm, that her companion was—
amused. Doubtless, she came here often; this shop

135

one of her favorites. It would be instinct, would it not, to bring a new acquaintance in need of clothes to one's favorite shop? And it would be an impertinence to call the judgment of one's host into question. Yet, how much more distressing to find that the guest could not meet her debts?

"I feel," she said slowly, "that I cannot afford anything that might be on offer here. My needs are modest. *Quite* modest," she added, firmly.

Her companion nodded easily.

"I understand perfectly," she said in Terran. "The first time I was here, I thought I'd melt into a puddle, I was so embarrassed. There I stood, great, hulking gel that I am, wearing not much more than my socks, and not a cash card to hide behind. I couldn't remember when I'd been so unnerved—and all for nothing! By the finish of it, I was almost enjoying myself."

"Yes, but—" Aelliana ran her thumb across the tips of her fingers; the hand-talk sign for *cash*.

"No, now, lassie, you mustn't worry about money." Anne put a gentle hand on Aelliana's shoulder. "You've plenty for this. The delm's orders to me were to find you a 'suitable' wardrobe, since you'd come away without. We can outfit you here with everything you need. They'll measure you, take note of your wants, put it all together and send it! In the end, it's much less tiring than going through half-a-dozen shops, looking for something ready-made that will do. Now." She tipped her head toward the expensive door. "If you find you don't like the place, after we've gone in, just give me a wink and we'll go elsewhere. Is that fair?"

It did seem a reasonable compromise between her own misgivings and the task given Anne by her delm.

Anne's *delm*.

Aelliana looked up into the other's face. "*Daav* doesn't pay for this, does he?" she demanded, shocked at how rudely the question fell on the ear. How did Terrans manage without mode to clarify intent?

Anne, however, appeared to have no trouble understanding that the object of Aelliana's concern was not herself.

"Daav isn't paying for this," she said calmly, and opened the gate.

It was as Anne had said: measurements were taken with such graceful efficiency that Aelliana scarcely cared about the necessity of disrobing before a stranger. After, she was given an undressing gown almost as nice as the green one Daav had sent to her. Tea and biscuits were served while she answered questions about her preferred colors and fabrics, and her usual occupations.

"My needs are quite simple," Aelliana explained. "A scholar is expected to show respect for her students; and a pilot, respect for her ship. Beyond that, my occupations are research, and writing." She glanced up at the frame, where a seemingly endless series of elegant clothing and cloaks faded into and out of existence.

"I fear that I bring no honor to your enterprise," she said, as a particularly entrancing lady appeared in the frame, wearing a midnight blue dress, its bodice cut low and its full sleeves slashed with silver.

The tailor followed her glance. "That dress would become you extremely, Pilot. You have a good eye."

"But no need at all for a such a garment," Aelliana said hastily.

The tailor smiled, made a note on her pad, and

inclined her head. "If you will excuse me, I must consult my database. Please, enjoy some more tea. When you are ready, you may dress and find me with Lady yos'Galan in the reviewing room."

Aelliana frowned as the order scrolled across the low screen. Surely, she did not need a dozen shirts? Beside her, however, Anne Davis inclined her stately head and murmured, "Yes, excellent" and "Very good."

"A cloak?" Aelliana exclaimed as that item scrolled past, accompanied by Anne's approving murmur. "I have no need of a cloak!"

The tailor extended a hand and froze the list in place. Anne turned to Aelliana.

"The word I had from the delm was that you were to have a complete wardrobe," she said mildly. "A complete wardrobe includes at least one cloak."

Aelliana considered her closely. She seemed, now as she had from the start, to be a sincere and open-mannered lady, intent on doing what she had been bid by her delm. It bore recalling, she told herself, that Anne's delm had also begged Aelliana to allow herself to be guided by the lady's judgment. Anne, more than Aelliana, knew the cost of things from this emporium where she was plainly a valued client. And Anne had assured Aelliana that she could afford what she purchased here, knowing that her purchases would include . . . a cloak.

"Thank you," she said, slowly. "I am . . . not accustomed to going about in the world."

"That is entirely understandable," Anne said, and looked to the patient tailor.

"I approve the suggested items for purchase," she said easily. "Please send them to Trealla Fantrol."

"Certainly, Lady." The tailor inclined her head deeply. "They will be with the pilot no later than tomorrow morning."

"That is well, then," Anne said, briskly. "Thank you for your consideration."

The tailor rose and bowed. "Thank you, Lady—and you, Pilot—for your patronage. You honor my shop."

Anne came to her feet, rising like a mountain into the day. She inclined her head easily. "Good day to you," she said, and turned to Aelliana.

"I believe I could eat some lunch," she said companionably. "Will you join me, Pilot?"

That, Aelliana thought darkly, was surely Daav's hand, but as it happened she was beginning to feel, just a little, hungry.

"I would be pleased to join you," she said.

. . . ✳ . . .

"If your lordship will review the documents, I believe you will find that a very satisfactory arrangement has been constructed with Bindan." Mr. dea'Gauss passed the first folder across his desk and into Daav's waiting hand. "The Balance with Pilot tel'Izak will, I hope, meet with your approval. It was necessary to liquidate a small personal fund, your lordship; after deducting your lifemate's portion, and funding this Balance."

"Am I destitute, Mr. dea'Gauss?" Daav asked lightly.

"Indeed, no," the older man answered, with one of his rare smiles. "Merely a trifle embarrassed."

"Hah." Daav inclined his head. "You are far too good to us, Mr. dea'Gauss."

"Nonsense, your lordship."

. . . ✳ . . .

The restaurant was scarcely a block away, on yet another quietly expensive street, its trim door two shallow steps above the level of the sidewalk. They stepped into a dim vestibule overlooked by a grey-haired woman of elegant bearing, who bowed welcome.

"Lady yos'Galan, how pleasant to see you again! The garden niche for you and your guest?"

"Only if my guest will humor me," Anne replied. "Allow me to make you known to her—this is Pilot-Scholar Aelliana Caylon. Aelliana, here is Vesa bel'Ulim, host of the Garden Gate Café."

"Pilot-Scholar Caylon, you honor my establishment!" Vesa bel'Ulim bowed as host-to-honored-guest. "Please allow me to commend the garden niche to you; it is quite the most secluded table in the house; one may be entirely shielded from the curious there."

"It is also the most pleasant seat in the house," Anne added, and awarded the host a small bow. "Or so I believe."

The other woman smiled. "Not everyone is as discriminating as her ladyship."

Secluded? She had, Aelliana realized, entirely failed to worry about her supposed notoriety. But—Daav had cared, hadn't he? And apologized for exposing her to gossip. Perhaps Anne's instructions from her delm had included shielding Aelliana—which would also explain the quiet, exclusive tailor shop. And, now that she thought of it, a place away from overwide ears would suit her, very much.

"It sounds quite pleasant," she said to Anne.

The tall woman smiled and inclined her head to the host. "Your eloquence carries all before it," she said. "Lead on!"

✳   ✳   ✳

The garden niche was delightful, Aelliana owned, concealed from the rest of the tables placed among the flowers in the extensive back garden by a screen of trellises, each overgrown with a particular flowering vine.

Aelliana waited until lunch had been served and tasted before making her request, low-voiced, and in Liaden.

"I wonder if I might ask you," she said hesitantly, "something of a . . . personal nature." She raised her eyes to Anne's lively, intelligent face. "Regarding your . . . the condition you share with Lord yos'Galan."

"Our lifemating, you mean," Anne said, sitting back with an air of satisfaction. "By all means, ask! I have been hoping you would!"

"Did you choose this place for its secluded table, hoping that I might?"

"I had been hoping you would ask," Anne said. "A secluded table offers opportunity, and the food is wonderful. Do you agree?"

Aelliana smiled. "Yes, I do agree. I had never used to care about food, until—until yesterday. Now, it seems that every meal is more delicious."

"That may be the effects of the healing," Anne said softly. "Wounds fester in strange ways."

"So I begin to discover. I look back upon—only two days ago!—and I am astonished at myself. Mere commonplaces filled me with terror—" She moved a hand, sweeping her digression away. "But that is neither here nor there! What I would like—very much—to know is—Daav had told me, you see, that the Healers discovered us—he and I—as natural lifemates. He said that you and his brother share a like bond, and count it a great happiness."

"It is the greatest joy of my life. However, at first, it was so...*strange*. You may laugh, but I thought I had quite lost my mind! Now, I look back and hardly know how I bore my life—before. I was so alone. It seems unnatural now—an illness that had been with me for so long I hadn't realized I was unwell, until, suddenly, I was healed." Anne raised her wine glass and sipped. "Similar, perhaps, to your condition."

Aelliana leaned forward. "It was not a smooth transition? There were—misunderstandings at first? Difficulties with the—the interface?"

Anne laughed. "Difficulties doesn't begin to say it, lassie!" she exclaimed, in Terran. She continued in Liaden. "It took time, and work, and *communication*. Understand me, the link with Er Thom is sunk deep into my heart. I think if it were taken away, now, I would die of it. But when we first discovered ourselves—*bound*, neither of us knew what was happening, nor how to make sense of it. We tried—*I* tried—to deny it, which only caused more confusion and needless pain." She nodded at Aelliana's plate.

"Don't ignore your meal, Pilot."

"No, of course not!" Aelliana picked up her tongs and once again addressed her plate. Long, thin noodles and chunky vegetables in a cream sauce, with spark-spice and lemon. She thought she'd never tasted anything so delightful. Of course, she had thought that of the sandwiches she had shared with Daav yesterday, at Healer Hall.

"Are you and Daav," Anne Davis murmured after a few moments, "having difficulty with the interface?"

"It seems that we—I—may have ... misunderstood—and became entangled in—expectation," Aelliana said slowly. She looked up. "Also, you know, it appears that our link may not be—operating entirely as it should. There was—trauma, long left untended, which may be disrupting ..." Her eyes filled abruptly and she looked down, blinking.

"Certainly, together, we can—we can overcome this difficulty," she whispered.

"Certainly, you can," Anne said, with a crisp return to Terran. "Neither one of you is an idiot. Now, what do you say to dessert?"

THIRTEEN

· · · · · · · · · · · · · · ·

Each one of a Line shall heed the voice of the thodelm, head of that Line, and give honor to the thodelm's word. Likewise, the thodelm shall heed the voice of the delm, head of the clan entire, and to the delm's word bow low.

Proper behavior is that thodelm decides for Line and delm decides for clan, cherishing between them the *melant'i* of all.

—Excerpted from the Liaden
Code of Proper Conduct

"WELL, THE BOOK," ANNE SAID, AS SHE DROVE THEM at a sedate and seemly pace down the valley road. "It has its detractors. There's not much support for a common root-tongue—since that would give us a common root. Too many people find *that* offensive."

"Yet the scholarship—"

"Oh, well, the scholarship!" Anne laughed. "Jin Del—Scholar yo'Kera, my . . . colleague. He had the proof. But you must have seen the articles in the Scholar Base, written by those who have their own proofs . . ."

"I had seen that there was some lively discussion," Aelliana admitted. "Has Scout Linguist pel'Odyare published her results, as yet? It seemed she felt your arguments might be supported."

"I've been in communication with Master pel'Odyare; we're doing a source match, in our spare time." Anne threw her an amused glance. "Which is why it's taking us so long."

Aelliana laughed.

"In the meanwhile, the delm had a notion, though I'm not certain I have the right of it, yet. It seemed he was for sending some of Korval's records along with the book to certain . . . influential thinkers. What came of that, I know not—and it's possible we'll never know. Ah, now! Here we are, home."

She pulled the car to a stop, and they got out, walking side by side across the lawn toward the patio door.

"Ma!" A white-haired child hurtled across the lawn and into Anne Davis' laughing embrace. She caught him under the arms and swooped him up, spinning in a tight circle. A grey-haired woman stood at a small remove, her hands folded and her face composed. The effortless stillness of her pose called *Scout* to Aelliana's mind.

Spinning, mother and child shouted with laughter, then the ride was over, and the boy was set on his feet.

"Aelliana," Anne said breathlessly, "here is my son, Shan yos'Galan."

She looked down into a thin brown face dominated by eyes of so pale a blue they seemed silver, and bowed as visitor-to-child-of-the-House.

"Shan yos'Galan, I am pleased to meet you."

"Shannie, this is Aelliana Caylon," Anne said. "Please make your bow and welcome the guest."

A bow was produced, recognizably child-of-the-House-to-visitor. "Welcome to our house, Aelli," he said exuberantly.

"*Aelliana*," his mother corrected.

"No, allow it," she said. "My youngest sister sometimes called me so."

"His father tells me he needs to learn the forms. Shannie, what is our guest's name?"

"Aelliana Caylon," he answered promptly. "Her sister calls her Aelli, and so may I."

"You, my son, are incorrigible." She turned her head. "Mrs. Intassi, allow me to make you known to Korval's guest."

The grey-haired woman came forward, walking with Scout silence and the unmistakable grace of a pilot.

"Aelliana Caylon, I am pleased to meet you," she said, her voice soft and soothing. She bowed a plain bow of introduction. "I am Mrs. Intassi, the heir's nurse."

"Mrs. Intassi, I am pleased to meet you," Aelliana said politely, returning the bow.

"Now, if you will excuse me, Pilot, it is time for this young student to apply himself to his numbers. Unless your ladyship would like him with you?"

"Numbers first," Anne said promptly.

"Very well." The nurse gathered Shan in with an glance. "Please make your bow to the guest and take leave of your mother."

"Bye, Ma!" the young gentleman said in blithe Terran. To Aelliana, he bowed with more intent than mode, and offered, "Until soon, Aelli," in Liaden.

"Until soon, Shan," she replied. "Learn your numbers well."

Nurse and student removed to the house, Anne and Aelliana following more leisurely.

"Do you have you a child?" Anne asked, her voice lazy and unconcerned in the chancy modelessness of Terran.

Aelliana blinked.

"Tiatha is my daughter," she said. "Fosters she at with? Lydborg."

"Maybe she'd like to come for a visit," Anne said, as they reached the patio.

Aelliana bit her lip. It was certainly possible that her daughter might like to visit; she could not say. The probability of such a visit, however, was . . . very slim. Lydberg must surely have a controlling interest in Mizel's nursery by now; the temporary arrangement between cousin-houses had long since become permanent. Tiatha would think of herself as a daughter of Clan Lydberg, which had cared for her and educated her, and would in time require duty from her . . .

"Now, would you like tea, or would you rather I show you to your apartment?" Anne asked. "I hope you'll like it; the windows look over the park. Sometimes in the evening, the *syka* come to graze at the treeline. And the birds! I—"

"Your pardon." Aelliana stopped. It was hard to breathe. For a heartbeat she was the woman she had been two days ago, her shoulders climbing up toward her ears, and her chest tight with misery.

"Your pardon," she said again, and took a deliberate breath, willing herself to relax. "You—are very kind, but I have rooms at Jelaza Kazone. My things—"

"All moved while we were shopping," Anne interrupted airily. "Your car was sent up, too."

Daav's hand there, Aelliana thought, and no other, gaming her as skillfully as if she were a counterchance marker. And she, the gamepiece, complicit in her own defeat, too meek to put herself before him immediately, demanding that they speak, and—*how dare he!*

Aelliana swallowed, for it was not fear, but *anger* that informed her. She took a deep breath and retreated into the constraints of adult-to-adult.

"I do not wish to be rude," she said. "However, I must—I *will* return to Jelaza Kazone."

"Forgive me," Anne replied, following her into Liaden. "The delm requires yos'Galan to accommodate Korval's guest at Trealla Fantrol."

"The delm," Aelliana said, with restraint, "is in error."

It seemed to her that her tall hostess smiled then, just a little, but her answer had nothing of levity in it. "As a member of the clan, of course I am bound by the delm's word. Your apartment has been readied, and—"

A shadow moved at the door, and Er Thom yos'Galan stepped onto the patio. His first glance was for his lifemate, and betrayed concern.

"Anne? Is there a difficulty?"

"Korval's guest wishes to return to Jelaza Kazone," she said calmly.

Both winged brows lifted, and he turned gravely to Aelliana.

"Scholar, the delm was most wonderfully clear: yos'Galan is to have the honor of hosting Korval's guest. Please be assured that your comfort is the first concern of our House. It is of course vexing to have only yesterday settled into one set of rooms, and be obliged immediately to resettle into another. However, that is behind you, now. I hope and trust that you will find your apartment here to be everything that is convivial."

"I am grateful to the House for its care," Aelliana said, careful to keep her voice steady. "I—beg you forgive my lack of address, and honor me by accepting plain words."

"Certainly, Scholar," he murmured. "Korval is no stranger to plain speaking."

"Plainly, then, sir: As much as the care of the House warms me, I do not wish to guest here—nor am I persuaded that Daav wishes it! I must return to Jelaza Kazone and—and speak with him. I fear—it is possible that his delm has measured with a heavy hand, and precipitously."

"Ah." Er Thom yos'Galan shared another glance with his lifemate. "The Code does tell us that the guest is sacrosanct, and that it is the duty of the House to meet the guest's reasonable desires," he said.

"So I have also been taught," Anne agreed.

"We should scarcely care to disoblige the Code, or the guest." He bowed, sweet as a flower dancing on its stem. "I will myself drive you to Jelaza Kazone. Do you leave immediately?"

Relief washed through her so strongly that she feared her knees would fail.

"Yes," she said, and cleared her throat. "Immediately."

Er Thom yos'Galan paused as they came into the garage, his bright head cocked to one side.

"*This* is the car that Daav put at your disposal?"

Aelliana moved her shoulders, impatient to be

away. "He had said the blue car, but, truly, sir, this is the first I have seen it." Her voice carried an edge unbecoming to a guest. She took a breath and inclined her head. "I hope that it is not improper," she added.

He seemed to shake himself, and awarded her a grave smile. "Not in any way improper, Pilot; and it is, since you are too nice to ask, a very good car. It was our mother's. But, come! I see you are in haste to return to Daav."

"Of course you understand that the duty of the delm is to care for and solve for those of the clan," he said some few minutes later, as they turned onto the valley road. "It is an uncomplicated *melant'i*, though stern, and with a tendency toward avarice. Therefore, it is the duty and privilege of we who respect the delm, but who hold Daav in our hearts, to be vigilant on his behalf, and ensure that Korval takes no more than the clan needs, and not so much that Daav withers and becomes nothing more than the demands of duty."

Aelliana swallowed, staring at the Tree, the clouds of evening tangled in its tall branches. Her anger had not yet cooled—a novel sensation. And yet, she recalled suddenly, in the days before her marriage and the damage done, she had owned a temper, and had sometimes defied Ran Eld from what their mother had styled as wildness, and her grandmother as high spirits. Still, it would not do, if her first words to her erring copilot were hard. She ought at least to—

"Wait," she said, turning to look at Daav's brother. "What if he will not see me?"

"He'll see you," Er Thom said, as the car crested the hill, and began the race down toward Jelaza Kazone. "If you will allow me, Pilot—plain speaking may serve you very well here." He glanced over, bestowing another of his grave smiles upon her.

"I fear the delm often measures Daav's portion with a heavy hand. Perhaps you may find a way to leaven that."

Aelliana considered him closely, this man who shared his soul and counted it a gift, and who was held dear—very dear—by his brother.

"Perhaps I may," she said.

· · · · ※ · · · ·

There was no reason for him to be sitting in his office, with the lights dimmed and the screen dark. Such Korval business as demanded the delm's personal attention was retired, and he expected no outburst of emergency. Indeed, the emergencies of the last two days were enough to sustain him well into the next quarter.

He should, he told himself, rise, rid himself of his business clothes and—do something. Work in the garden, perhaps; or there was that business of Kiladi's yet to be concluded. Or—he might call Clonak and propose a night on the port.

Alas, that last was ill-thought, for it brought him 'round again to the sad certainty that Clonak, possessed of the most susceptible heart on the planet, had irrevocably given it to Aelliana.

"That's two of us struck," he murmured, leaning back in his chair and closing his eyes. "And neither fit to comfort the other."

He sighed, and opened his eyes.

"Really, Daav—such melodrama. Stand up, do, and take a turn around the grounds."

After a moment, he did rise, and was halfway to

the door when it opened, quite suddenly, admitting
a slice of brighter light from the hallway along with
his brother, Aelliana herself at his shoulder.

It was quite ridiculous, the way his heart stuttered,
and his eyes filled. And it was everything he could do,
not to step forward and sweep her into an embrace
as she passed Er Thom, striding into the room as if
she had every right to be there.

Which, gods help him, she did.

Three steps away, Aelliana paused, her face turned
up to his, her hands tucked deep into the pockets of
her jacket. Chest tight, eyes burning, Daav looked past
her, to where Er Thom stood, relaxed but unsmiling,
in the doorway.

"Would you care to explain yourself?" he asked, his
voice harsh in his own ears.

Er Thom inclined his head. "Korval's guest asked to
be brought to Jelaza Kazone, so that she might speak
with Daav. As this request is in all ways reasonable,
I am delighted to bring her to you."

Delight—well, and so it could be. Er Thom had
previously demonstrated a willingness to put aside his
delm's word. Nor did either of them, both trained to
hold Korval, in case one should fall—neither of them
entertained an appropriate respect for the delm.

"What he does not say," Aelliana said in her clear,
fine voice, "is that I was quite rude. I don't know how
I shall ever show Anne my face again. However, I am
prepared to be rude again, for I will not leave here
until you and I have spoken on my topic."

That was plainly said, Daav allowed; and plainer
still was the determination that informed her stance,
her shoulders, and the angle of her chin.

"There is no need to deplete your entire store of rudeness in one evening," he said, not quite as mildly as he had intended. He glanced to Er Thom. "Pray, await Pilot Caylon in the library."

Er Thom bowed—honor-to-the-delm, damn him—and departed, closing the door quietly behind him.

It was scarcely latched when she launched her first strike.

"Why did you send me away?"

He sighed, and flung out his hands, speaking the plain truth, as copilot and as lifemate.

"Because it is dangerous for you to remain here. I cannot allow you to reside in peril."

"So you sent me away without even discussing it? Have I no choice in how much peril I will accept?"

"Aelliana, last night I overruled you—utterly. Surely you don't wish to wager your will."

"It is my will and my wager," she snapped, stepping forward into the pool of light cast by the desk lamp. Her eyes were was green as glass, and as sharp. "What right have you to take them from me?"

He raised his hands—and let them fall.

"No right," he said quietly. "My reason is that I love you and—"

"You do not love me!" she interrupted. "It is the woman I was two days gone that you love—craven, shaking, and in need of protection!"

Shock chilled him, followed hard by anger.

"I beg your pardon, but you will not tell me whom I love—or why!"

Aelliana's eyes widened, but she did not step back—and that, he thought distantly, was well. It was ill-done to run from a Dragon.

"You may not defame my lady, nor call her craven. Frightened she may have been, but craven she never was! She pressed on and did what was needful, with courage and generosity. Her care of her comrades, her joy in flight, her gallantry—how could I not love her? And if she was frail, she grew stronger with every new sun, and I never doubted it, that she would do what she had set herself—learn Terran, master her ship, and shake the dust of Liad from her wings!" He took a breath, deliberately cooling his anger.

"I know my heart, Aelliana."

"And now I know mine." She stepped forward, and extended a hand. "I loved you two days ago, if I dared not name it. I love you all the more now that I allow myself to know what it is that I feel. If we are, in fact, lifemates, then what is left us is to consider how best to run this board between us. Separating us solves nothing, and only wounds both."

"Dare I risk my will overtaking yours, even once more?" He blinked the tears away. "Aelliana, the peril here is all yours!"

"Then the choice to wager—how much and how far—is also mine."

"No," he said, quietly. "It is mine. I hold the power." He took a breath. "It is plain that the link between us has been damaged. My brother describes a free flow of emotion and thought between his lady and himself. What we see between us is that I—whom the Healers have already declared overloud—broadcast to you, wiping your signal out. I—" He paused, lifting a hand as the idea broke upon him.

"Daav?"

"How if I ask the Healers to block me? Then you would be in no danger."

"But I would lose the joy of...hearing your signal," she said slowly. "And it *is* a joy, new as it is to me. I propose a method of slow study." She stepped forward, one hand reaching for his.

He sidestepped, slipping away from her grasp like smoke.

"Be wary! Here is good reason for fear."

"I am not afraid of you!" she cried, her anger sparking truth from him, like flame from a firestone.

"Aelliana, sometimes *I* am afraid of me!"

She paused, and he thought that sense had at last won through. Then she shook her head, Terran-wise, and smiled.

"That's as may be, *van'chela*. I beg, however, that you will do me the honor of allowing me to love you, fearsome as you are. Please, let us at least try my method. If you see that I am overruled and lost, then you must disengage, as you did last evening. I depend upon you for this, for you will be able to see when I cannot. Is that a bargain?"

He licked his lips, scarcely able to look at her. His love, his lifemate. His pilot.

"What do you propose?" he whispered.

"Sit," she said, pointing to his reading chair, over near the window. "My neck is quite cricked from staring up at you."

"Very well." He did as he was bid and looked up at her, with eyebrows raised.

"Good," Aelliana said. "Now, what I propose is very simple. I will touch you, and take time to listen to your signal, so that I may learn to differentiate.

Once I am able to know your signal as distinct from my own, then I believe the level of risk for both of us decreases by a factor of six."

It was the sort of calculation that Aelliana might very well do, he thought. More than that, she might have a point. Certainly last evening they had taken no leisurely course to pleasure, but had tumbled helter-skelter into passion, each half-blinded with need. Well they might try this more modest approach, and he would do what he might to make the course less dangerous yet.

He took a breath, preparatory to activating the Rainbow.

"You will please not use any of the skills you have to calm or distance yourself from me," Aelliana said.

He lifted an eyebrow. "Why?"

"It will dull the signal," she said reasonably, and raised her hand.

· · · ·❈· · · ·

Daav's cheek was soft beneath her fingers, the flutter of his pleasure as apparent to her as the scowl on his face. Aelliana paused, concentrating on these new perceptions the Healers had given her.

Regarded in calmness, Daav's input was nothing at all like the emotions she felt for herself; she could differentiate quite easily. She ran her fingers lightly down the side of his face, across his lips, noting the growing warmth—his and hers, distinct. It was rather like simultaneously listening to chatter off the wideband and instructions from the Tower. At first, it seemed nothing other than a dreadful mixup of sound, but the ear very quickly learned to sort and make sense of each stream.

"Aelliana..." His lips moved beneath her fingertips; she felt herself warm agreeably, even as she received a flutter of trepidation from him.

"Hush," she murmured, and reached to stroke those strong eyebrows before placing both hands, gently, on his shoulders.

He was in tumult now: fear, longing, and a tangled skein of emotion she was too inexperienced to name. What a complex creature he was! Complex and utterly fascinating. Her blood was beginning to heat, slow and inescapable, echoing Daav's longing, yet distinct and very different.

It was therefore her own choice that she moved forward, put her knees on the chair at either side of him, and sat astride his lap.

"Kiss me," she said, raising her face to his.

"Aelliana, I don't—"

She snatched his long tail of dark hair and pulled it, hard.

"*Kiss* me!"

He shivered and she felt his fear strongly, *almost* as if it were her own.

Then she felt his resolve, his concurrence, his desire, and his lips, warm and knowing on hers.

· · · ·❀· · · ·

She was pliant against him, her mouth not so cunning as yestereve, but taking her lessons to heart. Daav went carefully, fear at first mixing with desire, slowly dissolving into passion.

Somewhere in the world beyond she and he, there was a sound.

The door had opened.

Daav lifted his head, felt Aelliana sigh and nestle her cheek against his chest.

Er Thom lounged in the doorway, arms crossed, a book tucked under one elbow.

"Pilots," he said neutrally, inclining his bright head. "I am going home, to my lady and to my dinner. Pray, do not disturb yourselves on my account! I'm certain that Mr. pel'Kana can find me a car." He straightened and lifted the book. "Brother, I will return tel'Jorinson's *Treatise on Trade* tomorrow. Pilot Caylon, I took the liberty of having your things brought down from Trealla Fantrol and reinstated in your quarters here. A fair evening to you both."

And with that he was gone, the door shutting quietly behind him.

"Is your brother . . . angry?" Aelliana murmured.

"My brother," Daav told her, with a certain wry humor, "is enjoying himself *far* too much."

"And you think that is both amusing and irritating."

He laughed. "So I do. What else do I think?"

He had meant it for a joke, but, Aelliana-like, she took it as it was asked. Or, perhaps her terrible new sense informed her.

"It is not terrible at all," she said, snatching the thought wholesale out of his head. "Indeed, I quite like it, though I must say, *van'chela*, that you're not half complicated!"

She sat up, displaying a complete disregard for the fact that her shirt was unsealed, and her hair tumbled every-which-way.

"Shall I become more simple?" he asked.

Aelliana smiled. "I would never ask it of you. As to what you think—I can't pretend to know, though I might guess. It seems that my guesses will gradually come closer to the mark, as I learn you better." She put her hand flat over his heart, her palm cool against his flesh.

"I hereby scry," she announced, singsong and unserious, "you are regretful, you are happy, you are desirous, and you are . . ." She paused, brows pulling together into a sudden frown. "Daav, are you—ill?"

Ill? He looked down into her face, seeing playfulness melting beneath concern.

"Not that I am aware," he said. "I will own to being tired, now that the alarms of the last few days are behind us. Perhaps it is that which you scry?"

She tipped her head, considering, and finally sighed, shaking her hair back.

"It may be," she said eventually. "After all, this is new to me." She smiled and leaned toward him. "Perhaps I need more practice."

He bent his head, not loath to assist in so worthy a goal.

There was a knock at the door.

Aelliana drooped against him, muttering.

"It will be Mr. pel'Kana," Daav said, "wanting to know our wishes for Prime, or—" He glanced to the window, noting with surprise that twilight had faded into evening. "Or perhaps he wishes to tell us that a cold meal has been laid for us in the morning room. Either way, we should acknowledge him, and let him seek his bed."

She sighed, but slid off his lap, and walked to the window, her back to the door, and her hands busy at the fastenings of her shirt. He rose and sealed his own shirt, scooped her jacket up and dropped it into the chair.

The discreet knock was repeated.

"Come," Daav called, walking forward to stand by the desk.

Mr. pel'Kana came two scant steps into the room and bowed.

"There is a cold meal laid in the morning room, your lordship," he murmured. "Do you or the pilot require anything else this evening?"

"I believe that I do not," Daav said composedly. "Aelliana?"

"Thank you, I am quite content," she said, her voice perhaps a little unsteady.

Daav inclined his head. "We will serve ourselves, Mr. pel'Kana. Please do not wait any longer on our account."

"Thank you, sir. Pilot. Good evening to you both."

"Good evening," Aelliana called. "Thank you."

"You are quite welcome, Pilot," the old man said, and left them.

FOURTEEN

• • • • • • • • • • • • • • • • • •

He found it in a desert, so he told me—the only
living thing in two days' walk. A skinny stick with
a couple leaves near the top, that's all it was then.

I don't remember the name of the world it
came from. He might not have told me. Wherever
it was, when his Troop finally picked him up, Jela
wouldn't leave 'til he'd dug up that damned skinny
stick of a tree and planted it real careful in an old
ration tin. Carried it in his arms onto transport.
And nobody dared to laugh.

—Excerpted from
Cantra yos'Phelium's Log Book

THIS WAKING WAS BOTH EASIER AND MORE DIFFICULT.
Easier because she had the memory of last evening's
pleasures to treasure; more difficult because she knew
before ever she opened her eyes that she was alone.

After Mr. pel'Kana's interruption, she and Daav
had taken a leisurely meal, sitting together on the
window seat and overlooking the nighttime garden.
They had not spoken very much—there seemed to be
no need. When they were through, she had helped

Daav clear what was left and carry it down the back hall to the kitchen, where he made quick work of stowing everything in its proper place.

Arms around each other, they walked slowly up the stairs. She had opened her door, thrilled and a little frightened after all, stepped inside and turned to look at him.

"Daav? Will you—come in?"

"Not, I think, tonight," he said, with a smile so regretful tears rose to her eyes.

"How if I overwhelm you, and both of us asleep?" he asked.

"*Van'chela*, we have spoken of this. Surely this evening's pleasures have shown you that we are safe together? I know you now, and will not mistake you for myself!"

"Even asleep?" he asked, and shook his head. "We cannot be certain. I suggest that we stay the course and keep to your plan of unhurried research." His smile this time was pure mischief. "And we have done prodigious amounts of research this evening, Aelliana."

She laughed then, and come back to him, claiming one more kiss.

"May a humble copilot suggest a course to his pilot?" he murmured, when they had done and she was once more inside her door.

Aelliana attempted a stern frown. "If you must," she said haughtily. "Though I may space you, if the suggestion irritates."

"That seems fair enough," he answered. "I merely suggest—most gently—that it may be worthwhile to use the Rainbow to anchor what you have learned this day."

It was only sense to use the tools she had in hand, and so, at last in bed, she had laid in the course, worked her way through the Rainbow—and fallen asleep.

And now, she was awake. Not only awake, but—

"I'm hungry," she said and opened her eyes, throwing the blanket back with a will.

Breakfast was again laid in the morning room, though Mr. pel'Kana was not in evidence. Doubtless, he had duties elsewhere, and Aelliana could certainly feed herself. She glanced toward the window as she approached the buffet, hoping for a glimpse of orange Relchin.

She was denied that pleasure. However, lying on the window seat, very much at her ease, was a cat with luxuriously long creamy fur, with startling blue eyes blinking inside a mask of sable brown.

"Oh!" Aelliana approached and offered a finger. "You must be Lady Dignity. I am most pleased to meet you."

Her ladyship graciously touched her nose to the tip of Aelliana's finger, and squeezed her eyes into slits—a cat smile.

"Thank you," Aelliana said. "I see that there's room on the seat for me, if you will share. Only a moment, while I gather some food."

The cat had accepted a bit of cheese, then curled 'round with her tail over her nose and closed her eyes. Aelliana ate the rest of her breakfast slowly, savoring the tastes and textures while she looked out over the garden.

So much had changed in the last few days—and not the least of it, herself. This connection with Daav—already so precious to her—complicated the course she had thought laid in and locked. Indeed, the very reason she had chosen so stringent a course—to leave Liad and all she knew—was now gone, vanished by a wave of Mizel's hand.

There was a commotion in the hall—a voice, somewhat familiar, asking in ringing tones for "Korval" and the sound of bootheels being set firmly against the wooden floor.

Lady Dignity's head came up. She listened to the noise for a moment, eyes wide in apparent consternation. Then she was gone, flowing off the window seat, and racing out the open door.

"If your ladyship will consent to wait in the small parlor," Mr. pel'Kana's voice was no less carrying, "I will fetch his lordship immediately."

"I will await him in the morning room," the lady said, above the racket of her progress. "You may tell his lordship that I will remain there until such time as it pleases him to give over playing in the dirt. If he delays himself until nuncheon, he will find me here. If he puts me off until Prime, yet I will await him. My topic will not be denied."

"I am certain that his lordship will be delighted to see your ladyship."

"Yes, of course. Do, please, fetch him as best you may."

A shadow moved at the door, and Daav's sister bore, noisily, in. Aelliana glimpsed Mr. pel'Kana's face over the lady's shoulder. He met her eyes and his widened slightly. Then, he was gone.

Aelliana sat up, juggling plate and cup; her movements drawing the lady's eye.

"Ah, *Pilot* Caylon," she said, executing an extremely brief bow in a mode Aelliana did not recognize. "We are well-met."

"I am pleased to hear you say so," Aelliana said in the mode of adult-to-adult. She rose and carried her dishes to the tray. When she turned back, she found Kareen yos'Phelium watching her . . . oddly.

She bowed, guest-to-one-of-the-House. "In what way may I serve you, ma'am?"

"It is I who may serve you, Pilot. Since we last spoke, I have researched yourself and your clan. Allow me to congratulate you for the astuteness with which you have improved your position."

Aelliana frowned, even as her stomach clenched. She was unskilled in social dueling. Yet, if she were not mistaken, Lady Kareen had drawn steel.

"Improved?" she asked, since one must say something. "I fear that I miss your meaning."

The other woman smiled, and inclined her sleek head.

"Certainly, to be under Korval's wing is an improvement over standing as the second daughter of an indigent and scarcely coherent clan, the minor children of which are already indentured to another House, and which has recently sustained the loss of its nadelm. I applaud your perspicacity and your call to action. But I wonder, Pilot, if you have thought this plan through?"

No, Aelliana thought suddenly, this game was well-known to her: Ran Eld had played it. He, at least, could often be drawn by a show of bewilderment. Perhaps Lady Kareen was vulnerable to the same ploy. Aelliana tipped her head and made her eyes wide.

"Truly, ma'am," she said, "I am in uncharted skies. What is this plan which I may not have thought through?"

Another smile, this one edged with perceptible malice.

"Why, I only mean to say, Pilot, that, if you wish to attach my brother more . . . permanently—but hold! Am I correct in supposing that you think of a lifemating? Certainly, I would do so, in your place."

Kareen did not know! Aelliana took a careful breath, and vowed to conceal the fact of her bond with Daav. There was no reason to place another weapon into her ladyship's hand. Even if one could not entirely see how something so straightforward could be given an edge, it was enough to know that she would use it to harm Daav, if she could.

"I had considered a lifemating, yes," she admitted.

"I had thought as much," Lady Kareen said, a note of satisfaction in her voice. "It is no secret that my brother is susceptible. He desires a lifemating, for his *cha'leket* has made one. It has ever been the case that what one of the pair has the other must have in equal measure. Further, it would seem that you have appealed to his natural inclinations. So far, you have done well—no, I will not stint! You have done brilliantly! However, before you take the next step, I ask you, most urgently, to review your scheme. You stand at a cusp point, Pilot. One wrong throw, here and now, and you lose all."

"I don't understand," Aelliana said, and if her voice was shaking, it was only just, for her legs were shaking, too. The emotion—perhaps it was anger, or disbelief. It was not, however, fear.

"Perhaps you do not, after all," Kareen acknowledged. "Look you, Pilot—Korval moves at the highest levels. As one who has been bred to that *melant'i*, as my brother has been, I cannot help but notice your lack of . . . polish. While my brother enjoys posing as a Codeless renegade, in fact he is a high stickler. In his way. Also, he is *Korval*, a *melant'i* that he carries as well as he is able, given the defects of his character. I will tell you that I know from bitter experience that he has no hesitation in separating close kin, whatever their feelings on the matter.

"You may wish to consider what might go forth if—I should say *when*, for surely the High Houses are chancy flying for even an experienced pilot—you make a misstep. For truly, Pilot, at these heights you are as a mouse among raptors. Your best chance of survival is to remain small, and to feast upon whatever crumbs fall your way."

The air in the room changed. Aelliana glanced to the door, and here came Daav, striding swift and silent, a pair of dirt-stained gloves gripped in his left hand. His face was utterly devoid of emotion, but the force of his anger struck Aelliana from across the room. She went back a step, her hand rising as if she would fend him away.

"Good morning, Kareen; you're about early today." His voice was ordered and calm; not welcoming, but neither did it deliver any hint of the fury that hammered at Aelliana's senses.

"Pilot," he said, his eyes still on his sister's face, "would you grant me a few moments alone with my kinswoman?"

"Certainly."

She bowed to Lady Kareen's honor and forced herself to walk calmly across the room. In the hall she met Mr. pel'Kana.

"Pilot—" he began, and stopped when she held up a hand.

"I desire to go into the garden," she whispered. She cleared her throat. "Of your kindness, point me the way."

. . . ✧ . . .

He knew where he would find her. Wherever the knowledge had come from, he did not doubt it—which argued for Tree-sense. Those born to Korval accepted such things as commonplace. Those who came to Korval from lives previously unburdened by an ancient alliance with a large, vegetative intelligence . . . took some amount of time to adjust. He was not entirely certain that Anne had yet come to an accommodation, or if her seeming acceptance was merely bravado.

He left the path and walked over the grass, taking care with the surface roots. Aelliana was pressed close against the massive trunk, soft cheek against rough bark, the lines of her body expressive of some tension, but not so much as he had feared.

Coming to her side, he spoke as gently as he might.

"Aelliana, you mustn't take my sister's words to heart. She is—we have a long history of despite, as much to my blame as hers. I fear that she does not count the cost, can she but land a strike upon me."

She took a breath, slim shoulders rising and falling. "Does this tree," she asked dreamily, "*speak* to you?"

Well, and *that* was no time lost, he thought.

"It speaks to all of us," he told her, and added,

with Kareen in his mind, "though some listen less closely than others."

For three heartbeats, she said nothing more, merely embracing the Tree so nearly it seemed that she might meld with it. Three heartbeats more, and he was becoming alarmed. If the *Tree* were to overwhelm her—

She straightened, and turned, holding a seedpod between thumb and forefinger.

"This fell into my hand," she said, sounding brisk now, and not dreamy in the least. "The Tree tells me that it is a gift, and good to eat."

"True on both counts," he allowed. "However, there is a third thing, which perhaps it did not tell you." He nodded at the pod. "The Tree ... *engineers* its gifts, from time to time. If you eat that, you may become bound to it."

"As you are," Aelliana said.

He inclined his head. "As we all are."

She held the pod out to him. "How does one proceed?"

He took a breath—but who was he to deny her the benefits the Tree's gifts so often bestowed? She was his lifemate, and thereby Tree-kin. She had a right to the gift.

Taking the pod, he cracked it between his fingers and returned the pieces to her.

"The kernel is what one eats," he said, and extended his hand, warned by a rustle in the leaves overhead. Another pod dropped into his palm.

He held it up, and gave her a wry grin. "I believe that we are being coddled."

"A little coddling may not go amiss, surely?" Aelliana murmured, as he cracked his pod. "Your sister—"

"Pray put my sister out of your mind," he said, teasing the kernel free.

Aelliana tipped her head. "This smells so—odd."

He lifted an eyebrow. "In what way?"

"Well, it smells not *of* something—like mint or spice—but rather of the *idea* that the food is good." She looked up at him. "Is it always thus?"

"No, sometimes they do smell of mint, or spice, or new leaves. I posit an encryption system peculiar to the Tree. These, though..." He paused to sniff his own kernel. "I believe they may have been produced especially for this event. And if that does not frighten you, then you are bolder than I am."

She laughed, her eyes brilliantly green, and put the kernel into her mouth.

"That's put me on my mettle," he said, and followed her lead.

Usually, when one ate of the Tree, the result was a pleasant taste, and perhaps a mild, pleasurable euphoria. This was not usual tree fruit.

His mouth cooled, as if he had drunk iced water, and the sensation flowed through him, informing each bone, muscle and cell, until his strength was frozen and he sat down, hard, and leaned his back against the massive trunk, eyes closed, shivering.

"I wish," he said, and his voice was shivering too, "you would at least give one warning. What have you done, wretch?"

"Daav?" Aelliana's voice was not shivering. Indeed, it was remarkably firm.

He opened his eyes and turned his head, carefully. She was kneeling at his side. Green eyes looked directly into his, mild concern apparent.

"Are you well?" she asked.

"I expect I will be," he said, breathless still, but gaining strength. "Surely it has no need to murder me today, and good reason to keep me alive for just a few days more."

She frowned. "I don't think the Tree means to murder you," she said seriously. "Though what reason?"

"yos'Phelium is grown dangerously thin. At least I must survive until I've done my duty to the bloodline. Unless, of course, it means to give over breeding yos'Pheliums entirely, which I might do, in its place."

The shivering had passed, leaving him slowly warming, and in a state of not-unpleasant languor.

Aelliana shifted off her knees and sat on the grass, her shoulder against the great trunk. Her expression was thoughtful.

"I had forgotten," she murmured, then seemed to shake herself. "*Van'chela*, perhaps the Tree means to—to repair the damage, and render you—able to hear me."

Well, and there was a thought—and not at all beyond its range. "Though one would still count it a kindness if a warning were issued before the blow falls."

A leaf floated from one of the lower branches and landed on his knee.

"Your concern warms my heart," he told it, ironically.

"*Are* you well?" Aelliana demanded.

He took a breath, and took stock. The languor was fading, though he felt no immediate need to rise and go about his day.

"In truth, I seem to have taken no lasting harm, and only a glancing blow to my pride."

She blinked. "Pride?"

"One does not like to appear a complete idiot before one's pilot, after all."

She smiled at that.

"Here," she said, and put her hand flat against his chest.

"Can you," she said, and he heard hope raw in her voice, "hear me?"

He closed his eyes, but if there was anything other than his own chaotic thoughts bouncing inside his skull, they were too faint for his inner ears to hear.

He put his hand over hers and opened his eyes.

"Alas."

She wilted, a little, then straightened resolutely. "After all, it is a complex problem and may require several attempts."

If it could be repaired at all, he thought, but did not say. Instead he smiled for her, and inclined his head.

"Very true."

She sighed, and took her hand away from him.

"Your sister," she said once more, and pressed her fingers against his lips, silencing him.

"Hear me," she said firmly, and he perforce subsided.

"I know that she wished to warn me away, but she built her argument on a foundation of fact. I am *not* High House, and hold but an indifferent acquaintance with the Code, despite my late adventures. I am not traveled, nor have I been accustomed to making decisions based on the best good for all. For too many years, my decisions were made from fear, and concerned only my own safety.

"While I do not believe that you would send me away from you for embarrassing the High House of Korval before the world, yet the High House of Korval *ought not to be* embarrassed."

Daav caught her wrist and lifted her hand away from

his lips to cuddle it against his shoulder. "I note that Thodelmae yos'Galan is Terran, and despite earnest study, does yet from time to time err in small ways. The world makes nothing of it."

"Nor should it. The fact that Anne is not of Liad is there for all to see. She cannot be expected to stand Code-wise and the fact that she errs only in small ways must be to her credit. But from one born to Liad, *van'chela*, more is expected."

This new decisiveness was fascinating.

"What solution do you propose?" he asked.

She drew a breath, her fingers curling hard around his.

"I propose that we return to my original plan, with appropriate emendations."

His heart sank. Of course she would fly her ship, nor was he the one to deny her, wing-clipped and planet-bound as he was.

"You wish to put *Ride the Luck* to space?"

She smiled. "I had always intended to do so—now more than before. Surely it must only improve my condition within the House, to captain my own ship. I might even undertake to learn the Code."

She leaned forward, looking deep into his eyes, doubtless seeing his hurt and his jealousy and all the small unworthy pains.

"Will you sit my copilot?" she asked.

His eyes filled, and he closed them, unwilling to allow even her to see him so vulnerable.

"Aelliana, I am Korval."

"So you are," she said briskly. "What has that to do with the case?"

His eyes sprang open in shock. "The clan's business ties me to Liad. A day or two away, I might arrange that, but—do you plan a trade loop? Or will you go for courier?"

"That is but one of the *many* things I had hoped to discuss with my copilot, who is far more space-wise than I," she said with some asperity. "Come, Daav! I don't know how it is done among the High, but among the Mid Houses, it is common for the delm to hold employment!"

He stared at her. "It has been . . . tradition," he said slowly, and so it had been, since they had grown so thin, and the dangers of space had begun to be counted as more compelling than its joys.

"It is an absurd tradition!" Aelliana said decisively. "And I see no reason why you should be made ill because of it—or that we be denied the joy of sitting the same board, as surely we are intended to do!"

"As surely we are," he said slowly, feeling her fingers gripping him tight—so tight. Not as certain as she sounded, his bold lady, and yet—her argument had merit.

"You must understand the cargo you would sign for, Pilot. yos'Phelium is a reckless Line. Had we not had the good fortune to fall under yos'Galan's care, we would scarcely have survived so long. When we grew thin, it was considered best that the delm not risk space."

"Thodelm yos'Galan trades," Aelliana said. "Anne told me he was to leave on a trip at the end of this twelve-day."

"So he does and so he is. Er Thom is the very spirit of discretion—and I, my lady, am very much his opposite number."

Surprisingly, she smiled. "Then I will learn that, too."

He laughed, and raised her hand to his lips. Teasing her fingers open, he kissed her palm, then looked into her face. Gods, she was beautiful, with her eyes reflecting the strength of her will, and her determination plain in her face.

"I will have to research it," he said slowly, "and I must speak with Er Thom. It seems to me that there was once a system that allowed Korval's delm to, as you say, hold employment. For today, however, let us assume that the thing might be managed, someway. Are you at liberty?"

"I am entirely at your disposal," she told him solemnly. "What do you propose?"

"That we take ourselves to Binjali's and inventory your ship. I lean towards courier, but I wish to refresh myself on certain measurements."

"*Our* ship," Aelliana said, and stood in one fluid movement, pulling him up with her. "Let us, by all means, go to Binjali's."

FIFTEEN

. . . .

Melant'i—A Liaden word denoting the status of a person within a given situation. For instance, one person may fulfill several roles: parent, spouse, child, mechanic, thodelm. The shifting winds of circumstance, or "necessity," dictate from which role the person will act this time. They will certainly always act honorably, as defined within a voluminous and painfully detailed code of behavior, referred to simply as "The Code."

To a Liaden, *melant'i* is more precious than rubies, a cumulative, ever-changing indicator of his place in the universal pecking order. A person of high honor, for instance, is referred to as "a person of *melant'i*," whereas a scoundrel—or a Terran— may be dismissed with "he has no *melant'i*."

Melant'i may be the single philosophical concept from which all troubles, large and small, between Liad and Terra spring.

—From "A Terran's Guide to Liad"

TRILLA, JON'S SECOND, WAS ON-SHIFT, WITH A SCOUT introduced offhandedly as "Vane," which was the mode, at Binjali's.

"Pilots, welcome!" Trilla called, riding a rope down from the catwalk. She landed lightly and came toward them, an unabashed grin splitting her dark, Outworld face.

"Pilot Daav, you're looking well. Pilot Caylon . . . you're looking very well indeed, if a sparring partner may say so! Have you a moment to dance?"

"I—" Aelliana hesitated, torn between the desire to try her new self against Trilla's skill and the desire to find *The Luck* and discover its part in her destiny.

"Perhaps . . ." she began—and stopped, turning her head to track the flicker of motion to her left, near the entrance to Jon's office—

A blur of leathers was all she saw, only that.

"Clonak!" she cried, entirely certain that it was he. "But—"

Daav caught her fingers; she felt concern, unhappiness, and worry. He released her with a smile that looked genuine, though surely, she thought, it must be false.

"I will go and find him, while you and Trilla dance."

"There's a bargain," Trilla said, a shade too heartily, to Aelliana's ears. "Come, Pilot, I've had a dull morning—enliven it for me!"

· · · · ·✦· · · ·

"Clonak."

Jon's office was dim, the only light the glow from the work screen. A stocky figure was outlined in that glow, shoulders rounded and face tipped downward, ostensibly absorbed in whatever was on the screen.

Three steps beyond the door, Daav paused and recruited himself to patience, counting slowly, his hands in plain view, his stance easy and comfortable. Nothing to challenge a heart-struck and dangerous man, should he look up to see who bore him company.

The stocky figure at the computer never raised his head.

On the stroke of one hundred forty-four, Daav took a careful breath.

"Old friend?"

For some moments more, the rapid click of keystrokes was the only sound in the room, their rhythm broken at last by a sigh.

"Good-day, Daav." Clonak's voice, usually ebullient to the point of lunatic, was cool, his stance behind the computer was nothing more nor less than a warn-away. If he had been a cat, Daav thought, his tail would have been bristling. "I'm quite busy at the moment. You understand."

He understood well enough. Twisted as their bond was, yet Aelliana and he acknowledged themselves partners, from the heart. That he dared long for the fullness of the link, when Clonak was denied even a taste . . .

Daav raised his hands, showing empty palms and fingers spread wide—the sign for surrender.

"Clonak, I am her natural lifemate."

The keystrokes stopped. The figure in front of the screen raised his head, his round face showing lines that had not been there, four days ago.

"Then it is neither your fault nor your blame, is it?" Clonak asked harshly.

Daav winced, and lowered his hands. Clonak bent his head again, but did not return to his inputting.

"Jon . . ." Daav cleared his throat. "Jon tells me you have an assignment. Where to, Scout?"

"Security detail for a trade mission to Deluthia."

Daav blinked. "Are the guild masters after that again? Don't they recall what happened last time?" Granting that it had been more than two dozen Standards in the past, but the last trade mission to Deluthia had resulted in the loss of two master traders and several support team members before the remainder had managed to win back to their ship and depart.

"Oh, they say the theocracy has mellowed," Clonak said, sounding for the moment almost like his usual, manic self. "They came to the masters with sweet words on their tongues, and interesting goods in their hands. The masters considered it worth a second risk, and asked for volunteers."

Volunteers.

Daav closed his eyes.

"It would be better," he said, around the ache in his heart, "if you exited this adventure intact. She would miss you, terribly—and I . . ."

"I'll come back, Captain," Clonak said softly. "I only need . . . something to occupy me for the next while."

"I do understand." He took a breath. "Be safe, darling. Come to us, when duty releases you." He turned. It was an ill parting from a lifelong friend, but he did not—he very much did not—wish to abrade Clonak's emotions further. He hoped, with all his heart, that their friendship might survive this—

"Daav!"

He turned back, as Clonak came 'round the desk.

"I—I haven't wished you happy, old friend. He opened his arms, and Daav stepped into the embrace, cheek to cheek.

"Tell her that I wish her so very much joy," Clonak whispered. "Tell her that, Daav."

A strike to the heart, that was. Daav closed his eyes, arms tightening around the other man.

"I'll tell her," he promised.

· · · ❁ · · ·

Trilla spun, sweeping her leg out in an attempt to catch and trip. Aelliana leapt, landing in a counterspin, her hand rising to block a blow at her dominant left side. What a pleasure it was to dance, to feel her muscles moving in concert, to know herself perfectly balanced and aware—

She caught the motion from the side of her right eye, a fist, striking without subtlety directly for the heart of her defense.

In former times, when she had danced *menfri'at* with Trilla, her immediate response to such an attack was to avoid it at all costs, even diving to the floor and curling into a ball, her arms folded over her head.

Today, without even a thought for the pain, she half-turned, accepting the glancing strike across her shoulder as she lunged back along that admirably straight line, her hand connecting solidly with her partner's chest. The force of the blow sent them spinning apart. Aelliana came 'round as fast as she was able, anticipating a blow from the rear, or perhaps a snatch at free-flowing hair. Ran Eld had caught her that way—

Trilla was standing flat-footed, her hand up in the sign for *pause*.

"Bravo!" she called. "You've been listening, after all!"

"I had always listened." Aelliana shook her hair out of her face. "It was only that today, I could—access what I'd learned."

"Well done." Daav's deep voice came from behind.

Aelliana turned, and smiled to see him lounging against a tool cart, his arms crossed over his chest, pride plain on his face.

"I think the pilot may be ready for the next level, Master Trilla. What say you?"

"I agree, Master Daav. I agree!" She gave Aelliana a grin of sheer deviltry.

"Come again tomorrow, Pilot, and we'll dance indeed!"

"Ought I to be terrified?" Aelliana asked, though the prospect exhilarated rather than frightened.

Trilla laughed. "It depends on how apt a student you are." She fished a rag from her back pocket, glancing to them each in turn.

"Your pardons," she said, and dabbed at the sweat on her forehead.

"Pilot?" Daav said. "Did you want to do that inspection, now?"

"*You* had wanted to do the inspection, as I recall it," Aelliana answered. "But I will gladly stand by and watch."

"Fair enough," he said, and came out of his lean with boneless grace, melting immediately into a bow to the pilot's honor.

"After you."

The walk to *Ride the Luck*'s coldpad had been quiet, with Daav abstracted. Twice, Aelliana began to ask after Clonak, and twice thought better of it.

When we reach the ship, she thought. *Then, surely, he will tell me.*

She climbed the ramp first, and slotted the key, looking up at him over her shoulder as the hatch slid open.

"We will need to have a set made for you," she said. "Do I apply to the Guild?"

"Jon can make another set of keys for you just as easily as the Guild—and charge you half the price."

"I will commission Jon, then," she said, turning 'round by the pilot's station. "My copilot should have access to our ship."

He closed his eyes briefly. "Aelliana..."

"No, we have decided it, *van'chela*. You shall sit copilot on this, our ship. It only remains to know our cargo and our destination."

"Simple matters," he said, giving her a smile that was, perhaps, not utterly false. He turned toward the corridor to the rear of the chamber.

"Well, then," he said, suddenly brisk, "let us survey what we—"

"Daav."

He paused, but did not look at her. Aelliana bit her lip, stomach suddenly tight. It was bad news, then. One did not like to think—no. One did not *know* what to think. And apparently Daav was not going to tell her what had transpired, absent a direct question.

"Clonak," she said, carefully. "What did he say?"

Daav sighed, and did turn to look at her, his face carefully bland.

"He said that he wished you every joy, Aelliana."

That was true, she felt that it was so. However, it was too thin a truth to hide the pain at the back of Daav's eyes.

"There's something else," she said, watching him; listening with all of her senses.

"Indeed. He leaves very soon on a mission—a security mission—and is much involved in preparation."

A chill washed over her, damply; she spoke before she had consciously named the emotion.

"That distresses you. Why?"

Daav sighed and walked toward her. "You are becoming far too adept at this," he commented, "else all my skills are failing at once."

She took a breath, tasting his dismay.

"I think—I think that I am still reaping the Healers' benefit," she said slowly, "and . . . perhaps . . . the Tree's."

One well-marked brow lifted as he shook his head. "I had warned you that the Tree was meddlesome."

"So you had," she replied with what calmness she could manage. "But you were going to tell me why you are so . . . very worried."

"Clonak volunteers as security to a trade mission bound for Deluthia, which, in the recent past, has demonstrated a certain . . . hostility to Liaden trade missions. The security team that supported the last attempt at Deluthia—fared badly."

But this hardly seemed like Clonak, Aelliana thought. For one who enjoyed his comfort so much to put himself into such peril?

"Why?" she asked. "Why is he accepting—*volunteering for*—so dangerous a mission? Surely, there are other—" It struck her then, full knowledge, as if the thought had passed from Daav's mind into hers.

"It's me." Her hand moved, her fingers gripped his arm, and she read the truth out of him.

"Clonak . . . loves . . . me? How is that possible?" Her

knees were weak—not fear, she thought, dully, but shock—and a tithe of shame.

"I must—" She groped behind her for the pilot's chair, spun it and sat, staring at the deck plates, her thoughts in turmoil.

After a moment, she looked up to meet Daav's eyes.

"I don't know what I must do," she said, her voice small in her own ears.

He dropped to one knee next to her chair, and looked seriously into her face.

"Nor do I, except to allow him to pursue his own destiny." A smile glimmered, far back in his eyes. "I did wring a promise from him, that he would endeavor not to get himself killed."

"That was well done," Aelliana conceded, with a ripple of her own humor.

"Thank you." He sighed. "Truly, Aelliana, Clonak is fully capable. I think we must trust him to come back to us, and in better condition than he now stands."

"Is he—badly hurt?" she asked.

"He has taken a wound," Daav acknowledged. "Serious, but I think not fatal."

"That I could— I would never harm him of my own will!" Aelliana burst out. She felt a sudden need to throw things, excepting that nothing lay to hand. "I—I honor him, and I value him. Perhaps it is love, of a kind, but…"

"It is possible," Daav said softly, "to love more than one. Greater or lesser is a clumsy ruler. So it is that I love Clonak, and Olwen, Frad and Jon, Er Thom, Anne, and Shan."

There was no need to ask it; she knew the answer. Yet it seemed her tongue had a will of its own.

"And—me?"

"You . . ." He lifted his hand and cupped her cheek. "If I measured each of my loves against what I feel for you, it would seem that I had never loved anyone at all."

A thrill of emotion accompanied that, all edges and pinpricks. Aelliana took a breath.

"*Van'chela*, this thing that we are—is it—*well*?"

He smiled, slow and warm. "I think it is very well, indeed," he murmured, and leaned over to kiss her.

The touch of his lips ignited her; she leaned in hungrily, with one hand pulling him close, and closer still.

Daav made a noise that might have been a purr or a growl, his lips on her throat now. He pressed forward; the chair began to recline, yielding beneath their combined weight.

Open, you stupid, mewling brat! Her husband's voice shouted from memory; accompanied by the sensation of being pinned by a weight greater than hers, her legs thrust wide—

Quick as a breath, the memory was gone, and it was Daav holding her, pressing her down, and she wanted, wanted—

She raised a hand and put it flat against his chest. "Wait . . ." she whispered.

He froze where he was; she felt the care he took, and what it cost him to straighten away from her and sit back on his heels.

"Aelliana, forgive me—"

She put her fingers over his mouth.

"There is nothing to forgive," she told him, "only . . . an accommodation. I—we—can learn this, *van'chela*." She came to her feet, reaching down to take his hand. "Come."

Hand-linked, they left the piloting chamber, and hand-linked they went down the short hall to crew's quarters. She put her free hand against the door on the right side of the corridor, and smiled when it slid soundlessly open.

The room beyond was decadent, reflecting some—though not all—of the former owner's . . . predilections. The ceiling mirrors had been sold, but the rest of the room was absurdly furnished for a working Class A Jump.

The floor was covered in thick, creamy carpet; the bed luxuriously outfitted with silks, furs, and an entire school of brightly colored pillows. It was, she thought, turning to face Daav, perfect. It belonged to no one, save her; and it was her choice that had brought him here. That was important.

Very important.

"Take off your jacket," she commanded.

One eyebrow rose, but he complied, dropping the garment to the rug.

"Take off *your* jacket," he countered, softly.

Ah, this was a game that Daav knew, was it? She smiled again, delight stitching through the bright threads of need, desire, and determination.

Her jacket slid down her arms. She dropped it next to his on the rug.

"Your shirt," she said. "Remove it."

He smiled and fingered the lacing loose, taking an inordinately long time about it, his eyes on hers the entire while, at last withdrawing the cord from its guides entirely and dropping it to the floor. His eyes still on hers, he slowly pulled the shirt over his head, and let it fall.

She stepped forward then, unable to stop, and ran her hands over his chest, delighting in the texture of his skin, stretching high to place her hands on his shoulders, her body pressed into his, and her face turned up.

"Kiss me."

He did that, and willingly. Hunger seared her; she angled her mouth against his, hard and demanding, and he responded—but with restraint; his embrace not as fierce as it might have been—she read it in him, that he did not wish to frighten her, and stepped back, shivering with need.

Her shirt had someway joined the muddle of clothes on the rug; she didn't remember how, and it did not concern her.

"Boots," Daav murmured, before she could draw breath. "Else this will quickly become a comedy."

She laughed, breathless, and sat on the edge of the bed to attend hers, then looked up at him, feeling suddenly not . . . quite . . . bold.

"Take off the rest," she said, her voice shaking. "And lie down on the bed."

He was a paradox—a dozen paradoxes; velvet skin over hard, lean muscle. Her fingers found scars; her lips found places that had him nearly weeping with delight.

This was far superior to their first encounter, when all she had known was what he had desired. This . . . *exploration*; this teasing out of sensual knowledge—she could do *this*, she thought, lazily running her fingers down the inside of his thigh, for days. She smiled at the catch in his breath, and moved her fingers again.

"Aelliana . . ." He reached for her; she caught his hands and kissed his palms, feeling his intent.

"Yes," she whispered. "It's your turn now."

Passion, pillows cascading to the floor, laughter, cries, and limbs entangled. She was astride him, aching for union, and there—there he came again, her husband, cursing her as he slammed her against the wall and thrust his member into her—

She shivered, the bed slipping sideways.

"Aelliana?"

Warm hands caught her and she shook her head, dashing the hateful vision away, looking down into his face, this, her most beloved friend, who shared her heart and her soul.

"Daav!" she cried and bent to kiss him most tenderly indeed.

She opened to him then, willingly, filling herself with him, as the two of them climbed, entangled, to the stars, to ecstasy, crying out with one voice, in fierce celebration of their union.

· · · ❄ · · ·

"The most beneficial model," Daav murmured, his cheek resting against her hair. They had adopted the coverlet as the heat of lovemaking began to fade, leaving them shivering in the ship's temperate air. Aelliana had slept for a few minutes, her head on his shoulder and her leg thrown across his hips. Upon waking, she had immediately demanded an analysis of the options open to *The Luck* as a working ship.

"The most beneficial model for a small ship embarked on trade is a fixed route, with both reliable suppliers and reliable buyers at each port. Er Thom could work out such a route for *The Luck*, if the pilot-owner wished to embrace that option. Indeed, I would venture to say that we would be hard put to deny Er Thom the considerable pleasure of putting together such a route."

"Mmm," she said, "but there is the option of courier. What benefit there?"

"Courier has the advantage of a certain freedom in flight," he said obligingly, this being the sort of data the child of a house old in both trade and piloting ingested with his porridge. "One need only have a client and a destination. One may set one's price, or refuse a commission altogether. With freedom, of course, comes heightened risk. One cannot be certain that there will be someone in need of the ship's services at the delivery port. Also, one may not know well in advance which port one will raise, or in what condition it will be found."

"Is it—more dangerous?" she asked. "Courier."

He considered that. "Not necessarily, no. A known trade loop with published stops holds danger as well— perhaps in equal measure, though there are safeguards built into the loop. If one does not arrive when scheduled, for instance—"

"I'm inclined," Aelliana interrupted, reaching up to brush his cheek with cool fingertips, "I'm inclined to go for courier. What do you think?"

He smiled, and craned his head to look down into her face, catching a glimpse of shining green eyes among the tangled strands of tawny hair.

"I think that I am inclined to go for courier, too."

She chewed her lip.

"We will need papers? A registration, or—a license to do business. Is that the Guild?"

"Ultimately, the Guild. However, Mr. dea'Gauss can do much of the ferreting and the filling out for you."

"He had said he would be pleased to serve me—when I met him in the hallway," Aelliana said. "At the time, I could scarcely think how he might. I will call upon him tomorrow."

"Fortunate Mr. dea'Gauss," he said lightly.

She laughed and sat up, the coverlet falling away to reveal breasts made pert by the cool air.

"We are in accord," she said, and leaned down to kiss him, her passion striking his from banked to bonfire in a heartbeat.

Gasping, he surrendered to her, and willingly let her have her way.

SIXTEEN

. . . .

Be aware of those actions undertaken in your name...
—From the Liaden Code of Proper Conduct

"THIS IS QUITE SUDDEN, SCHOLAR." DIRECTOR BARQ went so far as to frown into the screen. "I wonder if you have given any thought to the impact of your decision upon Chonselta Technical College."

As it happened, she had, and it grieved her. She had taught mathematics at Chonselta Tech for seven Standards, and the advanced seminar in practical mathematics, that her Scout pupils had called Math for Survival, for five. Surely, she owed Chonselta Tech much, for having hired her, trembling and timid as she had been; and for having been for so many years a refuge and a sanctuary.

And, yet, she told herself now, as she had told herself several times during a solitary, wakeful night— one had other tasks before one; an entire new life to explore. She had given Chonselta Tech fair measure.

"I regret the inconvenience; I appreciate that my decision seems sudden," she told Director Barq. Surely it would seem so to him; it having been her custom for so many years to simply reinitial her contract at the beginning of the Long Interval. This year she had put off that simple custom while she considered requesting a reduced teaching schedule, so that she might spend more time with her ship, learning that galaxy of practical detail necessary to a working pilot.

"I believe, however," she continued, in the face of the director's unremitting frown, "that there are many qualified to teach the mid-level courses. The seminar, of course—"

"Of course," he interrupted, and threw up a hand, as would one bested in negotiation. "I had meant to bring this to your attention previously, Scholar, but our paths scarcely crossed this last term. I am dismayed that I must tell you that the college failed to accurately record your ascent to the next level of compensation at the end of last school year—seven Standards with us, and all of them to our honor! Of course, we will be transferring the balance owing to your account immediately. Also, I think you will be very pleased with your bonus this semester."

Aelliana stared, a sudden and not-entirely-welcome thought forming at the back of her mind.

She had been accustomed to receiving a small bonus, most semesters, which reflected the continued success of the advanced seminar. However, she could not immediately recall that she had ever received an increase in her general compensation. Seven Standards, and she had been so grateful for a huddling place; a door to which Ran Eld did not hold a key; a place to think, and study, and write . . .

"Certainly," she said slowly, hating the thought that

she had been cheated; hating the woman she had been, who had been so poor a thing that she was *so easily* cheated.

"Certainly," she said again, to Director Barq's suddenly careful face, "if there has been an error, it should be rectified. I regret, however, that I remain unable to continue my contract with Chonselta Technical College. Necessity . . . necessity exists."

That was true, she thought defiantly. And if it was her own necessity and none of clan or kin, yet it did exist.

"I will come later today to remove my belongings from my office," she said. "If there are—separation papers that the college requires me to sign, I will be pleased to endorse them then."

Director Barq's face closed; he inclined his head.

"Of course, Scholar."

"Good-day, Director," she said sadly, and touched the disconnect.

She sat back in her chair, looking out over the morning garden.

You are as a mouse among raptors, Lady Kareen reminded her from memory.

Aelliana sniffed, and shook her head.

"I will learn better," she told the room at large.

A chime sounded, as if to underline her determination. Aelliana frowned, then rose to go hastily across the room.

The door slid open to reveal Mr. pel'Kana, a sizable envelope in his hand.

"This has just come for you, Pilot."

"Thank you," she said, receiving it. She glanced down; but all she saw was her own name, written out in elegant green ink.

"It was delivered from the office of Mr. dea'Gauss," Mr. pel'Kana murmured.

"I thank you," Aelliana said, not much enlightened. Surely, she had planned to call upon Mr. dea'Gauss today. Could he have anticipated her request? Or was this Daav's hand once more? She looked up to the waiting butler.

"Mr. pel'Kana, I will be driving into the city soon. Could you tell me where I might find... the car lent to my use?"

He inclined his head. "I will have your car brought 'round, Pilot. When do you anticipate leaving?"

"I—" She glanced at the envelope, then over to the clock. "In half a glass?" she asked.

"Certainly. Is there anything else?"

"Not at the moment. I thank you."

"Very good." He bowed and departed, walking stately down the hall.

The letter covering the packet gracefully directed her to review the enclosed account transfer forms, sign each at the place indicated, and return two sets of the three to the office of dea'Gauss, in Solcintra, address appended. She could, she learned, assign a password to each account and manage them herself, or she could assign management, in whole or in part, to Mr. dea'Gauss and his staff. Had she any questions, she was invited, most warmly, to contact him.

Aelliana flipped the letter over and riffled the first clipped set of papers, located an accounts list, with balances, among the appendices, and ran an expert's eye down the page.

Carefully, she pulled out the desk chair, and, care-fully, sat.

She flipped back to the first page, and was very soon in possession of the fact that certain monies (itemized list in Appendix A) were transferred from Daav yos'Phelium Clan Korval to Aelliana Caylon Clan Mizel to be hers fully, without restraint, and without condition, to use wholly as she judged fit.

There was more, language specifying that the grant was to herself *personally*, and a great deal of what she judged to be mere formality, in order to sanctify the contract in the eyes of another *qe'andra* and the Accountants Guild.

What there was not, was any explanation of why Daav should be giving her—*her personally*—so very much money, not to mention what appeared to be a small house or holding in the Hayzin Mountains.

Aelliana reassembled the papers and slid them back into their envelope with the letter from Mr. dea'Gauss covering all, exactly as it had been. She could not possibly accept so much—not from Daav. If this was some High House notion of seeing to her comfort—

She bit her lip, recalling Anne's reassurance that she could afford that exclusive, expensive shop. Daav hadn't paid for her clothes, no. He had merely given her the means to do so.

Well, she thought, pressing the seal on the enve-lope and rising from her chair, Mr. dea'Gauss had invited her to consult him with any question. How convenient, that she had already determined to call upon him with other business.

· · · ⚙ · · ·

Daav closed the door behind him, and sealed it before going deeper into the clan's closest-held library. Here were shelf after shelf of leather-bound volumes—Korval's Diaries, including the stained and rumpled book that had belonged to the very Founder, Grandmother Cantra, who had first lain down the rules of the clan.

Today, he thought, he need not go...quite so far back. He stepped up to a shelf holding more modern, less abused, volumes and ran his fingers down the leathered spines...

· · · · ❖ · · · ·

"May I," Aelliana said to the young man at the desk, "speak with Mr. dea'Gauss?"

The young man inclined his head, respectful, but not encouraging.

"Have you an appointment, Pilot?"

Aelliana's stomach sank. A gentleman so highly placed—of course she ought to have made an appointment, rather than rushing in as if—as if this fine office in Solcintra's business district was the Binjali Repair Shop, and someone of the regular crew certain to be about to aid her.

"I beg your pardon," she said to the young man. "It did not occur to me to do so. Perhaps I might make one with you?"

"Certainly," he said, his fingers touching the keys set into the desktop. "Your name, please?"

"Aelliana Caylon."

The young man's busy fingers paused.

"Ah..."

"I understand that there is a great deal of demand

upon his time," Aelliana began—and paused when he raised his hand.

"Pray forgive me, Pilot Caylon. I will inform Mr. dea'Gauss of your presence. Please, allow Ms. pen'Dela to guide you to one of the private parlors."

He must have touched a key, for here came a young woman who scarcely looked past halfling, dressed in sober business clothes, her face formal, and her bow precise.

"Pilot Caylon, please. Follow me."

"I—" Aelliana looked back to the young man at the desk. "Pray do not call Mr. dea'Gauss from his duties for me. Indeed, you are quite correct; I ought to come at his convenience."

The young man inclined his head.

"My instructions are that Mr. dea'Gauss will see Aelliana Caylon," he said.

"If the pilot will come?" Ms. pen'Dela added in a sweet, high voice.

Aelliana bit her lip, then inclined her head and followed the young lady down the hallway and into a small, graciously appointed parlor.

"There is tea," her guide said, showing her the buffet laid with cups and a small plate of pastries. "If you would prefer wine..."

"Thank you, tea is all that I require," Aelliana said hastily.

Ms. pen'Dela bowed.

"Certainly, Pilot. Mr. dea'Gauss should be with you very soon. In the meanwhile, if there is anything at all that you require, only press this button—" She placed her hand briefly next to the button in question,

discreetly set into the top of the buffet. "—and someone will come."

"Thank you," Aelliana said again. "I am quite content."

Her guide bowed and departed. A curtain woven
with the sign of the Accountants Guild fell across the
doorway, granting privacy as Aelliana sank into one of
the soft chairs grouped agreeably about a small table.

She took a breath, straightened her spine, placed
the envelope on her lap, and folded her hands atop it.
Mr. dea'Gauss had been very kind to her during their
previous meeting, she told herself. She would explain her
error, and beg his pardon—surely he would accept that?
Then, she would make a proper appointment, and—

The curtain across the doorway parted to admit a
man of very erect posture, wearing a bronze vest over
dark shirt and trousers.

Aelliana came to her feet and bowed low.

"Mr. dea'Gauss, please forgive this unseemly intru-
sion into your day."

There was a pause, growing rather longer than
courtesy permitted. She straightened, and met a pair
of speculative brown eyes.

"You do not intrude, my lady," he said, his voice
soothing in the mode of servant to lord. "I see that
you have the transfer packet. Please, allow me to take
you to my office. We may speak confidentially there."

Aelliana swallowed. Well, and if he would see her,
she thought, then he would. She would try to keep her
requests and her questions to the point and disrupt
him as little as possible.

"Thank you," she said, and took the arm that he
offered.

"Only a step down the hall," he murmured, keeping

yet to that mistaken mode, "and a short ride on the lift. It is a fine day, and the views from the windows are quite pleasant."

It was, Aelliana admitted some time later, a worthy view: Most of Solcintra City could be seen from the windows of Mr. dea'Gauss' office, an orderly gridwork of architecture and parkland. Indeed, if one took the right angle, one could see the Tower in Solcintra Port, nearly colorless against the bright sky.

"From the rear windows one may see Korval's Tree." Mr. dea'Gauss gestured toward an panel of opaqued windows. "Alas, this is not the best hour for such a viewing." He inclined his head, and continued, somewhat more briskly, "Now, my lady, what task may I be honored to perform for you?"

She hesitated. It was an impertinence to call another adult's understanding of *melant'i* into question. However, it was ... dishonorable to claim a place higher than where one stood.

"I fear that, in my ignorance, I may have misled you, sir," she said carefully in adult-to-adult. "I am the second daughter of the House, and Mizel—Mizel does not stand High. Scholar will do for me, or Pilot; each is a *melant'i* that I hold in my own right. I have, for a variety of reasons, accepted the protection of Clan Korval." She raised her hand to touch the pin in the collar of her jacket. "But I am not *of* Clan Korval."

"I see." Mr. dea'Gauss tipped his head, and moved a hand, indicating that she walk with him to the table where she had left the envelope. "Perhaps, then, Pilot," he said in adult-to-adult, "we ought to discuss your *melant'i* more fully. But first—" He used his chin to point at the worktable—"you have some questions regarding the transfer paperwork?"

"Yes," she said, pausing by a chair to allow him to seat himself first, as was appropriate, given their relative ranks. "And also, I have a—task for you, if you are willing to undertake it. Understand, I have no good idea of how much work is involved, so you must not hold shy of telling me if it will not do."

"That I will not, Pilot," he said calmly. He paused, and appeared to consider her for a moment before bowing slightly. "Allow me to fetch tea," he said smoothly. "Pray, make yourself at ease; I will not be a moment."

He moved toward the back corner of the room, where a buffet like the one in the reception parlor stood. Aelliana sat down, folded her hands on the tabletop, and glanced about.

Mr. dea'Gauss stood high, indeed, she thought, to have gained the right to such an office. A working desk holding three screens and several piles of hard copy occupied a windowed niche on the left-hand wall; the table at which she sat was one of three such placed about the room. The floor was old wood, with bright carpets here and there, like flowering islands adrift upon a dark sea.

"Now, we may talk comfortably," Mr. dea'Gauss said, setting a tray on the table. He poured for them, deft and neat, before taking the chair at her left hand. "Where shall we begin, Pilot? I am wholly at your disposal."

He did certainly seem to be so, Aelliana acknowledged. She sipped her tea—and sipped again in appreciation—before putting the cup aside.

"The task for which I would like to commission your consideration," she said carefully, "is . . ." She leaned forward, looking directly into his face.

"I own a Class A Jump—*Ride the Luck*—which is berthed at Binjali's Yard. It is—my intention to enter the lists as a courier pilot. I understand that there is paperwork—licenses to obtain, guarantees to be posted—in order to best serve and protect ship and crew along the . . . beyond Liaden space."

"You wish me to bring that paperwork together for you? That is perfectly within my scope, Pilot." He reached into the pocket of his vest and pulled out a notepad. Tapping the device on, he glanced at her. "A few questions, if you will."

"Certainly."

"Good—when do you propose to put your ship to work beyond Liad?"

"As soon as may be," she answered. "Much depends upon my copilot, who has some matters to put in order before he is cleared to fly."

Mr. dea'Gauss tapped a note onto the pad. "What is your copilot's name?"

"Daav yos'Phelium Clan Korval."

She thought his fingers missed a beat; if so, he recovered so rapidly that she could not be entirely certain.

"Of course. I have Pilot yos'Phelium's particulars on file, so there is no need for you to detail those. *Ride the Luck* is of course registered with the Guild?"

"Yes. I had only just thought! Will you need ship's archives?"

"Ship's archives are not required, though I have found that it is beneficial to include them as part of the supporting documentation," Mr. dea'Gauss murmured, his attention on his notes.

"I will transmit them to you this afternoon," Aelliana promised.

He glanced up. "You need not discommode yourself, my Lady. As the archive is in support only, its presence is not necessary for the completion of the primary documentation."

"It is no trouble at all," she said. "I will be taking *The Luck* to Chonselta this afternoon."

"In that wise, I will be pleased to have all necessary information immediately in hand," he murmured and looked up. "I anticipate that the completed and certified documents will be in your hands no later than Banim Third-day."

Aelliana blinked. "That's very soon."

"As a task, it is not difficult. There may be some delay upon the Guild's side, though we will of course do everything possible to expedite the matter."

He put his notepad on the table and gave her his whole attention once more. "I think we have this task well in hand, Pilot. What else may I be honored to do for you?"

She placed her hand on the envelope.

"I wonder if you are . . . able . . . to explain to me why I am awarded this—considerable!—settlement. Daav owes me nothing—it is I who owe him, more than ever I can hope to Balance."

Mr. dea'Gauss glanced down, perhaps at the envelope; perhaps at the Jump pilot's ring on her finger, then raised his eyes to hers.

"His lordship allowed me to know of the bond between you," he said slowly. "In . . . more regular circumstances, that bond would predicate a . . . social outcome."

"As it did with Anne and Lord yos'Galan."

"Precisely." Mr. dea'Gauss placed his fingers lightly on the edge of the envelope.

"Precisely," he said again, and paused, as if gathering his thoughts.

"His lordship," he said after a moment, "chose to honor the bond as if it is the social outcome, realizing that this may never come to pass. It is . . . an unusual *melant'i*, as he himself said, and one may therefore too easily err in proper action. One wishes to place honor—one wishes to place *regard* correctly, and to rightly value what is precious. His solution . . . I have spent many hours considering his lordship's solution, and I cannot find it in error, my lady, nor say that I might have counseled him differently."

The envelope was textured and tickled her palm. Aelliana took a breath.

"This is a lifemate's share."

"It is."

She closed her eyes, opened them and considered the man before her with his practical face and canny eyes.

"Mr. dea'Gauss, Daav and I are indeed lifemates-by-nature, as he told you. However, it is by—it is by no means certain that we can, or ought to be, lifemates-by-law. It is—I had hoped that this joint endeavor we undertake would clarify that point. You will know, sir, that Mizel is by no means High House. I would not damage Korval through my ignorance, nor would I make Daav vulnerable."

He inclined his head, but said nothing, apparently

waiting for her to continue, though what else she might say—

But, no, there was something else, after all, to say. She pushed the envelope to him and lifted her hand away.

"Please, hold these safe until I call upon you in order to sign them, or ask that you destroy them."

Again, he inclined his head, and Aelliana bethought herself of yet another question.

"In your judgment—ought I to make Daav half owner of *The Luck*?"

"My lady, you ought not," he replied promptly. "He is your copilot, and I believe you will find that satisfies him very well."

"Thank you," she said, and hesitated, for surely the question that next rose to her tongue was no concern of hers...

"Is there something else, my lady?"

"I only wonder," she said slowly. "This...employment as *Ride the Luck*'s copilot will mean that Daav will sometimes be...unavailable to Delm Korval and the business of the clan."

"That had mostwise been the case with Korval's delms until very recently," Mr. dea'Gauss said. "This firm has protocols in place to handle much of what Korval has been addressing personally. Korval's presence will naturally be required at the bi-annual meetings of the Council of Clans, but a good deal of the...lesser business may be handled by a designated speaker."

She frowned. "Does he—know this?" she asked, thinking of the sense of weariness and ill health that she had felt in him, bone-deep.

"It is my *melant'i* to assume that Korval is informed,"

Mr. dea'Gauss said delicately. "The conditions under which we currently operate are by instruction of Thodelm yos'Galan, acting as *Korval-pernard'i*, in the aftermath of the tragedy that cost Korval its delm and yos'Galan its a'thodelm. The instructions were never rescinded."

"I see," she said, and inclined her head. "Mr. dea'Gauss, I thank you for the gift of your time—and for your assistance."

"You are most welcome, my lady. Please consider me entirely at your disposal."

"You're very kind," she said and stood, Mr. dea'Gauss rising with her.

"There is," she said, suddenly recalling, "one more thing." She touched the collar of the shirt she was wearing, one of several purchased from Anne's favorite store.

"You will, I think, be receiving an invoice from the Crystal Flower. Please forward it to me when it arrives; it is my debt and I will pay it."

Mr. dea'Gauss bowed.

"Certainly, my lady."

SEVENTEEN

· · · · · · · · · · · · · · · · · · · ·

A room without books is like a body without a soul.

—Cicero

ER THOM WAS IN HIS OFFICE. GOOD.

Daav pushed the door open gently, pausing just inside the room to consider his brother, who had for so long been the first tenant of his heart. He made a charming sight, to be sure, with his head bent studiously over his work, and the light from the lamp making golden hair luster.

"You might be of some use, and pour the wine," Er Thom said, without raising his head. "I'll be through here in a moment."

Grinning, Daav crossed to the cabinet, unshipped glasses, and poured—red for Er Thom, and the same for himself, there being no *misravot* on offer.

"You stint me," he said, carrying the glasses to the table and disposing them.

"Does Pilot Caylon know you drink *misravot*?" Er Thom asked. He rose and stretched, hands over head, relaxing all at once, with a sigh.

"She may well," Daav said ruefully. "She may even know that I am not particularly fond of it."

"A perceptive lady, indeed," his brother said, coming forward. He looked into Daav's face, violet eyes shrewd. "When shall I have the felicity of seeing the announcement in *The Gazette*?"

"Perhaps not for some time," Daav said slowly. "My lady wishes to hone her edge."

"Surely she can acquire whatever edge she feels she lacks on the whetstone of the world," Er Thom murmured, picking up his glass and assaying a sip.

"She makes a compelling argument against that route," Daav murmured, tasting his own wine. "And offers an interesting proposal, darling."

"Which you are inclined to accept."

"Since it falls in with my own wishes and desires, of course I am inclined to accept. Which is why I've come creeping along yos'Galan's back hallways at an hour when we both ought to have put work away." He sipped, and lowered his glass. "I need your advice, Thodelm."

Golden brows rose slightly. "Shall I be alarmed?"

"You may well become so; who am I to know?"

"And is it," Er Thom asked carefully, "Korval come seeking yos'Galan's advice, on behalf of the clan's son Daav?"

Trust Er Thom to parse the *melant'i* thus. Indeed, he had himself spent a goodly portion of the afternoon attempting to untangle just that point.

"Scrutiny reveals that it must be Korval who seeks yos'Galan's wisdom—on behalf of Korval. There's no keeping Daav out of the equation, I fear, but the solving cannot be for the undutiful child alone."

"Hah." Er Thom pulled out a chair and sat, waving Daav to the other. "Tell me."

"Put most simply, and with the best good of the clan foremost in your consideration—does it seem to you that the clan might...thrive...should the delm choose to accept employment as copilot on a courier ship?"

"It does not immediately seem to me that the clan would founder and break apart," Er Thom said placidly. "yos'Galan appears to take no harm from the benevolent neglect of its thodelm."

"True. I will tell you that I have spent some time with the Diaries today, and learn that past delms have been...more lightly tied to Liad."

"So there is precedent."

"There is," Daav agreed. "Do you think it wise for both the delm and the delm's heir to be offworld at the same time?"

Er Thom tipped his head. "Did not our mother and my mother travel off-planet together in company with my elder brother?"

They had, Daav allowed—delm, thodelm and a'thodelm, together all. And when the trip was done, delm and a'thodelm were dead, with the thodelm crippled, and in mortal fear of her life.

"That is hardly an argument in support of the scheme," he commented.

"It is merely an observation," Er Thom said, frowning down into his glass. "We were already thin when that trip was taken—it was only after that we came to think of ourselves as *endangered*."

He lifted his head. "I think it was my mother, who came back to us so badly wounded, having lost her sister and her heir, who locked us down, brother, and insisted that the delm clip his wings."

Daav considered. In the terrible days after their losses, he and Er Thom had depended upon the clan's sole remaining elder for advice and guidance. Ill and grieving as she was, she might well have deemed it best to nail her reckless nephew to the ground, lest he risk his life and his bloodline.

"It may be that she was the author of our current situation," he said slowly. "Indeed, the entries in the Diaries would seem to support the supposition. Perhaps it was wisdom."

"Not wisdom," Er Thom said decisively. "Not malice, I think—but wisdom? No." He straightened.

"yos'Galan advises Korval," he stated, in the mode of subordinate-line-to-the-delm.

Daav inclined his head. "Korval hears," he returned, delm-to-subordinate-line.

"It is not the best care of the clan to huddle, safe, upon the homeworld. Korval is ships; Korval is pilots. If Korval allows fear to rule it, we become less than we are. More, we violate the law laid down for us by the Founder. Thus does yos'Galan advise the delm."

That the Founder would have found nothing wonderful in her heirs breaking faith, pirate that she'd been, Daav did not say. Instead, he inclined his head once more.

"Korval hears yos'Galan."

"That is well. Does the delm require further service from yos'Galan this hour?"

"I believe that our business is done," Korval responded.

"Excellent." Er Thom smiled. "Now, tell me how matters fare between yourself and Pilot Caylon. She must think well of you, if she considers placing her ship in your hands."

"Her regard humbles me," Daav said truthfully, "though there have been moments when I have wished that the Healers had meddled less with what was finished and done."

Er Thom tipped his head. "You speak of the bond? Truly, it is unsettling at first—who wishes to share his innermost self, with all one's flaws and pettiness? I swear you will grow accustomed, brother, and then you will wonder how ever you went on—before."

"Aelliana reports something very like," he admitted, setting his glass aside. "For my part—" He raised his head and met Er Thom's eyes. "The link is only one-way, darling. She describes a condition like to what I have heard from you and from Anne. For myself, I experience nothing of the sort—"

Er Thom shifted, pity on his face, his lips parting—

"No—hear me," Daav said, his eyes suddenly wet. "I do well enough—how many believe that Scouts are able to read minds, after all?"

"But the full sharing," Er Thom murmured.

"The full sharing—is perhaps not to be ours. That the link functions at all is—ought to be—a joy. Indeed, she says that she finds it so, and I—I would far rather sit copilot to Aelliana Caylon than anything else I can contemplate."

"That is well, then." Er Thom said, and leaned over to grip Daav's hand, his fingers warm and firm. "It *will be* well, brother."

"Of course it will," Daav said, and smiled, seeing

some of the distress fade from his brother's eyes. "How could it be otherwise?"

He had walked from Jelaza Kazone to Trealla Fantrol, wanting to have time with his thoughts. After leaving Er Thom, he was again glad of the walk, this time to soothe his unruly emotions. His last message from Aelliana was that she was Chonselta-bound and might not return until late. It may have been that which encouraged him to follow the more circuitous paths down-valley, though Jelaza Kazone rarely felt empty to him any more.

Whatever the case, the stars were well up by the time he opened a side door and stepped into a hall illuminated by night-dims—and a bar of bright light from the partly open library door. Frowning, he moved silently forward.

Aelliana was curled into his favorite chair, her head bent over some handwork. She was wearing the green silk robe he had sent to her in Chonselta; the ripple of tawny hair that hid her face from him was damp, the light casting the drifting dry strands into an aura.

He pushed the door wider.

She looked up, smiling.

"Daav. Good evening."

"Good evening," he answered, stepping into the room. The object she had been so concentrated upon was a remote, its screen dense with figures. "Am I disturbing your work?"

"Not at all," she answered. "I was waiting for you. This—" She shook the remote lightly—"is a notion I've been considering. Only let me close down."

Her fingers flickered across the small keypad; the

screen dimmed and she put the device on the table at her elbow. Daav came further into the room—*like a moth drawn to the moon*, he chided himself—and perched on the arm of the chair opposite.

"How went your errands today?" he asked when she looked up.

She sighed, very lightly. "Mr. dea'Gauss was everything that was accommodating and agreeable. Director Barq was...less so, I fear."

That dea'Gauss had been accommodating was scarcely surprising. Director Barq, however...

"Was there a difficulty?" he asked.

Aelliana moved her shoulders, as if she would cast the memory away.

"There was no difficulty," she said, "unless you count the realization of an unwelcome truth difficult." She looked down at her hands, folded tightly on her lap. "Director Barq had apparently felt that my decision not to renew was a...strategy, and that my... *relationship with Korval*, as he phrased it, had given me insight into the fact that I had in the past been neither advertent, nor careful of my own best good. And so I became someone whom it was easy and natural to cheat."

The set of her shoulders and the tight clasp of her hands told him precisely how profound was her unhappiness.

"We are all cheated, once," he commented, which was the truth as he knew it personally. "It is how we learn not to be cheated twice." He tipped his head. "Are you hungry?"

She glanced up at him, green eyes wide and misty. "I beg your pardon?"

"Are you hungry?" he repeated. "I confess that I am."

"Since you are so bold—yes, I am hungry. However, I didn't wish to disturb Mr. pel'Kana."

"No need," he said, rising and holding his hand down to her. "Come, we will forage for ourselves."

She put her hand in his and allowed him to pull her to her feet. "This sounds risky," she commented.

"Not in the least! You must learn to have faith in me, Pilot."

· · · ·✹· · · ·

"There's wine in the keeper," Daav said, jerking his head toward the rear of the kitchen, as he opened the coldbox. "If you would be so kind as to pour for us?"

Aelliana tightened the sash of her robe and moved off in the indicated direction, the floor tiles cool beneath her bare feet. By the time she had extricated a bottle of white wine by a process that could only be defined as True Random, Daav had taken over the corner of the counter nearest the stove, knife and cutting board to hand.

She carried her burden to what was obviously a wine station, with glasses and cups hanging ready over a table topped with stone. Reaching up, she unracked two glasses, unsealed the wine and poured.

"Where will you have it?" she asked.

"In hand," came the answer, so she took a glass to him.

He had it from her with a smile, sipped—and laughed. "Yes! This will go excellently!"

"I suppose I should have told you that I know nothing of wine," Aelliana said ruefully. "But my mission came upon me so quickly..."

"No, you have comported yourself with honor! It only remains for me to do my part."

Smiling, she drifted back down-counter, picked up her glass and looked about her. There were stools pushed under a high table set at an angle to the counter. She pulled one out and perched on it, watching as Daav deftly took four slices of brown bread from the loaf, sprinkled them with oil and set them on the flatiron he had placed on the stove. He unwrapped the block of cheese, and cut four thin slices from it, rewrapped it and pulled a second, smaller block to him. His motions were quick, but relaxed, without a wasted move, nor a stutter.

"Will you like sweet sauce?" he murmured, without looking up from shaving paper-thin slices from the second cheese. "Hot sauce? Jam?"

"Make them as you would for yourself," she told him. She sipped her wine—and gasped.

Daav looked at her over his shoulder.

"Is the wine not to your liking?"

"I— It is very much to my liking," she confessed, and raised her chin, determined that he not see her chagrined twice over the same bottle. "It will, I think, go very well with the cheese."

"I agree," he said, his eyes dancing. "I see that you give me close supervision."

"As to that, I haven't the first idea of how to make toasted cheese sandwiches! I find the process fascinating."

He grinned. "Watch well, then. The next time we require comfort, you will cook."

She shook her hair back, watching him ply the knife, so certain and so deft.

"I might very well make an error, and lose comfort for both."

"Little chance of that." He put cheese on two slices of the oiled bread, and pulled a small jar down from a shelf cluttered with such. Each slice was spread with a brownish sauce and capped with a second slice of bread. Daav lit the burner and reached for the turner hanging behind the stove.

"Every toasted cheese sandwich is unique unto itself," he said, picking up his glass. "Like art, there are no mistakes."

Aelliana sipped her wine, relishing the sweet flowery notes, and the bite of licorice beneath. Daav made a pleasant sight, his shoulders easy and his hips cocked, as he overlooked his project. He raised his glass for another sip, the muscles moving beneath his shirt, and she was suddenly, vividly warm, recalling the feel of his skin beneath her palms, his long legs, entwined with hers...

Flushed, she raised her glass and drank, perhaps more deeply than the wine deserved. At the stove, Daav used the turner, and the sandwiches sizzled against the grill.

Turning slightly, he put his glass down and reached into the cabinet to the left of the stove, pulling down two plates.

"In a moment," he said, over his shoulder, "we feast."

That was, she thought, a cue. She slid from the stool and retrieved his glass, carrying it with hers to the table before she fetched the bottle and refreshed both. The stool, she brought back to its proper place, and turned just as Daav arrived with the plates, each adorned with a toasted sandwich, cut neatly into halves.

"Now, Pilot," he said, folding his long self onto a stool, "I daresay you've never sampled anything like this!"

She laughed, watching under her lashes as he picked up a half sandwich and juggled it along his fingertips. That was not play, she found a heartbeat later, as she picked up one of her own halves; the bread was hot, slightly oily, and smelled delicious.

Carefully, she nibbled a corner, sighed and looked up to find him watching her.

"Well?" he asked.

"It's marvelous," she told him truthfully. "What is the sauce?"

"Apple butter. You don't find it too sweet?"

"Not at all," she assured him, and smiled. "Thank you, Daav."

"No need to thank me for taking proper care of my pilot," he answered, and turned his full attention to his meal, Aelliana following suit.

"Where," she asked, after the plates were empty and the glasses refreshed again, "did you go?"

"Ah. Daav visited his brother while the delm took counsel of his thodelm."

Aelliana felt her stomach tighten. "And the outcome?" she asked, striving for a calm voice.

"Thodelm yos'Galan is of the opinion that it is Korval's duty to show a bold face to the world. It is unbecoming of us to cower in the shadows, clinging to safety. He stops short of advising us to brawl in taverns and set up a business in the Low Port, but only just."

She considered that, sipping her wine gratefully. "Mr. dea'Gauss had said that there were protocols in place in his office, to accommodate those tasks that the delm now oversees," she said, looking up

into Daav's sharp, attentive face. "He says that there
is a promising younger on his staff whom he would
very much like to accept those responsibilities—with
oversight, of course."

"Of course," he murmured.

Aelliana sipped again, thinking of the papers that
she had left, unexecuted, in Mr. dea'Gauss' hands.
There was, she decided, no need to mention them to
Daav. After all, he had seen no need to tell her that
he intended to settle half his fortune on her.

"We are agreed, then? You will sit my copilot, and
we shall enlist *The Luck* as a courier?"

He smiled, and she felt her blood warm.

"We are agreed," he murmured. "How can we stand
against the advice of both yos'Galan and dea'Gauss?"

She laughed, and reached out to touch his hand,
feeling his amusement bolster her own.

"Now!" he said. "Would you like another toasted
cheese sandwich?"

She considered him, and the thought—the desire—
that had formed, seemingly of its own.

"I thank you," she said, "but no. I believe that I
would rather field—an impertinence."

Interest rippled from him, and perhaps a glow of
pride.

"And that would be?"

She took a deep breath, his hand beneath hers on
the table. "Might I see—your apartment?"

There was a flutter of— Daav slid his hand away.
Panicked, she looked up into his smile.

"There is not very much to see, but if that is your
whim—certainly. Let me clear the table while you
finish your wine."

* * *

His apartment was on the same side of the hall as hers; it warmed her absurdly to think that they shared a like view of the inner garden. He opened the door and stepped back to allow her first entry, as if she outranked him—or the place was hers by right.

She looked up into his face, which was perfectly and politely bland. She raised her hand—and let it fall before she touched him.

"Daav? If you had rather not..."

"You had wanted to see it," he murmured. "Please, satisfy yourself."

Thus commanded, and regretting her impertinence fully, she stepped into the room.

She had meant—when she saw how much it distressed him, she had meant only to *look*, and then to go away and leave him his peace. But the room drew her in, step by wondering step, and she with just enough sense to keep her hands clasped behind her. The shelves begged study—there were books, certainly, but also interesting stones, figurines, shells, and other things that she would need to ask him what they were, and what he thought of them.

A comfortably-shabby double chair covered in dusty blue sat at an angle to the fireplace, a book open, facedown on the seat. By the window, where in her apartment the computer desk held pride of place, stood a worktable of another kind, bladed tools were neatly set to hand; wood in different shapes, colors and textures were sorted to the sides. The comm unit sat on a table of its own; message light dark.

She moved on, her steps Scout-silent on overlapping

rugs, pausing as she came to a wall covered so closely with pictures that the wood could not be seen. A star map caught her eye, and a portrait of the Tree, drawn in a childish hand. A flatpic of a fair-haired woman with piercing blue eyes, and another, of a brown-striped cat...

Aelliana took a breath, and spun slowly, seeking to memorize this place that was so clearly and definitively *Daav's place*.

Her spin brought her 'round to face him, standing as still as a wild thing to one side of the open door, watching her from hooded black eyes. She bowed, as one who has been granted a great boon.

"Thank you," she whispered, and took a breath. She wanted to stay here in this room that seemed to embrace her and hold her close, but that would indeed be an impertinence. Daav, she understood suddenly, did not have people here. He had an entire house in which to entertain whom he would—friends, even lovers, need never come here.

"I will bid you good night, *van'chela*," she said gently. "Dream sweetly."

She moved toward the doorway.

"Aelliana." So soft, his voice. Almost, she thought she had imagined it.

She turned. He held out his hand, fingers slightly curled; she put her palm against his.

"Will you stay?" he asked, and she read his desire, that she *would*, and his fear—that she would refuse him.

She stepped forward, standing on her toes to lay her arms around his neck.

"Yes," she said, setting her cheek against his. "I want to."

EIGHTEEN

· · · · · · · · · · · · · · · ·

In an ally, considerations of house, clan, planet, race are insignificant beside two prime questions, which are:

1. Can he shoot?

2. Will he aim at your enemy?

—From Cantra yos'Phelium's Log Book

KILADI HAD ACHIEVED A THIRD DEGREE.

Now that, Daav thought, was unexpected in the extreme. He had been certain that the good scholar's plea for a remote defense, relying solely on the body of his work, would be roundly rejected by the Guardians of Knowledge at Dobrin University. However, it would appear that the existence of Scholar Kiladi's previous degrees had borne some weight with the accrediting committee. He opened the folder, barely glancing at the chip beneath its protective covering before running his eye down the short lines detailing the committee's decision.

Jen Sar Kiladi comes to Dobrin University already an accredited expert in comparative linguistics and diaspora dynamics. His numerous monographs and articles illuminate him as a scholar of rigorous and impeccable methodology. Therefore, though his request to waive a personal defense is unusual, it is the decision of this duly convened meeting of the Dobrin Guardians of Knowledge to honor the scholar's plea.

The Guardians and three unaffiliated Scholar Experts have closely examined the dossier submitted by Scholar Kiladi, taking particular care to scrutinize his sources and test his conclusions against the key literature in the field.

Having performed this examination, it is the judgment of the Guardians of Knowledge of Dobrin University that Jen Sar Kiladi is without a doubt fitted to be elevated to the rank of Scholar Expert of Cultural Genetics.

It was signed by all of the members of the Guardians of Knowledge and the three unaffiliated Scholar Experts, which display was significantly longer than the Statement of Certification.

Daav closed the folder, slipped it into an inside jacket pocket and pressed the seal.

A note would have to be written, of course. Kiladi was meticulous in such things. Indeed, he bordered on a little too meticulous, did Kiladi; it had seriously pained him to enter the plea for a remote defense. He *ought to have* gone to Bontemp and stood his defense; it was disrespectful of his colleagues in scholarship to have done otherwise, and yet—travel had become difficult for the good scholar of late, and common sense had at last carried the day.

Daav glanced at his watch, and turned his steps up-port, away from the little street of temp offices, noodle shops, and automated mail drops. He'd best be quick if he wished to be anywhere near on time to meet Aelliana at Ongit's for lunch.

He smiled slightly as he walked. Aelliana—what a marvel she was, to be sure! She grew—were he more loverlike, he would of course say that she blossomed, but hers was no coy unfolding, petal by shy silken petal. No, Aelliana hurtled skyward, branches spreading greedily, soaking up sensation, experience, *life* at a rate that was nothing short of astonishing. He would take oath that she changed even as she slept; he, proximate to that storm of constant alteration—he had changed, as well.

It was not to be expected that his growth would be so exuberant as hers; he was her elder—in years, and in experience. Yet with all of that, he felt lighter of late, as if his experience was buoying him rather than bearing him groundward.

Had he been asked, he most certainly would have said that he would never welcome another person into his rooms, privy to all his bad habits and distempers. Aelliana—he smiled and dashed across the street, dodging busy traffic. That they had not settled in her rooms—that, he thought, was understandable, for she had so little of her own to want about her. His suggestion that they choose another suite to make into *theirs* had dismayed her, and he had found himself... content to have her establish herself within his space.

Even, he thought, turning the corner into a street appreciably more prosperous than the one from which Kiladi collected his mail, he had accommodated himself—*almost* accommodated himself—to her ability to snatch his feelings and his thoughts straight out from the core of him. For himself, the more he observed her, the more he knew her mind and her heart—which was Scoutlike, and comforting.

For those other things that he desired... Aelliana remained adamant in her refusal to accept what she referred to as a "social lifemating"; nor would she sign the financial papers dea'Gauss had drawn up, and so make some comfort for herself. Those things grieved him, though not as much as her presence fulfilled him. Nothing, he felt, could break their bond, unequal as it was.

He negotiated a bit of crowded sidewalk, raising a hand to Gus Tav bel'Urik as he passed. The merchant acknowledged him distractedly, most of his attention on a lady of visible means, which was well, in Daav's opinion. As nearly allied as their clans were, yet he had no wish to exchange extended pleasantries with Merchant bel'Urik today.

Two steps more and he turned right, into Ongit's cluttered foyer, and smiled over a small sea of heads at young Pendra Ongit, who was on duty at the reception tower.

She gave him a grin and jerked her head to the left.

"She's waiting for you, Pilot," she called.

"My thanks," he answered and passed Scoutlike through the crowd.

Daav had arrived.

In the back booth, Aelliana straightened and craned to see him over the rest of the diners in Ongit's common room. Useless, of course. How she envied

Daav's height! Especially when he was not on hand to act as her lookout.

But there—a tall shadow was moving down-room, dark hair sweeping level shoulders, and the glint of silver at one ear. Aelliana smiled, feeling herself warm agreeably. It was thus, now: however contented or happy she had been by herself, that feeling was intensified sixfold by Daav's arrival. Today, she felt as if she might melt entirely, for she had been happy indeed, and all but ready to burst with her news.

Long legs delivered him to her quickly. He stood a moment, looking down at her, dark eyes bright, the merest hint of a smile at the corner of his mouth. For herself, she felt she must be grinning like a babe, too simple yet to control her face—and cared just as little.

"You are late," she said, striving for severity.

"And yet," he said, with mock seriousness, "you waited for me. How am I to take that?"

"I might easily have left," she answered as he slid into the booth next to her, rendering any such escape impossible.

"So you might have done," he allowed, and nodded at the wine bottle that had been left to breathe in the center of the table, two glasses standing sentinel.

"Is that your choice?" he asked.

"It was sent over by the red-haired pilot," she said, nodding to the right.

Daav turned his head, considering for a long moment the boisterous round table where the pilot sat with eight of his comrades. Aelliana blamed him not at all. The red-haired pilot made a compelling figure. Not beautiful, but *pleasing*, his demeanor somewhat reminiscent of Daav himself. Aelliana thought the similarity might stem from a familiarity with command, and wondered if the red-haired man was also a delm.

"The pilot has excellent taste, as I happen to know," Daav said, returning his attention to her. "We could scarcely be so churlish as to disdain his gift. Will you pour?"

"Certainly. Daav, I have—"

"Have you ordered?" he interrupted. "For I fear you are correct, and I am most shamefully tardy. If we're to keep our appointment at Tey Dor's, we may not linger long over our meal."

"I asked for salads and soup and bread to come when you did," Aelliana told him. "Felae assured me that there would be no difficulty."

Daav's left eyebrow quirked. "*Felae*, is it? Shall I be dismayed?"

She knew that he was teasing her. The proper thing to do was to answer in kind; she had learned that. She had even learned a certain pleasure in matching his wit. Today, however, she was too full of her news—*their* news—and simply shook her head at him, much as Anne did to Shan, when she wished him to behave.

"Cast into my place!" Daav mourned. "But at least I shall not starve."

"Pilots." Felae deftly swung the tray 'round, stopping it with a touch of his fingers. He sorted the plates and the utensils quickly before looking to Aelliana.

"Will there be anything else, Pilot?" he asked respectfully.

"Thank you, this looks to be everything," she said, and smiled at him. "You were very quick to notice that we were ready!"

The boy ducked his head.

"That was my sister's doing, Pilot. She pinged me from the reception station when your partner cleared the foyer."

"Excellent teamwork," Daav murmured approvingly.

Felae's pale cheeks darkened slightly, with pleasure or with shyness, Aelliana was not able to discern. He bowed, straightening to catch the tray as it began to wander aside.

"Enjoy your meal, Pilots," he said and off he went, veering to the left in response to a high-held hand.

"Bread, Pilot?" Daav murmured, reaching into the basket.

Aelliana sighed in anticipation.

"Bread would be good," she said, and it would be, here at Ongit's. Truly, she feared that she had acquired an addiction.

He broke the loaf with strong fingers, put half on her plate, kept the other and took up his spoon.

Aelliana reached—but no! Her news was too urgent. Even fresh-baked bread and Ongit's vegetable chowder paled before it.

"Daav," she said, breathlessly, "I have something very important to tell you."

Halfway to his mouth, the spoon stopped, reversed itself and made a soft landing in the bowl. She looked up, seeing at once that she had his undivided attention.

"*Very* important?" he repeated, head tipped to one side.

"Extremely important," she clarified. She reached into an interior pocket of her jacket and withdrew her prize.

"Just before I left Binjali's, I received *this*!" She held it up for him to see.

Whatever Daav had been expecting, she sensed that it had not been an envelope, no matter how luxurious against the fingers, or how elegant the script that adorned it.

"And that is?" he inquired politely.

"A job offer!" she said triumphantly. Since he made no move to take the envelope, she opened it and slipped the single sheet of paper free.

"We're to take an antique dulciharp to Avontai... complete instructions and an introduction to be provided when we accept the commission." She looked up from the letter. "Only think, Daav! We have a job offer."

"Allow me." He plucked the paper from her fingers. "You are not eating, Pilot."

"The job—"

"If the job cannot wait while the pilot takes care of her reasonable needs, it is not a job we may wish to accept," he said quellingly.

He recovered his soup spoon, and directed his attention to the letter.

Sighing, Aelliana tasted the soup—and was abruptly quite hungry indeed.

Daav read the letter—twice—while he pursued his own meal, then folded the paper and slipped it back into its envelope.

"What do you think?" she asked, breaking off a piece of bread.

"I think that we will have to fly like a Scout to make the proposed delivery date," he answered, pulling the salad toward him.

Aelliana moved her shoulders. "We could scarcely fly like anything else," she pointed out. "The fee?"

"Acceptable," he allowed, throwing her a bright, unreadable glance. "Though I would insist upon a bonus, if we deliver early."

"*Early*?" She did the math in her head and laughed. "There is a very small chance of that, *van'chela*—even if we fly like *two* Scouts."

He smiled. "Then the client will not mind the presence of the clause, since it is so unlikely that we will collect." He speared a bit of greenery; it broke with an audible crunch. "Besides, it is standard in our contract that we receive a three percent bonus for early delivery."

Aelliana considered him. "Is it?"

"From this moment forward," he said solemnly. "Pending the pilot-owner's approval, of course."

"Of course," she said, with the irony he had not supplied. "It is the pilot-owner's inclination to accept this offer of employment, unless my copilot has an objection, or knows ill of the prospective client?"

The prospective client—Dath jo'Bern Clan Hedrede—was High House. Aelliana had set herself to memorizing the Houses and Lines, a task she found remarkably agreeable with young Shan as her study partner, and more often, her tutor. However, as she had also come to understand, through listening to Daav and Er Thom's conversation, High House did not necessarily mean "wholly honorable."

"Your copilot sees no reason at all why we should not accept this offer of employment, to the enrichment of the ship and the enjoyment of the pilots. Let us by all means inform the client that she will be receiving our contract immediately."

She frowned.

"Mr. dea'Gauss has our contract on file," she said. "Is he likely to have put in such a clause on his own initiative? For I did not know to tell him."

"Doubtless Mr. dea'Gauss considers early delivery worth far more than three percent, pirate that he is. But! All may be known, as soon as we have a comm..."

"A comm..." she began, meaning to say that it would be a wonder, indeed, to find Felae or another server in this crush, but there. Daav had merely straightened; perhaps he lifted an eyebrow, but certainly not a hand, and here came the second Mr. Ongit himself, his blunt-featured face attentive.

"Service, Pilots?"

Daav glanced to her—which was of course, she reminded herself, correct. The captain ought to call regarding matters of the ship. She felt her cheeks warm.

"If I might trouble the House for the use of a comm?" she murmured.

"Certainly, Pilot. I will bring it myself."

Aelliana finished reading the contract Mr. dea'Gauss had obligingly sent to the screen. It seemed well-done enough to her, but, she reminded herself, only look how ably she had handled her employment contract.

She glanced to Daav, who was sipping his wine, eyes pointed at a spot slightly above the comm, his face perfectly neutral. Almost, she put her hand on his arm; something—perhaps it was pride—restrained her. Instead, she cleared her throat.

"Your opinion?" she asked.

He glanced to her, one eyebrow up.

"I see nothing egregious, but this is, after all, the pilot-owner's decision."

She frowned. He knew she was inept, and depended upon his advice, she thought, feeling rather put out. Why did he withhold himself?

The second eyebrow rose.

"Have I displeased the pilot?" he murmured.

Aelliana drew a breath—and let it out in a rush.

"Only by being correct," she said ruefully. "I need to learn how to be captain of my own ship—that is why we are undertaking this enterprise."

He gave her a small, sympathetic smile. "Being reminded of one's duty is endlessly irritating, is it not?"

She felt her mouth twist slightly—perhaps not quite a smile, but no longer a frown. "In fact, it is."

She touched the comm, recalling Mr. dea'Gauss from his exile off-screen.

"The contract is well, sir, saving that we stipulate a three percent bonus for early delivery, rather than five, as it is written here. We are young in this trade, after all. Perhaps, after we are established, we might revisit the clause and raise our bonus to be more in keeping with our *melant'i*."

Mr. dea'Gauss inclined his head. "The change shall be made, Pilot, and the contract dispatched immediately by runner to Lady jo'Bern. We will of course hold the executed hard copy at this office. Do you also wish a copy?"

She paused on the edge of saying "no," considering what sorts of proofs might be required, Outworld.

"Of your goodness, please send an electronic copy to *Ride the Luck*."

"It shall be done," he promised. "Is there any other service I may perform for you?"

"Not at the moment, I thank you." She glanced

to her copilot. "Daav, have you anything for Mr. dea'Gauss?"

He glanced to the screen and inclined his head. "Only my thanks, as always, sir."

Mr. dea'Gauss bowed.

"It is my pleasure to serve, your lordship," he said formally.

The screen went dark.

"Put in my place twice in the course of a single meal," Daav said mournfully.

Aelliana turned the comm off, and glanced to him.

"I think he meant respect, *van'chela*," she said.

His lips twitched. "Ah, do you?" he murmured, and turned his head.

Aelliana followed his glance, immediately spying the red-haired pilot, who had apparently dismissed his comrades. He approached their table slowly, both hands plainly in sight, fingers slightly spread in the pilot's sign for *no danger here*. His hands were innocent of rings, Aelliana saw, which was proof of nothing—Daav had used to leave off Korval's Ring when he worked his shift at Binjali's. This man's pale fingers were unmarked, however, as if he disdained rings in general. His face was also pale, and his eyes were very blue.

He was not, she realized with a slight shock, Liaden.

"Clarence," Daav said, his tone so even that Aelliana slipped her hand off the table and rested it on his knee.

She tried to be stealthy, but the red-haired pilot saw the movement, and stopped where he was, though he partially blocked the aisle. The emotions she received from Daav were—complex, even confused: wariness, affection, dismay, fellowship . . .

". . . it's good to see you," Daav continued, in Terran.

"It's good to see you, too," Pilot Clarence responded readily, and to Aelliana's ear truthfully. He glanced at her meaningfully, as if chiding Daav for his choice of language.

"Practice, I need," she told him, in her laborious Terran.

"In that case," he answered gravely, "I'm honored."

Beside her, Daav shifted slightly; she received a flutter of good-humored fatalism from him, even as he swept his hand out to formally show her their guest.

"Aelliana, this is Clarence O'Berin. You may hear him referred to as 'Boss O'Berin,' or 'the Boss.'"

Aelliana inclined her head. "Clarence O'Berin, I am happy to meet you," she said, which phrase in Terran had very nearly the same meaning as its counterpart, in High Liaden.

"Not as happy as I am to meet Aelliana Caylon herself," he answered gallantly. He glanced again to Daav. "I'm hoping the wine was acceptable?"

It was, Aelliana realized with a start, a bi-level question. She had not thought that such complexities were possible in Terran! In the flush of discovery, she almost missed Daav's reply.

"Half the pilots on-port have already bought Aelliana wine. I'm only amazed to find you among the half yet to do so." His tone was light now, as if he wished to set the other pilot at ease.

"Not any more," Clarence pointed out with a smile that perhaps betrayed relief.

"Kind it was," Aelliana said, feeling that she should do her bit for good will between pilots. "Thank you."

"My pleasure," the red-haired man assured her. He

paused, considering her out of sharp blue eyes. "Word on the port is you're looking to set up as courier."

She frowned slightly as she felt over the shape of the words. "Set up? Ah! I see. Yes, I am available as a courier pilot." There came a thrill of . . . something . . . from Daav, but she was too focused on the conversation to sort it out properly.

"I was a courier pilot, myself," Clarence said. "It's a grand life, but a dangerous one."

He spoke as one who had known such dangers at first hand, and Aelliana leaned forward eagerly. Here was a pilot she might learn from.

"I am . . . hearing this from even my copilot of danger, but I am also hearing that . . . no thing is absent of danger."

Clarence grinned. "Can't argue with that. You can mostly dodge the worst, if you're awake and noticing details. Sometimes, though, no matter how careful you are, you get caught out. Not so much a mistake as it is somebody else being a little cleverer than you are—this time."

Beside her, Daav stirred.

"But," Clarence continued, sending a bright glance into Daav's face, and shifting into the mode between pilots, "I had only come to make my bow to you, Pilot, and, I confess, to renew my acquaintance with your copilot. It has been too long, Daav."

"Too long and not long enough," Daav replied, surprisingly keeping to Terran. "Clarence. Is there something we should know?"

The other man sighed, his expression rueful. "There's something *off*, if you catch my meaning. Nothing a man can put his hand on and take away with him, but it makes the place between the shoulder blades itch, nevertheless."

She felt Daav's attention sharpen.

"Here?"

Clarence shook his head.

"Not that *I've* noticed," he said, and it seemed to Aelliana that the assertion held a secondary meaning, though she did not know what it might be.

Daav nodded. "But?" he prompted.

"But, I've got pilots—solid, port-worthy pilots who know how to keep clean—coming in from Out and Farther Out. They're telling the same tale, all independent of the other." He shrugged, bringing his shoulders high and letting them drop suddenly, nothing at all like a proper Liaden shrug. "Ghost stories—that's what I got."

Daav nodded again. "Thank you," he said gently. "We'll be careful."

"And if you happen to see something a little more solid than a wisp of smoke?"

"I'll let you know."

The red-haired man grinned. "Can't be any fairer than that."

He bowed, with pilot grace, though a little too quickly.

"Pilots," he said, back in Liaden again, "I take my leave. Good lift."

"Safe landing, Pilot," Aelliana answered, and felt Daav at last relax.

NINETEEN

· · · · · · · · · · · · · · · · ·

Those who enter Scout Academy emerge after
rigorous training capable of treating equitably
with societies unimaginably alien, some savage
beyond belief.

Scouts are by definition courageous, brilliant,
supremely adaptable and endlessly resourceful.

—Excerpted from "All About the Liaden Scouts"

THEY HAD FLOWN AFTER ALL LIKE A SCOUT AND A
brand-new first class, and so missed the bonus. On-time
delivery, however, was comfortably within their grasp
when Aelliana entered the code provided by the client
into the comm.

"Clan Persage, who is calling, please?" Though the
phrase was recognizably the familiar challenge to an
unknown caller, the words fell oddly on her ear.

Aelliana blinked and belatedly inclined her head to
the round-faced young woman in the screen.

"I am Aelliana Caylon, pilot-owner of *Ride the Luck*.
I have been engaged to deliver a package directly
into the hands of Bre Din sig'Ranton Clan Persage."

The young woman hesitated, as if the accent of

Chonselta was something exotic, and not readily decipherable. Then the moment passed, and she inclined her head.

"I am desolate to inform Pilot-Owner Caylon that Bre Din sig'Ranton is away from House." She tipped her head to one side, apparently debating with herself—and coming to a decision all at once.

"Bre Din plays music at the port, you know, Pilot. The place is called Bas Ibenez."

"I thank you," Aelliana said. "I will seek him there."

By the time they had exchanged the required parting formalities and Aelliana had closed the connection, Daav had located the listing for Bas Ibenez in the Avontai Port database and had sent the information to her screen.

"You are far too efficient," she told him, with a smile.

"Copilot's duty," he returned, as she scrolled down the listing.

"The club opens in the evening only," she murmured, with a glance at the board to check local time. Several hours, yet, until opening time.

"Still well within the client's necessity for delivery," he pointed out.

"True," she acknowledged, and sighed. "I suppose we might call and find if he's arrived early."

"Or," Daav murmured, "we might refresh ourselves, and rest, so that we do not come to the young gentleman in all of the disorder of travel." He met her eyes, his only slightly mischievous. "After all, he may have something to send in return."

Aelliana leaned back in her chair and ran her fingers through her hair. It was true that they had flown hard, pushing her limits, if not his, and more

with her training in mind than the bonus...But, it
had been the pure joyous rush of flying, even the
considerable bits where "flying" was Jump and the
screens showed nothing but grey—the joy of knowing
that she was at last working her own ship, just as she
said she would do—*exactly* as she had hoped to do,
with Daav sitting his board at her right hand. Oh, it
had been exhilarating, the lift to Avontai.

But it had not necessarily been conducive to either
rest or sleep.

"There is something in what you say," she admitted. "Who would entrust anything precious to such a
pair of scarecrows?"

She rose, stretching, and looked down into his face,
noting the subtle signs of weariness there. Daav had
kept good watch, as a copilot ought, and if he had
not been as flight-drunk as his pilot, yet he had not
gotten much more rest.

"I am going to take a shower."

He raised an eyebrow.

"A shower and a nap?" he suggested.

"Only if you will do the same."

He smiled, and a trickle of mischievous lust warmed
the air between them, lighting a slow fire in her own
belly.

"There's a rare bargain," Daav murmured, and rose
to his full height, formally extending his hand to her.
Korval's Ring glinted, almost as if the Dragon had
moved a wing. She rested her fingers on the back of
his hand—and gasped aloud.

"I thought you said a *nap*," she managed.

He smiled and raised their hands, bending his
head above hers.

"There's time," he whispered, and kissed her knuckles lingeringly.

His lips were cool, exciting in their remoteness, giving the lie to the passion licking across their nerves. She wanted to move closer, to achieve a fuller embrace, but their relative positions did not allow it. Daav completed his salute, unhurried, raised his head and turned, his hand still beneath her fingers.

Bland-faced, as outwardly indifferent as if they were two strangers about to go into a formal dinner together, he guided her across the piloting tower and down the short hall to their quarters.

The snow drifted prettily, glinting like mirrors among the lights of the port. The flakes were *cold*, which she had known they would be, but which still surprised, and she turned her face up into them, laughing as they showered burning kisses on her cheeks.

Snow play was limited to the air. Underfoot, the walk was heated and dry. Daav had approved of that, and settled the pack holding Hedrede's fragile treasure more firmly on his shoulder. She had protested that she could carry it just as well, but he claimed copilot's right.

"But that leaves me to protect you, and you know what my marksmanship is!" she'd protested, which had gained her one of his tightly edged smiles.

"I repose every faith in my pilot," he'd replied, which was no answer at all, but nonetheless put her on her mettle.

Avontai Port was not so large as Solcintra, nor even Chonselta, though it enjoyed good custom. The walks were crowded; gem-colored light from the shops splashed across the walkways, scandalously painting the faces of passersby.

Aelliana looked from right to left and back again, trying to see everything at once. Her first new world— with snow! Perhaps, she thought, they might take a day, after the package was delivered, and explore Avontai more fully.

It came to her then that Daav, too, was being watchful, but in an entirely different manner. She considered the side of his face and the set of his shoulders. Not worried, she decided, but on guard.

Cautiously, she looked about, trying to see what might have made him wary, but saw nothing untoward. She swayed a step nearer to his side, though she did not take his hand. There was a chance that such contact would break his concentration, which she in no way wished to do until she more fully understood their position.

"Does the port feel strange to you?" she asked.

He looked down at her, his hair starry with snowflakes.

"I have no comparison; this is my first time on Avontai Port."

Aelliana bit her lip, and glanced about, but all she saw were shops and shoppers and people moving quickly, as if they had an errand in hand.

"Your friend Clarence had said that he was hearing from pilots that the ports felt . . . odd. To me, Avontai feels unlike Chonselta or Solcintra, but surely that is as it should be and nothing *odd*?"

"There are certain things to notice, when one is on-port. Do the natives seem unconcerned or anxious? Are proctors or security very obvious—or absent entirely? Does it seem that pilotkind cling close to each other, or that there are too few about on the common ways?" He moved his shoulders. "I will try to be a better teacher, Aelliana, though I suspect an experience of several ports may be necessary to build a sense of what is *not* odd."

"That seems reasonable," she granted, and gave him a grin, inviting him to share the joke. "So, we see a necessity to raise *many* ports!"

Daav, however, did not laugh; rather, and unexpectedly, he frowned.

"There is a matter of *melant'i*," he said, slowly, his voice taking on a formal cadence, though he kept yet to the mode between comrades. "Clarence O'Berin is not my friend."

"But of course he is!" The words were out of her mouth before she had time to consider propriety. Who was she, to tell Daav's affections out for him? And yet—

"I beg your pardon, *van'chela*," she said more moderately, but with a degree of determination. "Recall that we were linked during the exchange with—with Pilot O'Berin. I grant that . . . I understand that there is a confusion of regard, but certainly there *is* . . . affection. Indeed, he must hold you likewise, else why step off of his path to speak of this . . . oddity among the ports?"

Daav sighed, and said nothing. Aelliana bit her lip. She had transgressed; she had feared it. She curled her hand into a fist so that she not reach out to him, and cleared her throat.

"It is ill-done of me to—to correct you on such a matter. As clearly as I might hear you, it is not I but you who must know best . . ."

"No, that will not do," Daav interrupted, very gently indeed.

His hand touched hers, and she gripped his fingers greedily. Wistfulness flowed from him, and a sort of wry amusement, thinly edged with resentment.

"We have what we have, and a pilot who wishes to survive uses the information in her hand, no matter how it comes to be there. So, there will be no forgive-mes, my lady, nor any regrets, though I may sometimes be abashed, or even embarrassed. I will engage to do my best not to become angry, but my temper is not always biddable."

"Nor, I fear, is mine," she whispered.

"Well, it's a pair of hotheads we'll be, then, and no help for it. As for Clarence . . ." He paused; she received the sense of him marshaling his thoughts.

"You are correct that I hold Clarence in some esteem—we are of an age, of like temperament, and bear the burden of similar *melant'is*. If circumstances were otherwise, we might indeed be friends. As it is, I have the honor to be Korval, and Clarence—is the final authority for the Juntavas based on Liad."

So, Aelliana thought, she had judged Clarence's *melant'i* rightly. As for the Juntavas; the Guild handbook would have them be thieves, grey-traders, and warned pilots away from their employ.

"Korval and the Juntavas," Daav continued, "have long ago agreed to a policy of . . . avoidance. Which means that, value him as I might, yet I cannot by policy assume Clarence to be trustworthy, nor may I consider that he holds Korval's best interest first in his heart."

"Nor should he," Aelliana murmured. "He must care for his own folk first."

"So he must and so I must. Thus we meet seldom, with pleasure tinged by regret." He glanced up into the dancing snowflakes. "Here is our street, I think."

Hand in hand they walked down a narrower and only slightly less-well-lit street. It seemed to Aelliana that Daav was easier now—less chagrined—yet still on point. She caught a glimmer of concern, and a thrill of pleasurable curiosity, growing more intense as they found the door.

It was recessed, hidden deep inside a series of arches, the first so black it seemed to swallow the light from the street lamps. The second arch was dark grey, the third foggy blue, the fifth ivory, and the sixth pure white, lit so brightly that no shadows were possible. The door itself was crimson, as bright as blood in the glaring light.

She felt Daav hesitate—the tiniest catch between one step and the next—then they were walking side by side down the short tunnel; at the end of it, Aelliana put her hand against the plate.

The door opened into a room dimly illuminated by red light. Aromatic smoke drifted between the tables; the servers moving languidly among them wore red shirts with billowing sleeves and tight white trousers.

Beyond the half-moon of tables was an open area floored in black tile so glossy that the ceiling was reflected in its depths. On the far side of the floor was a stage. Thick white smoke rose 'round it, mixing with the ruby light. Inside the resulting pink mist, Aelliana could see instruments set up on racks, awaiting musicians who had yet to arrive.

"Perhaps we should ask a waiter to take a message—" she began, but Daav was already moving, passing between the clustered tables like a wisp of smoke himself.

Sighing, she followed, neither so neat nor so invisible, and caught him on the far side of the floor.

"A warning before you move away," she said sharply, "would ease your pilot's mind. I am no Scout, recall."

"Forgive me, Pilot," he murmured, not noticeably contrite. "As our hour approaches, it seemed best for us to seek the young gentleman backstage and dispatch our errand before he is called upon to perform."

It did, she admitted, seem the only route to fly, outlined thus. Still—

"What if I were to lose you?"

He looked down at her, his face utterly serious.

"You will not lose me, Aelliana."

It was said so surely that the words had weight, as if he had placed six smooth stones into her hand.

She sighed, soothed despite herself, and went with him 'round the back of the stage.

Four figures dressed in grey and black turned toward them. Two held glasses half-full with dark liquid, one had a thin brown stick between two fingers. She watched them coolly as she brought the stick to her lips and drew on it, waking a sickly green spark at the tip.

The fourth member of the group came forward, hands moving decisively against the air, as if he were pushing them away.

"If you please, the band is preparing for the first set! You interfere with our art! Leave at once!"

Aelliana took a deep breath, tasting smoke and spice in the close air.

"It is not my intention to interfere with art," she said, speaking as she would to an excitable student.

"We will leave, and willingly, as soon as we have delivered a package to Bre Din sig'Ranton Clan Persage."

The young man paused, and glanced over his shoulder. Aelliana followed his gaze, and saw one of the three at the table—towheaded and plump, wearing a tight, sleeveless grey shirt and flowing black trousers—put his glass down and move slowly toward them.

"I am Bre Din sig'Ranton," he said. His voice was light and slightly blurry, as if they had woken him. "Who are you?"

"I am Aelliana Caylon, pilot-owner of *Ride the Luck*. I have been engaged by Dath jo'Bern Clan Hedrede to deliver a package directly into your hands."

The young gentleman paused at his comrade's side. His eyes were wide and very dark, and there was a— Aelliana blinked—there was a tiny red flower drawn high on his right cheek, near the edge of his eye. He was not, she thought, very much older than Sinit.

"Dath jo'Bern?" He breathed the words, though Aelliana did not know if it was awe or dismay that she heard.

"Indeed," Daav said. "Precisely Dath jo'Bern, young sir. I suggest, if we are not to further disrupt art, that you take delivery of this package, sign the receipt, and allow us to depart."

The girl holding the smoking stick laughed, sharply.

"He has you there, Rose. Sign for the package and finish your juice."

Bre Din moved his shoulders, as if shaking off her voice.

"Where?" he demanded, taking a deliberate step forward.

Aelliana drew herself up, determined not to show

concern in the face of his intensity, despite the sudden tightness of her chest.

"Here," Daav said, swinging the package off his shoulder and holding it out. "There's no need to stalk the pilot."

Color drained from the boy's face, it seemed to Aelliana that he swayed . . . then he steadied, fairly snatching the package from Daav's hands. He spun back to the table, shoving glasses and other clutter roughly aside. Hands shaking, he unsealed the outer protective layer, and scattered a second layer of frothy tissue-glitter to reveal a carven wooden case.

He paused then, as if he feared to continue. The boy who had tried to shoo them away drew closer to the table, shoulders hunched, as if he had caught the other's tension. The first girl lifted a mocking eyebrow and drew on her stick.

"Make haste, Rosie," the second girl chided. "Or leave it until after the set!"

"Peace," he murmured, but it seemed to Aelliana that he was advising himself more than her. Slowly, and with infinite care, he lifted the lid away.

Nestled in silk, the dulciharp took fire; pegs flared, light ran along the strings, ivory keys gleamed.

"Ah . . ." The second girl leaned close, extending a hand, as if to touch.

"She's a beauty," the first girl said grudgingly, blowing smoke out of the side of her mouth. "From Liad?"

"From Liad," Bre Din sig'Ranton asserted. Reverently, he reached into the box and had the instrument out, cradling it against his shoulder like an infant. His fingers moved, and the strings whispered, loud in the quiet dimness.

"But—why?" asked the first boy.

"Yes, why?" the second girl repeated. "Who is this—" She glanced aside, at *them*, Aelliana realized "—this Honorable jo'Bern? Why is she sending you gifts?"

"Not a gift," Bre Din murmured. "Not a gift, Veen. A promise." He stroked the strings again, and sighed.

"Dath jo'Bern is my grandmother's *cha'leket*. When my grandmother died, the dulciharp went to her, as a death-gift. I sent her—gods, *relumma* ago!—I sent her a recording, and I asked her—I asked her, if she would sponsor me to the Conservatory on Liad, and, if she thought I was worthy, to return me my grandmother's harp."

"What's this?" Veen plucked a slim folder from inside the case and flipped it open.

"Tickets," she said blankly, "and a bank draft."

Cheek against wood, Bre Din sig'Ranton smiled.

"If I'm to study at the Conservatory, I need to travel to Liad, Veen."

"But—" She stared at him, the folder forgotten in her hand. "What about the band?" She took a hard breath. "What about—"

"If you please," Daav spoke up, placing his hand on Aelliana's shoulder. "There is a confirmation of satisfactory delivery to be signed."

Obedient to her prompt, Aelliana reached inside her jacket and withdrew the card.

"Certainly, Pilots." Bre Din turned, the harp still cradled against him, and pressed his thumb onto the card's surface. "My thanks; you have—you have changed my life."

Aelliana bowed, and stepped back to Daav's side, slipping the card away into the safety of an inner pocket. As one, they turned toward the door, which opened smoothly under Daav's hand.

"Bre Din!" The second girl's voice was sharp. "Will you turn your back on—"

"Leave it until after the set!" the first girl interrupted. "We're on!"

The door fell shut, Daav turned to the right, opposite the direction they had entered, and Aelliana, wordless, followed.

TWENTY

. . . .

Norbear—Size: 16–22 cm; Weight: 121–180 g. Furred quadrupedal mammal with a burrowing habit; soft dense coat, ranging in color from grey, brown, black, orange, white and mixed. Herbivore. Fearless and lively disposition, natural empath. Adapts well to domestication. Banned on certain worlds. Check port rules before importing.

—Courier Wildlife Guide, Fourteenth Edition

THE BACK DOOR OPENED ONTO A SERVICE PLATFORM overlooking a thin alley harshly lit by vapor spots. Aelliana stood quietly at Daav's side, doubtless trying to figure out what it was that he saw which eluded her.

In fact, he saw only an empty alleyway, and some bits of trash fluttering in the corner made by the intersection of ramp and foundation.

"It's stopped snowing," she observed.

"So it has."

"I wonder, *van'chela*, why we exited this way, rather than by the main door?"

It was a fair question, and one that a new pilot might with honor ask of a port-wise comrade. The pity being that he had no answer nearly so fair to offer her in return. Scout instincts, pilot instincts— things learned through bone and blood, recalled by the deep mind, acted upon, and never questioned... How did one explain, without seeming to be perfectly demented? Worse, how did one *teach*, except as one had been taught—by trial and error, and the occasional laceration or broken bone?

Still, he told himself, rallyingly, there must have been a reason, mustn't there have, Daav? Only take a moment to reflect, and no doubt it will come to you.

He cast his mind back to the main room: the dance floor, the charmingly attired wait staff, the tables made private by the wafting smoke. *Had* there been a potential for danger, an... oddity, damn Clarence *and* his ghosts! The tension in a shoulder; the attitude of a head? Some small thing set slightly out of place? An object that *ought* to have been there, noticed only by its absence?

He sighed.

"I don't know," he admitted. "Forgive me, Aelliana."

She looked up into his face, her eyes deeply green in the sulfurous light.

"Forgive you? For heeding your training, which has kept you safe on dozens of ports, and in far stranger places? I can scarcely find that a fault, *van'chela*, nor any cause for forgiveness. Had your training been less thorough, or yourself less advertent, I might never have met you, nor known what it was I lived in lack of."

If, indeed, her brother had allowed her to live so long. Horror shivered through him; it had been so near a thing, their meeting so much a matter of chance...

"Daav? Is there something amiss?"

"Nothing amiss," he said, forcibly shaking off the chill, and producing a smile to soothe her. "I was merely thinking that the luck moves along strange pathways."

"So it does," she agreed, and glanced about them once again. "If there is nothing here for us, do you think that we might leave?"

"In fact, I do!" He preceded her down the ramp, in case the fluttering litter should suddenly turn feral, and nodded to the left as she joined him on the alley's floor.

"I propose that we find us a convivial place for a glass and a bit of supper, now that we're at leisure."

Aelliana tipped her head, her stance wistful. "I had hoped to see more of the port."

Of course she would, he chided himself; this was her first new port—her first world that was not the homeworld! Who would not wish to walk such streets and marvel that she had come so far?

"There's no requirement that we find supper at the first shop displaying a glass," he pointed out, and was rewarded by her smile.

"There isn't, is there?" she said. "We are free to meet our own fancy. Let us, if you will humor me, walk." She held out her hand, inviting, and he stepped forward to take it in his own.

"By all means, let us walk and observe the port! It has been an age since I've been at leisure to tour."

· · · ❖ · · ·

They bought bowls of stew from a cart outside of a greens market, and fresh-squeezed juice from a stall inside. Leaning on the railing at the observation window, they ate while watching pallets of vegetables being offloaded from rail cars, to ride the conveyors into the vendor area below.

After, they went back out onto the port and walked, taking turns choosing their direction. At some point in their meanderings the snow began again, riding a freshening breeze. Aelliana shivered and turned up the collar of her jacket, curling her hands into warm pockets.

They found a bakery open at the edge of what might have been a day-side business district, ate lemon squares and drank hot tea at a tiny round table while in the back the baker prepared the next day's dough.

Warmed by tea and sugar, they went on the prowl again, pausing by a map board so that she could discover the locations of such landmarks as the Portmaster's Office, the Pilots Guild, Healer Hall, and Port Security. There were pointers to various ferries: the Ocean Line, the Mountain Line, the City Line—and the shuttle to the Pleasure Quarters.

"The Pleasure Quarters?" she murmured. "What do you suppose that is?"

"I am without information. Shall we find if the shuttle is running and explore?"

Her laugh was swallowed by a yawn.

"Perhaps tomorrow," she said. "For tonight, *van'chela*, I think it might be time to seek our ship, and our bed."

"Well enough," Daav answered. "It's always good to have a plan for the morrow." He considered the map briefly, and raised a hand to trace out a route.

"If we go north, past Avontai Port 'change, we'll cut the corner of the Entertainment District, and so come back to the public yard." He glanced down at her. "Or shall we find a cab?"

"I think I can walk so far—unless you're chilled?"

"My legs are long, and walking keeps the chill away."

"Then we are in accord. Lead on, sir."

He smiled and led them back across the square.

"I remember when you insisted on *sir*," he said.

Aelliana chuckled. "And I remember when *you* insisted on 'Daav'—or 'pilot,' if I must." She slipped her hand into his pocket and curled her fingers 'round his. "Each as stubborn as the other—even then. I wonder..." She paused.

"Wonder?"

"The boy to whom we delivered the dulciharp. I wonder how he will go on, in his changed life. If he will be happy, or become a master, or if his delm will bid him stay..."

"Ah, but it is the fate of couriers never to know the end of the tale. We fly in, deliver our package, take up our cargo—and fly out. We are agents of change only insofar as we have adhered to the terms of our contract. Those things that we set in motion go on to their fruition, without our knowledge and beyond our aid."

They crossed a boulevard that must, Aelliana thought, be very busy by day, and turned down a street sparsely illuminated by the spill of night lights from sleepy shop windows. The snow had stopped again, leaving glittering arabesques around darkened signs, icy scallops at the edges of windows.

"Asleep, Pilot?" Daav murmured, when they had traversed the block in companionable silence.

"Merely content. It's very quiet, isn't—"

"No!" The cry shattered the crystalline quiet, like a knife thrown through glass. "No, give it back!"

She felt a jolt of adrenaline, a shock of necessity, and she was running, hot on Daav's heels, *toward* the scream, which was, one small, rational part of her mind pointed out, surely unsafe. They ought to be running *away*, to find a call box, or a proctor—

"Don't let it get loose!" That was another voice, angry and perhaps a little afraid.

She rounded the corner, swinging out so that she not slam into Daav, who had frozen into near invisibility, watching.

Halfway down the thin alley, a pilot was on his knees in a drift of snow, arms raised, hands reaching, every line etched with desperation. Before him were ranged five port toughs, their ranks opening to receive a sixth, carrying a bag that had surely been reft from the downed pilot.

"Give it back!" If words could bleed, these did. "I have money . . ." He reached into his jacket, pulled out a pouch, his hand shaking so that the coins jangled clearly.

"Take it—the jacket, my boots—take what you like, but return—"

A rock smashed into the wall just beyond the pilot's shoulder. He cowered, throwing his hands up, a small, broken sound escaping from his throat.

"Please . . ."

"Please . . ." One of the six sobbed, mockingly. "We saw what you have in this bag and we know how to deal with it!"

"No! Give it back! I'll take it offworld!"

Another rock came out of the cluster of tormentors. The pilot gasped when it struck his arm.

"Stop that!" someone shouted, her voice strong in the Command mode. Aelliana was standing at the downed pilot's side before she realized that the voice was hers, and that her position was unsafe in the extreme.

"Another one!" "Is she holding another?" "Search her!" "Take them both down!"

A rock flew toward them, its trajectory flat and purposeful. Aelliana saw its course unwind inside her head, saw that it would strike the pilot's unprotected head, and danced sideways. She snatched the missile out of the air as if it were a bowli ball, allowing the energy to spin her, releasing as she came back around, sending the rock back, low and fast, into the crowd, directly to the one who had thrown it—

Bone broke with an audible crunch, followed by a scream and a disturbance among the crowd.

"My ankle! She broke my ankle!"

"Enough!"

That voice brooked no disobedience; the crowd froze, the screams subsiding to moans. Aelliana maintained her position between the wounded pilot and harm, as Daav strode toward the crowd.

"You!" he snapped. "Surrender the pilot's case!"

"Oh, no you don't!" came the returning snarl. "It's a norbear in here, and it's bound for the river with a rock in the bottom of the bag to keep it company."

Behind her, Aelliana heard the pilot whisper a scream.

"Give me the bag," Daav repeated. "I am a Scout captain. I hereby take possession of the contraband item and will dispose of it in the prescribed manner." He paused, his hand extended. "Which is *not* throwing it in the river."

"It'll take over your mind," someone else in the crowd shouted. "Scout captain or not!"

"If he *is* a Scout captain!"

"Am I not?" Daav demanded and flowed forward, swift and silent, his hand suddenly on the bag holder's shoulder.

"Surrender the norbear," he said softly. "You do not wish to incite my pilot to further violence against you."

There was a general mutter, a moan of "My ankle..." and that quickly the bag was in Daav's hand and five of them backing away.

"But what about *him*?" demanded a voice from the rear. "The proctors will have business with *him*, bringing that perversion here!"

"We will take care of the pilot," Aelliana heard her voice assert. She bit her lip.

"I suggest," Daav said, stepping to her side, "that you disperse. One of your number has injured herself and requires medical attention. That is your first order of business and your closest concern. These other matters will be taken care of appropriately."

Perhaps it was the absolute certainty of Daav's voice; perhaps it was the continued whimpering of their downed comrade. Whichever, the crowd faded away, and very shortly they were alone in the alley with the wounded pilot.

"Thank you, Scouts, thank you...I am in your debts..."

The pilot thrust clumsily to his feet, slamming his uninjured arm against the wall with no regard for bruises. He extended an unsteady hand.

"I'll be off now. I swear, we will be off-planet before dawn, and never come back here. Just be good enough to hand me the case—"

"You're wounded!" Aelliana protested. "Daav, we must find him a medic!"

There was a small pause, then Daav went to one knee on the alley floor. He opened the top of the case, just a little, and peered inside. A furry hand crept over the edge, and gripped his finger.

The wounded pilot whined, high and futile in the back of his throat.

Daav sighed.

"You're quite safe," he told the bag, at his most matter-of-fact. "Recruit yourself now and allow us to do what must be done."

He closed the bag and swept gracefully to his feet. The glance he spared for wounded pilot was ... not kind.

"My pilot and I will escort you to the Healers," he said, which, Aelliana thought, was sensible. The Healers would have an autodoc, and it was plain that the pilot had sustained other, less visible injuries. He shook where he stood, and his posture was of one who expected a blow to fall at any moment. Aelliana swallowed against a sudden surge of tears. So had she been, and look what wonders the Healers had wrought for her.

"There is sense in what the Scout says," she said gently. "Come, let us go to the top of the street and hail a cab."

The Healers kept a small house in the port; barely larger than the bakery at which she and Daav had eaten their lemon squares, hours or days ago. What they lacked in scope, however, they more than made up for in action. Scarcely had the door opened to them than the wounded pilot was whisked away upstairs, while they and the case were left to stand in a chilly parlor considerably less spacious than *The Luck's* piloting chamber.

"Perhaps," Aelliana said, when half a glass had fallen

and no one had yet come to speak with them. "We should simply leave the ... case, *van'chela*, and return to our ship."

The item under discussion was sitting on the floor against his leg. He glanced down thoughtfully. "That might, after all, be—"

"Nay, nay! The case and its contents must go, and also the noisy empath! You, my lady mathematician, are just the woman to take them both in hand!"

A thin man with a well-lined face and fading ginger-colored hair swept into the parlor, pale robes trembling about him.

"I beg your pardon?" Aelliana stammered. "We are here in aid of another pilot, and—"

"Yes, yes! It was well that you brought him to us; we can assist—but *not* until that creature is well away, and you!" He spun to stare up into Daav's face. "*You* are disrupting every Healer in the Hall!"

"My apologies to the Hall," Daav murmured.

He took a breath, closed his eyes, and seemed to—to step away from himself. Aelliana gasped, for truly he burned less vividly inside the dingy little room. He opened his eyes, and her heart cramped; his gaze was remote, as if he looked across a distance too great to bear interest, or humor, or love.

"*Daav* ..."

She stepped forward, hand rising—her wrist was caught by the Healer, his bony fingers surprisingly strong.

"Yes, that is well done and I thank you!" he said snappishly, apparently to Daav. "Maintain yourself thus, and give respite to those who shielded themselves in time to avoid a headache! Pilot—"

He turned to Aelliana, releasing her with a small bow. "As improbable as it seems, this man will do as you tell him. Tell him, I implore you, to take up the norbear and go away with you, back to your ship and off of Avontai, immediately!"

"We had thought," Daav said, in a too-calm voice, "to leave the norbear in the care of the House. The Healers on Liad often take charge of such strays."

"This is not the homeworld!" the Healer snapped, and sighed. "Forgive me—you are not informed. We dare not keep the creature here, Pilots. Avontai has a horror of such things as mind control—*we* are barely tolerated—and only if we are careful not to interfere too much! To hold a norbear would be to destroy the Hall. We cannot allow even such limited aid as we may offer to falter on one life—*any* life. You have interfered in an alleyway brawl, which you surely know better than—and now you must pay the price. Remove yourselves to a place of safety greater than Avontai. We have summoned a cab—go now!"

Aelliana met Daav's remote black gaze and shivered.

"What is your name?" she asked the Healer.

"I am Hall Master Ver Sev. Feel free to use my name with the Portmaster. Now, will you *go*? Every moment those two linger here is a moment that those in pain are without surcease."

She could, Aelliana thought, scarcely be so cold-hearted as to remain in the face of such distress. She cleared her throat.

"Daav?"

"Aelliana, it is well," he told her in that too-calm voice.

She doubted it, but there again, if departing this

place won him wholly back to her, then she wished
to tarry not one heartbeat longer.

"If you please," she said, her voice hoarse. "Bring
the...norbear and let us go."

Calmly, he bent and picked up the case.

The Master Healer sighed, noisily. "Just through
there, Pilot. The cab awaits."

Carrying the case, Daav left the parlor first. As
Aelliana followed him out into the foyer, she heard
Master Ver Sev say, softly, "Thank you, Pilot."

The Luck's hatch sealed securely behind them, and
Aelliana spun, fright and confusion flaring into anger.

"Daav yos'Phelium, stand forth and tell me what
has happened!"

He tipped an eyebrow; she thought his gaze was
sharper now, but he maintained a reserve that was
both unfamiliar and unwelcome.

"What would you know, Pilot?"

"What is that—that norbear? Why must we take it
off-world? Is it dangerous? Where are we to take it?
What happened to you?"

"A comprehensive beginning list," he murmured,
and his eyes *were* sharper; his expression sardonic,
his whole self coming back into focus.

"As for the norbear..." He dropped to one knee
and opened the bag wide.

"Come out now, rogue, and show yourself to the
pilot. Understand, I can do nothing if she decides to
space you, or to bake you and serve you up for tea.
She is the final authority here, and it is she whose
patronage you must win."

As before, a small, furry hand rose to grip the

side of the case. The hand rested for a moment, was joined by a second, and then a pair of round ears, a round head and large, liquid eyes. It paused with its nose level with the case, as if giving her a moment to accommodate herself.

"It understands?" she asked Daav.

"To a certain point. The questions being—which point, and whether he also *mis*understands or only ignores one."

She frowned at the creature, knelt, and tapped the deck before her with a forefinger.

"Come here, norbear."

It blinked, as if considering the request, then all at once it was scrambling out of the case, sliding and hitting the deck firmly on its rounded rump. Undeterred, it performed a graceless somersault, got all four feet oriented and bumbled toward her. It tried to stop on the spot she had indicated, but its claws got no purchase on the decking and it slid the last distance, bumped into her hand, skittered a little, and sat, one paw braced on the deck and the other on her knee.

She stared down at it. A less offensive creature would be difficult to imagine, yet neither the crowd's horror nor the Healer's fear had been feigned. It bore her scrutiny with the good humor that seemed its chiefest characteristic; not so large as a cat, nor yet so small as a mouse, its brown fur was shot with ripples of orange. Aelliana bit her lip, fighting a desire to laugh—and another, to gather it up and rub her cheek against its plush fur.

Instead, she raised her head and looked to her copilot, who was watching the proceedings with interest.

"*This* is a creature so dangerous that it must be

put to death on sight, and all of its kind are banned from Avontai Port?"

"From Avontai entire, if I understood the Master Healer correctly. As for dangerous—there are some humans who are susceptible, and some of norbear kind, I expect, who are rather *loud*—"

The norbear turned its round head to regard him, as if wounded.

Daav grinned and inclined his head. "As one who is also *loud* may say without prejudice. The pilot we found was, I expect, extremely susceptible, and our rogue there has already admitted to loud."

"But—mind control?"

"Norbears are natural empaths. If you are melancholy, a norbear may help you feel . . . better. If you are frightened, a norbear may leach your fear. Someone who is in . . . a great deal of pain—as I suspect our rescued pilot was—might quickly become addicted. After all," he added softly, "there are few delights more poignant than the absence of pain."

Aelliana looked at him sharply, felt the discrete prick of claws through the fabric of her trousers and looked down.

The norbear met her eyes, and stood up on its hind legs, reaching one hand high.

Barely considering, Aelliana picked the creature up and brought it up to her shoulder, where it settled itself as if it were the most natural thing in all the worlds. It caught a disordered lock of hair in its hand and leaned companionably against her ear. There came a contented buzzing, growing slightly louder.

Aelliana looked to Daav.

"It's purring."

"Apparently he does not wish to be served up for tea."

"That's all very well, but where are we to take it? Liad?"

Daav frowned slightly.

"I think not," he said eventually. "But I may know better, later."

"Oh? And how will that be?"

"I propose to retire with our guest to the acceleration couch, to make sure of his comfort while you lift us to an outer orbit. It may be that two loud empaths will share dreams during such a time. At the very least, we may all rest once we are safely off-world, and be able to make better plans on the morrow."

Aelliana closed her eyes, feeling a certain creeping weariness.

"It has been a full evening," she said, and rose, the norbear riding her shoulder easily.

Daav rose as well, and moved toward her, face watchful.

"*What happened to me*," he said softly, "is a . . . method, somewhat like the Rainbow. It's true that my presence sometimes dismays Healers, especially those already under stress. I was not absent from you, Aelliana, only . . . at rest."

She sighed, not understanding, but lacking the energy to pursue the topic further at this moment.

"Very well, sir. If you will take our passenger and render—him?—safe and comfortable, I will call the Tower and postulate an urgent packet from Master Ver Sev at Healer Hall."

Daav smiled. "Excellent, Pilot."

TWENTY-ONE

. . . .

Happy is one who finds a friend on every port.
—Liaden proverb

THE NORBEAR'S NAME WAS, REPORTEDLY, HEVELIN, and he had once "been employed," as Daav had it, at a Traveler's Rest or a Guild Hall, or some similar establishment, possibly in the Far Out.

Daav had the grace to admit without much prodding from her that this information, while interesting, was...rather vague. He had also some hours later been prompted to say that he knew of a person whom he thought "might answer." Hevelin, on the occasion of this individual being...*described* to him, or *felt at* him—Aelliana sighed, for the dozenth time retreating before the problem of how one communicated with a creature that had no language, excepting an extremely nuanced vocabulary of emotion.

However it was done, Daav's description of this personified solution had excited Hevelin's interest.

Which was why they were here, on Staederport, walking, guns on belts, in the warm, slightly sticky rain, down a thin street crowded with tall Terrans. Aelliana clung to Daav's side, he being taller than she, though in comparison to the company they moved through, even he seemed . . . undergrown. Still, he had the trick of claiming space upon the walkway—a particular way of holding the shoulders, and a certain swagger in his usually smooth gait—and neither she nor the bag he carried over his shoulder were unduly jostled.

"Here we are," he murmured, turning them in toward a grey storefront like all of the others they had passed.

No, Aelliana corrected herself—not like all the others. The autoscroll over the door of this establishment read, in alternating Terran and Liaden: GUILD TEMP OFFICE. ACCEPTING APPLICATIONS AND UPGRADES.

A buzzer sounded as they entered a small room bisected by a counter holding several screens and a large green plant.

"Be out in a sec!" a voice called from beyond the screen on the far side of the plant.

Daav put the case on the counter and propped an elbow on it. Aelliana climbed onto the tall stool at his side, resisting the temptation to lean against him. She was not, she told herself, afraid.

Perhaps, she was a little uneasy, but surely that was reasonable? Although she spoke the language—enough, at least, to be understood—she could not feel but that her grasp of culture, especially in regard to what might be held as an insult, was firm. Of course, she thought, shifting carefully on the stool, it was that way among Liadens, also. One could not hope to know the necessities of a stranger's *melant'i*, and error was always possible. It was absurd to have felt as if she was at home on Avontai, only because it was a Liaden world. She had no more call upon grace from a Liaden than a Terran.

A shadow moved behind the screen, and an apparition stepped up to the counter. He was tall—she had expected that. What surprised her was how broad! He made two of Daav on the vertical and three on the horizontal! His hair was confined to a hand-wide bristle of black along the very top of his skull, and his skin—crown, face and hands—was ruddy and freckled.

"Mr. Peltzer," Daav said in Terran. "Just the man I'm wanting."

The big man put his big hands flat on the countertop. "Well, now. Maybe that's not as disturbing as it sounds at first hearing," he said, and jerked his head toward Aelliana. "Standing sponsor?"

"Pilot Caylon holds a card," Daav murmured. "But yes, a sponsor in some suit."

"Pilot Caylon, is it?" The big man looked at her with renewed interest, and inclined his head with gentle courtesy.

"Pilot, I hope you won't think it's rude of me to say so, but I'm glad of the opportunity to thank you in person. Those Revisions of yours saved my bacon at least twice that I know of, and probably more that I was too space-brained to recognize."

He held a big hand out in her direction, palm up.

"I'm Bruce Peltzer, Circuit Rider for the Terran Guild."

His face was earnest; plainly he was offering courtesy, and she gathered nothing from her lanky copilot save a relaxed amusement. She glanced down at his hand, held steady and patient, raised hers and placed her palm against his.

His skin was warm and slightly moist, as was everything she had thus far encountered on Staederport.

"Happy I am to meet you, Pilot Peltzer," she said, forming the Terran words with care. "I am Aelliana Caylon, Pilot First Class."

He smiled, briefly covered their joined hands with his free hand and released her before she had time either to take offense or to become alarmed.

"Well, then," he said, turning his attention back to Daav. "If you're not sponsoring this pilot, why are you here—and should I have you thrown out?"

"Perhaps you should," Daav said cordially. "But before you call the guard, allow me to present to you Hevelin, who stands in need of a position."

He opened the top of the case and reached inside, placing the norbear on the counter midway between himself and Bruce Peltzer, keeping his hands in a loose semicircle about the plump creature.

"I represent him to you as an individual of exceptional character: observant, polite, and able to recall what he has observed. He has, I believe, been previously employed in an establishment similar to this one."

He lifted his hands away, leaving Hevelin to face the large man alone. For a long moment, they regarded each other, the norbear standing tall on his back feet, the man with his elbows folded atop the counter, his head tilted, brow knit in concentration.

"Hevelin, huh?" the man asked, without looking away from the object of his study.

"So he has said," Daav murmured.

"Sharp, too. That's good. Where'd you get him, Smokey?"

"Pilot Caylon rescued him from a crowd on Avontai Port who were bent upon murder."

"Be just," Aelliana protested. "A pilot in peril, I saw. Of norbears, what did I know?"

"Avontai's no place for a norbear," Bruce Peltzer said. "Where'd the pilot who had him get him?"

"That," Daav said, "we were unable to determine. The pilot was in need of medical—and other—attention. We delivered him to the Healers, thinking to find sanctuary for Hevelin there, as well—"

The big man snorted.

"Precisely. We were encouraged to depart—quickly—and as a life was the stake, Pilot Caylon made haste to do what was necessary."

Daav extended a finger to touch a round, furry ear. "From himself, I received the dream of previous employment and a desire for more of the same."

The other pilot was silent for three heartbeats, then gave a gusty sigh. "That pilot must've been stupid as stone, taking him onto the port."

There was a tremble in the air; Hevelin stiffened where he stood. Aelliana slid her hand across the counter toward him, meaning to offer comfort. He flicked an ear and reached down, enclosing her forefinger in a surprisingly strong grip. For a moment, it seemed as if there was something more than the norbear's wariness trembling on the edge of her awareness, then it faded and she looked up into Bruce Peltzer's watchful eyes.

"Ill," she said, not quite knowing where the word, or the conviction, came from, yet certain that it needed expression.

"Ill," she repeated and moved her shoulders. "Needing more comfort than gives a norbear."

The big man nodded, slowly.

"Well, he seems a likely yoster," he said. "Couple things remain before I can accept him permanent. First being, does he take to me like he's apparently taken to Captain Smoke and yourself?"

He extended a large hand, palm up on the counter—and waited.

Hevelin stood very still, gripping Aelliana's finger. For a heartbeat, she thought he would dash away and scramble back into the safety of the carryall. She felt a thrill then, of what might have been determination, and her finger was released. Dropping to all fours, he bumbled across the counter with his usual cheerful insouciance and climbed into Bruce Peltzer's hand.

"Bold lad. Let's you and me get acquainted, eh? Maybe you can tell me a little more about your previous circumstances." He looked at Daav.

"If you pilots would like to take an hour's tour of beautiful Staederport, or stop over at the Repair Pit for a bite to eat? I'll have something to say when you come back."

Daav inclined his head. "Of course."

He stepped away from the counter, leaving the bag where it was. Aelliana slid off of the stool, and hesitated, looking once more to Hevelin. He did, she allowed after a moment's study, seem to be engaged and not at all nervous. That was good.

She turned and followed Daav out into the warm drizzle. Behind them the door sealed with a loud *snap*.

Startled, she turned.

The autoscroll now read: CLOSED FOR LUNCH.

· · · ❖ · · ·

Daav scanned the street, finding no dangers more immediate than becoming waterlogged in the incessant drizzle, and glanced at his companion. She was, he thought, ridiculously appealing with her rain-flattened hair and drop-spattered face, despite which he sensed that she was about to tax him hard.

"You have a question, Pilot?" he murmured.

"In fact, three," she answered, holding up her thumb. "What is 'bacon'?" Forefinger. "Why does he call you 'Smokey'?" Second finger—"Why should we be directed to a garage for lunch?"

Well, it was not an unreasonable list, he conceded. "If it is all the same to you, I propose to address the last question first, as I am most wonderfully hungry."

"So long as they are *all* answered, sir, and no stinting on the count!"

He grinned. "I will do my best to keep every card in play," he promised, looking about them again. The very casualness of the suggestion argued that the Repair Pit stood close at hand; that it had been mentioned specifically, surely indicated that Bruce felt it to be a reasonably secure haven for two pilots new on-port, and who were also Liaden.

"Ah." He'd spied the end of a scroll message in the gap between two shops. "Just a very short walk, and I believe we may satisfy our—or, at the least, my—craving for food."

Aelliana fell in beside him without comment. She kept watch, too, also without comment, and he smiled again, with pride of her. At this rate of gain, she would be as port-wise as any courier might need to be inside of two *relumma*.

Not, he reminded himself, that they were to be

traveling so long. They ought, indeed, to turn their wings toward Liad, as soon as Hevelin's affairs were settled.

"Daav?" Aelliana put her hand on his arm.

"Ah, your pardon! I was thinking how delightful it will be to again raise the homeworld."

She snorted lightly, eloquent of disbelief, but all she said was, "Of course. Now. You were answering three questions, without stint, beginning with the third."

"I don't know how it is that I keep forgetting that you are a teacher," he murmured. "However, I will not be seen to step back from my word! The answer to the third question is that 'Repair Pit' is—a joke, Aelliana. A play on words."

He might never be able to share her thoughts, but he could—and did—feel her thinking, sorting through her store of Terran words and meanings, fingering each as if it were a bright stone . . .

"So one repairs to the Repair Pit in order to repair the deficiencies of hunger and thirst," she murmured, slowly. Then, more quickly, her voice bright with excitement: "It is another multiple meaning!" She tucked herself closer against him, her fingers tightening on his arm.

"At first, you know, I had thought Terran a flat language, with all of its information on the surface. It is . . . delightful to find that I have been wrong, though it is somewhat difficult to know how to fathom the depths."

"That is precisely what makes learning a language so perilous," Daav murmured. "For one must have the culture, in order to understand that there *are* depths. Often," he added, looking down into her luminous face, "the depths are treacherous."

"Certainly they must be! And the assumption that one has—or has not—understood the whole of the information being granted..." She sighed. "It seems to me that the Scouts set themselves an impossible task, *van'chela*. How can you hope to fathom all?"

"No one ever fathoms all; even the most astute of native speakers sometimes err. It is...often... enough to be aware of the depths, and to tune the ear for nuance."

They paused to let a lorry clear the street, then crossed to the entrance of the Repair Pit, where Aelliana was disposed to dawdle, observing the windowless exterior and the scrollbar over the door.

"It only displays in Terran," she commented.

...and thus they might be looking at a subtle warn-away, Daav thought, pleased that she had caught the hint.

"We may go elsewhere if you like," he said. "I will say that I do not believe that Pilot Peltzer would send us into a situation he considered to be less than secure. It is, however, the pilot's choice."

Once again, he caught the intensity of her thought, then she nodded, once, in a gesture she had undoubtedly learnt from Anne.

"I am hungry, too," she said. "Let us by all means accept the pilot's suggestion."

"Now," Aelliana said after they had found seats in the crowded room and entered their meal selections into the data board bolted to the side of the table. "The next question, if you please."

Daav glanced around the room, admiring Bruce Peltzer even more than he had done previously. The place was set up as a garage with multiple work-benches. Each table ordered through the data board; the meals were delivered via a slightly lunatic conveyor system. There was no reason for those seated at one work bench to interact with the occupants of another. Thus, one might be certain of one's own space, one's own custom, and one's own language over the meal. Such an arrangement greatly reduced opportunities for taking—or giving—offense.

"Daav..."

"The next question—what is bacon?" he said, turning back to her with a smile. "Bacon is a condiment—a cured meat served in thin strips, hot. However, in the usage 'saved my bacon,' it is meant that one's life was preserved." He held up a hand as her lips parted. "I do not know how one leaps from the first to the second, and can only in this instance repeat what I have been told by a native speaker—in fact, by Pilot Peltzer."

She sighed, clearly unsatisfied, but... "We shall, of course, abide by the pilot's explanation. Though I believe I will ask Anne when we return home."

He grinned, picturing the conversation. "Do that."

A discreet clatter drew his attention to the conveyor belt, where two trays were on course for their table.

"Our meal approaches," he said.

"Smokey?" Aelliana asked, before she had even sampled her "Rimrunner's Stew" or her lemon water.

"A call-name," he said promptly, eying his "Space Jockey Special."

"Yes, but—why not *your* name?"

The absence of utensils argued that the foodstuff on his plate was intended to be addressed with the fingers, though he scarcely knew how he was to escape without becoming well sauced, indeed.

"My name was unknown in the initial transaction," he said, picking up the first overflowing bun gingerly. "And one must call a man *some*thing. Also, there appeared to be a complaint regarding my comportment, in that I kept fading in and out, like smoke. I was inclined to put that aspect of things down to the head injury, myself, but one must not be churlish in these matters." He glanced over to Aelliana, who was holding her spoon near her mouth, an expression of not-entirely-pleasant surprise on her face.

"How is your meal?" he inquired politely.

She took a deep breath, lowered her spoon and reached for her bottle of lemon water.

"The word may be 'decisive,'" she said. "I had not expected something so *warm*. And yours?"

"I have not yet recruited my courage," he admitted. "Hold but a moment."

He assayed a small bite, finding it not bad; the sauce sweet, but not overly so, and the filling agreeably chewy, despite being every bit as messy as he had feared.

"Not inedible," he told Aelliana. "If you cannot support yours, take from mine, do. I cannot imagine that I can accommodate the entire plate."

"Perhaps the second spoon will be less surprising," she said, determinedly. "After all, one cannot always have toasted cheese sandwiches."

Daav laughed. "Now that," he said, "is not a very Liaden outlook."

"I suppose it isn't," she agreed, and assayed her soup again.

✳   ✳   ✳

"The yoster and me have reached an accord, and he'll be staying on," Bruce Peltzer said. He nodded at the green plant on the counter. "I'll be doing better for him, of course, but for now, he's taken that for his bunk. Last I saw, he was having a bit of a nap, but if you'd like to say your good-byes..."

"I see no reason to disturb his dreaming," Daav murmured. "He'll recall us, and we'll recall him, each for as long as we can."

"That's right." The big man cleared his throat. "I didn't do any better getting a fix on his previous bunk. Seems clear he was lifted, though, and took off without permissions." He shook his head. "Boy that took him had some troubles—like the pilot said, more than a norbear could fix. They were both lucky you two happened by."

"Work he will do for you?" Aelliana asked. Bruce looked to her.

"Don't you worry, Pilot, I'm not going to let him slack off! Norbears are useful to have around the place. Not only are they what you might call a calming influence, but they're real good on knowing when somebody's thinking about walking out a hatch without a suit. You don't often get 'em as sharp as Hevelin; he's going to be a real asset to the circuit rider's office."

"Good," Aelliana said, and Daav heard the tears in her voice. "We do well for him."

He reached out and took her hand. "We've done what's best for him," he said, and gave Bruce Peltzer a grin. "And for you, too."

"I'll allow a good turn," the big man said comfortably, and stuck his hand out. "Good to see you again, Smokey."

"And you." Daav put his palm against the other man's, watching as it was swallowed and released. "Fair travel, Pilot. Walk carefully, port-wise."

"That I'll do—and the pair of you, as well. Pilot Caylon, it's an honor."

"Thank you," Aelliana said, inclining her head slightly. "Good lift, Pilot."

"Safe landing," he replied.

They were passing a bookstore on Duty Free Street, all but in sight of *The Luck*, when the unanticipated occurred.

The door opened as they strolled by; Daav registered the impression of an ordinary-seeming Terran of perhaps an affluent habit, his belt innocent of weaponry, and a package with the bookstore's name emblazoned upon it cradled against his chest.

In a word: harmless.

Hand in hand with his pilot, his love, Daav took a step.

"Professor!" Excitement, only that. Nothing to concern one.

Daav took another step.

"Professor Kiladi, wait!"

There was no excuse for it; the merest Scoutling might have acted with more finesse. His heart stuttered, his step faltered...

...he snatched his hand away from Aelliana's.

"Professor!"

Discovered, he thought, *after all these years. And*

yet, the thing might still be recovered, if only you can rally a bit of credence, Daav.

Slowly, an expression of what he devoutly hoped was cool and slightly offended curiosity on his face, he turned. Aelliana, who must have felt that first jolt of horror as clearly as if it had been her own, turned with him, her face wary, and one hand on her gun.

The man approaching them, already out of breath with his hurried dozen steps, was younger than Daav, his pale hair glued to his head by the rain. His eyes were tight at the corners, as if he spent long hours before a text screen, or bent over the pages of books. He came on, oblivious to Aelliana's threat, a smile of purest pleasure on his not-entirely-forgettable face.

"I beg pardon, sir..." Daav said, suddenly recalling the face as it had been, much younger, rounder, less drawn—third row, second quadrant, he thought. Dobson. Chames Dobson.

"...you have the advantage of me," he concluded.

The man paused at the proper distance for speech between non-kin, Daav was pleased to note, and performed quite a credible bow to the master.

"You *are* Jen Sar Kiladi, are you not? I—of course, out of so many students, you wouldn't remember me. Chames Dobson, sir. I was in your class on comparative cultures at Searston University, and it—" He blinked, and appeared at last to see the man who stood, broadly puzzled and perhaps losing patience, before him; his leather well worn, and his partner standing at backup.

"I... It is I who beg your pardon," he said slowly. "You—you might be his brother, sir, but I see that I am in error. You are not Jen Sar Kiladi. Please accept my apologies for disturbing your peace, Pilot."

"Please," Daav said, carefully, as would a man who had been surprised, but after all not threatened, and by one who had some grasp of proper manners. "It is a simple error. I have made it myself, when on a strange port, and hoping, perhaps, to see a friend."

Dobson's face relaxed into a smile, and for a moment he was entirely the earnest young scholar he had been.

"Yes, exactly. I just got word—well. Say that circumstances brought him to mind—and I wished that I could share my news, and tell him how much his teaching had meant to me. Then I saw you as I came out of the bookshop . . ." He shook his head, half amused, half regretful, and stepped back, lifting his free hand politely.

"Safe lift, Pilot."

"I thank you. May your day embrace joy."

Chames Dobson turned and walked off, a trusting man.

Daav braced himself for the question that, alas, was not long in coming.

"Who," Aelliana asked sternly, "is Jen Sar Kiladi, and why did you lie to that man?"

TWENTY-TWO

. . . .

"Liaden Scout" must now be seen as a misnomer, for to become a Scout is to become other than Liaden. It is to turn one's face from the homeworld and enter a state of philosophy where all custom, however alien, is accepted as equally just and fitting.

We are told by certain instructors that not everyone may aspire to—nor all who aspire, attain—that particular degree of philosophical contrariness required of those who are said to have "Scout's eyes."

For this we must rejoice, and allow the Scouts full honor for having in the past provided refuge for the disenfranchised, the adventurous and the odd.

> —Excerpted from remarks made
> before the Council of Clans by
> the chairperson of the Coalition
> to Abolish the Liaden Scouts

"A WAGER," AELLIANA REPEATED. "YOU FABRICATED AN entire person—for a *wager*?"

"Well," he said apologetically, "at first, it didn't seem so difficult—comparative linguistics was near enough

to a portion of a Scout's course of study. By the time
the wager had come against its deadline, Kiladi had
defended his first degree and taught a seminar or
two, and it seemed impossible that I just *stop*. He
had colleagues, correspondents, students—in a word,
he would be missed, poor fellow. I could scarcely
murder him out of hand." He sipped, and admitted,
"Besides, I was curious to know how long he might
support himself."

Aelliana reached for her glass and sipped wine. It
was not very good wine, being what was on offer at
the Pilots Mart, but it was well enough for its purpose.

"How long has Scholar Kiladi persisted?"

He sighed. "Nearly fifteen Standards. I admit, it will
be hard to end the Scholar's life." In fact, it was remarkably dismaying, the thought that Kiladi would no longer
be with him. It was not as if the scholar had been a
constant companion; his needs were modest: time and
resources for his researches, and leave to produce his
papers and keep current with his correspondence . . .

"Why must you?" Aelliana asked, fortuitously breaking this increasingly bleak line of thought.

"The terms of the wager were that the fabrication
might continue only until it was discovered. Even
though he has far outlived the circumstance that birthed
him, he has been found out, and thus is forfeit."

She shook damp hair back from her face.

"But he has *not* been found out," she said. "The
man on the port just now—Chames Dobson—he
admitted a likeness, but was convinced at the last
that you were not his teacher."

"Be it as may be, yet *you* are wise to Kiladi's
secret, Aelliana."

"Yes, but I am your lifemate," she answered serenely.

"Are you?" he asked, softly.

She frowned. "Am I not?"

"In the eyes of the world, you are not until there is a contract between us," he said, and wondered at himself, that he pushed this point at her now.

Her frown became more pronounced.

"That is a separate issue," she said sternly. "Which I am not prepared to discuss. At the fore is Scholar Kiladi's life. Has he a résumé? A bibliography?"

"He has. Shall I download his file for you from the Scholar Base?"

"There is no need to trouble yourself; I have an account."

She rose, taking her glass with her.

It was no small effort to keep his tongue behind his teeth and his posture inoffensive. Aelliana was plainly annoyed with him and he had no wish to provoke her further.

"I will want an hour alone," she said.

He bowed his head. "Of course, Pilot."

· · · ·✴· · · ·

Jen Sar Kiladi's bibliography was extensive. She was by no means an expert in his fields, but that mattered not at all. His work had been studied—not to say scrutinized—by those who *were* expert, and had formed the basis for further illuminations and scholarship.

The words *brilliant*, *radical*, *original* were more often than not the descriptors applied to Scholar Kiladi's work. There was of course a leavening of *popinjay*, *recluse*, and *dangerous madman* from his detractors, but those served more to relieve than alarm her. A scholar who did not make collegial enemies was a scholar who was not exercising his intellect to its fullest extent.

It might seem odd that a Liaden had taken all of his degrees at Terran universities, but it appeared that Scholar Kiladi had originated upon a Terran world which also housed a lesser Liaden population. This early living astride two cultures, so he had written in his supplication letter to the Admitting Officer at Dobrin University, was what had first excited his interest in the field of cultural genetics, an interest that had only deepened as he pursued his degrees first in comparative linguistics and then in the dynamics of diaspora.

She requested half-a-dozen papers from various stages of his career and skimmed them, finding evidence of a supple mind and subtle thought. His arguments were solid, his presentation confiding and occasionally playful. His conclusions, while sometimes risky, in her sample never lacked the support necessary to their weight.

In fact, Scholar Kiladi was brilliant, Aelliana thought, leaning back in her chair and looking at last to the copilot's station, where Daav sat cross-legged; freshly showered and relaxed in a long-sleeved sweater and soft pants, his hair loose and fresh along his shoulders.

No, she thought—not relaxed. Daav was awaiting her judgment, and he was . . . concerned of what it might be.

She sighed again, ran her hands through her rain-sticky hair, and wrinkled her nose, feeling grubby.

"*Van'chela*, you cannot deny the galaxy the gift of Scholar Kiladi's thought," she said slowly. "You are . . .

Daav, you are"—she waved her hand hopelessly at the screen, *brilliant, radical, original*—"a jewel."

He shook his head. "Not I, lady of my heart."

"Is it not you, at base?"

"It may be," he said slowly. "I consider Kiladi to be—other than myself. We have points of similarity, and I read his papers, among dozens of others, with interest, for we overlap in our areas of expertise. Daav yos'Phelium does not write papers, nor hold any degrees, saving his survival of Scout Academy and ascendancy to the rank of captain. But, *melant'i* teaches us, does it not, that we must tailor ourselves to fit the role in which we stand?"

Aelliana felt a slight, not entirely pleasant thrill, recalling the man he had become out on Staederport; the man who was so definitely, to the eye of the admiring student, *not* his beloved professor. It had been stance, she thought, and a dozen subtleties that had remolded Daav, her copilot, her lover, her lifemate—remolded him into a rough pilot, perhaps a little chancy in his temper, perhaps, even, just a tiny bit the worse for his wine...

"You have never seen me stand fully as Korval," Daav murmured. "It is necessary from time to time, and one must be...convincing. It comforts me, that I feel less in common with the delm than I do with Kiladi."

"I want to see him," she said abruptly. She spun the chair around, her hands gripping the armrests. "Scholar Kiladi."

Daav lifted an eyebrow, and drew in a long breath. He unfolded his legs and stood, closed his eyes and let his breath go.

Aelliana leaned forward in the chair.

It was not so marked a translation as that in the port, yet she had the uncanny certainty that she was beholding a man similar in form to her lifemate, yet undeniably someone . . . other.

Like Daav, Scholar Kiladi was an upright man, proud without being prideful. It seemed that he was not quite so tall as Daav, nor, when he opened his eyes, so bold or ascertaining in his glances. He looked into her face, then courteously looked aside, as would a newly acknowledged colleague. He seemed younger than Daav, or perhaps, Aelliana thought, it was the lack of Korval's weight burdening his *melant'i*. A mere scholar, no matter how many times an expert, was a simple thing, compared to Daav yos'Phelium.

"Walk," she whispered. "If you please, Scholar."

"Scholar," he murmured, and turned, walking from the copilot's chair across the chamber, toward the hall.

His step was light, but by no means silent; his carriage easy, even graceful, but it did not cry out "Pilot!" nor even whisper "Scout."

"Stop," Aelliana said, wrenching herself out of the chair. She approached him, and looked boldly into his eyes. The gaze that returned hers was intelligent, polite, inquisitive. The eyes and the face of a stranger.

"You can support this?" she asked. "For how long?"

An eyebrow twitched. "Your pardon, Scholar?"

She took a breath, recalled herself and bowed. "Forgive me, Scholar; I misspoke. I met one of your students today on the port. He spoke of you warmly and with genuine regard. The message he sends is that he has recently received great news, and that it was the influence of your teaching upon his life which had brought him to this happy circumstance. His name is Chames Dobson, though he doubted you would remember him, as indifferent a scholar as he had been."

He smiled with unfeigned pleasure, and inclined his head. "My thanks to you, Scholar. Chames was— an earnest student. One is gratified to hear of his success, unspecified as it is. To have one's teaching credited with so much, must of course bring joy to a teacher's day."

"Exactly," she murmured, and stepped back, suddenly exhausted, and of no further mind to have a stranger on her ship.

"Daav."

Jen Sar Kiladi melted; she could not have pointed to the moment when he was gone entirely and Daav yos'Phelium stood before her, his face etched in an exhaustion that echoed hers.

"I can support it more easily at length," he said softly. "It becomes worn in, like a favorite sweater."

She nodded, and sighed, and raised her hands again to her sticky hair.

"I am going to have a shower," she announced. "If you please, find us a meal and some tea. While we eat, we shall plan our best return to Liad."

TWENTY-THREE

. . . .

The most dangerous phrase in High Liaden is *coab
minshak'a*: "Necessity exists."
                              —From "A Terran's Guide to Liad"

"UNCLE DAAV!"

A missile hurtled out of the branches of the decora-
tive tree they strolled past. Aelliana twisted sideways,
heart in her mouth, the outcome of the child's trajectory as obvious to her as if he had already struck his
head and snapped his neck. She was too far away to
catch him!

However, Daav was not.

He spun in a graceful arc, arms extended, as unhurried as if there were no possible danger, swooped the
hurtling body out of the air and continued his spin,
faster now, the child slung over his shoulder scream-
ing with laughter.

Daav slowed, coming to a halt with his back toward
her. Shan grinned at her, blithely upside-down.

"Hi, Aelli."

"Hi, Shannie," she returned, over the frenzied
pounding of her heart. "Perhaps next time you might

consider an approach less fraught with peril. How if your uncle had missed you?"

"Uncle Daav never misses," Shan said comfortably.

The subject of this encompassing trust gave a shout of laughter, snatched the child off his shoulder and set him upright on his feet.

He dropped to one knee, and peered down into the small face.

"Even the quickest pilot sometimes misses," he said, seriously. "And it is not *at all* the thing to be ambushing your kin from the shrubberies."

Shan frowned uncertainly. "No?"

"No," Daav said firmly. "Also, you had frightened my pilot, a circumstance of which I am required to take a very dim view, indeed."

Silver eyes sought hers.

"Were you frightened, Aelli?"

"Yes," she said, kneeling beside Daav on the grass. "I could see the path of your fall, and I could see that you would strike your head, and that *I* was too far away to catch you."

"Oh." Shan looked down, frowning ferociously.

"You see numbers," he said at last, looking up again. "Like sparkles."

She had previously been introduced to the concept of "sparkles," by which Shan would have one believe that he could see another's emotions. It said much for the change in her circumstances, that she had not found this odd in the least, though he was young, so Anne had told her, to be showing Healing talent.

"Perhaps, a little," she admitted. "Recall that I cannot compare directly, for I do not see sparkles."

He nodded, and abruptly bowed.

"Forgive me," he said formally.

Aelliana inclined her head. "It is forgotten," she answered properly.

"Very well," Daav said, rising. "Now, if you please, young pirate, lead us to your parents!"

Their arrival was greeted with embraces, and exclamations about timing and the luck. It transpired that Er Thom had only arrived home himself within the last two-day, and had scarcely, as he told Daav with perfect solemnity, had time enough to sort through his mail.

Shan being returned to the care of his nurse, with whom Daav had a quiet word apart, the adults repaired to the patio overlooking the twilight wild park, where a cold meal was served, over which she and Daav were quizzed on every detail of their trip.

Anne asked the majority of questions, while her lifemate contented himself with studying Daav's face, his displaying what Aelliana could only say was tenderness. It was very much pilot and copilot work, Aelliana thought, though she could not have said for certain who sat which board.

"No more!" Daav protested at last, falling back in his chair and raising his hands, as if in surrender. "You now have every crumb upon which we had hoped to dine out for the next *relumma*!"

Anne laughed.

"We won't tell a soul," she promised. "Besides, you know that Lady yo'Lanna refuses to believe anything she hears of you, unless it comes from your own lips."

"Whereupon she disbelieves it doubly! But, here—turnabout is fair play. Tell us all and everything that has happened to you while we were apart! And mind you tell it well!"

"I'm to be interviewer and interviewee? What will *you* do?"

"Sip my wine and be entertained," he retorted. "I hope you don't believe that I memorized that long list of inquiry."

She laughed, and shook her head, brown eyes dancing.

"If you want it then, laddie, here it is—I was dull and held at home, teaching my classes and playing with my son while Er Thom went out on the route. He came home once, between, and then we were merry."

"A pleasant tale, if a short one. Brother? Have you nothing with which to embroider this spare narrative?"

"A single thread, I fear, though perhaps it will please."

He extended a hand to his lifemate, who received it with a smile so brilliant Aelliana felt her eyes tear.

"yos'Galan will soon welcome a second child into the house."

Anne laughed.

"Don't let him cotton you," she said. "I'm only just caught, so it's more 'eventually' than 'soon.'"

A ferocious joy struck Aelliana from across the table, nearly unseating her. Daav being Daav, it was nothing so simple as *only* joy, no matter how fierce; it carried envy on its back; hope, anticipation, delight, and a single dark stroke of fear.

"The clan increases!" he cried, and it was joy only that informed his face and his voice. "May we reap much delight from Korval's new child!"

✳ ✳ ✳

They arrived at Jelaza Kazone with the rising of the stars, and went first to the inner garden, walking hand in hand along the flower-choked path, toward the center, and the Tree.

"I see that I shall have to free the pathways," Daav said, "else random strollers will become engulfed."

"Do we have many random strollers?" Aelliana asked, letting his happiness marry her own. The result was a gentle euphoria, edged with excitement.

"We do from time to time host gathers, and the garden is of course open to our guests. I will lead here, Pilot, in case there is a savage beast lying in wait..."

He stepped forward without relinquishing her hand and led her safely past a tangle of twigs, leaves glossy and black in the starlight.

When she was able to walk beside him again, she murmured, "I like the garden wild."

"As I do. I swear that I envision no such pretty tribute to the landscaper's art as we might see in the city. Though they have their place, it is not *this* place. No, I merely wish to widen the trail so that two may walk abreast."

They left the path altogether then, and walked across the root-woven grass to the Tree. Daav put his free hand flat against the broad trunk, and she did the same.

Immediately, she was aware of warmth, of a sense of welcome, and of a gentle probing, as if the Tree asked how did she go on.

"Very well, thank you," she murmured. "I hope you have not been lonely."

The leaves directly over her head fluttered, though there was no breeze—laughter, so she thought. Intense focus sizzled along her connection with Daav, and her fingers grew quite warm. She did not pull away, and after a moment the heat faded.

Daav moved, retreating two deliberate steps from the trunk, pulling her with him. From high in the boughs came a clatter of leaf, as if a rock had been thrown from inside the canopy, then two seedpods plummeted out of the Tree, striking the ground precisely—one at Daav's feet; the other at hers.

"It seems we are welcomed home," Aelliana murmured, bending to retrieve her pod.

"So it does," Daav murmured. "Shall I open that for you?"

"Please."

She lifted the first of the neat pieces to her lips, abruptly and ravenously hungry, though the meal with Anne and Er Thom was only recently behind them. Tonight's nut smelled of sweet cedar, the taste... If hot and cold were tastes, it would have tasted thus. The first morsel left her hungry for the second; the second for the third, and the fourth—sated her entirely.

Fulfilled, she looked to Daav, who was watching her with a quizzical tilt to his eyebrow.

"Have I forgotten to say that you are a thing of astonishing beauty," he murmured, "the love of my life and the guiding star of my heart?"

She smiled up at him, shivering with delight. "I believe you may have mentioned it once or twice," she said. "But how unhandsome! You leave me with no words to say at all, *van'chela*, only a wish to stay always at your side."

"A rare compliment," he said, "considering how many will have nothing at all to do with Korval."

He turned and bowed to the Tree—honor-to-a-master—straightening just as Relchin, orange-and-white-striped tail held high in welcome, burst from the shrubbery and ran to them, burbling excitedly.

Aelliana laughed, and bent down to offer her finger. Relchin rubbed his muzzle, eyes slit in ecstasy.

"Now here's an enthusiastic welcome!"

"Indeed," Daav said, rubbing an orange ear briskly. "I wager Mr. pel'Kana has forgotten to fill the food bowls. Only see the poor creature, with his ribs on display!"

It was no such thing; Relchin was as sleek as ever he had been beneath her stroking palm. Aelliana gave him one skritch on the chin and straightened.

"We should go inside, then, and check the bowls."

"We should go inside," Daav corrected, taking her hand as they started back to the path, "and deal with our mail."

Aelliana sighed comfortably as the warm breeze gently dried her, then she reached for her robe and belted it loosely around her. She paused in their bedroom to brush out her hair before going to the parlor.

Daav, resplendent in a house robe embroidered with gloan-roses, was sitting on the floor with his back against the couch, long legs stretched before him, Relchin leaning companionably against his knee. The disordered clutch of mail she had last seen him with had been reduced to several tidy piles.

"I should have given it out that we were not expected to return," he said, looking up with a rueful smile. "Er Thom has the right of it—the worst of coming home is dealing with one's mail."

She sat down by his shoulder and leaned forward. His hair was loose on his shoulders, damp and smelling distractingly of sweet cedar. She wanted to comb her fingers through it, bury her face in it... Aelliana took a breath and forced herself to focus on the tidy piles.

"What a lot of invitations you have," she said, eying the stack of square ivory envelopes. "I suppose you can't just throw them out?"

"More's the pity—however! I am not alone in having mail to sort, my lady." He rummaged briefly and produced two invitations and an envelope.

"These," he said, putting them into her hands, "are for you."

"For me?" She couldn't remember when she had last received an invitation. Before her marriage, surely. After—she had not cared for going among people, and if she had shown any disposition for society, she thought, with a surprisingly hot spark of anger, Ran Eld would doubtless have forbidden her the pleasure.

Daav rested his head on the cushion at her side, and gave her a lazy, upside-down smile.

"That robe is quite fetching," he murmured.

"You gave it—" she began, and then realized that her position had allowed the loosely-wrapped garment to fall somewhat open, thus revealing certain of her holdings.

"Fetching," he repeated, softly, and reached up to pull on the sash, which obligingly gave up its knot; the robe opened more fully, falling away from one breast entirely.

Clearly, a countermeasure was called for.

She bent down and kissed him, as thoroughly as she knew how.

His desire rose to meet hers; she leaned closer, hungry for his mouth, his hands, for *him*...

* * *

"The mail is all mixed up again," she said some while later.

She was lying across his back, breast against shoulder, cheek against cheek, his hair and hers thoroughly tangled together, with only the vaguest notion of how she had gotten there.

His other cheek pressed against the carpet, Daav sighed.

"Torn from virtuous industry by a ravishing temptress; all—all—to be done over!"

"Ravishing temptress? Who was it opened up my robe?"

"Who ravished whom?"

"That's not the point."

"No, only give me a moment to recruit myself!"

She laughed.

"If I let you up, will you comport yourself as a gentleman?"

"For how long shall I be bound to *that* hideous fate? It may be that I will prefer death by ravishment."

"Did I offer that alternative?" she asked, the sternness of her voice marred by a giggle. "You shall be bound for the time that it takes us to read our mail."

"I suppose I may last that long. Am I allowed the comfort of a glass of wine?"

"Certainly," she said grandly. "You may fetch me one, too. Have we a bargain?"

"We do, cruel lady."

"Rise, then," she said.

"After you."

She rolled to her feet, glanced about—and found

her robe cast all everyway across the reading chair. She slipped it on and tied the sash *firmly*, while Daav likewise reassembled himself and moved off toward the kitchen alcove.

Aelliana knelt on the rug amid the disorder of envelopes and picked up an invitation.

By the time he returned with the wine, she had gathered the invitations into one pile, and discovered most, but she felt not all, of the letters.

"My lady wishes to make my time in bondage as short as possible," he murmured. "Perhaps she is not cruel, after all."

"Merely pragmatic," she said, rising to receive her glass. "I fear that some of the letters may have taken refuge beneath the furniture."

"Fear not, I will recover all. Please, rest from your labors and attend to your own matters."

Her correspondence had remained aloof upon the sofa cushions, where they had been joined by Relchin, who was asleep with his chin on an ivory card. She smiled, put her glass on the occasional table, and slid the letters free. The cat opened one eye, muttered and went back to sleep.

"Thank you," she said politely, retiring to the corner and curling against the pillows. She broke the seal on the first invitation, which was marked with the sign of a snake wrapped 'round a moon.

The gift of your time is solicited for a select gathering of friends at an informal midmorning tea in the garden at Glavda Empri on Metlin Eighthday of the current relumma. *Acceptances only to Ilthiria yo'Lanna, Thodelmae.*

"Who," Aelliana wondered, "is Ilthiria yo'Lanna?"

Daav looked up. He had resumed his seat on the floor and was engaged in dividing the invitations, still sealed into their envelopes, into two piles.

"Ilthiria yo'Lanna is my mother's best and oldest friend," he said. "Why do you ask?"

She held up the card.

"She invites me to a picnic on the grounds of Glavda Empri, but—surely not. It is in three days! I have not been introduced to the lady, and will know no one—"

"Ah, but there you are out!" Daav riffled the envelopes in his hand and held one up so that she could see the Snake-and-Moon. "Unless she has lost her touch—which is *not* the wager to take—this is my invitation to the same event."

"That was clever of her," Aelliana acknowledged. "Shall we go?"

"I should think that we must. She's very likely enjoyed herself immensely in choosing the guest list so that she may be the first to make you known to those whom you may find charming, interesting, or of use. We could hardly be so churlish as to deny her so much pleasure."

Aelliana frowned down at the card, trying to read intent into the few formal lines.

"Of use?" she murmured.

"Indeed. Lady yo'Lanna is nothing if not a pragmatist. You see? Already you share ground in common! It appears that she is willing to ease your way into the world."

She looked up. "This is—a kindness?"

"So I believe, yes."

A kindness. Aelliana sighed.

"Tomorrow, I will write Lady yo'Lanna a note, accepting her kind invitation and thanking her for her notice."

Daav grinned. "I shall do the same. In my own hand, mind, or I will have such a peal rung over me that it will be heard in the Low Port!"

She tucked the card back into its envelope, placed it on the side table, and sipped her wine before turning her attention to the other invitation.

The embossing was Korval's familiar Tree-and-Dragon; her name was written in glossy black ink in a hand so firm the pen had scored the paper.

She broke the seal and drew out the card.

Since their second, not entirely cordial interview, she had not again met Daav's sister. Indeed, it might have been said that, busy as she had been with other matters, the lady had slipped her mind altogether.

Alas, she had not been similarly forgotten.

She drew a breath.

"Ah, Kareen," Daav murmured, "so subtle."

He held what she could only suppose was a like card; shaking his head at it sadly.

"I will not be attending this *formal evening gather*," Aelliana stated.

Daav looked at her, one eyebrow up. "Whyever not?"

"Because it is a trap. Lady Kareen warned me that I would not be able to hold my place among the High. Now, she seeks to prove her course and shame me publicly. I will not attend."

"Don't you wish to prove her wrong?" Daav asked, with every appearance of seriousness.

"I fear that I will rather prove her correct."

"No, only think! Lady yo'Lanna's picnic is well

before this evening gather. Recall that you will at that event be introduced to people whom she thinks you should know. I will grant that not all will be High House, but some will. Very certainly some, if not all, of those whose acquaintance you will make at Glavda Empri will also be present at Kareen's affair. And, you know, you will probably receive other invitations between—Kareen having been so kind as to give us more than half a *relumma* to prepare."

She considered him. "You wish me to enter battle?"

"Not in the least. Only attend and demonstrate to Kareen why her equations are faulty." He tipped his head. "If you refuse to attend this gather, she will only have another, you know. Refuse again and it will surely come to be known that *Korval's dependent* shows scant gratitude to the House."

It took the breath away, that summation, but Aelliana had to admit that nothing he said struck her as being beyond Kareen's scope. Certainly, it was to the lady's benefit to publicly discover her rag-mannered and worse. Not to mention that such a public humiliation must also score a strike upon Daav.

Stomach tight, she returned that card, too, to its envelope and put it with the first.

"Tomorrow," she said unwillingly, "I will send an acceptance." She looked up and met his eyes. "In my own hand."

He smiled, pride evident.

"We play on," he said and inclined his head. "Of course, I shall accompany my pilot onto this chancy port."

He placed his sister's card onto the smaller of the two piles, dropped the three remaining in his hand onto the larger, and picked up his other correspondence.

Aelliana sipped her wine, watching him lazily as he opened the first, and drew out a sheet of pale violet paper. He could have read no more than the first two lines before he dropped it, too, into the larger pile and opened another envelope.

Smiling, feeling very much at peace, Aelliana turned her attention to her own letter. The envelope bore the ship and planet sigil of the Liaden Scouts over the words *Verisa pel'Quinot, Scout Academy*. She broke the seal and withdrew a single sheet of white paper, light and crisp to the touch.

The letter itself was brief, consisting merely of a proposition, and a request for a meeting, if the proposition pleased.

Aelliana smiled. If it *pleased*? Of course it pleased! The inevitable presence of Scouts in her Math for Survival seminar had never failed to delight her. To be offered an entire student contingent composed only of Scouts and those whom the Scouts thought it worthwhile to train—

"Now there's the smile of a conqueror," Daav murmured. "One rarely sees so much delight on a single face."

"I have cause, I think," she said. "Scout Academy writes to ask if I would consider teaching the advanced seminar there."

"A coup, indeed! Will you accept?"

"Certainly, it is tempting. I very much enjoyed working with Scouts. At least I must speak with Scholar pel'Quinot and see what she envisions."

"If talk comes to contract, recall that you have dea'Gauss to call upon."

She began to say that she would scarcely trouble

the gentleman with so trivial a matter, but pressed her lips together without uttering the sentence. Only see how well she had done with her other employment contract!

Perhaps it would be a . . . good idea to ask Mr. dea'Gauss if one of his staff might be available for the task.

"I will remember," she said, picking up Scholar pel'Quinot's letter once more.

"I swear that the man is prescient," Daav murmured, his tone an interesting mixture of humor and resignation.

She looked up. "Is there something amiss?"

"Likely not," he said, giving her a half grin. "Mr. dea'Gauss has a matter which requires my personal attention, and asks that I meet with him at my earliest possible convenience."

Aelliana glanced toward the dark-filled windows.

"Which will be," Daav said, folding the letter back into its envelope and placing it on the smaller of his two piles, "tomorrow." He lifted an eyebrow.

"We have finished reading our mail," he said, his voice low and intimate.

Aelliana felt her belly tighten, and her breath came ridiculously short. She tried not to let him see these things, however, and calmly put her letter with the others.

"Your geas is lifted," she said coolly, raising her glass for a sip.

Daav smiled. "Then I am no longer required to be a gentleman."

Effortlessly, he came to his feet and approached her comfortable corner, his eyes on hers. She could not look away from his face; she could not move...

Gently, he took her glass and placed it on the table, keeping her hand in his. She found that she could move, after all; he raised her and she stood shivering and breath-caught as he loosened her sash. The robe fell open and he bent to kiss her breasts.

TWENTY-FOUR

. . . .

Love is best given to kin, and joy taken in duty
well done.

—Vilander's Proverbs, Seventh Edition

THEY HAD BREAKFAST ON THE BALCONY OVERLOOKING
the inner court, at not a particularly early hour. Daav
had gone in to dress while she dawdled over her
second cup of tea; he returned, overneat in his town
clothes, to join her for a third.

"Is there anything that I might bring you from the
city?" he asked.

"Nothing springs immediately to mind," she answered.
"Please convey my best regards to Mr. dea'Gauss."

"Certainly. It may be that I will return in time for
lunch; it may be that I will not. Mr. dea'Gauss was
not as plain as he might have been regarding the
nature of our business."

"Mr. pel'Kana will see that I don't stint myself," she
said, smiling at him from a vast inner contentment.
"In the meanwhile, I have my letters to write, and
an appointment to fix. After that, I may walk in the
garden, or find Lady Dignity and stroke her."

"It sounds a full day, yet not overly fatiguing," Daav acknowledged with a grin. He rose and kissed her, sweetly, on the cheek. "Will you sleep with me tonight, beautiful lady?" he whispered, his breath tickling her ear.

Aelliana shivered.

"Eventually," she said.

He laughed at that and went away. She finished her tea as she wrote out her acceptances, taking especial care with the note to Kareen yos'Phelium, then dressed and placed a comm call to Scout Academy.

By the time she came belowstairs, portcomm under arm, it could fairly have said to have been midday. She stopped in the kitchen to ask for an apple, some cheese and a bottle of cold tea, and carried these out into the garden, where she made camp on the bench surrounded by gloan-roses. She opened the computer and was very soon lost in the complexities of sub-rational mathematics.

It was there that Mr. pel'Kana found her more than an hour later, her lunch forgotten on the bench beside her, the sunlight threading her tawny hair with gold.

"Your pardon, Pilot," he said softly. "This was brought, express. You left no instruction..."

Immersed as she had been, it took a heartbeat, or longer, for her to understand the words.

"Express?" she repeated, frowning up from the screen. "I did not ask for—an express what, Mr. pel'Kana, if you please? I fear I am—somewhat fuddled."

"Your pardon," he said again, and held up a letter for her to see. "This arrived for you by express messenger, Pilot. I thought you would want it. If not, I will take it away and place it with the rest of the correspondence."

"Oh, I see! I will take charge of it. It was kind of you to bring it out."

"Not at all, Pilot," he said, placing the envelope into her hand. "May I bring you anything else? A muffin, perhaps?"

"No, thank you, I am quite well-provisioned."

"Of course, Pilot," he answered and left her, walking as if he were not quite accustomed to grass.

She glanced down.

Mizel's seal leapt at her from a field of too-bright white; her name written out in blue ink in her mother's familiar hand.

Aelliana's stomach clenched. For a moment, she thought of merely tearing it up, unread, and scattering the bits among the roses.

But that would be craven; unworthy of a pilot, and to refuse a letter from kin—that was smaller than she knew herself to be.

She broke the seal, and withdrew a sheet of paper that felt unpleasantly smooth against her fingers, and unfolded it.

It was not, after all, a letter from her mother.

It was a command from Mizel.

It is the judgment of the Delm that Aelliana Caylon has been too long separate from Clan and Kin. Her duties have languished for lack of another to carry them out, and any further absence is to Mizel's disadvantage.

Aelliana Caylon is therefore commanded to return to her Clanhouse no later than Zeldra Seventhday of this present relumma, *bringing with her such items as legitimately belong to her, and nothing else. She will herefore consider the House of Mizel her natural and permanent residence, and Mizel's care and protection her natural right.*

It has further come to the attention of Mizel that Aelliana Caylon owns, in her name alone, a spacegoing vessel and a viable courier business. These things will pass properly into the care of the Clan, and any profit realized from them will be divided by Mizel equally among the members of the Clan.

"No!" The word burst from her. She raised a hand and pressed her fingers hard against her lips, lest there be more, and stronger, to dismay the garden's peace.

Mizel's patience had run out, and she was summoned home, all her goods forfeit to the clan, as was proper and according to custom. Well, and she had known that it might happen—that it *would* happen. She had hoped for more time for circumstances to further resolve themselves, but she saw now what her choice must be. Really, there had never been a choice at all.

She glanced down again to the letter.

It has further come to the attention of Mizel that Aelliana Caylon owns, in her name alone, a spacegoing vessel and a viable courier business.

Yes, well.

She stood, folding the paper without much attention to the process and sealing it into her sleeve pocket.

Her ship would not be compromised, nor would it be dishonored.

And she would not—she would *never*—return to Mizel.

Deliberately, she gathered up the portcomm, and her ignored lunch, entering the house by the kitchen door. The cook was elsewhere; she stowed the tea bottle and the cheese in the coldbox, left the apple on the counter and continued on course, walking briskly down the hall and up the stairs to their apartment.

Not more than two minutes later, she ran lightly down the stairs, jacket on, keys in hand. She let herself out the side door closest to the garages, and was very shortly away, on a heading for Solcintra Port.

. . . ❖ . . .

Daav read the letter twice, not because a single reading had failed of putting him in possession of the pertinent facts, but because the sheer audacity of the thing had left him breathless.

Not to say angry.

"So," he managed at last, lifting his head to face Mr. dea'Gauss decently, "Mizel accuses Daav yos'Phelium of kin-stealing. How refreshing."

In fact, it was, and showed a small glimmer of wit. By naming him *personally* responsible, rather than Clan Korval, Mizel swept half of his pieces from the board and made the game much more equal.

"Alas, there is some merit to their argument," his man of business said gently.

Of course there was. Aelliana Caylon did not belong to Korval. By custom, Daav yos'Phelium had no call upon her. He was not her employer—far the contrary! The world would see that he held her out-of-clan for his own pleasure, while using his *melant'i* as Korval to insure that none would interfere.

How many times had she said that she would not return to Mizel? Nor *should* she return to a clan that valued her so little, to a delm who would make certain to remind her every day that her brother had died on her account.

"Can we stall?" he asked, and only realized that he had spoken in Terran when he saw the incomprehension on Mr. dea'Gauss' face.

"Your pardon, sir. I meant to say: Can we stand against this?"

"Ah." The other man folded his fingers together before his lips, as if he would prevent any unfortunate words from escaping, and gazed thoughtfully down at his desk before finally speaking.

"There are certain...delaying tactics which might be employed, your lordship. I will detail them, if you wish."

Daav considered him. "I would be interested in hearing your estimation of the probable success of these tactics."

"We may delay," Mr. dea'Gauss said promptly and far too certainly, "but we will not prevail. It will be expensive, and—forgive me—your lordship is not in funds."

Daav took a breath.

"Does Pilot Caylon remain steadfast in her refusal of a...formal lifemating?"

"She does not wish to speak of it," Daav said neutrally.

"Ah. If I may then offer a suggestion on what is, most naturally, a most delicate matter..."

"You know that I value your advice, Mr. dea'Gauss. Please, speak plainly."

"Thank you, your lordship. I wonder if a contract marriage might be proposed to the pilot. This would win time—for all—and be...considerably less expensive than entering into a *stall* with Mizel."

It would win time up front, Daav thought. But

when the contract was done, Aelliana would be bound
by law and custom to return to her clan.

That was unacceptable, he thought—and thought
again. A contract marriage would buy them time, yes.
More importantly, it would buy *her* time, to ready
herself and her ship.

And *that* might be a fair line of play.

He rose. "Thank you, Mr. dea'Gauss. I will speak
with Pilot Caylon. Now, if you might produce a very
small *stall* on my behalf. Pray allow Mizel to know
that I am only last evening returned to planet, and beg
another day's grace so that I may craft a formal reply."

Mr. dea'Gauss inclined his head. "Of course, your
lordship."

TWENTY-FIVE

· ·

The pilot's care shall be ship and passengers.
The copilot's care shall be pilot and ship.
—From the Duties Roster of the Pilots Guild

MR. PEL'KANA WAS PLAINLY DISTRESSED. NO, THE PILOT
had left no word. He had brought her a letter—yes,
sir, Mizel's seal—brought the letter to her in the
garden. She was deep in her work; had he known it,
he would never have disturbed her, but she had left
no instructions, and—an express message. He had
followed House protocol...

"Of course," Daav soothed. "You did exactly as you
ought, Mr. pel'Kana. But I wonder, did it seem the
letter disturbed her?"

"Truly, sir, she scarcely regarded it. She took it
in hand, but did not even glance at the mark, and
thanked me for bringing it. I asked if she wished for
anything else, but she said she was well-provisioned
and dismissed me. I—Cook and I were in the back
room, inventorying...neither of us heard her come
in, or leave. She left no message in the house base;
the garage reported her car out..."

"I see," Daav said, keeping his voice calm and his face noncommittal. "Doubtless it slipped her mind; she is sometimes forgetful of commonplaces when she is at work. I have no doubt she'll be back with us soon, never thinking that we would have missed her. Thank you, Mr. pel'Kana."

His butler hesitated.

"She is a fine lady, sir," he offered tentatively, "gracious and sweet-tempered. Staff is pleased to serve her."

Well, here is a recommendation! Daav thought. First, Mr. dea'Gauss and now Mr. pel'Kana. Aelliana conquers wherever she goes.

"Indeed, she is a fine lady," Daav answered. "To my mind, there is none finer."

Mr. pel'Kana bowed.

"Sir," he murmured. "Will you wish to sit for Prime meal, or—"

"I will wait, I think, until Pilot Caylon has returned," he said smoothly, as if he had no doubt that she would do so, and soon.

"Of course, sir," Mr. pel'Kana said, and went away.

Alas, it appeared that Daav had been unreasonably optimistic in his assessment. Hours passed and Aelliana did not return, nor did she send any message. In order that the servants not be subjected to his increasingly disordered state, he retired to his apartment, where he paced, and searched the house base for any message she might have left for him that may have gotten misfiled. When he tired of that, he humiliated himself by checking her closet, and so found that her jacket was gone, which comforted him not one bit.

Sitting down at his worktable, he tried to calm

himself with carving, but his thoughts wandered so that he was a danger to his own fingers, and soon set the knife aside.

He went out onto the balcony where only this morning they had shared breakfast and she had outlined her plans. A pleasant day it had seemed she intended, before the arrival of Mizel's letter.

Mizel's *damned* letter, of which he had found no trace, though he had found her portcomm and the empty envelope on the desk, with the cards she had written out that morning.

Mizel had threatened her; he was more certain of that than he was of his next breath. The shape of the threat scarcely mattered; it had been enough to send her flying out of their house without a word to any who might try to prevent her, without even a message for him in the house base, explaining—explaining...

What?

That she was taking her ship and fleeing, refusing both the dominion of Mizel and Liad? Or that she was returning to her clan, hostage to his honor?

He hoped for the former, if, indeed, she *had* left him. If it were the latter...

...he could not abide it, if she had returned to her clan in order to protect him, and he became yet another stick for her delm to beat her with.

The racket of the night birds mocked him. He went back inside and resumed pacing.

To leave, without so much as a word... He thought to bring up the departure log from the port feed, but froze with his fingers on the keys, certain that his heart would break, if he found *The Luck* gone; and nothing proven, if she were still at dock.

He thought then that he would call Mizel, but refrained from that mad start, as well. In his current state of mind, he would only worsen a desperate situation. Any calls should rightly be made by dea'Gauss, to whom Mizel at least must speak on the subject of an open complaint. Daav yos'Phelium had no right to speak to anyone enclosed by Mizel's honor, and an attempt to do so could be shown as harassment.

It was past midnight when, nerves exhausted, he at last sat down in the reading chair. With nothing more useful than a cat to occupy him, he tried to think what he would do, if Aelliana were well and truly gone from him.

She was his lifemate. If she had lifted, intending to make her own life, still he might ease her way. If she would not take his money, she might yet accept work sent to her through Korval channels. He would need to be careful of her pride, but he need not despair of being some use to her.

If she had returned to Mizel, the opportunity to honor her fitly was . . . much more difficult. He supposed he might commission Mizel assassinated, which would be the best service he might render her . . .

Across the room, the door to their apartment opened.

"Daav?"

Aelliana stopped, staring at him, huddled in the chair with Lady Dignity, his face etched with—

"*Van'chela*, are you *weeping*?"

She moved forward, and he snapped to his feet, dropping the cat unceremoniously to the floor.

"Aelliana..." His voice was hoarse. "Aelliana, where have you been?"

"At the port," she said, sweeping toward him. Such grief; it must—no, surely there was no ill news from Anne?

"What's amiss?" she demanded and took hold of his arm.

Agony scorched her; fear froze her. She gasped and snatched her hand away, staring up into his face.

"dea'Gauss," he said, and for once his voice was neither calm nor steady. "dea'Gauss had received a letter from Mizel, demanding your joyous return to clan and kin, else Daav yos'Phelium would be revealed before Council as a kin-stealer. I came home, and there had been another letter from Mizel, which precipitated your headlong flight from our house..."

"You thought I'd left you," she said, disbelieving. "Daav..."

Deliberately, she stepped forward, slipped her arms around his waist and pressed her body against his, trying to warm him, trying to *force* him to feel her love for him. She put her forehead against his shoulder, shivering with his fear.

"*Van'chela*, I would never go away from you without at least leaving a message!"

His hands came lightly 'round her waist. He sighed and some of the frightful tension left his body.

"And yet," he said softly, "you did just that."

Yes, she thought guiltily, she had done just that. So focused upon her own necessities that she had not thought of his, or what he might think—a letter from Mizel arrives, which surely Mr. pel'Kana would have told him, and Aelliana flies. Absent a message, even setting aside his own dire letter, what else was he to think, having heard her say time and again that she would not return to Mizel?

"I'm sorry," she whispered the Terran phrase against his shoulder. She raised her hand to his cheek. "Daav, please forgive me; I never meant to cause you a moment's care. I swear to you now that I will never leave you; I love you too well."

One of his hands left her waist. He stroked her hair back from her face.

"It is forgiven; it is forgotten," he whispered. "Aelliana..." He cleared his throat. "What were you about at the port?"

"A tale hangs there," she said, "which might be better heard sitting down."

He released her immediately. She stepped back, keeping a grip on his hand and pulled him back onto the reading chair.

"Sit," she murmured, and when he had done so, she sat across his lap, leaning companionably against him. He was so *cold*; she was desperate to warm him.

"Mizel's letter to me was something like your own," she murmured. "I had been too long absent from duty and therefore commanded to return to my natural place. It was also noted that I held free title to a ship, and to a business, both of which I would be required to relinquish to the clan. I could thereafter expect to receive my proportionate share of any profit realized from either."

She felt a snarl of anger from Daav, which was better at least than the cold.

"Yes," she said, comfortably settling her head against his shoulder. "It was very stupid, for of course I had to act in my ship's best defense, whereupon I went to the port, *van'chela*, in order to see Jon dea'Cort."

"One wonders—why did your mind turn to Jon?"

"You'll recall that he holds a note for the repair and installation of the nav-comp units."

"Ah, yes, so he does. Did you pay him, then?"

"Pay him?" She raised her head to look into face. "*Van'chela*, I fear you have become overtired. I cannot afford to redeem that note. No, I asked Jon to put a lien against *The Luck*."

Delight shot through them. Daav threw back his head and laughed.

"Yes, of course you did!" he gasped, when he was able to speak at all. "And Jon was pleased to comply, I assume?"

"Not precisely at first," she confessed. "But once I had made him familiar with the case, he was eager to assist in any way that he could. We went to his woman of business—and it was there that time began to slide away from me, *van'chela*, for the matter was not as simple to effect as it was to envision. Additionally, there were some points upon which Jon stood adamant, and still other complications introduced by his *qe'andra*. Did you know that a ship must be inspected and certified before a third-party lien can be set against it?"

"Actually, I did, but only because Mr. dea'Gauss does insist upon explaining these matters to me as we go along."

Aelliana laughed softly. "Well, I wish *I* had known! However, it was all eventually done, signed, and filed. After, we fetched Trilla and Mistress Apel and all went to find something to eat, which I see now that I should not have done—"

"No." He raised a hand and put his fingers lightly over her lips. "A call would have sufficed. Had I only known that you were with Jon and not lifted for the Out..."

"Without my copilot?"

"The ship must come first, for the pilot."

"So it must," Aelliana agreed, and added the phrase she had lately learnt from Anne. "But there is not only one way to skin a cat."

Daav laughed. "So I learn. Your copilot, I am sad to report, is a lackwit."

"No, that I cannot allow. My copilot had other matters to concern him. How does Mr. dea'Gauss suggest we respond to this absurd charge of kin-stealing?"

"Mr. dea'Gauss is inclined to believe that Mizel can carry the day, does it come to that. He advises that I propose contract to you, Aelliana, which buys us more time together, all by Code and custom."

"Contract?" she repeated, around a sudden gone feeling in her stomach. "But—that merely puts off the inevitable! When the contract is fulfilled, I will be required to return to Mizel." She shook her head.

"He cannot have thought the matter through. The better solution is for us to cry lifemates, pay Mizel its price, and sign the lines."

A rush of emotion so powerful she could scarcely hold onto her own soul swept 'round her in joyous chaos.

"You had, I thought," Daav murmured, "no wish to be Korval."

"Nor do I," she answered warmly, "and I shall doubtless make many bitter errors. However, it appears that I must have Korval, if I am to attain Daav, and so I accept the handicap, if you can accept my ignorance."

"You are not ignorant," he told her. He touched her cheek with fingers that trembled. "I say to you, Aelliana Caylon, that your solving this day—rather, your solving of yesterday!—is masterful. Only consider Korval your ship and you shall do very well for all of us!"

She laughed and shook her head.

"Truly, Daav, it was all I could think to do!"

"Your instincts," he said solemnly, "are good."

He tipped his head, and she felt a returning flutter of fear, paired uneasily with doubt.

"Tell me true, Aelliana, for I would not see you trapped: Do you think that you may bear it?"

"Bear it?" she repeated. "Since the first time we flew together, I had wanted nothing but to sit board with you, always. If Korval is the ship we have to fly, then—better together than apart."

She felt his pride in her, and a certain feeling of awe, which, she thought hotly, would never do.

She reached up to take hold of the long tail of his hair, pulling his face down to hers.

"Kiss me," she commanded.

TWENTY-SIX

. . . .

> Balance must be maintained in all things. Debts
> must be paid promptly and in full.
> —From the Liaden Code of Proper Conduct

"GOOD MORNING, MR. DEA'GAUSS. I HOPE I FIND YOU
well?"

There were in Daav's office, downstairs, he in the
chair and she standing behind, both within range of
the screen.

Mr. dea'Gauss inclined his sleek head. "Good
morning, your lordship; my lady. I am perfectly well,
I thank you."

"Excellent," Daav murmured. "Please forgive me
for accosting you in this uncivilized manner. My only
excuse is that we are summoned in an hour to Lady
yo'Lanna's side, and I have something rather urgent
for you to undertake on Korval's behalf."

"Of course, your lordship. I stand ready to assist,
as ever."

"I will be brief. Pilot Caylon has found a simple
solution to our dilemma of yesterday, sir. She suggests

that she and I sign as lifemates before the world, and thus place Mizel beyond distress."

Mr. dea'Gauss blinked, and raised his eyes to Aelliana's.

"Yes," she told him, with a smile. "It must be so, Mr. dea'Gauss. If you please."

"Few things which I have undertaken in the service of Korval have pleased me so much, my lady. I will, of course, make this my first priority." He gave a seated bow. When he had straightened again, he looked to Daav.

"Korval will offer the life-price of a first class pilot, and a scholar expert?"

Aelliana stirred, meaning to say that it was too much; she had been a scholar expert during her whole adult life. Had matters fallen otherwise, she supposed she would have remained a scholar expert until Mizel's Ring passed and the new delm had made her a whore.

Daav inclined his head. "Korval seeks to place value appropriately. We have no reason to stint Mizel and every reason to be generous."

"Very good," Mr. dea'Gauss murmured. "This business ought to take no more than a few hours. It is perfectly possible that I will have the concluded contract in hand this afternoon."

"We will come to you," Daav said, "when Lady yo'Lanna releases us. Pilot Caylon had been wanting to visit the shops in any case."

Oh, had I? Aelliana frowned down at the top of his head, which was as helpful as one might expect. When she looked back to the screen it seemed to her that Mr. dea'Gauss was smiling.

"Very good, your lordship," he said. "I will not to work immediately. Good morning, my lady."

"Good morning, Mr. dea'Gauss," she said.

The screen went dark.

"Why do I want to visit the shops in Solcintra?" Aelliana asked.

Daav spun 'round in his chair and smiled up at her.

"Why, to purchase a dress worthy of Lady Kareen's formal gather, of course! I advise that you place yourself entirely into Eyla dea'Lorn's hands."

Aelliana sighed lightly.

"Who is Eyla dea'Lorn and how shall I find her?"

"She is an artist, and I will guide you to her, directly we have concluded our business with Mr. dea'Gauss." He tipped his head, his smile broadening into a grin.

"Where will you wish to go for our honey-trip, Aelliana? The mountains or the sea?"

"Do you know?" she said reflectively. "I think I had considered the trip to Avontai our honey-trip. Though I should," she admitted, "like to see an ocean."

Daav's grin twisted a bit. "Have you never been to the sea?"

"No, never," she said, and touched his cheek, reading ebullience, relief, delight... "I was waiting for you to take me there, you see."

"Then I shall," he answered more seriously than perhaps the moment warranted, and came to his feet.

"Come, let us collect your guest-gift and be on our way! It will never do to be late!"

She eyed him.

"Are we in danger of being late?" she asked.

"Not if I drive like a pilot," he answered, looking down at her quizzically.

"Drive like a Scout," Aelliana whispered, and stretched up on her toes to kiss him.

· · · · 🟐 · · · ·

"Aelliana Caylon Clan Mizel." She straightened and looked boldly into Lady yo'Lanna's face, offering the bouquet of gloan-roses and gladoli they had gathered from Jelaza Kazone's gardens.

"Please accept a small token, ma'am, to commemorate our first meeting."

"I thank you." Lady yo'Lanna received the bouquet into her hands, and gazed at it for a long moment.

"Gladoli were my friend Chi's favorite flower," she murmured. "I have always been partial to gloan-roses. It is well-chosen."

"I had good advice," Aelliana said, and Lady yo'Lanna smiled.

"Of course you did," she said, and glanced aside with a smile that could only be said to be sardonic.

"Daav, it is good to see you among my guests once more. I think you know everyone who has come. Please do me the favor of reacquainting yourself, while I make Scholar Caylon known to all."

He bowed, of course; there was nothing else he might decently do.

"Certainly, ma'am. Is there anyone in particular you would like to have drowned?"

She appeared to give the question serious consideration, head tipped to one side, and eyes dwelling on the flowers she held. "No, I thank you. I believe that today I am in charity with all the world."

He bowed again. Lady yo'Lanna slipped her hand through Aelliana's arm. She cast him a single look

over her shoulder from wide green eyes as she was
led away, and he smiled as if he were perfectly comfortable with the arrangements.

He was not, to say true, *completely* comfortable with
the arrangements, but that had more to do with his
desire to be private with his lady, rather than sharing
her among a dozen.

"How long," asked a voice at his shoulder, "is that
going to continue, young Korval?"

Daav turned to confront Delm Guayar, Clonak's
father, coincidentally Lady yo'Lanna's brother.

"Good morning, sir. As long as your lady sister desires,
I should think, but surely not upwards of a day or two."

"Pfft!" Guayar frowned sternly. "The last time we
met, I did you a good turn, sir. Do you intend to
repay me by coming lack-witted and tedious?"

"Of course not! I hope to repay you properly in
kind. Is there a bit of news I might drop delicately
into one certain ear alone for you?"

Guayar considered him.

"I know what ails you," he said at last. "You haven't
any wine." He slipped his arm companionably through
Daav's and turned him toward the center of the garden.
"Come, let us rectify that immediately. While we are
on our way to the wine table, you may tell me how
long you intend to allow the enchanting pilot to style
herself 'Mizel.'"

"As it happens," Daav said slowly, "Mr. dea'Gauss
is currently in negotiation. We hope for a speedy, and
joyous, resolution."

Guayar inclined his head.

"It relieves me to see you moving to consolidate
your strengths," he murmured. "I counsel, if it does

not offend, that Korval can afford to be generous. When one wishes to acquire a jewel beyond price . . ."

"I concur," Daav said.

Perhaps he spoke a bit too sharply, for Guayar inclined his head and said no more.

They began to meet other guests. Daav made his bow to Lord Andresi, another of his mother's staunch allies, and to Nasil tei'Gasta Clan Idvantis. Seeing him on Guayar's arm, neither detained him long, and soon they were comfortable again, just the two of them.

"How does Clonak go on?" Daav asked.

Guayar moved his shoulders. "I assume he thrives, as the Scouts have not notified me of his attaining a less satisfactory condition. One never does hear from Scouts when they are at duty, you know. Your mother and I had used to speak of it, often."

"Indeed," Daav said, properly chagrined. "One might suppose I would be accustomed to that circumstance by now."

"When the heart is anxious, the mind grows forgetful," Guayar murmured, and slid him a sidewise look. "In my experience."

Daav inclined his head.

"Ah, at last! The wine table! Let us turn you up sweet, young Korval. Have some of Ilthiria's canary; it is excellent."

He took the older gentleman's advice, finding it good, as it so often was, and mingled with the guests who lingered in the area, pausing to speak with Thodelm Wespail regarding the latest vagaries of the market in aleut and the sudden popularity of *vya* among the Terran ports.

When he next glanced about him, Guayar was gone.

. . . ⚙ . . .

Aelliana and Lady yo'Lanna met quite a number of people in the course of their unhurried stroll. Aelliana had done her best to commit faces to memory, as she would memorize the faces that filled each new class. Most pleasantly, they had spoken with Len Sar Anaba Clan Gabrian, who was a trader, and knew Er Thom well; and exchanged bows with Lady Sera tel'Kai Clan Vakmont. Vakmont, Aelliana told herself, with a certain feeling of pleasure for knowing it, was High House.

"Do you mean to keep Korval on your string very long?" Lady yo'Lanna asked.

Aelliana felt her temper spark, and took a careful breath.

"Ma'am, I fear you are misinformed," she said quietly. "Daav had said you were his mother's best and oldest friend, so I have no hesitation in telling you that he and I are natural lifemates. We stand each at the side of the other because we must. *That* lifemating, ma'am, cannot be undone."

"I had wondered if that were the case, given the clan's history," the lady said smoothly. "But there are other matters, Pilot, which may only be captured correctly by paper and ink. I cannot imagine why Chi's son has not yet cemented his advantage."

"He has been convenable and patient," Aelliana murmured. "There were those things which I needed to find of myself, for myself, before I would allow even discussion of contracts."

"Ah. And now?"

Aelliana smiled. "Mr. dea'Gauss is speaking with Mizel now."

Lady yo'Lanna did not go so far as to smile, though she did press her lips together for a brief moment.

"That is excellent news," she said. "May I be the very first to wish you happy."

"The contract is not set yet," Aelliana protested.

The Lady laughed softly. "My dear Pilot Caylon, with the dea'Gauss in negotiation, success cannot be far behind." She used her chin to point at a man in a very fine tunic, coming toward them up the path.

"Now, here we come upon my good friend Etgora. You will doubtless find him pleasant enough, but pray be aware that he will look first at your rings and calculate from there."

Aelliana glanced down at her hands. She wore her Jump pilot's cluster and the silver puzzle ring she had from her grandmother.

"I have no shame in my rings, ma'am," she said composedly.

"No," Lady yo'Lanna said, sweeping forward, "nor should you."

· · · · ❖ · · · ·

". . . it was Plemia lost an elder pilot in the Out," yo'Taler was saying. "The most curious affair imaginable. She had delivered her cargo, and taken on the return, went onto the port for a bite and a glass—and never returned to her ship. It was like the port swallowed her up."

"The ship?" Daav asked.

"Ah, there's Korval! No, sir, you'll rejoice to hear that the ship was unharmed. It paid the docking fees until its account ran dry, which is when Port Admin noticed something amiss, and by then the pilot's trail was cold. No one came forward with her ID or a ship key, or any likely tale for taking what they knew was aboard. Nor could anyone recall seeing the pilot after she left with another, before port middle night."

"She might as easily have fallen into the lake," Wespail murmured. "Pilots do get drunk."

"Did anyone find her companion?" someone asked.

"Yes. And he was as astonished as any other to learn that she had vanished. He was employed by the yard where her ship was docked and had come to tell her that there might be need of a rebalancing. Left her at the gate, is what he told the proctors, and none to disbelieve him."

"The pirates are getting bold," Len Sar Anaba said. "Even here in Solcintra, there are cargoes going missing as a regular thing—from beneath the noses of trained guards! Down in the Low Port, it's said that the Juntavas rules all. Pilots are in particular peril, and many never return to their ships."

Daav looked up, warned by a sense he had not known he had.

Aelliana and Lady yo'Lanna were walking toward their little group, escorted by Delm Etgora. He murmured an excuse and moved out of the intent knot of discussants.

"Daav, the gardens are quite beautiful!" Aelliana greeted him, abandoning Lady yo'Lanna's arm for his.

"Yes, they are very fine. Glavda Empri wins awards every year, for its artful and pleasing displays."

Aelliana moved her hand, showing him Etgora.

"This is Hin Ber del'Fordan, who has the honor to be Etgora."

"We have met," Daav said, giving his fellow delm

the courtesy of the bow between equals. "It has been some time, sir."

"It has. You are looking well, young Korval. Pilot Caylon, please, call upon me at any time."

"Thank you, sir," Aelliana said.

"Yes, all very well," Lady yo'Lanna said. "Etgora, I am thirsty. Pray find me a glass of the canary."

"Certainly, Ilthiria." He inclined his head and led her to the wine table.

Aelliana sighed, and wilted a little on Daav's arm.

"How do you go on?" Daav asked her. "Do you wish to leave?"

"Not just yet," she said. "We must give Mr. dea'Gauss time to work! But I would like a glass of wine. It is a vast garden, Daav! And I think I must have walked every step of it."

"In that case, you must, by all means, have wine, and perhaps even a small plateful of food. Let us see what delights are laid for us."

As he turned with her toward the buffet, he saw several pairs of eyes following, not him, but her.

Aelliana conquers all, he thought, and only just managed to keep his smile to himself.

TWENTY-SEVEN

. . . .

Nothing is as easy as it looks.

—Terran Proverb

MR. DEA'GAUSS WAS NOT HAPPY; AELLIANA KNEW IT
immediately they entered his office. *How* she knew
it—well, likely the knowledge was Daav's, whose fingers
were interlaced with hers.

"Your lordship. My lady. May I bring you refreshment?"

"Thank you, no," Daav said gently, as if the apprehension she felt from him did not exist. "I think
you had better just tell us, sir. Has Mizel refused
our offer?"

There was a pause—and a sigh.

"Not . . . precisely, no."

Mr. dea'Gauss moved his hand, showing them chairs,
and did not take his own until they were seated. "Mizel
has produced a . . . counteroffer, your lordship. Quite
an extraordinary counteroffer."

Daav had taken his hand from hers as they were
seated, but Aelliana felt a flutter of hope on her
own behalf. A counteroffer. Surely, that was only

339

expected? Contracts were after all about negotiation and compromise.

"If they are still talking, then there is hope," Daav murmured, in echo of her thought. "With what have they countered?"

Mr. dea'Gauss drew his notepad to him and touched the screen.

"They ask . . ." He cleared his throat. "They ask high for the life-price, though had that been the only obstacle I might have counseled your lordship to accept, in order to have all done soonest. They ask, also, for the life-price of a nadelm, and they—" Mr. dea'Gauss looked up, but it was her eyes he sought, not Daav's.

"They *demand*, my lady, that you return to your clan-house until the negotiations with Korval are complete."

"No!" She raised her hand, fingers spread. "That I refuse."

Mr. dea'Gauss looked even more unhappy.

"There is custom behind it, my lady. Mizel's *qe'andra* informs me that you had been called home by your delm ere this negotiation had begun. You are thus constrained, as a daughter of Mizel . . ."

"I will *not* return to that house!"

Panic clawed at her throat. That house, with Ran Eld behind every door, and her mother, with his ghost in her eyes! It would happen again—her life would be torn from her, the House would wear her down, they would demand—demand duty done, demand that she give Daav over, demand—

"No! I will not go back there to be ground down and destroyed! I will not be a prisoner to Mizel's incompetence! I have appointments—engagements! I—"

"Aelliana."

Calm and beloved, his voice. She shook her hair away from her eyes, startled to find herself standing and halfway to the office door. Her legs were shaking and her stomach was . . . quite unsettled. It came to her that she was weeping.

"Aelliana."

Daav held his hands out, palms up, offering himself to her.

"We will find the route, Pilot. I swear it."

Shakily, she stepped forward, put her hands in his, fully expecting to feel the force of his anger, but instead there was only and truly—

Calm.

She closed her eyes.

"Yes," he murmured. "Take what you need."

The panic wilted before this encompassing calmness. She felt peaceful, and alert . . .

"Mr. dea'Gauss," she heard Daav say.

"Your lordship."

"Korval perfectly comprehends Mizel's natural wish to guard the well-being of one of its precious children. Further, it is Korval's wish, as of course it is Mizel's, that there be no coercion or threat brought to any of the principals of these talks. Pilot Caylon will therefore remove from Jelaza Kazone—"

"No," she whispered, her fingers tightening on his, but he went on as if he had not heard her.

"She will remove from Jelaza Kazone, to Trealla Fantrol. If that discomforts Mizel, then to Glavda Empri. If yo'Lanna finds no favor with Mizel, then Pilot Caylon will go to Healer Hall in Chonselta City, remanded to the specific care of Master Healer Kestra.

In no case will Pilot Caylon be a prisoner, held to her rooms, or forbidden to have visitors. She will be free to go about her business, honoring her appointments and her social engagements as an adult and fully responsible person."

"I will see it done, your lordship."

"Thank you, Mr. dea'Gauss," Daav murmured. "Aelliana?"

"The price of a nadelm," she murmured. "It's blood money. For Ran Eld."

There was a startled silence. Mr. dea'Gauss spoke first.

"Are you certain, my lady? It was told to me that Mizel named you as nadelm."

"She did not," Aelliana said, daring to take her hands away from Daav's and approaching the table.

Daav slipped a hand under her elbow and helped her regain her seat before taking his own. He and the accountant shared a troubled glance.

"If—that is a dangerous precedent," Mr. dea'Gauss said slowly. "It imperils the future negotiations of all, and muddles the lines between restitution made in Balance of a death, and the price paid to adopt a member of one clan into the ranks of another. As a Master of the Accountants Guild, I—forgive me, your lordship—I cannot allow that precedent to be set."

"I understand entirely, Mr. dea'Gauss, and I would not ask it of you." Daav sighed.

"Thank you, your lordship." He sighed, and leaned back in his chair, pushing the notepad aside.

"Mizel's *qe'andra* allows me to know that Mizel will deal in earnest when Korval's good intentions are shown."

Aelliana swallowed. "I must remove from our house before Mizel will begin to talk?"

"That is the essence, my lady."

Aelliana closed her eyes.

"What do they have to gain?" she whispered.

Mr. dea'Gauss cleared his throat.

"If I may venture a guess . . . I believe that it may be that news of the attachment between yourself and his lordship has come to Mizel's ears."

"They hope that separation will disorder us," Daav said. "Thus we will not negotiate as well or as carefully as we should, and Mizel will achieve an advantage."

Mr. dea'Gauss inclined his head. "That is my belief, yes."

"Well, then." Daav put his hand over hers on the table. "We depend upon you to keep us careful, Mr. dea'Gauss, and to guard us from all harm."

TWENTY-EIGHT

. . . .

The guest is sacrosanct. The welfare and comfort of the guest will be first among the priorities of the House, for so long as the guest shall bide.

—Excerpted from the Liaden
Code of Proper Conduct

OF COURSE, MIZEL HAD CHOSEN THE HEALERS. AELLIANA supposed she ought to be relieved, that they had chosen at all.

She flew *The Luck* to Chonselta solo, and even on so short a lift bitterly felt the lack of his calm, solid presence in the other chair. But it would not have done, Mizel's further condition being that she should have no congress with Daav yos'Phelium. If they were chance met, as say, at Kareen yos'Phelium's formal gather, some weeks from now, they were to bow with appropriate courtesy and separate themselves as quickly as possible.

And it would not have been any easier, Aelliana thought, sealing *The Luck* and walking down the gantry with her bag over one shoulder, to leave him at Chonselta Port than it had been to leave him—at home.

"Three days, at most," he had murmured into her hair, as they embraced for what she would *not* think of as the last time. "Now that this is begun, it should end quickly. I'll wager you'll be back home well before Kareen's gather, and will not have the occasion to impose upon Lady yo'Lanna after all."

Aelliana smiled slightly as she came to the ground and walked on in the direction of the main thorough-fare. Lady yo'Lanna had immediately fallen in with the suggestion that Aelliana's dress be delivered to Glavda Empri, with Eyla dea'Lorn, too. Aelliana would then take herself there for dressing. "For," Daav had said, with great common sense, "you would not want to crush your skirts in the pilot's chair."

She came out of the yard into a side street. Ahead, the sign for a taxi stand glowed gently against the afternoon light.

Scarcely had she touched the call switch than a car pulled up, back door open.

"Service, Pilot?"

"Yes, thank you." She tossed her bag inside and slid in after it.

"Healer Hall, if you please."

She was shown into a side parlor, with assurances that the guide to her quarters would be with her very soon, and left alone. Aelliana sighed, put her bag on the seat of the nearest chair and wandered over to the table. There were several decanters and glasses set ready, but she did not wish for wine. Continuing her prowl, she came to a bookshelf scantily filled with old novels and out-of-date periodicals. She flipped through them, and had just decided that she ought to choose one of the garden magazines to while her time when the door opened and a woman whose face was immediately familiar to her entered the room and bowed.

"Kestra, Master Healer," she said briskly, and straightened with a smile. "Pilot Caylon, how good it is to see you looking so well..." Grey brows pulled sharply together.

It seemed to Aelliana that the Healer looked past her face, indeed, that her gaze was fixed slightly above her head.

"Yes," Kestra said, considerably less brisk, "it is wonderful to see you looking so *exceptionally* well. This is beyond anything we had dared to hope for. How does your lifemate go on, if an old woman might inquire?"

Aelliana tipped her head. "He fares very well by my accounting. However, my eyesight is not so sharp as your own. It may interest you to know that it has not been given him to... experience me fully."

"No? But surely—" The Healer sighed sharply and moved her hands in a gesture vaguely akin to *forgive* in hand-talk. "I am but seeing half the pattern. With the wholeness before me, I might see the flaw and the flow, but even then—perhaps not. There is a great deal of flash and brangle about your partner, which makes it difficult—but there! You are not here to satisfy my vulgar curiosities, though you must permit me to say again that it is gratifying to behold you thus. I had hoped that our work would give you some ease. That you have been able to take what we began and unfurl your wings so far..." She bowed again, gently, as one who has beheld a wonder.

"Thank you, Pilot."

"Surely, it is I who should thank you. Had you not made a beginning, I should—I should not have been able to build upon your work." And, she added silently, she would not have been made privy to the complex, tricksy creature who was Daav yos'Phelium, without whom—

"We are both in debt to the other," Master Kestra said.

"And so the debts cancel," Aelliana said, and inclined her head. "When this current business is done, if you like, you may come to us at Jelaza Kazone, to view the whole of the pattern."

"That at least would satisfy an old woman's curiosity. However, you remind me, most gently, of our current business. Allow me to show you to your lodging." She turned with a sweep of her hand and crossed the room to the door. Aelliana stretched her legs, snatched up her bag, and followed.

"The Hall Master felt that you and those of our order would find more comfort if you were at some remove from the house. We hope that you will find it worthy. It has its own entrance onto the street, so that your visitors may come to you without recourse to our doorkeeper; and you may come and go about your business as it may be necessary. It is, admittedly, not convenient to the dining facilities in the main house, but there is a small and well-stocked kitchen. We can of course provide companionship. The guest need only ask."

Master Kestra produced a key from her sleeve and used her chin to point at the stone cottage nestled in the far corner of the Hall's inner garden. Flowers surrounded it, and a small tree with long trailing branches covered with pale pink flowers half-concealed the doorway.

Aelliana paused, and took a breath against the tightness in her chest. The breeze brought her the sweet scent of flowers and a faint, musical tinkle.

"Wind chimes," Master Kestra said. "We can remove them if they annoy. If this arrangement is not convenient to you, there is an apartment available within the house..."

"No, it is—please do not remove the chimes on my account," Aelliana said quickly. "As for the situation itself—I think that I will like it extremely. I have been—accustomed to having a garden, of late."

"Perhaps you should look inside before making a final decision," Master Kestra said, preceding her up the two shallow steps and sliding the key into the reader on the door.

There came a small beep, the door opened and the Healer stepped back to allow Aelliana to enter.

It was no bigger than their private apartment at Jelaza Kazone: a single large room divided into three areas by painted screens. The kitchen was small, but, as promised, well-stocked; the bedroom comfortable, the 'fresher unit slightly cramped but entirely usable. In the main room, a desk sat near the window; behind, an upholstered chair, a chaise and a double sofa were grouped companionably by a low table.

Another table, near the bookshelves, held a comm unit and an entertainment screen. The floor was covered with woven jute over which other rugs had been deployed with haphazard charm. At the very back of the room, beyond the bookshelves, was a short hallway. Aelliana opened the door at its far end, and stepped out onto a thin porch, three stone steps above street level. A modest hedge and a wooden gate separated her from the public walkway.

She closed the door, locked it and returned to Master Kestra, waiting patiently by the window.

"Of companionship," she said, "I thank the Hall for its care. One would welcome a cat, if possible. The house—"

She looked about her once more, pleased and in some way soothed. "The house will do excellently." She bowed gratitude to the house. "I thank you. Please convey my pleasure and gratitude to the Hall Master."

"We are delighted to hear that the guest is pleased," the Healer said, with no noticeable irony. She extended her hand. "If you please, Pilot?"

Aelliana put her palm against the other woman's soft flesh. Perhaps she felt a slight tingle of energy; perhaps it was merely her fancy. Whichever, it was only a heartbeat before Kestra broke contact.

"Felicitations," she murmured.

Aelliana frowned. "Felicitations?"

"Indeed. Korval and all who wish them well must be gladdened to know that the heir has been conceived."

The heir? Aelliana pressed her hand against her breast, recalling Daav, the first day they had shared the tree's bounty, felled by his morsel, and his voice breathless with some exultation that had not been fear: "Surely it has no need to murder me today, and good reason to keep me alive for just a few days more."

She took a hard breath and stared at the Healer, her face so calm and her eyes so knowing.

"Daav had kept fertile," she said stringently, "for he was to have wed. I, however—had no such necessities."

"Ah," Master Kestra inclined her head. "Have you, perchance, eaten of the fruit of Korval's Tree?"

"Yes, certainly. It is able to bypass the safeguards?"

"It is able to do a great many things, apparently, and it is invested in a Korval heir, more than many."

Well, and Daav had told her that, too. She had not thought, not even while she was asking it to engineer some way for them to fully share themselves...

Whether it was at all reasonable, she owned herself annoyed, though not quite utterly horrified. Why couldn't it do as it was asked, she thought irritably, instead of playing mischief with one's sureties and arranging for an heir, too—

She gasped.

"Master Kestra."

"Yes, Pilot?"

"I must ask you to hold this information in the strictest confidence. Tell no one! If Mizel—Mizel will see even more advantage in delay, if it becomes known that I am pregnant beforetime."

Kestra inclined her head. "It is forgotten," she said solemnly.

"I thank you," Aelliana said fervently.

"Is there anything else the guest desires," the Healer asked, "excepting a cat?"

Daav, Aelliana thought, around a knife thrust of longing so intense she thought she might be ill. As pleasant and cozy as it was, she foresaw that the cottage might very soon come to seem vast and echoing.

Forcefully, she put these thoughts behind her and shook her head.

"I thank you," she said to the Healer. "I am well-content."

"Then I will leave you. Please recall that you are welcome in the house, if you care to join us for meals or at another time. There is a list of activities on the house-net."

"Thank you," Aelliana said again, and it was all she could do, to hold the tears decently at bay until Master Kestra had made her bow and departed.

Aelliana closed the door, and made sure it was latched, then leaned her forehead against the friendly wood and allowed the tears to have their way.

Uneasy with the silence, she had found a music feed on the entertainment unit and turned up the volume until it could be heard in the furthermost corner of the little house. She washed her face, arranged the portcomm on the desk, and hung her clothes away in the wardrobe, working methodically and taking care to think only on the task in hand.

Unhappily, she had not brought clothes enough that she would be occupied all evening by hanging them away. She sighed, leaving the green robe draped across the foot of the bed, and went back into the main room. Leaning over the desk, she touched her screen—and jumped at the sound of a firm knock.

The knock came again—from the garden-side door, which meant that her visitor was a Healer—perhaps even the Hall Master, come to see how the guest was faring. It would not do, she told herself sternly, to simply ignore the summons, though she was not at all certain that she wanted company.

She opened the door.

"Well met, Pilot Caylon! The House offers companionship!"

The woman on the step had chocolate brown hair and light blue eyes. She was holding a lanky grey cat stretched across her body from hip to shoulder, one hand supporting the lean belly, the other gripping just beneath the upper legs. The cat's head was against her shoulder. There was something about the long muzzle that suggested at least temporary resignation; the very tippiest tip of the scruffy tail was twitching. Slowly.

Aelliana stepped back. She had, after all, requested a cat.

"Please bring her in," she said hastily, "and put her down before she becomes angry."

"He," the other woman corrected, stepping into the house with a will. "Close the door, or he'll hide in the garden and it will take days to coax him back out."

Aelliana complied, and her visitor placed the cat on the sofa.

"Now, Mouse, behave yourself. Pilot Caylon had specifically desired you."

Mouse, however, having been granted liberty, wasted no time in leaping to the floor and taking refuge beneath the chaise.

The woman sighed and turned to Aelliana, her hands raised chest-high in a gesture that looked like the sign for surrender. Since she was wearing a shirt cut very low over round breasts, the gesture was beguiling—as perhaps it was meant to be. Her smile grew softer as she lowered her hands, and wider as Aelliana followed them to a trim waist.

"He'll come out in a while—whenever it suits him. He'd been living wild in the business district, and not doing a very good job of it. One of the desk workers found him fainting and desperate and brought him to us. He hasn't been here long, and isn't very trusting of people yet." She took a step toward Aelliana, her presence somehow heating the air between them. "My name is Jen ana'Tilesty, Pilot."

"I am pleased to meet you, Healer," Aelliana said, breathing deeply against the sudden warming of her blood. "Thank you for bringing the—for bringing Mouse. I had scarcely expected him so soon."

"The way the house works is that whoever is at liberty takes up the next task in queue. Mouse was at liberty and I was, so here we both are. Master Kestra said you wished companionship."

Companionship. And Master Kestra made sure to send a woman, Aelliana thought, so that the heir's parentage was not for a heartbeat in contention.

"It may be," she said slowly, "that I, in my ignorance, gave Master Kestra faulty information. Certainly, she had offered companionship, and I had said, yes, meaning that I wished for a cat. She may have heard differently, with Healer's ears."

"That's likely," Jen ana'Tilesty said seriously. "Even I can see—well. I'll never be a Master Healer, no matter how much you polish me."

"But you are," Aelliana said, "a Healer."

"I'm a Healer. I teach Empathic Sensuality, and tutor those whose clans don't want them going ignorant to their contract beds."

She had never considered . . . certainly *she* had gone ignorant—desperately so—to her contract bed. Such a tutor might have shielded her from the worst of the damage inflicted by her husband. So much time wasted, thinking that what was happening to her was what everyone endured . . .

"I've stirred up something bad," the other woman said. "Forgive me, Pilot."

"There is nothing to forgive. I was merely remarking to myself that I wished I had known that such persons as you had existed . . . many years ago, now."

"We all learn what we're meant to learn, when the time is ripe for learning," Jen ana'Tilesty said. "You know I exist now, and I'm pleased to offer whatever will ease you."

Aelliana considered her, glanced beyond her to where the cat named Mouse was only a pair of glowing green eyes, underneath the chaise.

"I wonder," she said, looking back to Jen ana'Tilesty's wide-cheeked face, "if you would like a toasted cheese sandwich."

The sandwiches had turned out moderately well. She was, Aelliana thought, gaining some skill on that front. Jen had proved a convivial companion, knowledgeable on subjects which Aelliana scarcely knew existed. After the meal was eaten, they cleaned up the kitchen, saw to the needs of the as-yet-invisible Mouse, and played several rounds of Modes, Aelliana having declined to play cards against a novice.

Just after midnight, they parted amicably on a three-and-three split, with promises on both sides for a rematch. Aelliana had then sought the bed behind the painted screen.

It was a very wide bed; the sheets were chilly; the pillows by turn too soft and too hard. She lay on her back and deliberately closed her eyes, but she was anything but restful. Now that it was quiet, thoughts crowded upon her. The Tree—how could it have circumvented her protection! Worse, could a child born from such unguessable tampering be—well? Or ought it be aborted in favor of a more-regularly-got child?

Alas, her expert on Korval's Tree was beyond her for these next few days—surely no more than a few days!—and that was an unhappy thought, indeed, for it brought to mind precisely the very many ways in which she missed him, and how much she wanted him with her this moment, in this terrible, strange bed, placing his hands thus and his lips so, and doing that particular—

Aelliana snapped up, forcefully pounding the too-hard pillow before curling onto her side. Her blood was hot, now, and she missed him even more for knowing that he would not tonight at least be slipping into bed behind her, curling his long body around hers; his skin so warm, soft over hard, wiry muscle, and his hands so knowing...

She fell at last into an uneasy doze in which it was not Daav but Jen ana'Tilesty who had curled 'round her, and teased her onto her back, offering a round breast to suckle while she guided Aelliana's hands, teaching her—

Unfairly, she woke again, hot and disordered, before the lesson was well completed, and retreated from the bed. Belting her robe around her, she went past the screen and into the common room.

Mouse's eyes still glowed from beneath the chaise.

Aelliana sighed and sat down on the floor, her shoulder against the chaise and her legs curled under her.

"I had used to be a mouse, you know," she murmured. "Utterly craven. I hid from my own reflection and would scarcely have spoken at all, saving that I had students and one must, after all, teach. I thought that my cowardice would save me; but in the long term, it did not answer. Those whom my existence threatened demanded ever more mouselike behavior. Willingly, I gave my strength away, but I was never safe, and I was always—*always* afraid.

"My fear almost killed me, though by then I had been growing bolder. But I had given so much of my strength away...it was a near thing, and I take no credit for my own survival. What I have learned is—mark me now!—life is not safe. Random action threatens us all. The choices we have are between fear and boldness, between joy and terror.

"If at all possible, I believe it is necessary to choose joy. One may survive no longer, nor ever be safe, but one's life will be worth living."

She sighed, and rested her head against the side of the chaise.

"I don't presume to make your choices for you," she told the cat, her eyelids drooping. "I merely offer the fruit of my own experience."

She allowed her eyes to drift shut. It was very quiet in the little house. On *The Luck*, such silence would be horrifying, signaling the loss or malfunction of vital systems. Here...she was very tired, and the silence allowed her to hear quite small sounds, such as the beginning purr of a cat.

Aelliana sighed and settled her head more closely against the upholstery.

When she opened her eyes again, the room was filled with sunlight, her legs were stiff, and a rangy grey cat was curled up snugly asleep in her lap.

TWENTY-NINE

. . . .

Friends are a costly necessity.

—Anonymous

"YOU'RE ABOUT EARLY," ANNE SAID, LOOKING UP FROM her screen.

Daav came up onto the patio and perched on the arm of the chair across from hers.

"It is too glorious a morning to simply lie abed," he told her, earnestly.

Normally, such a performance would have gained him a peal of Anne's ready laughter and a change of subject. This morning, he caught a sharp look and a small shake of the head.

"I'd like to know what's going on in that woman's head," she said, darkly.

That woman, Daav surmised, was Mizel. He sighed.

"She merely wishes to gain the best advantage for her clan. It is what delms do, you know."

"If she wins Korval's annoyance for her clan, what's best there?"

"No, you misapprehend. In the usual way of things Korval and Mizel would have . . . very little to do with each other. Our means are so far apart that it must be so. Once this—very rare—bit of business is done, we will each drop back into our appropriate orbits and scarcely heed the passing of the other. That being the case, Mizel must look to immediate gain."

"Which is to say, cash," Anne said sourly. "Wouldn't there be benefit in alliance?"

"There might have been, but you must recall that it was I who provided the means to expose the nadelm's villainy, leading to his death. An alliance with the murderer of one's son—well! I don't say that I could do it, no matter how much Korval stood to gain."

He leaned forward to glance over the top of her screen. "But, come! What is it that occupies *you* so early on this lovely morning? Not more student work?"

"No, I'm saving that for a treat after lunch," she said seriously. "This morning, I'm sorting applications from universities that want to host a Gallowglass Chair."

"Ah." This was a pet project. When it had eventually borne in upon Anne precisely how much discretionary funding was available to her, as a full adult member of Clan Korval, she had lost no time in setting up a trust to fund a university chair to be filled by scholars who excelled in the teaching of comparative cultures, cultural genetics, or any other of a very short list of diversification studies.

Once she, and more importantly, Mr. dea'Gauss, was satisfied with the terms of the trust, universities galaxywide had been solicited to apply for a grant.

"We have two chairs already in place—at University, of course, and also at Delgado—which is a coup!"

He remembered the excitement generated by the receipt of the application from the University of

Delgado, a catalyst school with a stellar reputation in the academic galaxy.

"What have you now?" he asked. "More than one, else there would be no need to sort."

"Bontemp has applied—a well-established school with a strong cultural diversities component already in place. It seems we'll have them, if they meet the financial test, which I'm certain they will. No, what's interesting is that we have an application from Islington College, which is very small and very...Terran. I can't imagine they'll pass the financials, but—the opportunity! We ought to try to accommodate them...somehow."

"Perhaps a co-op?" Daav murmured.

Anne frowned. "Co-op?"

"Indeed. Perhaps three or four worthy but under-funded institutions of higher learning can between them more than adequately support the Gallowglass Scholar? Might they make a joint application, with the understanding that the scholar would travel between schools?"

"That..." She snatched at her screen and made some rapid notes. "We don't want to muddy the waters around the Gallowglass, but that's a good notion you have there, laddie. Let me think about it a bit."

"Certainly," he said, absurdly pleased to have been of use. "Remember to consult with Mr. dea'Gauss."

"You'd best believe it! That young man's a fountain of ideas."

Since Mr. dea'Gauss was, in fact, a good dozen years Anne's senior, Daav supposed "young man" to be a pleasantry. He therefore smiled and rose, inclining his head slightly.

"As much as I would like to sit here in the sun

with you all day long, I fear that duty calls. Is there a commission I might discharge for you in the city?"

"Not a thing, my dear; thank you for asking. Will you be seeing Mr. dea'Gauss today?"

"We have an appointment after midday," he admitted.

"Fingers crossed he'll have good news for you," Anne said, with another unusually sharp glance up into his face. "If it happens that the news isn't as good as you'd like, you know you can stay here."

All of Korval's houses were open to the delm, of course. Still, it warmed him that she offered—a gesture of sisterhood the like of which he was unlikely to receive from his own sister.

"I know," he said, bending to kiss her cheek. "Thank you."

Eyla dea'Lorn had provided him with several bits of fabric—a slip of misty green silk and a finger-length of silvered lace. These he set out on the board between himself and Master Moonel, and waited while the artist considered them.

"Tell me about her," he said, stroking the lace with a delicate, scarred fingertip.

Daav settled himself on the stool and glanced about the shop. No pretty client room, this, but the Master's own workshop, tools hung to hand, calipers, alembics and scales set out on the tables, amid the bits and pieces that would, soon or late, become one or more of the most sought-after pieces of jewelry on Liad.

"As one looks at her, she seems frail," he said slowly. "Her face is thin, the bones show clearly at her collar, impossibly delicate. I can span her waist with my two hands. Her hair is light brown, shot through with gold, yellow and amber, like a Porthian tapestry. Her eyes—" He leaned forward to touch the bit of foggy silk.

"Her eyes are green, gloriously so; when she is troubled, or very deep in thought, they seem to mist over, like fog shading the ocean.

"When one comes to know her, it is obvious that she is very far from frail. She has strength of purpose enough for the captain of a starship, wit, humor—aye, and a temper. She flies like a Scout and mathematics is her first and truest language." He raised his head, but Moonel was not looking at him. He was sketching something with a bit of chalk onto a torn sheet of dark paper.

"Naturally, Mistress dea'Lorn did not feel that she could safely entrust the details of her design to me. However, she asked me to say that she awaits *your* call, Master."

Moonel did not look up from his sketching, though he was heard to vent a small chuckle.

"It is always a pleasure to speak with Eyla," he murmured. "Will you be wanting a ring?"

"I think not. She holds two—a Jump pilot's cluster and an old silver puzzle ring. More would overpower her hands."

"She will wear the cluster, of course," Moonel murmured, perhaps to himself. "We may echo." The chalk moved once more, delicately, and the Master at last looked up.

"I will undertake it," he stated. "The jewels will be delivered to you in good time. Good-day."

Daav came immediately to his feet and bowed, as novice-to-master.

"Good-day, Master Moonel. I thank you for your favor."

There was, after all, no good news from Mr. dea'Gauss. Korval's counteroffer, reiterating the life-price of a pilot-scholar and a bonus, as that scholar was the author of the ven'Tura Revisions; plus the life price of an accountant, which Mizel might put toward the adoption of an adult to replace the nadelm—Korval's counteroffer was spurned with so little discussion that it must seem that Mizel considered it an insult.

"Mizel's *qe'andra* is not permitted... discretion in the negotiation," Mr. dea'Gauss had murmured. "I have produced another offer, along the lines which your lordship and I had discussed previously. If it is likewise rejected, then we must assume that the desired outcome is that negotiations fail and Pilot Caylon remains as a member of Mizel."

That chilled the blood, that did. Daav sat very still until his heart resumed its normal rhythm and he felt that he might, with some care, manage a breath.

There was no law or custom that dictated that an offer of lifemating must be accepted. After all, a delm must act for the best good of the clan, and to accept an offer that would cripple the clan...

He closed his eyes.

He was a fool. He had depended upon Korval's *melant'i* to win everything; indeed, he had behaved as if everything he wished to accomplish was already so, as if the laws and custom of Liad were so many inconvenient trivialities. To have high-handedly removed Aelliana from her clanhouse, thereby making her delm his enemy...worse than a fool. Yet, what else could he have done? Out of the question to allow her to remain, newly Healed, and vulnerable. He might have—he supposed he might have prevailed upon the Healers to aid them, pled his case at once and—

No. She would not have accepted him; she would not—*they* would not—have known the extent of their bond, the depth of their love. They must have had that time with each other...

"Your lordship?"

He started, reminded that he was not by any means alone. Carefully, he took a breath, and opened his eyes.

"Your pardon, Mr. dea'Gauss."

The other man took a breath at least as careful, and inclined his head. "We will prevail, your lordship."

Of course they would. As long as Mizel preferred to play games, there existed the possibility of a win. It was, therefore, imperative that Mizel not be brought to the point of uttering the single syllable that would kill all hope, forever.

No.

"I repose every faith in you, Mr. dea'Gauss," he murmured, which was true. He rose and bowed. "Thank you for your efforts on Korval's behalf—on *my* behalf and that of my pilot."

Mr. dea'Gauss rose from behind his desk and returned the bow.

"It is my very great honor, your lordship."

Daav shifted in his chair in one of Ongit's private inner parlors. He had chosen one of the smaller, unthemed rooms for this *tête-à-tête*. For the business he intended to negotiate, a thunderstorm or a waterfall would only be a distraction.

Alas, his guest was late; verging, indeed, on very late. Normally, he might not have minded, but in the extended solitude it was far too easy to wonder after Aelliana, her probable state of mind, and what, if any, damage might come to her through their continued separation. It was she, after all, who bore the weight of the gift. She—he had no idea how much she depended upon the receipt of his "signal"; if such contact nourished her in some manner that only their separation would reveal.

Based on his own experience last night, he doubted that she had slept—but there! He was forgetting where she guested. Most assuredly, the Healers would have provided comfort, to the limit of the Hall's considerable ability. He hoped she had not held shy of accepting such comfort, though—was it only he with whom she might share such comforts and pleasures? If Mizel withheld agreement, was Aelliana doomed yet again to an existence devoid of all joy?

He came to his feet, eyes stinging. Damn Mizel, he thought, dispassionately. Damn Liad and the ties of clan and kin.

And damn most of all this small, empty room where he had waited too long in vain for companionship of his own. He had been, he thought, in Anne's peculiar phrase, *stood up*.

He turned toward the door.

Which opened, admitting a slim, red-headed person, wearing a leather jacket over a dark sweater—and limping. Limping rather markedly, in fact, off of his left leg.

"Clarence!" He caught the other man's arm, offering support to the nearest chair.

"Gently done," came the murmur, as between comrades. At least, Daav supposed that Comrade had been the intention; the mode was just slightly off. He shivered and looked to where the elder Ongit tarried yet by the door.

"Wine, if you will—the house's preferred red. Also, the plate that I had ordered may be brought now."

The Ongit bowed and went away, soft-footed. It was the most discreet who served private parlors, which is why he had suggested meeting here, but—

"A message saying that you were wounded would have found me, you know," he said in mild Terran.

Clarence laughed, just a bit breathless. "No, now, it was only a fortunate fall. My own fault, too, so I'm doubly dismayed."

Daav moved forward and placed another chair across from him.

"Thank you." The other man brought his leg up, stiffly, and settled his boot on the chair seat with a sigh. He smiled up at Daav. "It's good to see a friendly face."

"That fall may have been less fortunate than you suppose," Daav said, but could not bring himself to frown.

The door chimed softly, and opened to admit their server, bearing wine, glasses, and platter. He disposed them about the table, bowed, and retired, the door sealing behind him.

Daav poured, handing the first glass to Clarence. Cradling the second, he settled into his former chair.

"To fortune," Clarence said, raising his glass with a shaky flourish.

"To the luck," Daav agreed, holding his glass high.

They sipped—and Clarence sipped again. He sighed, shifted in the chair, and nodded.

"Now, then, what's on your worry plate this evening?"

Daav nodded at the elevated leg. "I think we may be on my topic. It comes to my attention that pilots are once again hunted in Low Port. There are attending lesser tales of cargoes going missing, ships disadvantaged, and crew bewildered. The culprit, according to my information, is the Juntavas, which has grown out of reason bold, and the lightest word from the boss' lips held as law."

Clarence laughed and shook his head.

"Now, if *that* were the way of it . . ." he murmured. He raised his free hand and rubbed his eyes, tiredly.

"I'll admit it sounds like we've got the same old problem. It isn't me causing concern—which I'm bound to say and you to take with as much salt as you like. That done, I'll admit there's some of mine mixed into it. If I don't find out who—and soon—then I'm going to have to choose . . . and I'll tell you, that's a course I hate to fly. Bad for business."

Daav sipped his wine, chose a savory, and pushed the platter closer to Clarence's hand.

"Thanks," he said absently, helping himself to a cheese square.

"Surely," Daav murmured, "you must have something. A hunch?"

Clarence snorted. "Oh, I had a hunch, didn't I just!" He shifted the bad leg meaningfully. "Much good it did me."

Daav put his glass down.

"But—"

"Concealed gunman, and me not close enough to my best guess to be able to be *sure*. Nothing wrong with my hearing, at least—" He sent Daav a bright, unreadable look. "A fortunate fall, and no mistake."

Daav let his breath out slowly.

"My crew lit out after, but lost them—that's been the story lately." Clarence shook his head. "I want them off my port, mind you; they're causing no end of trouble."

"I agree," Daav said. "Perhaps we can pool information?"

"That's all right by me. I'll send what I have tomorrow by public courier—acceptable?"

"Perfectly acceptable," Daav said. "Clarence—"

"It's late, you know," the other man interrupted. "Shouldn't you be going home to your wife?"

"I haven't a wife," Daav said, his voice much cooler than he had intended.

Clarence shot him a hard glance. "No, now, that's not the way to go about it! Get yourself home, man, and make it up."

In spite of himself, Daav laughed. "It sounds as if you've been married."

"Happens I was," Clarence said, soberly. "We were too young for it, o'course. I had my second class, doing in-system work, but still, a lot of lonely nights for him and me not there. We worked at it, but then—it was a hard world, and money wasn't easy, even with both of us working like we did. The fees on a pilot's labor—" He glanced down at his glass.

Daav lifted the bottle and poured, adding some more to his own glass.

"Thank you. In any case, I'd flown my hours and

was burning for first class, but we'd never afford the buy-in. Come a woman to port offering to pay it all, and hire me when I had my ticket, if I agreed to do her a favor, if you understand me." He shook his head. "He wouldn't stand with that, not at all. It was terrible, that fight, but in the end I chose the ticket, and the doin' of that favor." He drank, deeply.

"And that's how I come to work for Herself as a courier pilot, before she come here to be Boss; before she got transferred and I did..." His voice faded out and he looked down at his hand where it rested on his knee.

"And your spouse?" Daav asked, though surely it was no business of his, if Clarence kept a harem.

"Eh?" The other man looked up, eyes distant with memory. "Oh, he left me, and right he was to do it. The doin' of favors, well. Look where it's got me." He shook his head and offered Daav a half-feral grin. "The choices we make, those're what shapes us. You go on home, now, and make it up with her."

"In time," Daav said softly. "Do you have someone here to escort you?"

"Several someones," Clarence assured him. "They're outside."

"Then the first thing I will do is see you safely into their care. After, I will indeed go home."

"If you're of a mind to coddle, then I'm not the one to stop you," Clarence said. He put his glass on the table and rose, gingerly, most of his weight on his uninjured leg.

Daav offered his arm. "Off we go now, two comrades, deep in our cups."

Clarence laughed as they turned toward the door.

"Y'know, I'd rather that was the reason. Gods, I hate being stupid."

"Stupid would have seen you dead," Daav said, opening the door and guiding him into the hall.

"They're watching the shadow door?" he asked, meaning Ongit's discreet—and well-guarded—back exit.

"Yeah. *That* stupid, I'm not."

THIRTY

· · · · · · · · · · · ·

Absence makes the heart grow fonder.
— Terran Proverb

IT WAS EARLY EVENING WHEN SHE RETURNED TO THE
Hall, the meeting at Scout Academy having gone longer
than she had supposed it would. As had become her
custom, she passed through the front parlor of the
house itself, in order to collect her mail. The fact that
she received mail—invitations, almost exclusively—had
at first bemused her. But, after all, she had met a
great many people at Lady yo'Lanna's picnic, and it
was, as she had learned from Jen, the season to be
giving parties.

Today, there were no invitations, but a letter.

Aelliana froze, staring down at the word "dea'Gauss"
and her direction, written out with dainty precision:
Aelliana Caylon, in care of the Healers, Chonselta City.

Mouth dry, heartbeat pounding in her ears, she
stared down at the envelope. It was impossible to
deduce whether it held good news or bad. Her hand
moved, as if she would break the seal, but she clenched
her fingers tight, and forced her arm to her side.

Not here. Not where her elation or her despair would discommode the work of two dozen or more.

Slipping the envelope into her sleeve, she went down the hall, meeting no one, which was perhaps a blessing, and stepped out into the garden.

She hesitated again, once she was out-of-house, but forced herself to walk on until she came to the cottage and let herself in.

There, her back against the door, she had the letter out, snapped the seal and let the envelope fall as she unfolded the single sheet.

Mr. dea'Gauss wasted few words on pleasantries. He wrote, so the lines ran, to apprise her of the state of negotiations to date. Mizel remained adamant in its demands, refusing all counteroffers tendered by Korval. They were therefore about to embark upon a new tactic, which held some increased risk. He did not wish to proceed without first soliciting her thoughts on the topic, as she was a principal in the case, and stood to lose the most, should the stratagem fail.

No, Aelliana thought, *he cannot know what Daav will lose, if Mizel will not be persuaded.*

She focused again on the page. In brief, Mr. dea'Gauss proposed to challenge Mizel on the harm done to the lifemate bond, harm taken directly from the actions of Mizel's former nadelm. He would intimate that perhaps a hearing before Council was in order, to determine to whom the bond belonged and what Balance might be owing for its damage.

Aelliana gasped. A bold move, indeed! To shout the fact of their link, and its deformed state, to all the world—yes, small wonder that Mr. dea'Gauss begged that she contact him at any hour of the day or night, using either of the comm numbers he provided, should she have questions or concerns.

He closed kindly, naming himself her most devoted servant, and bidding her to be of good heart.

She put the letter on the desk and went into the kitchen. Deliberately, she put the kettle on, refilled the cat's water bowl and food dish, took down a mug—and froze.

The sound came again. A knock—not Jen's robust rap, but a hesitant, trembling sound scarcely audible over the roiling of the kettle.

Some instinct guided her to the other door, that gave on to the shaded, unbusy street. She opened it, looking out and then down, to the hedge and the gate, and the thin hand on the latch—

"Sinit!"

Tea, the tinned cookies from the very top cabinet, cheese and rye crackers made a very worthy guest tray, Aelliana thought—and a welcome one, too, judging by Sinit's attentions.

"More tea?" Aelliana murmured.

"If you please," Sinit said, indistinctly. She swallowed. "These cookies are very good, Aelliana, you should try one!"

"I've only just had lunch," Aelliana murmured, which was true. Also, she had found of late that sweet things did not please her, which she did not say. Merely, she took a bit of cheese onto a cracker and nibbled it while Sinit disposed of four more cookies.

At last, her sister sighed, and leaned back into the sofa cushions, her teacup gripped tightly in both hands, as if she feared it being snatched away from her.

"Thank you," she said.

"You are very welcome. I'm glad I was at home when you came. Your timing was fortunate; I'd just gotten in from a meeting in Solcintra."

"To visit . . . your ship?" Sinit asked, with what Aelliana supposed was meant for delicacy.

She smiled. "Indeed, no. My ship is berthed at Chonselta Port; I flew it to Solcintra and met with Verisa pel'Quinot, at the Scout Academy. From today's discussions it seems fairly certain that I will be teaching Math for Survival, and an advanced course in general mathematics. The contract must be drawn and reviewed, of course, but—"

"Scout Academy?" Sinit interrupted. "But . . . you'll still be teaching at—at your usual—"

"I resigned my position at Chonselta Tech," Aelliana said gently. "I had determined to set up as a courier service, you see, and the demands of that employment are incompatible with the academic calendar. Scout Academy proposes an intensive course of study that will occupy me and my students fully for a *relumma*, thus leaving three in which to fly." She sipped her tea, considering Sinit's face.

"What news from home?" Aelliana asked, when it seemed that the silence had stretched too long.

Sinit glanced down into her cup. "Voni's married again," she said slowly, "so it's only me and Mother in-house. She keeps to her office, though I see her sometimes at meals. My tutor was dismissed; I've signed in with the Virtual Classroom—accounting courses, mostly, and comparative cultures. I— Oh! What a beautiful cat!"

He did, Aelliana supposed, cut a handsome figure,

with his plumed tail held high and his whiskers a-quiver, as if he had no notion that there was anything improper in perusing the cheeses on the guest tray.

"He was rather disordered when he first came, but he has cleaned up nicely," she said. "Extend your finger, slowly—yes. Now wait for a moment."

The cat considered, then stepped forward, daintily avoiding the tray, and bumped his head forcefully against Sinit's finger.

Aelliana laughed. "He wants his head rubbed, I fear."

Sinit willingly performed this service, also skritching his chin when it was presented.

"What is her name?"

"His name is Scout," Aelliana said, leaning forward to put her cup on the table. "He had been called Mouse when he first took up residence, but he has grown so bold that it no longer suits him."

Scout stepped away from the ministering hand, stretched a back foot in salute and jumped to the floor. Sinit did not look up; her voice when she spoke was very quiet, and far too serious for a girl of nearly fifteen Standards.

"Are you coming home, Aelliana?"

She sighed and shook her head. "No."

"Is it because—Mother says it's because Korval makes itself free of everyone's treasures."

An argument that would bear more weight, Aelliana thought sharply, if Mizel had valued her, at all. She sighed.

"It is because I do not love Mizel, nor can I forgive its failures." She spoke carefully, for to say such a thing—such things were not said. To be outside of the clan was to be dead to the clan. Exactly thus had Ran Eld been deprived of life and every human comfort. She looked to her sister, who was slightly pale, though her eyes were steady.

Aelliana inclined her head. "In addition, Daav yos'Phelium and I are—natural lifemates, bound soul to soul. That Mizel conspires to separate us does not bring the clan nearer to my heart."

"Mizel is . . . not well," Sinit said seriously. "I asked if she should have the Healers, for it seemed—it seems that she grieves too much, and she—" Tears rose in the brown eyes. "She struck me, Aelliana."

She took Sinit's hand, speechless.

"The reason I set myself to accounting is that—I looked in the House records—"

Aelliana stared. "Sinit!"

"I had to know! Mother—the delm—I scarcely know who! She speaks of merging with Lydberg and she swears that you are the clan's only hope of survival, and I know that you do not—cannot—come back to us, Aelliana! But surely there is something—" Tears started down the pale face; Sinit's fingers gripped her so tightly that Aelliana was certain she would have bruises.

"I *do* love Mizel and I don't wish to see us fail! We need to reclaim the nursery and—and bring ourselves into profit. If I become an accountant, I will know how to do these things; I will have access to the Accountants Guild's mentoring programs and—and Mother won't say that I'm a useless drain on the clan . . ." she finished in a whisper.

Aelliana moved, wrapping her sister into a hug.

"You are *not* useless," she said fiercely. "You are Mizel's last and best hope."

Sinit sniffled. "I don't—"

"What would you be willing to do," Aelliana interrupted, "in order to salvage Mizel? Would you be willing to—to—" An idea was coming into shape. She didn't have all of it, yet, but she had . . . something. She could taste it, like the solution to a knotty math problem.

"Would you be willing to be fostered into a clan that might teach you about management and how to forge alliances?"

"Yes!" Sinit pushed against Aelliana's embrace, and sat up, her face set and her brown eyes fierce. "Aelliana, I would do *any*thing within my power." She blinked. "Your face is— Aelliana, what are you planning?"

"I don't quite know myself," she admitted. "I need to think."

"I—" Sinit looked up. "Gods, the time! Aelliana—"

Aelliana looked at the clock, astonished at its report.

"Come," she said, rising and pulling Sinit up with her. "We'll catch a cab."

The cab was easily caught, but Sinit would not allow her escort.

"If Mother sees you, she will compel you to come in-House," Sinit whispered. "You dare not risk it. I will be quite safe."

From this position she would not be moved, and at last, not without relief, Aelliana let her go, first paying the fare to Raingleam Street and a bonus, for the driver's trouble.

She watched the taxi out of sight, then slowly went back inside.

To think.

· · · ❄ · · ·

Jen Sar Kiladi had been particularly prolific these last weeks. It seemed the man thrived at night. Who would have known?

The most recent paper polished to a high gloss, the professor's attention wandered and himself after it, leaving Daav yos'Phelium yawning in his chair.

It was very late—or very early, depending, he supposed, on whether one was still awake or just risen. He—was still awake, and had really ought to engage the Rainbow in the service of getting some sleep.

He rose from behind the desk and stretched, feeling cramped muscles catch, then loosen.

Well.

"Sleep," he told himself. "Now."

He turned away from the desk—and immediately turned back as the comm chimed.

Who, at this hour? he thought, but his fingers had already accepted the call, and there was Mr. dea'Gauss in the screen.

"Good morning, your lordship," he said peremptorily. "Necessity dictates that you hear two things, immediately."

Daav sank back into his chair. "You have my attention, Mr. dea'Gauss."

"Excellent. The first thing that you must hear is that Aelliana Caylon Clan Mizel has accepted the portion settled upon her some *relumma* past by Daav yos'Phelium."

Daav's heart stuttered. Here it is, he thought. She has had enough, and who can blame her? A pilot's first care is for her ship, and a ship—a ship needs money.

He inclined his head.

"I hear," he said, formally.

"Yes," Mr. dea'Gauss sighed. "The second thing you need to hear, your lordship, is rather complex. If you would prefer that I come to you—"

"We have begun, sir," Daav interrupted. "Let us by all means continue until we reach the end."

"As you say." There was silence for the beat of three. In the screen, Mr. dea'Gauss glanced aside, as if gathering his thoughts. It was then that Daav saw that his man of business was not calling from the offices downtown, but from what appeared to be his private rooms.

"The following is proposed, as an offering to Mizel," Mr. dea'Gauss said at last. "There are five specific points."

Five points? Daav wondered. But what use had they for points, or for appeasing Mizel in any way if Aelliana—

"One. Korval will pay to Mizel the life-price for a first class pilot as set down in the Accounting Standards. That sum will be paid in full at the time the contract is signed.

"Two. In six years, Korval will pay to Mizel the life-price for a scholar expert as set down in the Accounting Standards.

"Three. Sinit Caylon will be fostered into yo'Lanna for six years in order to complete her education."

Daav sat forward in his chair.

"Four. In acknowledgement of the fact that Mizel is grown dangerously thin—and made thinner yet by reason of Three, above, a dea'Gauss will be placed into Mizel's service for a period of six years, to perform those tasks that would, in the proper order of things, fall into the nadelm's honor.

"Five. Aelliana Caylon will pay the blood-price for Ran Eld Caylon's death, which debt properly falls to her, when Sinit Caylon takes up Mizel's Ring."

It was a thing of broad and scintillant amazement, Daav thought; a solving worthy of a delm. Saving one or two small details.

"Mr. dea'Gauss, I stand in awe of Pilot Caylon's solution. However, I cannot help but notice that your Line has become entangled in Korval's contract, which we surely cannot have—"

"Your lordship of course is not conversant with all the details of our House," Mr. dea'Gauss interrupted. "I therefore hasten to assure you that this is the very solution toward which I have been groping for a Standard or more. There is one of my House, who serves in the firm, for whom this proposed assignment is—in a word, your lordship, perfect." He inclined his head. "I welcome this opportunity to further strengthen the bonds between our clans."

There could be no doubting his sincerity, Daav thought. He inclined his head.

"Very well, Mr. dea'Gauss. I also see that we have involved yo'Lanna in this. It is perhaps unworthy of me to suppose it, but I fear my mother's dear friend will not share your generous impulse."

"On the contrary, your lordship. Pilot Caylon reports that her ladyship would be delighted to assist in this matter. She asserts that it is not to yo'Lanna's benefit to see Mizel dissolved and further states that it is the duty of the High to assist those who stand below."

Daav gave a shout of laughter.

"Exactly," Mr. dea'Gauss said solemnly. "I should add," he said after a moment, "that Pilot Caylon was

kind enough to calculate the seed money needed
for the proposed future payouts, and to cite several
funds paying interest enough to grow the seed into
payment in full."

Daav bit his lip. "No doubt the exercise afforded
considerable pleasure to Pilot Caylon."

"She seemed very much in spirits," Mr. dea'Gauss
said quietly.

Daav took a breath against the sudden stab of
longing. Below the desk, out of sight of the screen,
he clenched his fists until his knuckles screamed.

"I am pleased to hear it," he said, steadily. "Mr.
dea'Gauss, in your considered opinion—is Mizel likely
to take this?"

"There lies the genius of the plan, your lordship. If
Mizel does not take it, then the delm must surely be
brought before her peers and closely questioned as to
her reasons. As Lady yo'Lanna states, it benefits no one
to allow a clan to dissolve. In offering this, Korval is seen
as looking to the best benefit of Liad." Mr. dea'Gauss
inclined his head. "Which is according to its charter."

Daav bent his head and considered the plan. It
posed, in its way, just as much risk as the one he
and dea'Gauss had produced, yet carried a greater
likelihood of success, if Mr. dea'Gauss was to be
believed, and an avenue of legal recourse open to
them, if Mizel balked.

"It is well," he said, raising his head. "I do not
need to ask you to bend your best efforts, I know.
Please, proceed as you see fit in negotiating these
new terms. The dice are in your hand."

Mr. dea'Gauss bowed.

"I shall do my utmost, your lordship."

THIRTY-ONE

. . . .

The wages of spite are well-earned.

—Liaden Proverb

DAAV GAVE HIS CLOAK TO KAREEN'S BUTLER AND PAUSED a moment to order himself. He wore a misty grey coat and silvered lace, in complement to Aelliana's colors. That he arrived alone, and yet constrained by Mizel's whim, angered and dismayed him.

Still, he reminded himself, he would at least be able to see her, a pleasure that had been denied him for too long. If he were very lucky, they might meet in a condition demanding that they exchange a brief greeting with the bow. It frightened him, how much he ached to hear her voice.

Well, and standing out here in the hallway would serve nothing, save Kareen's spite. He gave his lace another, unnecessary, shake, and moved down the hall to the reception room.

He had arrived somewhat behind time, wishing to avoid a long dawdle in line before he paid his respects to the hostess and was passed inside. Thus, he found

Kareen alone in the reception hall, with only her good friend Scholar Her Nin yo'Vestra to support her.

He made his bow properly: guest-to-host, augmented with the hand-sign between kin.

"Good evening, younger Brother!" Even in the High Tongue, Kareen sounded positively cheerful, which could not, Daav thought, be a good sign.

He straightened warily.

"Good evening, Sister," he replied, speaking in the Low Tongue more from habit than from any particular wish to annoy her this evening. He inclined his head to her support. "Scholar yo'Vestra."

"Korval," the man answered, with a certain sternness, as he was every bit as much of a stickler as Kareen. Indeed, the two of them sat together upon the League for the Purity of the Language—two cornerstone members.

"Do go in," Kareen urged him, smiling. "You will of course find many here whom you know."

Yes, he thought, his stomach tightening, *too cheerful by far.*

He bowed again and passed into the great room.

It was not quite a crush, he thought, pausing to survey the room. That would change over the course of the evening. He had only been somewhat late, and that in service of his own convenience. There were those others who would time their entrance so that the most eyes fell upon them.

At the moment, he saw the usual and expected assortment of guests. Kareen had drawn almost exclusively from the High Houses for this entertainment, with a few of the more . . . ambitious of the Mid Houses, nor had she stinted herself in the matter of ostentatious display. The hall had been repainted a velvety gold, with new rugs to match. It was rather like standing inside a jewel box, with the guests acting the part of the jewels.

Daav took another step into the room, meaning his path to intersect with that of a server wearing a wide-sleeved gold shirt and carrying a tray full with glasses, when the crowd shifted, only a little; he saw Lady yo'Lanna, surrounded as usual with the beautiful and the amusing, the woman at her side perhaps the new favorite—

He went taut, even as the breath was crushed out of his lungs. Joyfully, he accepted the bolt of her beauty and he stood there, transfixed—no! Breath returned with a rush; his heart slammed into overdrive and there was nothing, there was no one but her, to whom he must go immediately. He took a step...

Aelliana turned, her eyes wide and fey. Her hand rose, lace flowing away from her fingers like water, as she, too, took a step—

His arm—the grip was firm enough to pierce the glaze of enchantment. The voice was overloud, commanding attention.

"Young Korval!" Guayar told the room. "Just the man I was wanting to see!"

Daav shook his head, unable to move his eyes from her face, the compulsion painful now, so that his breath came short, and he—

"Daav..." That was lower, almost a growl. "Command yourself."

"I—" His voice died. Gods, *he* would die, if he did not go to her now, *now*, and damn the consequences—

"Come with me," Guayar said. "You want wine."

"No," he whispered. "No, I *don't* want wine."

The grip on his arm was firm enough now to bruise. He scarcely felt it, in the greater agony of his soul.

"Very well, then," Clonak's father said, with quiet patience, "you want a glass of *tea*. Come with me, please, you are becoming an object of interest."

Lady yo'Lanna extended a hand; leaned close and whispered something to Aelliana. She—Aelliana turned her back on him.

"Daav?"

"Yes," he said raggedly, turning painfully toward his own rescuer. His body ached, as if he had been thrown onto sharp stones from a height. "For the gods' sweet love, sir, do not loose my arm."

Guayar sighed, but held firm. "No more than a dozen steps, there is an alcove provided with refreshments," he said, in normal tones. "We may be private there. I swear that my small bit of business will go no longer than is required to drink a glass of tea."

· · ·✵· · ·

"Will you lose everything for one unguarded step?" Lady yo'Lanna whispered in her ear.

Aelliana shivered. She could not move, except to go to him. She would die, if she did not touch him.

"Turn around." Lady yo'Lanna gripped her arm.

"I cannot," she whispered.

"You *will*," the older woman said, her voice conveying absolute conviction.

Daav—Delm Guayar was speaking to him. She saw the longing in his face; *felt* the effort it cost him, to stand in one place, trembling, as she was trembling, soul on fire and heart a-stutter ...

She closed her eyes. The pain did not abate. *I will not lose,* she thought. *I will not forfeit my life.*

Shaking, she turned away.

· · · ✦ · · ·

Shaking, he put himself into the alcove's farthest corner, closed his eyes, and concentrated on being very still. Now that it was aroused, the compulsion did not fade as he had hoped it might. He knew where she was; blindfolded, he could walk to her side, through walls, if he must . . .

"Here is tea," Guayar said.

He opened his eyes, and received the glass with both hands. The liquid sloshed and rippled unnervingly.

Apparently, Guayar thought so, too, for he sent a sharp look into Daav's face.

"Attend me, please," he said, as if he were speaking to a child yet in nursery. "You are to remain *precisely there;* you will not endanger your clan or your lady or yourself by word, action or deed while I am away. Do you swear it?"

Daav took a hard breath. "How long will you be gone?"

Guayar awarded him another sharp look.

"I am going to fetch your brother."

Daav inclined his head. "On my honor, I will wait here until my brother comes."

"Excellent."

Alone, Daav closed his eyes, and felt for the steps that would bring him to that place of quiet peace. He could not concentrate; the imperative to *go to her* shattered his thought, flooding him with agony.

Biting his lip, he reached for the Rainbow, but

the colors slid away from his thought, leaving him bereft and ill.

A light step alerted him. He opened his eyes.

Er Thom was in sapphire and ivory. He stood in the entry to the alcove, the golden light from the main room limning his slim figure, throwing his face into shadow.

"Karoon will be angry if you break that glass," he commented. "It's part of a set."

"I'll buy her a new set," Daav answered, horrified to hear how his voice quavered.

"Best not to call attention," his brother said, and came forward, walking easy and soft. "Brother, what pains you?"

Daav took a breath, keeping his eyes on Er Thom's.

"I am compelled," he said.

"Ah." His brother inclined his head. "I understand."

Of all the beings alive, Daav thought, his brother would understand. More the pity, that Er Thom's brother had not understood when a similar compulsion had been visited upon him.

"Brother, I owe you a profound apology."

"Nonsense," Er Thom said briskly. He slipped the glass from Daav's hand. "Let me fetch you something more fitting to drink."

"Not wine!" he said sharply.

"Of course not. Come out of the corner, Daav, do."

Come out of the corner, he thought, blinking back tears; *as if it were simple*.

. . . and yet, it was Er Thom who asked it; Er Thom, who knew precisely what it would cost.

Daav straightened his shoulders and stepped away from the wall. His knees trembled, but he could stand.

His hands were cold, and his lungs ached as if he had been running at the top of his speed for far too long.

"Here you are," Er Thom said, stepping to his side and handing him a wineglass filled with pale yellow liquid.

Daav shook his head. "No wine," he repeated. "Brother—"

"Taste it," Er Thom commanded.

Goaded, he assayed a sip—a *small* sip—and sputtered a laugh.

"Lemonade?"

"It is perfectly adequate lemonade," Er Thom said, sipping from his own glass. He wrinkled his nose slightly. "Who could have supposed that Kareen would have it too sweet?"

Daav snorted, then sobered.

"I promised that I would support her here," he said, without any need to explain who that might be.

"Of course you did, and so you shall," Er Thom replied, offering his arm. "Come, Brother, let us tour the room."

· · · ❖ · · ·

Lady Kareen had detached her from Ilthiria yo'Lanna, precisely as that lady had predicted.

"You are so new among us, Scholar Caylon, that I am persuaded there are many here who are strangers to you. Come! Allow me to make you known to the room."

Aelliana looked to Lady yo'Lanna, which had not been part of what they had decided between them, but did not, Aelliana thought, do them a disservice. What Lady yo'Lanna felt was not to be known, as she simply waved a negligent hand and issued an airy,

"Do allow Lady Kareen to introduce you to those to whom you are not known, Pilot. No one knows her guests so well as the host."

The first person the host guided her to was an unfamiliar man with a triangular face and severe grey eyebrows. Aelliana's stomach, already unsettled, grew more so.

"Ixin, allow me to make you known to Aolliana Caylon Clan Mizel, Scholar and Pilot. Scholar Caylon, here is Lus Tin ven'Deelin, who has the honor to be Ixin."

They exchanged bows, each accepting the other's introduction, while Lady Kareen stood back, her face watchful beyond, Aelliana thought, what became even the most careful host.

"Scholar Caylon, how glad I am to meet you!" Lus Tin ven'Deelin said. "My niece had only praise for you and for your course. But—" he looked suddenly conscious—"you have had so many students, perhaps you do not recall—"

"Rema was one of my best students," Aelliana murmured. "Of course I remember her, and—if a teacher may say it—with great fondness."

"That is kind of you, Scholar. I will be certain to tell her father of your notice. Also, allow me to add my own thanks for the gift of your genius, and for your care, Scholar."

"You are too kind," Aelliana murmured.

"Not at all," he protested gallantly, and they parted, with bows, he to proceed down the room and she to accompany Lady Kareen.

"How fortunate that you were acquainted with Ixin's niece," Kareen murmured.

"Trebly fortunate," Aelliana allowed.

"Ah, now, here is—"

"Is it Pilot Caylon?" a woman's high, sweet voice interrupted Kareen. "How well you are looking, ma'am!"

Aelliana turned and bowed. "Lady Sera, how good it is to meet you again."

"Had I the least idea you were to be here, I would have offered you my escort. I hope you were not constrained to come alone. Really, this matter inconveniences everyone—don't you think so, Kareen?"

"Certainly, it is an inconvenient situation," that lady answered smoothly, "and not at all regular."

"Well! But it is Korval, ma'am, and—aside yourself, of course—irregularity would seem a mark of the House. Pilot Caylon, how are you situated? It would please me to offer you guesting. My house is quite near."

"Thank you," Aelliana said, inclining her head. "Lady yo'Lanna kindly allows me to guest with her."

"Ah, does she? You're well taken care of then." She tipped her head. "I wonder, Pilot, your jewels. Moonel, I assume?"

"Yes," Aelliana said, who had not known the artist existed until that very afternoon, when Lady yo'Lanna had brought Daav's gift to her. The Master had used every jewel in the Jump pilot's cluster to make what seemed at first viewing to be a meaningless tangle. Once about her neck, however, it was revealed as a star route, with the Jump points marked out in grey pearl—three Jumps, in fact, to Avontai, and three more, to Staederport.

Lady Sera sighed. "You are very fortunate, ma'am."

"So I believe as well," Aelliana murmured, which gained her a sharp look from the lady, and an insincere smile.

"Why there is Etgora!" she said brightly. "I must have word with him before he vanishes into the crowd again. Kareen, you have achieved a crush!" A hasty bow and Lady Sera was away.

"How came you to meet Sera tel'Kai?" Kareen asked as they moved across the crowded floor together.

"We were guests together at Lady yo'Lanna's morning picnic some weeks back," Aelliana murmured. "She was kind enough then to give me her attention."

"I see." Lady Kareen took her arm, as if she were afraid that Aelliana might escape. "I hope you will humor me, Scholar. There is one of my guests that I particularly wished you to meet. I fear that the tel'Kai is correct, however, we have achieved a crush and will scarce be able to find ourselves, much less—Ah! There we have her!"

· · · · ✳ · · · ·

One did not, Daav found, grow accustomed so much as one found ways to cope. He coped by allowing Er Thom to steer them from one pleasant acquaintance to another, and by concentrating on seeming precisely as usual. vin'Tael made some comment meant to call into question the *melant'i* of those who did not immediately acquiesce to the demands of High. He was, however, in his cups, and was easily quelled with a stare.

That his brother's route down the room was modeled on Aelliana's progress, Daav knew by the burning of his nerves. He ignored it, as much as he might, and tried to be content with the occasional glimpse of her face, or her tawny hair, swept back into a deceptively simple knot, revealing her face entirely, and exposing her delicious ears.

Eyla had done well with the dress, he thought. It was a simple thing, with clean lines and matter-of-fact elegance. Beside her, Kareen seemed subtly overdressed.

Moonel's necklace—well, what could be said? The man was a genius. Daav wished he had been able to give it himself, so that he could have seen whether it pleased her. That, alas . . .

"Kareen is on the approach to mischief," Er Thom murmured. "Shall I go?"

Daav looked out over the room, beyond Aelliana's present location, and drew his breath in sharply.

"Yes, and at once," he said, releasing Er Thom's arm. "For if I go, I will surely murder her."

· · · · ·❖· · · ·

"You must allow me," Lady Kareen said, hurrying her toward a pair of ladies—one elder and stern-faced; the other young enough to perhaps be her daughter, with a face more resigned than stern, and her stance shouting *pilot*.

"You must allow me to present Gath tel'Izak, who has the honor to be Bindan, and Samiv tel'Izak. Delm and Pilot, allow me to introduce Aelliana Caylon Clan Mizel."

Face stiff, Bindan inclined her head, Aelliana scarcely heeded that. She stepped forward, slipping her arm free from Lady Kareen's grasp and bowed profoundly.

"Samiv tel'Izak!" she exclaimed. "I have been wanting to meet you, and to thank you! To have risked so much on my account—and never even knowing who I was! I am in your debt, Pilot. Deeply so."

"Indeed not!" the younger lady protested. "Pilot

Caylon—it is apparent to the meanest intelligence precisely who you are. I am honored, and if I may say so without offense, delighted, to be able to speak with you. The last I had known, your case was desperate, and then I fear"—a sweep of lashes in the elder lady's direction—"I became immersed in my own affairs."

"I understand entirely, Pilot," Aelliana assured her. "We should make time to sit with each other. I am presently situated at Chonselta, but I am at your service, Pilot. Only—" A shadow moved at her shoulder—*not Daav*, an inner voice told her—and she turned her head.

Not Daav, no, but welcome, nonetheless.

"Er Thom!" She caught his hand and brought him forward. "Do you know Pilot tel'Izak?"

"I have had the felicity," he said, with an easy bow. "Pilot, I am pleased to see you looking so well." He glanced to the other lady and accorded her a more rigorous salute. "Bindan."

"yos'Galan," the delm said sourly.

"Aelliana," Er Thom said in his soft, sweet voice. "I had seen that you were unrefreshed. Might I fetch you something? Pilot? Ma'am?"

"Thank you, no," Bindan said, with, so it seemed to Aelliana, scant courtesy. "Samiv, there is Midys, to whom we must speak. Forgive us, yos'Galan, Lady... Pilot; duty calls."

"Certainly," Er Thom said, inclining his head. Aelliana looked to Samiv.

"A message in my name to the offices of dea'Gauss will find me, Pilot. Please, do not forget."

Bindan moved sternly away, Pilot tel'Izak dutifully in her wake. When they had been swallowed by the crush of bodies, Er Thom turned again to Aelliana.

"May I bo of use to you?" he asked, and turned his head slightly. "Or to you, Kareen?"

"There's a rare offer," Lady Kareen said, her voice light, as if it were a joke between close kin, but her eyes angry, indeed.

"Worth all the more, then," Er Thom answered. "What may I be honored to fetch you?"

Lady Kareen drew a breath, and smoothed her hands down her skirt. "Nothing, I thank you, kinsman. Indeed, I have neglected the balance of my guests quite long enough! If you will forgive me, Scholar?"

Aelliana inclined her head. "Of course, ma'am," she said, carefully. "I thank you for your care."

"You are quite welcome, Scholar," the lady replied, her voice also careful. "Kinsman."

Er Thom bowed. "Kareen."

"Please, you must tell me how Daav goes on," Aelliana said rapidly, the instant the lady was away. "I—we saw each other, and it was as if I had taken a bolt. I could scarcely think anything, except that I must go to him at once. He was similarly struck, I saw—Delm Guayar took him in hand. But—"

"He suffers," Er Thom murmured, taking her arm and moving her carefully through the crowd—*away from Daav!* she thought, with a wrench—"he suffers as you do, and will continue to do unless and until this is solved." He flashed her a look. "I speak, as you know, from experience. It may perhaps seem unnecessarily harsh, but it is my opinion that Mizel ought to be flogged. If, as we suppose, she knows that you and Daav are linked..."

"She cares very little for that—indeed, how could she know what it meant, when we ourselves discover it as we go along?" Aelliana shook her head. "I have such a report of her state of mind from my sister that must concern anyone. I had hoped that the solution I proposed would move her, but it has been a twelve-day now, and no word."

Er Thom was silent for a few slow steps.

"Daav had promised to support you here," he said suddenly.

"Yes, and so he has done, by sending you to me," she told him warmly. "I am very happy to see you, Er Thom, but I think—I think it would be best to take me back to Lady yo'Lanna so that you may return to Daav." She smiled, half-amused. "We shall each have our rock, and our comfort."

He returned her smile, violet eyes flashing. "Aelliana, I may have been remiss—have I said that I like you extremely and am grateful to find you in care of my brother's heart?"

Her eyes filled, and she pressed her fingers gently against his arm.

"Thank you," she whispered.

"No—thank you." He put his hand briefly over hers, the Master Trader's ring flashing purple lightnings. "Come, let us return you to her ladyship, so that we may all be civilized for one hour more."

· · · ·⚜· · · ·

"Anne, we are well-met," Daav said. He slipped his arm through hers. "For the love of the gods, whatever you do, do not let me go."

She smiled and patted his hand. "Where's Er Thom got to?" she wondered in Terran.

"Gone to rescue my darling from my sister's spite,"

he answered, gladly embracing her choice of language. "Since I am disallowed from performing the service myself."

"Scholar yo'Vestra is making his way very deliberately in this direction," Anne commented. "Should I move us?"

"Not in the least," Daav returned. "It will do me good to have a worthy target."

Anne laughed, and then the scholar was upon them.

"Lady yos'Galan, I offer myself in place of your present escort, who is wanted on business of the utmost urgency to Korval."

Daav considered him.

"Do you bear a more explicit message, Scholar?"

yo'Vestra bowed. "The dea'Gauss awaits you in Lady Kareen's office, sir."

THIRTY-TWO

. . . .

A Dragon will in all things follow its own necessities,
and either will or will not make its bow to Society.
—From the Liaden Book of Dragons

DAAV TURNED THE LAST PAGE OVER, AND LOOKED TO
Korval's man of business, sitting straight-backed and
attentive on one of Kareen's damned uncomfortable
visitor's chairs.

"Mizel accepts all," he said, scarcely believing what
he had just read, "and even adds a date by which Miss
Sinit must be welcomed into yo'Lanna's keeping." He
extended a hand, and flipped up the last page, half
afraid that he had imagined it—but, no. Mizel's line
was signed, witnessed, and sealed. All that remained
was to apply his signature and Mr. dea'Gauss his, and
the thing was done.

At last.

"I have a pen, your lordship," Mr. dea'Gauss murmured, rising and reaching into his jacket.

Of course he had a pen. Daav received it with a nod.

"My thanks yet again, Mr. dea'Gauss. I regret this
disruption of your evening."

"It is nothing, your lordship. What *I* regret is the length of time it has taken us to arrive at this very welcome port, and the unnecessary distress with which Pilot Caylon and yourself were burdened."

Mr. dea'Gauss did not usually indulge in anger. That he was angry at this—but of course he would be. The misuse of *melant'i* and the waste of time and opportunity yes, those things might well anger Mr. dea'Gauss.

Daav addressed the paper, inscribed his name, and handed the pen to Mr. dea'Gauss, who wrote, brief and neat, noting also the time and date. He then withdrew a seal from his case and appended it in the proper place.

"It is done."

Relief pummeled Daav so that he sank back in his chair, exhausted. Done. Aelliana.

Aelliana was in the next room, and there was nothing now to lose by acquiescing to his compulsion to go to her.

He put his hands on the arms of the chair, meaning to rise immediately—

"If your lordship pleases," Mr. dea'Gauss said.

Daav grit his teeth.

"There is more, Mr. dea'Gauss?" he asked, managing to keep his voice level.

"I have with me other papers as well, your lordship, should you and Pilot Caylon wish to embrace the fullness of opportunity."

Daav blinked. *Other papers* could only be the lifemate lines. It was customary to invite allies and guests to a gather during which the lines were signed and witnessed by all who dealt with Korval.

Most of whom were gathered right here and now.

Kareen would not thank him for turning her party to his own ends. On the other hand, as their mother had often said, The shortest route to done is through begun.

"Yes," he said, rising more slowly than he had intended. "Let us have it done now, and done well, before all the world."

Necessity was placed before Kareen's butler, who immediately grasped what was needful and proper for the occasion and took all in hand.

A table materialized at the landing overlooking the gather hall, covered with a tapestry depicting the Tree-and-Dragon, pen, book, and glasses arranged according to Code. Servers were sent out among the guests below, to ensure that everyone held a glass.

Behind the table stood Anne and Kareen; the latter irreproachably solemn, the former frankly beaming.

Daav was escorted to his place by Er Thom, who would stand as his second. There was a wait, then, for Mr. dea'Gauss had gone to find Aelliana and explain the procedures to her. Now that he had leisure, he worried, for she had no kin here to support her, nor even any friends. Perhaps he should not have rushed this, and yet—

And yet.

Below him, the amassed witnesses began to move; folk took a half-step aside, or turned sideways, opening a path—a path wide enough to accommodate two slender women, arm in arm and heads high, both walking with pilot grace, neither faltering.

Aelliana, and Samiv tel'Izak.

Unhurriedly, but with purpose, they climbed the stairway, and it seemed that the room held its breath. Upon achieving the landing, Aelliana took her place before the second book, with Samiv beside her and one step to the rear.

Daav shivered. The desire, the *need* to touch her nearly overwhelmed his senses. His breath came shallow and fast. Gods, it would not do to swoon, and if he, who shouldered the least part of their bond, was thus afflicted, what must *she* be feeling?

He dared not turn his head to look at her.

Below, the crowd shifted again and Mr. dea'Gauss mounted as high as the third stair, where he turned to address those assembled.

"We are called to bear witness to the joining of the lives, the hearts, and the souls of Daav yos'Phelium and Aelliana Caylon. From this moment onward they shall share one clan, one purpose, and one *melant'i*." He paused for the space of two agonizingly long heartbeats.

"Let the lines be signed."

Their shared pen sat in its holder in the exact center of the table; a fanciful creation of silver and jet that was perhaps meant to evoke an old-style fin ship, the book open on the cloth before it. Aelliana, superbly coached by dea'Gauss, extended a hand, the jewels in the Jump pilot's ring winking like remote stars. From the side of his eye, Daav saw her pluck up the pen, write in the book, and replace the pen in the holder.

Daav took up the pen, signed his name, and replaced the pen.

Er Thom and Samiv stepped forward in time, as if they had practiced the move, each taking up the lesser pen at the table ends, and leaning over to sign their names, before stepping back to join Kareen and Anne.

"Let the book find its proper owner."

This, thought Daav, was going to be delicate. He closed the binder, fingers caressing smooth leather, and turned at last to face Aelliana.

She was . . . glowing; her eyes were beyond emeralds, her face transcendent. He raised the book and softly kissed the leather, his eyes never leaving hers.

There was a murmur, perhaps he had outraged those below. He did not care.

He placed the book into her hands.

"For my pilot."

"No," she answered, her voice flowing out over the room. "We fly together."

Silence from the gathered onlookers and now there was only one more thing to do.

Daav raised his hand, showing Korval's Ring to those gathered.

"Korval Sees Aelliana Caylon, beloved friend, pilot, lifemate, delmae." His voice wavered slightly, but he hardly cared. He closed the space between them, and placed his hands on her shoulders. She looked up at him with so much love in her face that he felt his soul seared, aflame and exalted all at once.

"The Clan," he said, loud enough to be heard in the farthest corner of the room, "rejoices."

He bent his head, and kissed her.

The room exploded into greenness, the air was scented with leaf. He stood on his toes, stretching into the kiss; he could feel the nap of his coat sleeves under his fingers, a heaviness in his womb, and passion poised like lightning.

Daav . . . he heard her voice, inside his head, and abruptly it was *his* head again, and his hands cupping silk-smoothed shoulders. It was Aelliana who ended the kiss, and stepped back from him, her hands gripping his arms, and her smile enough to dazzle a blind man.

Together, they took a deep breath and looked out over the room, where Kareen's guests stood, as if ensorcelled.

"It is done," Mr. dea'Gauss announced, and turned on the stair.

Deliberately, and with exquisite timing, he bowed: honor-to-the-delm.

The last guest had filed by to offer felicitations, and they were momentarily, at least, alone.

"Daav," Aelliana leaned into his side. "I must tell you something."

He looked down at her, dared to raise a hand and touch her lips.

"You're pregnant," he said, recalling that moment, or hour, when he had known her as entirely as himself. "The Tree is a brute."

"Indeed, it is," she said warmly, "and so I shall say to it! However the means, the babe was got beforetime. Master Kestra gave me the news when I came to the Healers. I could not speak to you and did not wish to disturb Mr. dea'Gauss with the matter, fearing to introduce too many factors into his calculations . . ."

"I understand," he murmured. He brushed his thumb over the high curve of her cheek. Gods, she was so beautiful—and now they fitly belonged to each other . . .

"Daav?"

He shook himself out of the growing reverie of passion.

"There is precedent," he managed to say, fairly calmly. "Shan preceded yos'Galan's lifemating by several Standard years, after all. We need not be concerned with the Tree's sense of humor in this, except, to chastise it for circumventing your wishes."

Relief washed over him—her relief. He caught his breath.

"*Van'chela*?"

"All's well," he said, unsteadily, his hand cupping her cheek. "Aelliana, I can—I have your signal."

Joy flared, and he nearly lost his balance. Aelliana pressed closer to him, her joy joining with his, arousing him—and her...

"Perhaps," Er Thom's voice came quietly from just beyond his shoulder. "Perhaps you had best go home."

Daav turned his head.

"Brother, we expect a child."

Er Thom's eyes took fire, and he extended a hand to each, his grip fierce.

"The clan rejoices," he said. Releasing them, he stepped back.

"Go now. I will make your apologies to the host."

"Kareen!" Aelliana brought her hand to her lips, and Daav felt her chagrin.

"The whole purpose of this gather was to show the world how unsuitable I am."

"She failed," Er Thom said. "If Kareen were less ruled by spite, she might succeed more often." He bent gently and kissed her cheek.

"Welcome, Sister," he murmured, and stepped back. "I will deal with Kareen, and with *The Gazette*. Now, if you please, take your lifemate home before he embarrasses us all."

THIRTY-THREE

. . . .

> Korval is contract-bound to stand as Captain to
> all the passengers until released by the Council of
> Clans, the successor to the Transition Committee.
> I should've written that contract looser, but who
> knew we'd even survive?
>
> —Excerpted from
> Cantra yos'Phelium's Log Book

THE WINDOW WAS OPEN, ADMITTING THE SOUNDS OF
the nighttime garden. Inside, the room was cozily
bathed in butter-yellow light. Daav was stretched on
his side on the sofa, reading his letters. Aelliana, on
the chaise, with Lady Dignity's chin on her ankle,
looked up from her screen, and considered him.

"Did you say something?"

He raised his head, black eyes dancing.

"I did not, though I might have done." He rattled
the paper in his hand. "Here's an invitation for Kiladi
to teach a guest seminar on cultural genetics. Impossible, of course, but one cannot help to be proud of
his accomplishments and the notice he receives from
his peers."

"Why is it 'impossible, of course'?" Aelliana asked. "Scholar Kiladi has much to offer. Some of his students at least found him to be of use."

"*One* of his students," Daav amended, shaking his hair back from his face.

Aelliana smiled. He had thought to cut his hair when they became lifemates, which was the custom of the tribe of the grandmother whom he honored. He had allowed, however, that the decision ultimately rested with his wife and that the grandmother would never gainsay the mother of another tent.

"You may drag a *crimson fish* across my path, but I will not be diverted," she told him, pleased to recall Anne's phrase. "Even to alter the thought of a single student is sometimes enough reward for all a teacher's efforts. It is the duty of scholarship to share, and to illuminate. Scholar Kiladi publishes—and so he ought!—but that is no substitute for teaching."

"To teach, Kiladi would need to absent himself— and myself, his willing vessel—for somewhat more than a *relumma*."

Aelliana moved her shoulders. "There's no trick to that. We have already established that we may absent ourselves from the homeworld in the service of our courier business—which I have no intention to give up, you know! If Scholar Kiladi must remain a stranger to your kin, then it is simplicity itself to take ourselves out and away, and offload the Scholar at whatever port he likes. In the meanwhile, I will hire me a Guild copilot and work the ports, returning for the Scholar at a prearranged time and place."

Daav smiled and her heart constricted in her chest.

"You've given this some thought, I see? Who knew you would take so well to subterfuge?"

She bent a serious gaze upon him. "I had a good teacher."

Daav laughed, and folded the letter. "Well, it is a plan—but a plan, I think, for the future. Let us first have our child in arms. I do not wish to be apart from you when the event occurs, nor do I wish you to be in the hands of a hired copilot, docked on a third-tier world, when the child decides."

He was worried still, Aelliana thought. They had had a Healer and a physician, neither of whom felt that the birth was beyond her. She suspected that his concern had root in her past, to which he now had access, as she had access to his. The heightened sensitivity, the Healer had said, was an effect of her pregnancy and would become less potent once the child was delivered. How much less potent, he had not ventured to say, nor whether Daav would retain his late-found ability to experience her as she did him.

"Perhaps Scholar Kiladi might plead a prior commitment," she said, "and ask them to place him on the lists for next year,"

Daav nodded. "I will suggest that course to him," he said, and smiled again, tenderly. "I love you, Aelliana."

It was enough to bring tears to her eyes. She blinked them clear.

"I love you, Daav."

Having mutually renewed their bond, Daav returned to his mail and she to her paper. They worked comfortably for some time; Aelliana so immersed that it was not until she reached the end of the section and had closed her screen that she realized that Daav was very still, indeed, and that he had been so for some time.

Carefully, her eyes on him, she put the screen on the table next to the chaise, and shifted her ankle from beneath Lady Dignity's chin. There was a taste in the air, sharp but not unpleasant, like ozone, which she equated with profound thought.

"Is there something that requires solving?" she asked, rising. She smoothed her robe, watching him. So *very* still...

He sighed sharply and looked up.

"Alas, it appears that the little difficulty in the Low Port is beginning to drift upward to Mid Port. Clarence's efforts are all for naught, which leaves me not knowing precisely what to think, as my most constant source of information in the matter is Clarence."

Someone was targeting pilots in the Low Port; she had read Clarence's dispatches, as well as some less detailed reports from other persons of Daav's acquaintance.

"Do you think that Clarence is lying to you, *van'chela*? What could be his reason?"

Daav shook his head, brows drawn, which made him look fierce, indeed. She received, as if wafted on the breeze from the window, one scent among many, a sense of frustrated dismay, and a hard edge of—

"Daav!" She stepped forward, more quickly than she had intended, one hand extended, as if to ward the very thought. "You cannot consider assassinating Clarence!"

He grimaced and held his hand out. She took it, and allowed herself to be brought down to sit on the sofa, her back against his belly.

"I would very much rather consider assassinating any number of other people, rather than Clarence. Alas, he puts himself in harm's way."

"You do not know that!" she protested.

"No, I don't. However, Clarence is not usually so ineffective. Time and again, he closes—only to find himself grasping a fistful of smoke. If this culprit is so clever as to elude him consistently on what he likes to call *his port*, that is very worrisome, and it may be that Clarence requires some aid which he is too proud—or too dismayed—to ask for.

"If, on the other hand, it is Clarence's office that is the source of these instances of pilot disappearances, cargo thefts, and shipnappings, it benefits him to provide false information."

He fell silent; Aelliana, leaning comfortably against him, felt the force of his intelligence at work, and something else. Something—a memory?

"What is it? Has this happened before?"

Daav breathed a laugh, which she read as carrying an undercurrent of resignation.

"I have no secrets from you, my lady."

"Indeed," she said, "there must be a way for you to have them, if they are vital to your joy. We ought to explore the subject with a Healer. For the moment, however—"

"Yes." Daav sighed.

"Many years ago," he said slowly, "my mother was still alive. She had heard of a situation in the Low Port of which she could not approve. Someone, you see, was stealing pilots. Clarence was newcome to Liad and to his station as Boss. My mother did not know him, as she had known his predecessor—and to be fair, she probably did not expect that he would last more than a *relumma*, following the pattern of the two replacements previous to him."

Aelliana held up a hand. "This predecessor. Would your mother have asked her for information, had she still been in office?"

"Very likely; they had a very good working relationship. However, Boss Toonapplo not being available, and Clarence an unknown; she sent me down to Low Port to gain the lay of the land and to see what I might find.

"To keep a long tale as short as I might—I found a pilot-taker *and* Clarence, he having been on the same scent. We took her together, but alas, we could not keep her. As I was shortly thereafter called back to the Scouts, Clarence mounted a thorough inspection, aided by my mother, and the predations—stopped.

"I had until this day always believed that Clarence was as earnest in keeping *his port* safe for pilots as was Korval, and that the thief we had taken together—was as little of his as she was Korval's. Now, these reports, they raise suspicions, and while I am not happy to entertain them, yet they must be invited in and scrutinized, despite—or even because—I would rather not."

Aelliana twisted, drawing her feet up and he shifted to allow her room to lie down, her back tight against his chest, her head under his chin. He put his arm around her, his hand resting on the mound of her belly.

"You intend to do something," she murmured. "What is it?"

"Can't you read it?" he teased.

"I can't," she confessed. "Which makes me believe that you don't know."

"Well reasoned. In fact, the only thing I can think to do is as my mother did before me: Send me down to Low Port to spy out what I might."

That was accompanied by a thrill of positive dread, whether it was hers or his scarcely mattered.

"Low Port is very dangerous," Aelliana murmured. "You had said it yourself."

"So it is, but I am stealthy."

"Will you go with Clarence?"

"That would rather defeat the purpose," he pointed out. "In fact, I would hope to pass through and come out again without him knowing I had ever arrived."

"You will take Er Thom, then."

"What? With Anne about to be delivered?"

"It is nearly six weeks before the child is due. Surely, you don't plan that long a visit?"

"I don't," he said shortly; she read clearly that there was no moving him on that point.

She took a breath, considering the problem. Surely, he was correct; if some agency operating out of Low Port was taking pilots and endangering ships, then that agency must be discovered and destroyed. However—

"You will take me, then," she said, firmly.

He was silent and perfectly still for the space of two heartbeats. Then, he rubbed her belly gently and spoke. "That I will not."

"Daav—"

"Aelliana, it is not as if this were my first foray; I have been to the Low Port many times. I intend to go in, look, listen, and speak with a few people who are known to me. At best, I will find a clue that Clarence's folk have overlooked, or a route that they have not explored. At worst, I will verify that we stand against ghosts who lure the unsuspecting into the mists and steal their self-will. I do not say that I will be as safe as I am this moment, nor that it will be possible to avoid a fight. However, I do think that I may contrive to come away again with nothing more distressful than a dirty face, and in good time for the birth of our own child."

"To go without a partner is not wise, *van'chela*. Consider Avontai, where one of us would not, I think, have prevailed. The situation required both."

"Ah." He relaxed slightly. "At Avontai, we had to step forward. In Low Port, I will keep to the considerable shadows, and become the most invisible Scout you never did see." He rubbed his chin against her hair.

"While it is often wise to be partnered, in some instances, it is best to go quickly, quietly and alone. Two draw the eye in Low Port. One, who does not wish to be seen, is . . . less likely to fall into peril. And, you know, it is not as if I were entirely without backup. You know where I am going and that I intend to deprive myself of no more than two nights with you. If I fall astray, you will do as you see best, Delmae."

He would not be argued and there didn't seem to be, she thought, any way to stop him, short of holding him at gunpoint. Nor, in truth, was she at all certain that she *should* prevent this foray. The situation was serious, and growing more so. Korval was ships, and ships required pilots, never minding the clauses in the ancient contract between the Captain and the passengers which she had only lately been set to study, along with the various diary entries that must be known to the delm.

"When do you go?" she asked quietly.

He sighed. "Tonight."

THIRTY-FOUR

. . . .

Speak softly and carry a big stick; you will go far.
                                    —Terran Proverb

"BOSS?" ROF TIN WAITED UNTIL THE DOOR WAS COM-
pletely closed behind him. "There's a lady here to
see you."

Clarence looked up from his screen. Rof Tin had
been in the front office for about a local year; quite
a distance from the Low Port honeycomb he'd come
up in. His Terran was vernacular, his Liaden low
class, and his understanding—usually—quick. There
wasn't much that rattled him, but right now, Clarence
decided, he looked decidedly uneasy.

"A lady?" he asked, probing for more information.

Rof Tin ducked his head, halfway between a bow
and a formal inclination of the head. "She says she's
a friend."

Clarence sat back. On the one hand, the Friendly
Lady was an old, old ploy. He thought his various
enemies on-world and off had moved beyond the
basics, but maybe there was somebody new testing
the Boss' defenses.

There was always somebody new.

On the second hand...

"It'd be a shame and a discourtesy to keep a friend waiting," he said, setting his screen to one side, and giving a thought to the hideaway nestled snug up his sleeve.

He nodded. "Show the lady in."

Rof Tin bowed, triggered the door and stepped into the foyer.

"Please," he said, in a mode recognizably that of child-of-the-House-to-guest; "Boss O'Berin will see you."

The lady stepped inside, both hands out in plain sight, good pilot leather on her back, and pretty far gone in a family way.

The door closed.

Horror threw Clarence to his feet and into the dialect of his youth.

"For the love o'space, woman! What's he thinking to let you come down here to me?"

She tipped her head, green eyes considering. Before he could wrap his tongue around the proper Liaden, she had smiled and inclined her head.

"From New Dublin you are?"

New Dublin was a lawful world, as far away from where he'd come up as Rof Tin's honeycomb was from High Port.

"No, lassie," he said, gently. "I lived in deeper than that."

"Ah. It is you speak as Anne speaks, in Terran."

"Not surprising. The Gaelic Union seeded a lot of colonies." He shook himself and stepped 'round the desk to set the chair more comfortably for her.

"Sit down, do," he said, finding his Liaden again in the mode of Comrade. "Would you like some tea?"

"Thank you, no."

That was prudent, at least, he thought, trying to approve her sense. But—

He sat down again behind the desk. "Aelliana, why are you here?"

"I have urgent business with you," she answered, as if it were the most reasonable thing in the galaxy.

"Very well. But, I advise: If it happens again that you have urgent business with me, send a message and I will meet you at Ongit's. It's not seemly for you to come to me."

Also, he added silently, it was damned dangerous. What the *blue blazes* was Daav thinking?

"Surely it is seemly, when I must ask you to grant me a boon."

He stared at her, suddenly chilly. "What boon?"

Aelliana inclined her head. "You are the delm of Low Port. I ask safe passage."

"I'm not the delm of Low Port, I'm the Juntavas Boss on Liad," Clarence said, grateful that Comrade allowed one to instruct without insult. "There's no guarantee of safe passage through Low Port, Aelliana. Not even for me."

She touched her tongue to her lips, and took a breath.

"Daav is on the Low Port," she said, and he could hear the strain in her voice, even under the kindly mode. "He left two nights ago and he has not come back."

Which explained a lot of things and confused a few more.

"His brother wishes to go after him. I— *The delm*— has disallowed this." Her lips quirked.

"So *the delm* wants to go in, instead?" Clarence shook his head. "I'm not such a fool as to risk both of you—your pardon—the three of you."

Aelliana raised her chin. "If you are not the delm of Low Port, can you prevent me?"

Clarence grinned at her. "Yes. Remember where you are."

Her lips tightened, and it gave him a pang, but dammit, she couldn't just come waltzing onto dangerous ground, like—

"He is alive," Aelliana said. "I can go directly to the place. I think."

"Might be he'll just walk out himself, after whatever business he's doing is done. If you surprise him in the midst, it might . . . disturb the balance, and place all in peril."

Aelliana shook her head. "I—he is not . . . well, Clarence. I think that he would walk out, if he could."

Ah, hell.

"If you would grant an escort, someone who is wise in the streets," Aelliana was saying. "Daav said that two draw the eye in Low Port, but I think that the risk—"

"You are not going to Low Port," Clarence interrupted. "I forbid it and I have the ability to enforce my will in this." He held up a hand, as her lips parted.

"Allow me a moment," he said. "If you are likewise lost or taken, to whom does the Ring fall?"

"To Er Thom," she said promptly.

"Correct. As much as I honor him, I do not want Er Thom yos'Galan to wear Korval's Ring. He measures with a far heavier hand than his brother, and I fear the consequences—for Korval, for the Juntavas, and for Low Port itself— if he is required to Balance the loss of three of the Line Direct."

She sat quiet for a long time, looking down at her hands folded on her lap. He gave her time, and at last she looked up.

"I withdraw my original boon," she said. "But I ask another."

Clarence inclined his head. "I hear."

She stared into his face as if, Clarence thought, she was trying to read his mind. Almost, he felt as if she could.

"I ask that you yourself and your most trusted crew fetch Daav home."

That was a favor more to his liking, and in fact he had already decided on it.

"You said you know where he is. Tell me and I'll go in now and pull him out."

Aelliana laughed. "I know where he is in the sense that I can go there. Street designations, shop names— those, I cannot tell you."

He thought about that. "Map?" he asked, reaching to turn the screen around.

She rose and came to the desk.

"It's worth a try," she said in Terran.

· · · ·✷· · · ·

The guard was Terran, and she knew his name—at least, a Terranized form of what might be his name. When he was aware, which he was only briefly from time to time, she had a tendency to chatter.

She was chattering now.

"Word's come down that the boss is on the way, David. You'll be glad of that, won't you? Get you in the 'doc, patch that leg up, give you a touch of detox. This time tomorrow, you'll be feeling as spry and as sassy as you were when you broke Jady's neck for him. Providing you're polite. The boss likes everything nice. You take some advice and be nice."

He was hazy on which of the four who had beset him had been the late and apparently unlamented Jady. He thought he had accounted for two, but the quarters had been close and the lighting confused. Nor had whoever struck him across the back of the head employed any unnecessary gentleness.

Not to mention whatever was in the hypo his guard—he thought her name was Kitten—used on him whenever he had been awake too long.

"Boss said to hold you awake," Kitten confided. She patted his broken leg, firmly.

He ground his teeth and failed to scream.

"Tough guy," she said, apparently approving. "Bounty's been out on you for a long time—dead or alive. Lucky thing the high price was for *alive*, or Jady'd just drilled you from the roof 'cross the way and not had us all down to dance."

She leaned over, making sure of his bonds. Satisfied, she patted him again, more intimately, laughing when he glared.

"You liked it good enough when you was under," she said. "All you got to do now is take it easy. Boss'll be here inside the hour. In the meantime, if you want anything, just whistle."

She left him alone in the tiny alcove that was his prison. In happier times, he thought it had been a closet. It was big enough for the cot to which he was bound, his broken leg strapped to a board in rough first aid. A small mercy, that, and one for which he was grateful.

Daav closed his eyes. "The boss" argued for Clarence, though what he could possibly hope to gain by maintaining Daav alive—he took a painful breath.

If Daav was a prisoner, he was a guarantee of Aelliana's compliance. And if Clarence had decided to expand his operations, as this harvesting of pilots seemed to indicate, then he would very much need Korval compliant.

If—

Fire ran his nervous system, and he spasmed against his bonds, gasping—then collapsed, boneless, panting, and soaked in sweat.

Kitten appeared briefly in the doorway.

"Yeah," she said. "That'll be the withdrawal from the drug. You can expect more of the same until you get another jolt of the good stuff, or that detox like the boss might have for you."

She vanished, then, closing the door behind her.

Fire arced through him . . .

· · · · 🌼 · · · ·

They swept in carefully, and this time it paid off. The second-story crew took the gun on the roof across from the place Aelliana had showed him on the map without even raising dust. There were two on the door; one bolted, and fell to a trank gun; the other ran into Rof Tin's fist.

Upstairs, a burly woman in a faded orange mechanic's coverall drew a gun—and dropped it, jerking her head at a sealed closet.

"Put her to sleep," Clarence snapped, remembering

the first time, when he and Daav had lost the reaper to a poison tooth...

Standing to one side, gun ready, he triggered the door to the closet. What was inside—

For a moment, he thought he'd come too late; the form on the cot lay so still. Then he saw the chest move, heard the harsh sound of panting, and yelled for the kit.

They hit him with a general detox, full-spectrum antibiotic, and got a balloon brace on the leg. It was only then that they turned their attention to the cuffs, Clarence picking one and Sara on the other.

"Boss." The word was raw, barely above a whisper. Clarence looked down into half-crazed black eyes.

"Daav."

"It was you, harvesting pilots. She said you were coming..."

"You," Clarence said in Terran, "have just spent the last day or two in hell; there's drugs I don't care to think too close on soaking up your blood and your good sense, and you've no business thinking anything at all."

"She said—"

"You'll tell me what she said later," Clarence said firmly. "I'm here to fetch you home to your wife, laddie, just like she asked me to do. You've been gone too long, and she's having the devil's own time keeping your brother to the High Port."

Daav drew a sharp breath.

"That was my thought, too," Clarence said comfortably. "Now, listen to me, Daav. You're a fair mess and I don't want to distress Aelliana any more than she already is. We'll make a stop at my office and get you half-patched, then we'll all have a nice chat at Ongit's. Does that suit you?"

It probably scared the heart out of him, Clarence thought, but Daav yos'Phelium wasn't one to let mortal terror stop him.

"It suits me," he said in a raw, rasping voice. He shifted on the bed, newly freed hand groping along his belt.

"What's missing?" Clarence asked, though he thought he knew.

"Gun."

"Right." He slid his spare out and put it in the other man's hand. "You're welcome to mine. Have a care; it's loaded."

Daav nodded, his arm, with the gun in his hand, stretched along the edge of the cot.

"Thank you, Clarence."

He stood and motioned to Sara that she should take up her end of the cot.

"No trouble at all, laddie," he said. "Not a bit o' trouble at all."

· · · · ✷ · · · ·

She hadn't told Er Thom where she was going or whom she was to meet. It was foolish; she knew it was foolish and yet she did it. Which was, she thought, taking her seat in the private room deep in the heart of Ongit's, precisely what Daav had done and for precisely the same reason.

Korval was too thin. The former delm had not gone to Low Port herself, she had sent her heir. His loss would have wounded the clan, but it would not have crippled it. There was no heir or maiden uncle for

Korval's present delm to send upon difficult missions. Every life was precious, and the combination of duty and necessity put them all at risk. The delm's duty, to preserve the clan, became the duty to preserve the future of the greater number of the clan, thus increasing the delm's personal danger.

She could see the graph inside her head; she could trace the lines of causation, and—

There was a tap at the door, and the elder Mr. Ongit stepped in, followed by Clarence, moving slowly, to accommodate the comrade who leaned hard on him, face drawn, and eyes haunted. Weariness flowed out from him, and a toxic wash of horror, pain, shame, and self-loathing.

She spun to where the elder gentleman waited by the door.

"Of your goodness summon a Healer immediately. Say that Korval is in need—wait!" She spun back to Clarence. "Yourself?"

He shook his head, and offered her a smile so weary it barely curved the straight line of his mouth. "I'm good, thanks," he said in Terran.

She nodded and looked back to Mr. Ongit. "One Healer—as quickly as you can."

He bowed and was gone. Aelliana turned again, finding that Clarence had gotten Daav seated and dropped into the chair opposite.

"Well," she said, taking the last chair, "which of you has the strength to tell me what has happened?"

Clarence laughed tiredly and shook his head.

"Short form, there's somebody else trying to set themselves up as boss. Whoever that is has a hit list and a nice crew of reapers. Daav's name was on the list and they took him down for the bounty, as Daav says his keeper told him. I'll know more after I've had a couple of good chats with those we brought home with us. When I do, I'll send the report along by courier, if that suits."

"It does," she said, with a glance at Daav, who was sitting where Clarence had put him, his head against the back of the chair and his eyes closed.

"He's had a bit of a bad time," Clarence said, following her gaze.

"It could have been worse," Daav murmured, sounding very nearly like himself.

"That's right," Clarence allowed, and rose with a wince. "I'll be taking myself off, gentle people." He bowed. "Aelliana, your servant. Daav—"

He moved a hand without opening his eyes. "Do not, I beg you, say so, or you will be doing nothing else with your time aside fetching me out of dreadful scrapes."

Clarence grinned. "I could branch out into bodyguard."

"So you could. Clarence—" He lifted his head with an effort Aelliana felt in her own muscles, and opened his eyes. "Thank you. I am in your debt."

"No, now *that* you're not. There are no debts between us. It's forgotten, and of your kindness you'll do the same."

There was a small silence, then Daav sighed, his mouth curving slightly.

"You drive a hard bargain, Pilot. Yes, that is the course of wisdom. Let it be so. Good lift."

"Safe landing."

He crossed the room, reaching the door just as it opened to admit Mr. Ongit, with the Healer.

THIRTY-FIVE

· ·

A clan's treasure is its children.
　　—From the Liaden Code of Proper Conduct

THE TREE HAD GIVEN SEVERAL PODS, WHICH DAAV HAD eaten without hesitation, and with every evidence of enjoyment. Aelliana was apparently judged well enough, for nothing fell to her hand. That was, as far as she cared, as it should be. Her concern at the moment was all for him.

Though he had received benefit from both the Healer and the autodoc, he seemed to her . . . tired; his signal, normally so clear, was subdued. The Healer had said that he might find it difficult to concentrate over the next few days, which was an artifact of the drug his captor had used to enthrall him. Aelliana gathered that there were crueler drugs that they might have used, but not very many.

She sighed, her back against the tree's comforting trunk, and looked down into his face.

Almost, she thought, *almost, I had lost him.* Her heart trembled, and she extended a hand to trace the stark line of his cheek.

"I love you," she murmured. "*Van'chela*, I love you so much that it frightens me."

"I know," he whispered. He opened his eyes and gazed up into her face. "You're weeping. It all came out well in the end, Aelliana."

"This time," she acknowledged unsteadily. "And yet it could have gone wrong in so many ways. They—"

He raised his hand and pressed his fingers gently against her lips.

"No. Do not consider what they might have done, nor even what they have done. They failed; we prevailed. That is what we recall."

She took a breath; nodded.

"That is well," he murmured. "Now, attend me, for I have been remiss and thus placed the delmae into danger. In the past, when the delms of Korval and the Boss of Liad have found it necessary to share information, a message is dispatched and a mutually acceptable time is found for them to meet at Ongit's. There is no reason for Korval to go to the Boss, or, indeed, for the Boss to come to Korval."

"Clarence said the same," Aelliana admitted. She laughed slightly. "Truly, Daav, I have seldom beheld someone so honestly horrified to see me."

"Clarence has a great deal of good sense," Daav murmured, and turned his head away, as if listening.

"Oh, dear." He sighed. "I believe we are both about to be scolded masterfully."

Aelliana frowned. She heard the breeze in the leaves, the repetitive call of a to-me, the bright burst of a rindlebird's song—and footsteps, light and quick, growing more distinct.

Er Thom appeared 'round the bend in the path, and crossed the grass to them.

With neither ceremony nor greeting, he dropped to his knees and leaned forward to look closely into Daav's eyes.

"Brother, how do you go on?" he asked.

"Well enough. The Healer did his work well."

"Good." Er Thom drew a hard breath, and sat back on his heels, his mouth tightening.

"I am going to murder you myself and save the toughs of Low Port any more losses," he said, his voice hard and distinct. He looked up, sparing a glare for her.

"And you! Do you have no better understanding than to place yourself and Korval's heir into the hands of one of the most dangerous people on this planet?"

"Neither then nor now," Aelliana said, meeting his anger with softness. "Clarence did well by us. It was he who brought Daav out of Low Port, which I don't think anyone else could have done. He was as distressed to see me in his office as you could have wished him to be, Er Thom, and lessoned me well. I honor him."

Er Thom closed his eyes and took a hard breath.

"Stipulate," Daav said, before his brother could speak again, "that we are idiots of the first water, polished and ready to be set."

There was a moment of silence before Er Thom sighed and opened his eyes.

"Stipulated."

Daav smiled. "Excellent. Now tell me, do, what else I might have done, given the contract and the ever-more-disturbing reports coming from our sources in the Low Port."

"There is no reason for you to go yourself," Er Thom said. "You might have done as our mother often did, and sent another of the clan as her eyes and her ears."

"I might have done so," Daav agreed. "Who would you suggest?"

"Myself."

Daav laughed. "Oh, yes! Twelves better!"

Er Thom looked goaded.

"They had Daav's name," Aelliana said, before he started in to brangle again. "It does speak to your point, that he should not have gone alone. But he could not have known that there was a bounty on his head, and the entire Low Port on the hunt for him."

Er Thom glanced to Daav. "Your personal name."

"In fact. Interesting, is it not? Clarence has kindly sent us a transcript of a conversation he had with my jailer, one Kitten Sandith. Kitten would have it that Terran Enterprises, Galactic is setting up headquarters in the Low Port, recruiting pilots and seeking to supplant both the Juntavas and, in her terms, 'the Liaden overlords of trade.'"

"Replacing both of those groups," Er Thom murmured, "with itself?" He sighed. "How is it that Boss O'Berin—whom I allow to be a canny man with a careful eye to his own best health—how is it that he has failed to notice the incursion of this group into his territory?"

"Because they're *wingnuts*," Aelliana explained, proud to have remembered Clarence's precise terminology.

Er Thom stared at her, before looking again to Daav.

"A wingnut is a small bit of hardware which is used to cap a screw."

"'Technically correct," Daav admitted. "However, in the vernacular usage, a wingnut is a person of lamentable understanding who is unlikely to be able to find his way, unaided, out of a paper bag."

"Ah. I am to understand from this that Boss O'Berin knew of the group's presence, but unfortunately underestimated the level of threat they posed to his operations and to the pilots on the port?"

"That fairly states the case."

"Now that he is aware, what does he ..." Er Thom paused. "No. Let us return to a former point. How came these ... persons ... to have your personal name?"

Daav sighed. "You will understand that Kitten is not a philosopher, nor is she disinclined to do a bit of freelancing from time to time. It would appear from the transcript that the Terran Party has taken strong exception to my gift to them of the gene maps from Grandmother Cantra's log book, and has offered a bounty. So far, they are the only organization to have paid the least attention. I suppose I ought to be gratified."

Er Thom frowned. "We had known it was a risk, which is why the gift was sent anonymously."

"Yes, and *that* makes for interesting speculation. Who informs the Terran Party?"

Daav was becoming agitated; the peace that the Healer had put on him was beginning to fray. Aelliana felt it, and did not approve.

"Perhaps," she said, stroking his hair back from his forehead, and sending Er Thom a hard glance, "the Terran Party is not entirely comprised of wingnuts."

"Now, that," Daav murmured, "is a truly terrifying thought."

Something was wrong. She—he—they felt a pain—a contraction of the belly and—

"Aelliana." Daav sat up, his arm around her shoulders.

"No," she gasped, around a second contraction. "Daav, you are making yourself ill."

"Not ill," he said softly. "The child has decided, I think." He took a breath and she felt him focus, his attention like a breath of cool air on her face, which was suddenly much too warm.

"Brother, of your kindness, go ahead of us and summon the Healer."

"Yes," Er Thom agreed, and was gone, running at pilot speed.

"No," Aelliana said. "It's too early, *van'chela* . . ."

"Not so early as that," he murmured. "Now, I am going to carry you, my lady. I pray you will bear with me."

The contractions were coming closer together now, and she remembered this part, with sudden vividness, with the med tech hovering, concerned for her pain, and she thought—she remembered that she thought, *But every step of the getting here has been pain, what else should there be at the end?*

The med tech, that was it, and her husband, sitting where she could see him, whenever she opened her eyes. Just that, the med tech and her husband, and the air stitched with pain. The med tech had called for a Healer, she remembered that, too.

But the Healer never came.

The pain struck again, like a wave—isn't that what they had said it was like? A wave? Arcing high and higher, milky green, with lace frothing at the fore, she remembered that, too, from when they had—and then it vanished, like snow, not like a wave at all, and someone was talking, very softly, so that they wouldn't wake her, but she wasn't asleep, she could hear them perfectly well. They were talking about sending him away, just into the next room, so that she would not be endangered—and he was going—

"Daav!" She tried to sit up, reaching—he caught her hand; she felt the power of their bond, buoying her like a leaf atop the next wave.

"Your lordship, you must leave," the Healer's voice was urgent. "I cannot give her what she requires from behind a shield."

"No." She gripped his fingers. "Daav stays. The Healer may—the Healer may be excused."

"Aelliana," he murmured, taking her other hand.

She opened her eyes, and he was there, kneeling beside the birth-bed. She looked up into his face—he was worried, exalted, wary, adoring—she saw it all; felt it all. "The Healer is here to make the birth easier for you, beloved," he said. "You do not wish to begin your relationship with our child in pain."

"Our child," she panted, meaning to say that they had both made him and ought both to welcome him, but there came the next wave—a towering monstrosity that reared its back halfway to OutEight, and she a leaf, floating atop. "Stay, *van'chela*. You do us well . . ."

"She does seem to take solace from your presence," the Healer murmured. "You do as well as I could." There was a rustle, soft footsteps. "I will be in the antechamber, if the lady calls."

Another wave, another and another, coming hard and close now, a rippling mountain range of waves, over which she glided, exultant, on dragon wings, borne up by starwind. She looked aside, and there he was, flying wingtip to wingtip: her love, her mate, her second self. She laughed, seeing the pattern of the winds across the foaming mountaintops, understanding their meaning and utility.

She tipped a wing and spiraled upward, daring him to follow her, up, and further yet, into the starweb, their wings stretching wide and wider, their bond forging into adamantine, until she was he, and he, her, and the both of them as ineluctable as—

"Aelliana..." Her voice. No. *His* voice. The wind fell; she set her wings and glided down the mountainside, feeling him nestled in her soul even as she swept into her body, and knew exhaustion, felt the birthing bed enclosing her, and her hands lying folded together beneath her breast.

"Aelliana," Daav said again.

She smiled to hear his voice, stirred a little, and opened her eyes.

He was kneeling at her side, his face filled with tenderness and amazement, a green blanket cradled in his arms.

"Aelliana," he murmured, "behold our son."

THIRTY-SIX

· · · · · · · · · · · · · · · · · ·

Each person shall provide their clan of origin with
a child of their blood, who will be raised by the
clan and belong to the clan, despite whatever
may later occur to place the parent beyond the
clan's authority. And this shall be Law for every
person of every clan.
> —From the Charter of the Council of Clans
> Made in the Sixth Year After Planetfall,
> City of Solcintra, Liad

THE CHILDREN WERE OUTSIDE ON THE BALCONY, WHERE
they had gone, so Luken phrased it, in his gentle way,
to enjoy the beauties of the day. Aelliana thought
that they had rather gone to remove themselves from
beneath Kareen's eye, which took a dim view of such
things as coloring, reading, and the launching of toy
spaceships.

Aelliana had remained in the birthing parlor until
she felt the need to escape Kareen's eye, and stepped
out onto the balcony, with a murmured excuse about
wanting some air.

She doubted that Kareen, who was speaking at,

rather than to Luken, heard her. Daav, who had stepped over to talk with Mr. pak'Ora, surely did.

The balcony overlooked a formal lawn and a far lacery of lesser trees. A flowering vine grew along the railing, trailing tendrils down onto the stone seat where the children—those being Pat Rin and Shan—were playing with—Aelliana squinted, trying to see—ah. Playing with dice.

Pat Rin shook the dice.

"Three," he said and threw them. They tumbled, stopped—and Shan shrieked with laughter.

"Do it again!" he cried.

Obligingly, the older boy picked up the dice and shook them in his fist.

"What number would you like?" he asked.

"Nine!" Shan said decisively.

Pat Rin bit his lip, and threw.

Aelliana drew close. The dice came to rest, showing seven on one face, and two on the other.

"Nine, it is," she said approvingly. "How clever."

"Aunt Aelli!" Shan crowed, leaping from his seat and throwing himself against her legs.

Pat Rin rose more seemly and made a bow.

"Good afternoon, Aunt Aelliana," he said, his voice and face far too formal for so young a child. "May I fetch you some—some wine, or some juice?"

"Thank you, no; I've only just finished a glass of juice. I came out to take the air." She considered him—grave face and wary brown eyes. "May I see your dice?"

"Of course." He caught them up off the bench and offered them to her.

She weighed them in her palm, but they seemed

to be honorable—no clover weights or shaved corners.
Bending, she shook them and released with a practiced
snap of the wrist. The dice behaved precisely as they
ought, revealing no concealed magnets or tiny gyros.

"Roll three, Aunt Aelli!" Shan cried, climbing back
on the bench.

"I'll do my best," she said, "but there's no guarantee."

There were, in fact, some tricks one might play
with spin and friction. She gave it her best but—

"Five," Shan said, disappointed.

Aelliana picked up the dice and held them out to
Pat Rin, standing by so quietly.

"Will you roll three for your cousin?" she asked.

"Yes," he said without hesitation, and took the dice
from her hand.

He shook them briefly, and rolled. Shan shouted
with laughter.

"Three!"

Aelliana sat down on the bench and picked up the
dice again.

"This is my specialty, you know," she said, shaking
the dice gently in her palm. "Pseudorandom mathematics, it's called. It means I study things like how cards
fall within ordered systems. I've concentrated on card
games—my dissertation was about card play—but I've
done some study of dice, as well." She looked into
Pat Rin's wary brown eyes. He looked—interested.

"My study has led me to understand that—even
given the random nature of events—dice do not
always display the number that we wish they would.
In fact, very seldom. One might be able to predict, if
one had very quick eyes and could count the sides as
they tumble, but to call the number before the dice

hit the cloth, and be correct, every time—that," she said carefully, "is not how dice operate."

Pat Rin said nothing.

Aelliana held the dice out. "I'd like to perform a test, if you will help me?"

"Yes," Pat Rin said. "I'll be pleased to help."

"That's very kind of you. I wonder if you would be so good as to roll for me. I'll call the number, as Shan was doing. I would like to do this—a dozen times."

"All right," Pat Rin said. He took the dice from her hand and looked up at her expectantly.

"Two," Aelliana said, and he released the dice.

They did it a dozen times; two dozen, and only once did the dice fall other than the call—and that was because Shan, overcome by excitement, tried to catch them when they struck the riser of the bench and bounced back.

Aelliana took the dice back.

"Now you call," she said.

The dice behaved normally on her run of twelve, so whatever he was doing depended upon his controlling the dice. She suspected a supple wrist and an unusual but not unheard of run of felicity, but—

"Perhaps Luken will let me come and dice with you again," she said. "That is, if it will not distress you."

"No," Pat Rin said slowly. "I find it interesting. When I think of my number and throw, I feel that the dice have—" He shot her a conscious glance. "I feel that the dice have *listened*. When I think the number and *you* roll, I don't feel that they've heard me at all." He frowned in thought. "I wonder why that is."

"Sparkles," Shan said, who had long since gotten

bored with the dice and had retired with his spaceships to the middle of the balcony.

Aelliana looked at him. Was it possible, she thought,
that there was a...Healer talent that encompasses
manipulating chance? She would have to ask Jen.

"Aelliana."

Daav stepped out onto the balcony, his face alight,
his eyes fairly glowing.

"We may see Nova now."

He extended a hand to Pat Rin. "That means you,
too, Nephew. We must make your new cousin feel
welcome."

"Yes," said Pat Rin, taking Daav's hand with a grave
smile. "Father read to me out of the Code and we
talked about what might be best. Since she's a little
baby, and not accustomed to gifts, Father said that I
should bring a kiss."

"A most excellent gift," Daav told him.

Aelliana rose, and held her hand down to Shan,
still busy at his toys.

"Don't you want to say hello to your new sister,
Shannie?"

"Yes!" he announced and sprang to his feet. "Father
said I had to be quiet," he confided, as they followed
Daav and Pat Rin into the parlor. "But he didn't say
for how long."

Anne lay in a chaise, her face sweetly peaceful,
her eyes languid. She held a small, blanket-shrouded
form against her breast.

"Such a crowd," she murmured. "When Shannie
came there was only Jerzy and Marilla."

Er Thom touched her cheek.

"Beloved, here is the delm, come to See our child," he murmured.

"Of course there is," Anne said dreamily.

Aelliana stepped forward at Daav's side, took the small bundle that Er Thom handed her and cradled it, in an accommodation that was already second nature.

She folded the blanket back, turning so that Daav could also see the tiny face and the halo of golden hair. Her eyes were open—violet, like her father's.

"Korval Sees Nova yos'Galan," Daav said in the Delm's Mode.

"The Clan rejoices," Aelliana added, and felt that she had never said anything else so true.

THIRTY-SEVEN

. . . .

Do not stand between a Dragon and its Tree.
—From the Liaden Book of Dragons

DAAV SMILED AS HE KNELT BESIDE AN OVERABUNDANT bank of darsibells. The bed should have been thinned some time ago, but he had put the task off, pending the discovery of an appropriate overflow location. Jelaza Kazone's head gardener having only yesterday expressed a need and named an appropriate location in the formal gardens for something very like darsibells, he was now pleased to do the needful.

Aelliana was on an errand at the port, and had taken their child with her. He supposed she would be home soon. They had tickets to the opening of the High Port Pretenders later in the evening.

As always, working in the soil soothed him. The sun warmed his back through his shirt, contributing to a feeling of pleasant dislocation, his thoughts drowsy and slow.

It was a wonder how quickly time fled before joy. The weeks when Mizel had held them apart from each other had each seemed a twelve-year, while the years that had passed since they had at last signed their lines scarcely seemed to encompass days. Indeed, if it were not for the visible evidence of Val Con's growth, he would swear that Kareen's ill-conceived, yet so-useful gather had been but the night before.

He laughed softly. One very long night, in order to properly encompass the courier contracts accepted and fulfilled, Kiladi's seminars taught, Aelliana's papers delivered, and the endless delight of their love for each other.

And then there was their child—another order of joy altogether, mixed liberally with astonishment and dismay. So far, Val Con ruled the nursery in splendid isolation. Not that he was by any means isolated; he spent considerable time with his cousins, and with the nursery crew at Glavda Empri, where one or six of Guayar's next generation was also likely to be found. He was a quiet boy, stubborn, merry, and kind to cats. He was quick with his numbers, as one might expect of Aelliana Caylon's child, and had only to hear a song or a story to be able to repeat it, all but verbatim.

Other things had changed over the long night: The ports had grown chancier; Terran ports, if one were Liaden, chancier still. *Ride the Luck* carried weapons now—weapons, as Aelliana had it, worthy of Korval's pirate founder, gentle Grandmother Cantra. The Low Port pushed at its limits, reaching stealthy fingers out toward Mid Port's plump pockets, to the point that the Portmaster fielded more proctors, and the Pilots Guild offered warnings to those newly arrived, on a street-by-street basis.

But those were distant shadows, even *The Luck*'s arming merely the prudence of pilots who were properly concerned for the well-being of their ship.

He smiled, plying his trowel with a will. Each

flower clump united by a common root ball that ho
excavated, he placed in the moss-lined basket at his
side. If it was darsibells Master Rota wanted, it was
darsibells she should have.

Turning back toward the bed, he paused, head
cocked to one side, listening.

Yes, there were footsteps—two pairs. One pair was
running, lightly but not quite evenly; the other walking quick and soft. Aelliana had very nearly acquired
Scout steps.

He put the trowel down, set the basket back, and
turned to face the path, kneeling as he was. No sooner
was he settled then his small son burst 'round the corner, shirttail flying and a tear in the knee of his pants.

"Father!" Val Con cried excitedly, hurtling into
Daav's arms. "Father, we saw Clonak!"

Hugging the small, wiry body tight, Daav felt his
heart constrict. Clonak had returned to the homeworld
several times since the Deluthia affair had relinquished
him, unscathed. To all appearances, his sojourn among
danger had mended his wounds, and opened for him
a new career path. One for which, he said, with true
Clonak style, he even possessed a talent.

"How did you find Clonak, *denubia*?"

"Funny!" Val Con wriggled and Daav loosed him,
setting him carefully on his feet and keeping a hand
beneath a sharp elbow.

The small face turned up to his, green eyes trimmed
with long dark lashes, the low sun striking red from the
depths of the dark brown hair. Daav sighed. He was
going to be a beauty, this one. All his mother, there.

"He is also," Aelliana said, and dropping easily
to her knee at Daav's side, "at liberty for an entire

relumma. I would not let him go until he had agreed to come to us for Prime."

"Now I understand what kept you," he said, returning her smile.

"No, what kept me was the young gentleman you see before you. He wished to insist that he accompany us, when next we lift out."

"Oh, indeed?" Daav looked down into his son's face. "Has he anything to recommend him?"

"Do we allow willfulness to count?"

Daav kept lips straight with an effort. "Only to a point, I think."

"I know my numbers," Val Con told him earnestly. "I can help."

"Doubtless you could. However, the pilot had denied you, in which case there is no more to be said. The pilot decides first and best for her ship."

"I *want* to go," Val Con said, lower lip becoming prominent.

"That is a different pot of tea," Daav said. "We do not always get what we want."

"Unless the luck is kind," Aelliana added, settling on the grass beside Daav. "Have you forgotten your promise, Val Con?"

Green eyes opened wide, and he was seen to rummage in his pocket, from which he eventually withdrew three seedpods.

"The Tree gave them, when we stopped to say good-day," he explained, holding them out on an only slightly grubby palm.

"That was kind of the Tree, to be sure," Daav murmured, eying the offerings. "But which belongs to whom?"

Val Con looked down at his palm, brows pulled together, then suddenly smiled and put a finger on a pod.

"This one," he said triumphantly, "is for me."

"Very well, then, have it off the table! Which is your mother's?"

Val Con bit his lip, and looked up. "I don't know," he admitted.

"Ah," Daav considered the two pods yet on offer, and shook his head. "I confess that I don't know, either. However, I do know mine."

He plucked it up, feeling it fair vibrate with pleasure against his skin, while Aelliana took the pod remaining, and handed it to him.

"If you please."

"It is," he assured her, "my very great pleasure." He opened the pod and gave her the pieces.

"Val Con-son?" he asked.

The boy sighed and handed over his pod, too.

"I want to be able to open my own," he commented.

"Then you will want to grow stronger," Daav told him, returning the pieces.

"Yes," Val Con said. He sat down without ceremony on the grass and began to eat his treat.

Daav looked to Aelliana, who had disposed of hers while he had labored, and smiled.

"How was Clonak?" he asked, breaking his own pod, and taking up a bit of kernel.

She tipped her head, considering.

"I find him changed, but cannot say precisely how," she said slowly. "I believe that security must suit him. He spoke of standing captain of a team."

"Good," Daav said. "Having folk to care for is a tonic."

"I would wish him more than a tonic," Aelliana said.

"Clonak said I looked just like you, Father," Val Con stated.

Daav lifted an eyebrow. "Much as it must pain me to say so, it seems that the Scout's eyesight has betrayed him. You, my child, look like your mother."

"I look like myself!" Val Con asserted.

"More so every day," Aelliana agreed, reaching to comb her fingers through his hair.

"Indeed, one sees signs of an emerging style," Daav added, eying the torn pants leg.

He glanced at Aelliana. "This state of disarray is notable, even given the source. I hesitate to ask, but feel that I must."

"I fell," Val Con said, matter-of-factly.

Again? Daav did not sigh.

"Well, then, that explains it. Falling is historically hard on the wardrobe." He tipped an eyebrow at the boy. "Would you like a flight upstairs to display yourself to Mrs. pel'Cheela?"

Val Con fairly danced. "Yes!"

"Very well. All aboard the *Dragon Flight*!" He swooped the thin body up and onto his shoulders. Val Con shouted his laughter—and again, as Daav surged to his feet.

Aelliana rose with him, the basket of darsibells in hand.

"I'll just drop these off with Master Rota and meet you in our rooms, shall I? We're promised to the play tonight, recall."

"I do recall," Daav told her.

"Jets full!" Val Con commanded, and perforce the good ship *Dragon Flight* took off down the path, flying low and fast.

*   *   *

He came out of the 'fresher to find her in a charming state of half dress; her hair wisping about bare shoulders. She smiled at him and came forward, running her palms over his chest in teasing circles before stretching high on bare toes and fitting her mouth over his.

The kiss was long and thorough; he, a surprised but willing participant, fair panting by the time she was done with him.

Or perhaps not quite done with him. She leaned against him, snug in the circle of his arms, cheek on his shoulder, breasts pressed against him, shivering.

"Aelliana," he managed, his voice nothing like steady.

She moved her head, idly nuzzling the skin beneath his collarbone.

"Aelliana, we will be late."

Her lips moved, trailing fire. She sighed and looked up at him, eyes as bright as he had ever seen them.

"Daav," she murmured. "I think we should have another child."

He considered her. "Do you plan on murdering the one we have, or is this to be in addition?"

"In addition," she said.

"Very good. I approve in principle."

Her hand slid inside his robe, and he gasped, ready all at once.

"Are we," he asked shakily, "to begin construction at once?"

Aelliana smiled, her fingers moving maddeningly. "I think that would be perfect."

"I can scarcely argue with a lady who has a plan. However, I point out that we will miss the play, which means we must on the morrow write a note. I mention this only because I am aware of how little you like to write notes."

Her other hand crept up 'round his neck and pulled him down to her.

"We only have to miss the first act," she whispered.

· · · · ❊ · · · ·

Aelliana slipped her hand through Daav's arm, letting the familiar and ever-new wash of his signal buoy her. They had parked in Korval's usual space by the theater. Ahead, she could see the intermission crowd just beginning to return to the theater, for the beginning of the second act.

"There," Daav said. "We shall be seen by all the world; no notes need to be written—truly, a most satisfactory outcome!"

Something moved in the shadows ahead. She felt Daav take notice, but no more than just that—notice. They walked on, quickly enough that they would merge with the last ripple of returning theatergoers, thus making it appear that they had been there for the entire time. They would go up to Korval's box and—

From behind them, a shout. Daav half-turned; she felt the stab of his concern.

A shadow stepped out of the shadow ahead; a tall, broad-shouldered man—a Terran, she thought with cold clarity. He brought his gun up, unhurried and certain.

Aelliana saw him acquire his target. Inside her head, she saw the bullet's trajectory, saw Daav's head explode. She jumped, twisting, striking Daav with every bit of her strength, throwing herself forward and up—

The last thing she knew was satisfaction, and the beloved sense of him holding her close, and forever.

THIRTY-EIGHT

. . . .

Al'bresh venat'i...

"DAAV."

From the silent, freezing dark of outspace, he took note. Of the word. And of the voice.

"Daav."

He drifted closer. The word had a certain familiarity; there was a worn feel to the voice. It was not, perhaps, the first, or even the fiftieth, time it had spoken that word.

"Daav." The voice caught. "Brother, I beg you."

He was close now; close enough to know whose voice it was—one of two in all the universe, that might have called him back.

"Er Thom..."

He felt—a grip. Fingers closing hard around his— around *his hand*. Yes. He gasped, groped, as if for controls, and opened his eyes.

For a heartbeat, there was input, but no information. Colors smeared, shapes twisted out of sense, a whispery keening disordered the air. The strong grip did not falter.

"A moment, a moment. Allow the systems to do their work, Pilot..."

He had weight now, and a form that stretched beyond his hand. The colors acquired edges, the shapes solidified, the keening—*he* was producing that noise, dreadful and lost.

"Daav?"

He blinked, and it was Er Thom's face he saw, drawn and pale, lashes tangled with dried tears.

He licked his lips, and deliberately drew a breath.

"Brother..."

The keening stopped, unable to fit 'round the fullness of that word, but the sense of it remained at the core of him, jagged with horror, blighted by loss.

Fresh tears spilled from Er Thom's eyes. He raised his free hand, and tenderly cupped Daav's cheek.

"*Denubia*, I thought you were gone from us."

"Where?" he asked, meaning, *Where would I have gone?* but Er Thom answered another question.

"High Port Medical Arts."

The hospital.

"Why?"

Er Thom moved his hand, smoothing Daav's eyebrows, brushing tumbled hair from his forehead.

"The response team brought you both in, of course," he whispered; the tears were running freely now. "They—there was no visible wound, and yet—you did not wake. Your life signs grew weaker, and the Healers—Master Kestra herself—said she would not dare to intervene, for she did not know what she was seeing."

The horror at the core of him grew toothier. He

tried to pull his hand away, but Er Thom hold on like a man with a grip on a lifeline.

"Aelliana?" he asked, and that was an error, for as soon as he spoke, he remembered: the shout, his turn, the sound of the gun, and Aelliana leaping, graceful and sure—her body torn by the blast, slamming into him, and a vortex of absence, sucking him out, out, alone, gone, dead...

"Aelliana!"

He twisted, prisoned by the bedclothes, desperate to escape the agony of loss.

Er Thom caught his shoulders, pressed him against the bed and held him there while he flailed and screamed, and at last only wept, weakly, turning his face into the tumbled blankets.

His brother gathered him up, then, and held him cradled like a babe, murmuring, wordless and soothing, and Aelliana, *Aelliana*...

"Another child," he whispered. "She had said we should have another child. We were late..."

"He thought he had missed you, going in," Er Thom murmured. "The gunman said as much before he died of his wounds. He thought to wait until the end of the play and catch you as you came away."

"Wounds? There was no one but us, on the street, who would have wounded—"

"You," his brother said. "The medics found your hideaway by your hand, and that prompted them to look for another who might be in need."

Had he been quicker, had he been more alert—he might have preserved her life.

"He said," Er Thom murmured, "that you were the target. That the Terran Party has a price on your head."

"She saw him," he whispered. "Timing and trajectory were blood and breath to her. She deliberately put herself into harm's way. Gods, Aelliana..."

"Pilot's choice," Er Thom said, though his voice was not by any means steady. "Brother, will you come home?"

Home? The rooms, her things lying where she had left them. Their apartment, with her scent and her imprint on everything. He could not... And yet where else was there to go?

His heart was beginning to pound. He drew a hard breath, and forcefully turned his thoughts to other questions; questions that Er Thom would expect.

"How long have I been—unconscious?"

"Three days," Er Thom answered, adding carefully, "Val Con is with us."

Val Con. Another bolt of agony shuddered through him. What was he going to tell their child? How could he begin to comfort Val Con, when he could scarcely hold himself rational from heartbeat to heartbeat?

"Daav?"

"Yes." He raised his head and kissed his brother, softly, on the lips. "Let us by all means go home."

Of course, it wasn't as simple as merely going home. The med techs needed their time with him, running suite after suite of diagnostics. He was found to be well-enough for a man who had sustained what the head of the tech team termed "a massive shock to the nervous and circulatory systems." One received the distinct impression that med techs had not expected him to survive.

If only he had not.

Blackness seized him; his breath went short; the

room, the med tech, the instruments all and every
thing smeared into a blur of senseless color. Dislocated,
he fell—and his knees struck the vanished floor.

The jolt focused him; he gasped for breath; heard
the med tech call out; felt a hand beneath his elbow.

"Are you in pain?" the tech asked.

Was he in pain? Daav felt something like laughter,
if laughter were bleak and bladed and chill, snarling
in his chest. He gritted his teeth and denied it.

"I am—a thought unbalanced," he managed, breath
coming easier now. "A momentary lapse."

"Ah," the tech said and spoke over Daav's head.
"Let us assist the pilot to the chair, please. Then,
rerun the room readings for the last six minutes."

He allowed them to lend him support and crept to
the diagnostic chair on their arms, like a toddler taking
his first steps on the arms of fond family. Once he
was seated, the shorter med tech left them, doubtless
to find the room readings, as she had been directed.

Daav leaned back and closed his eyes, spent.

"Blood sugars critical," the tech murmured. "Sys-
tolic . . ."

He took a soft breath. "Attend me, Pilot. It would
seem that you have suffered yet another potent shock
to your system. Please rest here. The chair will give
you several injections, to assist in balancing your body's
systems. I will return in a moment."

He departed. Daav lay limp in the chair, scarcely
caring when the injections were administered. Over
in the corner, he could hear the techs speaking quietly, they thought. His hearing had returned with
his eyesight, however, and he heard how worriedly
they discussed plummeting blood pressure, a sudden,

unexplainable crisis of blood sugars, and a glittering moment of cranial pyrotechnics.

"Seizure," the team leader murmured.

Fear flooded him, very nearly drowning the horror of his loss. If the med techs could prove brain damage, he would never fly again. He stirred in the chair.

"I am," he said, and stopped, shocked at how weak his voice was. He opened his eyes. Both of the techs were watching him, alarm clearly visible.

Daav took a deep breath.

"I am," he said again, "the surviving partner of a true lifemating."

The techs exchanged a glance.

"I suggest," Daav continued, "that I be released into the care of my kin, with whatever regimen will, in your professional opinions, best restore my strength. When I have had some time to become..." His breath grabbed; he deliberately breathed deeply, "... some time to become accustomed, then I will return for another series of diagnostics."

"If you have another seizure," the head tech said, "you will immediately return here."

"Agreed," he said, feeling considerably more awake. The injections from the kindly chair at work, no doubt.

"Very well," the head med tech said, motioning his subordinate out of the room ahead of him. "We will call your kinsman to you, and bring a mobile chair. Please remain in the diagnostic chair until the mobile arrives. The room is awake and watching as well."

And would certainly report another seizure or any other small infelicity, Daav thought. As it happened, he was content for the moment to rest where he sat.

"I understand," he told the med tech, who gave

him one more hard look before he, too, departed, leaving Daav alone.

Carefully, wishing neither to think, nor to invite yet another state that might cause a med tech even the smallest concern, he began to review the Scout's Rainbow.

In general, he had only to think of the Rainbow in order to achieve its benefits, as accustomed as they were to each other. Now, however, he deliberately slowed the process, visualizing each color particularly and fully before moving on to the next.

He was contemplating, with difficulty, the color blue when he heard the door cycle, and opened his eyes, fully expecting to see Er Thom.

But it was not Er Thom.

He straightened sharply in the chair, his heart jolting in what he could only hope was an unalarming and perfectly usual manner.

"Go away, Master Kestra," he said, his voice harsh. "I don't want you."

The Healer raised her hands, fingers spread wide.

"Peace," she said softly. "I had only come to look, now that you are aware again."

She paused, her eyes focused on some point just above his head, as Healers were wont to do.

"Well," he snapped, "and what do you see?"

"I am not certain," she answered, dreamily. "I note that I am neither blinded nor deafened in your presence, and that we both know the Rainbow is not potent enough to quiet you. Normally.

"I see your pattern, and I see your anguish, and I see the abyss that you carry within. Apparently, choice is available to you."

She blinked, her face sharpening as she looked directly into his eyes.

"You are not brain-burned, if that soothes you, Daav."

"If I continue to have seizures, it will scarcely matter why," he pointed out. "If I continue to have seizures, the Guild will have my license, and rescind my right to fly."

"And you still care about that," the Healer murmured.

"Deeply."

Anger licked through him, and he took a deliberate breath.

"Master Kestra, are you through looking?"

She bowed, gently. "In fact, Korval, I am. In this, I am timely. Your brother approaches."

With no further ado, she turned and walked toward the door, triggered it and stepped back, allowing Er Thom to enter first, in deference to his rank, and then the chair, in deference to the inept driver.

"Master Kestra," Er Thom murmured, pausing to give her a bow. "Have you business with my brother?"

"Our business is done," she said, inclining her head. "He does not accept my assistance. If it should come about that he requires it, please have no hesitation in sending for me."

Er Thom bowed. "Our House is grateful."

"Of course," she said, an edge of irony on her voice. "In the meanwhile, by all means take him home. Hospitals magnify every ill and pain; it is better to heal among kin, especially of such wounds as his."

She bowed then, and passed through the door. Er Thom turned to Daav and offered his arm.

"Daav."

Anne's embrace was sisterly and enveloping. He

leaned his head against her shoulder and for a heart beat simply accepted the comfort that she offered, feeling her warmth and her true affection.

She held him lightly, as would a woman accustomed to handling wild things, or small children, and released him the instant he lifted his head.

"Er Thom will have told you that the boy's with us," she said, in her lilting Terran. "He and his cousins have been having a fine time of it, running Mrs. Intassi ragged. I took it on myself to have some of your things brought up and a room made ready. You're to stay with us for as long as you want and wish to, understand me, laddie?"

"I understand," he said. "Thank you, Anne."

"No thanks," she said severely, and gripped him by his shoulders, forcing him to look up into her face. "No blaming yourself, either—do you hear me? She knew what she was doing."

"I think so, too," he whispered, and cleared his throat, blinking his eyes to clear them.

"Now, you'll tell me what you need to make you comfortable—a bite of food, maybe?"

"No," he said, striving not to sound as if he found the thought of food nauseating. "No, I—I thank you. I think that I wish . . . to be alone for a time." He paused and added, "I'm very tired," which had the felicity of being perfectly true.

She glanced over at Er Thom, who was leaning quietly against his desk. He straightened and came forward.

"Of course you are tired," he murmured. "Come, let me show you to your rooms."

Daav glanced back as he followed Er Thom out

of the room and saw Anne watching him, a look of naked concern on her face.

"Would you like to stop by the nursery and speak with Val Con?" Er Thom asked, as they mounted the back staircase.

Val Con, with his green eyes, and his face so like hers . . .

He took a breath and shook his head.

"Not just—yet, please."

There was a pause before Er Thom said, "Of course," and sighed.

"You should know that Anne had told him that we had bad news from the port, and that his mother . . . would not be returning." He shot Daav a sidewise glance.

"Val Con refused to believe Anne's information," Daav said slowly, "and may have . . . lost his temper, just a little."

"Mrs. Intassi reports a display of epic proportion," Er Thom agreed. "She said that she was reminded vividly of yourself."

Daav said nothing, and they walked down the hall in silence, turning the corner into the family wing.

"Here," Er Thom said.

They had given him Sae Zar's old apartment; he recalled coming here once or twice as a child, with Er Thom. It was a gentle choice: on the family wing, yet removed enough from Anne and Er Thom's suite that he could be private in his comings and goings.

Daav put his hand against the plate, sighing as the house recognized him, and opened the door.

"Good evening, Brother," he murmured and took one step forward.

"Daav."

Nerves grating, the longing for solitude a thirst, yet he turned back to face his brother.

"Do you want me to stay with you?" Er Thom asked. He reached out to stroke Daav's cheek, a gesture that moved them both to tears. "Daav? I—I fear for you, alone."

I fear for me, alone, as well, Daav thought, even as he shook his head.

"I swear that I will do nothing . . . irrecoverable tonight," he said, and felt that, perhaps, he would be able to honor that oath. "And you—*denubia*, you are as exhausted as I am—more!—for it fell to you to do all that had to be done, for—for her, and for me. I—" He leaned forward and kissed Er Thom on his damp cheek.

"Go to your lifemate, darling. I—I will come to you tomorrow, and be as seemly as may be."

Er Thom bit his lip. "I cannot imagine," he said, his voice so low that Daav could scarcely hear him. "Beloved, I—" He moved, pilot fast; his embrace swift and fierce.

"Do as you must," he whispered. "I love you, Daav."

"I love you, Brother," he answered, but Er Thom was already walking away, back to his lady, so Daav devoutly hoped, and there to take what rest and comfort that he might.

Deliberately, he stepped across the threshold; closed and locked the door.

The suite was much as he recalled it from childhood: agreeable rooms of good size, overlooking the topiary maze. He found his clothes in Sae Zar's closet; the books that had been occupying his attention on the table beside the double chair; his knives and wood pieces—the worktable itself!—set agreeably before the window; the computer in the office niche displaying a secure connection to Jelaza Kazone's network and to his private sub-net.

Restlessness took him to the bedroom, neat and not overly ornate. His brushes and his jewel box were disposed atop the bureau. Idly, for no better reason that he must be doing something or he would surely go mad, he opened the lid of the jewel box.

Green flashed at him, and a gaudy rainbow of jewel tones. Extending a finger, he touched the emerald drop—the very one she had been wearing when they— his mind veered, and for a long, long moment he wavered on the edge of the abyss.

I can, he thought, feeling the coldness in his own mind, *control this. I have a choice—Master Kestra said as much, did she not?—I do not have to fall into a seizure.*

I do not have to die.

It came to him, then, the fullness of the choice that he had been given. He did not have to die. Nor did he have to live.

He took a breath . . . another. A third, and he was able to look again into his jewel box, seeing the Jump pilot's cluster gaudily flaunt a ship's ransom, and a humbler sheen, like moonlight seen beside the sun.

He picked it up—the old silver puzzle ring that she had had from her grandmother, as a death-gift. His eyes filled as he raised it and slid it onto the smallest finger of his right hand.

"Aelliana," he whispered, bending his head as his tears fell more rapidly. "*Van'chela*, how could you not know that I would have rather died a thousand times in your stead?"

I could not bear to lose you, Daav.

Her voice was so clear, with that wistful tone she adopted when stating something of extreme obviousness. He spun, lips parting for a reply, before he remembered that he would never see, nor hear her again . . .

Horror ripped through him and he saw it all again: her leap, the pellets striking; the stink of blood, the coldness of extinction . . .

He dropped to his knees, unable to stand, put his hands over his face and sobbed; long, wracking sobs torn from the depths of him, until he crumbled facedown on the rug, exhausted; weeping silently now, and, finally, weeping no more.

When he felt he was strong enough to stand, he climbed to his feet, and, grimacing at himself in the mirror, fetched out his robe and strode into the 'fresher, emerging some time later clean, exhausted, and by no means interested in sleep.

He went out into the main room, pausing in the corner kitchen to pour himself a cup of cold water. Kneeling by the table, he sipped while sorting through his books, hoping to find something that might hold his interest.

There was a slight sound, as of a cat scratching at a door unfairly closed against it.

Daav frowned. Presently, there were no house cats at Trealla Fantrol, though there were several who worked the grounds.

The sound came again—a scratching, no doubt— and, yes, at the door.

He rose and crossed the room; touched the plate and opened the door.

A cannonball took his legs out from under him. He snatched, caught, and rolled until he stopped, on his back, halfway to the window, his small son clutched to his breast.

Across the room, the door closed, for lack of instructions to the contrary.

"Father!" Val Con struggled; Daav held him with one arm and stroked his back with the other.

"Softly, my child, I am not at the port."

"Father, you were gone so long…" That was said more seemly, excepting only that the boy's voice shook so.

"It was unavoidable," he said. "I never meant to distress you, *denubia*." He cleared his throat.

"I cannot help but note that it is well beyond that time when you should have been in bed. Did Mrs. Intassi bring you?"

That seemed unlikely. On the other hand, it also seemed unlikely that a small child, no matter how clever, could have slipped away from Mrs. Intassi, who was wise in the ways of childhood stealth and knew all the faces of deceit.

"Mrs. Intassi said I had to wait until tomorrow to see you," Val Con said. "But I had to see you *now*. Nova went to talk to Mrs. Intassi. Shan showed me how to unlock the door. We were supposed to be in bed."

The recounting of successful mischief was soothing; the child was beginning to relax, his muscles loosening under Daav's fingers. He lifted the restraining arm away. Val Con sat up, straddling Daav's chest, and looked down into his face, green eyes foggy.

That was a knife to the gut: Just so did his mother's eyes fog, with worry or—so seldom since they had embraced each other—with fear. Daav took a hard breath—and another as his son leaned forward and put one small hand on each cheek.

"Aunt Anne said that Mother wasn't coming home," he said huskily. "That's wrong, isn't it, Father? Mother lifted, but she'll come home."

Oh, gods. He raised his hand and stroked the back of his fingers along the boy's silken cheek.

"Aunt Anne is, unfortunately, correct," he whispered, feeling tears slip down his cheeks. "Your mother has—has died, Val Con."

The boy stared at him, foggy eyes full. "Like Relchin?" he asked.

The orange-and-white cat had died in his sleep last year, full of years and valor. If only Aelliana had been granted that same grace.

"Yes," Daav told his son. "Like Relchin."

A shudder ran through the thin body and Val Con began, silently, to cry. Daav caught him in both arms and sat up, cradling his child—Aelliana's child, *their* child—against his breast.

He rocked and put his cheek against the boy's soft hair, letting him weep, and weeping himself, in earnest.

Gradually, the boy's sobs lessened, and Daav found his tears less, as well.

"*You* won't die, will you, Father?" the boy's voice was blurry.

Daav sighed and cuddled him close. "Not for so long as I may," he whispered. "I promise."

Val Con sighed, apparently satisfied; and lay limp and exhausted. Daav kissed a damp cheek, and closed his eyes.

The gunman had been after *him*, Er Thom had

said. Daav shivered and held his son closer. Was he a danger, then, to all his kin? Dare he never again walk on the port with his brother, his niece—

His son?

He needed—he needed to think. Gods, he needed to talk this over with Aelliana to—

Not Aelliana, he thought carefully. *You will never speak with Aelliana again.*

It seared, that thought, but the abyss did not open at his feet.

Of course not. He had promised his son that he would try to live.

Cradling Val Con against him, he rose, and carried him into the bedroom. He settled the boy snug under the covers, then lay down next to him, one arm over the small body. He closed his eyes, not expecting to sleep.

The next thing he knew, it was morning.

THIRTY-NINE

. . . .

I have today received Korval's Ring from the hand of Petrella, Thodelm yos'Galan, who had it from the hand of Korval Herself as she lay dying.

My first duty as Korval must be Balance with those who have deprived the clan of Chi yos'Phelium, beloved parent and delm; as well as Sae Zar yos'Galan, gentle cousin, a'thodelm, master trader. There is also Petrella yos'Galan, who I fear has taken her death-wound.

Sae Zar fell while defending his delm. All honor to him.

Chi yos'Phelium died of a second treachery and in dying gave nourishment to her sister, my aunt, who alone of the three was able to win back to home.

The name of the world which has fashioned these losses for Korval is Ganjir, RP-7026-541-773, Tipra Sector, First Quadrant.

This shall be Korval's Balance: As of this hour, the ships of Korval and of Korval's allies do not stop at Ganjir. Korval goods do not go there; Korval cantra finds no investment there. And these

conditions shall remain in force, though Ganjir
starves for want of us.

   . . . I note that my mother is still dead.

      —Daav yos'Phelium
         Eighty-Fifth Delm of Korval
         Entry in the Delm's Diary for
         Finyal Eighthday in the first
         Relumma of the Year Named Saro

"I THANK YOU FOR YOUR GENEROSITY TO MY LIFEMATE.
With her death, your gift returns to you." Daav extended
the Jump pilot's ring.

Jon dea'Cort hardly spared a glance for it; his attention was on Daav's face.

"How are you, child?" he asked, his voice more than
normally gruff.

"Alive," Daav answered, the ring still extended.

"The pilot's ideal, right enough," the elder Scout
acknowledged, and pressed his lips tight.

"Jon," Daav said, perhaps too patiently, "take the ring."

The elder pilot sighed, and finally did look down at
the thing, sparkling like a galaxy against Daav's palm.
Slowly, he raised a hand and took the ring away. He
clenched his fingers, hiding the glitter and the promise
of it, and looked back to Daav, his eyes swimming.

"Don't forget your comrades, Captain. We're here
when you need us."

"I know," Daav whispered, swallowing against rising
tears. "Thank you, Jon."

"No thanks needed between comrades; you know
that."

"I do, and yet—she would have had it so."

The other man bowed his head. "That she would have." He cleared his throat. "Will you be working today?"

He felt equally horrified and tempted—a sensation that had become wearingly familiar. Binjali's was a safe place—for him and, later, for Aelliana. They had met right here in the garage; had learned to trust, and to love, each other...

"Not just today," he managed, around the ache in his chest. "I do not by any means forget my comrades, Master. I—certainly, I will have a shift before the next *relumma* is done."

Jon inclined his head. "As you will."

As he willed. Daav swallowed against the terrible noise that was not laughter, and inclined his head in turn.

"Soon, Jon. Be well."

"And you, child," the old Scout murmured. "And you."

The door cycled as he approached, admitting a familiar, pudgy form.

"Daav." His hand was caught, and he was drawn into an embrace as gentle as it was speaking. A heartbeat only before Clonak released him.

Daav stepped back, raising his hands with fingers spread wide.

"I am just on my way away," he managed.

Clonak nodded and turned with him, back to the door.

"I'll walk with you, if you'll have me," he said.

"It's only a step to my car," Daav murmured, "but if you crave the exercise..."

Outside, it was a sunny, cloudless day, chilly but virtually windless. Aelliana had been dead for thirty-three days.

"Old friend," Clonak murmured, as if he had heard Daav's thought, "there are no words to express—"

Daav's hand shot out on its own, and gripped the other man's arm, tightly—and released him. "Don't, Clonak."

There was a small silence, before Clonak nodded. "I will of course respect your wishes," he said stiffly.

Daav bit his lip, ashamed of his churlishness.

"Forgive me, old friend," he said, with what gentleness he could muster. "You loved her, too—"

Clonak took his arm. "I loved her—and love her yet. However, my concern of the moment is my friend, who seems to be fading as I look at him. Are you *well*, Daav? Do you need—note, I do not say 'want'—a Healer?"

He shuddered and tried to pull away, but Clonak did not relinquish his arm.

Trapped and goaded, he sighed. "The Healers will cause me to forget those things that—that perhaps cause me not to thrive. I—we had so little time! How can I forfeit even one moment?"

"Get down!" Clonak shouted, augmenting the command with a firm push.

Daav hit the ground, rolling, into the shelter of a delivery van, pulled his weapon, and peered out.

A pellet struck 'crete six inches from his nose, cutting a tiny gouge in a spurt of dust.

"Stay down," Clonak snapped from beside him, "and do *try* not to be a target."

"Too late," Daav murmured, though he did withdraw to a position of more prudence behind the van.

Clonak slid something back into his belt. "My crew will be here soon," he said. "Just keep your head down, Daav."

"Crew?"

"Security crew," Clonak said briefly. "I'm team leader."

"So—a practice run."

"Practice makes perfect," Clonak said in Terran. "Who's marked you out as a target, Daav?"

"The Terran Party."

Clonak frowned and shot him a glance. "The Terran Party..." he began.

"...are wingnuts," Daav finished. "Yes, I've been told. They do, however, carry a grudge, and apparently believe that killing me will kill the proof of a common ancestor for Terran, Liaden and Yxtrang."

Clonak stared at him. "They're a little late getting the message, aren't they?"

"Most of the organizations the information was sent to ignored it, so far as I am aware. The Terran Party went to the trouble of finding who I was and setting snipers on me." A pellet struck the side of the van they sheltered behind. "Also, they were kind enough to murder Aelliana."

Clonak said nothing. No one came to claim the van they sheltered behind; no pedestrians or other traffic disturbed them.

No one shot at them.

The device on Clonak's belt vibrated; Daav heard the faint hum.

"Got them," Clonak said. "Want to come along and hear what they have to say?"

He thought about that, weighing the anger that was twisted, twined and inseparable from his grief.

"Yes," he said.

* * *

It was, as he had suspected, the information packet he had sent out to various Terran and Liaden supremacist organizations, detailing the common root. The Terran Party had taken umbrage and word had come down that "Daav yos'Phelium" needed to be taken out.

Hidden, he had listened while Clonak questioned both of the . . . people . . . the team had harvested—questioned them closely. Their target was "Daav yos'Phelium," dangerous madman. Clans meant nothing to them, nor did the Scouts or Solcintra University. It was as if they truly believed that the annihilation of Daav yos'Phelium would destroy the information they found so alarming.

Idiots, he thought, stalking along the river path in Trealla Fantrol's wild garden. He had made his excuses to Clonak when it seemed that he must rise and kill them with his own hands.

Balance—but of course it would not have been Balance. The two women taken by Clonak's team were ignorant; they followed orders and collected their pay. Killing them would have as much to do with answering Aelliana's death as drowning two kittens.

When his mother had been murdered, and Sae Zar, he had removed Ganjir from Korval's trade routes, forever. It had caused some difficulty, he had heard, which had failed to gratify him. Had the planet died, its population starved to answer Korval's deaths, yet it would not have nullified those deaths, nor returned Chi and Sae Zar to the arms of their kin.

So it would be with Aelliana. Balance with the Terran Party could accomplish nothing.

Might not Terra take exception to the wholesale slaughter of her folk? Aelliana asked.

"Assuredly she would," he answered, "and to pot Korval against Terra is something that we are surely mad to contem—"

He ground his teeth together, looked around him at the empty pathway and crossed to an agreeably placed bench. Sinking into it, he closed his eyes.

This happened, too often. He had thought, with time, his halved soul would grow weary of attempting to simulate what was lost. Dreading the day it happened, yet he had supposed that the instances of his "hearing" her would grow further apart, and eventually, over . . . time . . . fade entirely.

Instead, he seemed to hear her voice more often, and more clearly, as he gained in strength. He tried to suppress it, to hear through it, but the effort left him exhausted in heart and soul. He told no one, not even Er Thom—especially not Er Thom—and that subterfuge further exhausted him.

Perhaps—perhaps, he thought, he should have the Healers. They would . . . Aelliana would be wrapped in mists, as if an old memory that no longer had the power to move him. He would forget the sound of her voice, her phrasing, her laughter; forget the color that mounted her cheeks when she was angry. He would be—reft and alone, the joy they had shared something that need no longer trouble him.

He took a breath and brought his attention forcefully back to the problem at hand. Daav yos'Phelium had a price on his head—he was in fact a hunted man who endangered those remaining of his loved ones by his very existence. Did Daav yos'Phelium vanish, then the hunt would cease.

It would, naturally, need to be a widely publicized

disappearance, but he thought he might manage that. There was also the matter of Aelliana's Balance. Certainly, the woman he loved would never have agreed to the slaughter of innocents, even if he found himself willing to pursue such a course.

No, he thought, recalling the interview with the two women. The enemy here was not Terra—it was ignorance.

He might, after all, be able to deal with ignorance.

Sighing, he settled himself more comfortably on the bench, his head resting against the trunk of a silver ash.

Perhaps he fell asleep. Perhaps it was another sort of seizure, which ceded comfortable oblivion, rather than pain and terror.

The stab of a headache brought him to himself again, but he was not drowsing on the bench by the river path.

He was sitting on the family patio at Trealla Fantrol, Val Con tucked onto his lap, the two of them bent over a book. By the count of pages, they had been reading together for some time.

Of the time between his stopping on the bench and this moment, he had no memory . . . at all.

"Father," Val Con scolded, leaning forward to tap the page. "Here. *The nighttime garden was full . . .*"

Daav caught his breath.

"Your pardon, my son; I am . . . a little sleepy. So—" He focused on the page.

"The night-time garden was full with moonlight, and the brown cat had no lack of partners for her dance . . ."

*   *   *

It was not a perfect solving—far from it. And yet, they could not find a better, he and his brother and Mr. dea'Gauss between them.

True, it removed a source of danger from within the heart of the clan, and undertook a Balance in Aelliana's behalf that moved Mr. dea'Gauss to a murmured "Excellent..."

Unhappily, it separated Daav yos'Phelium from every source of comfort and rare joy left in his life. That Daav yos'Phelium was sliding daily into a benevolent madness was something he did not choose to mention. There had been two more episodes of waking into a situation he did not recall; and the instances of hearing her voice were, he was certain, increasing. Sometimes, in the drifting grey mists between sleeping and wakefulness, he would feel her lying beside him, her head on his shoulder comfortably. He would scarcely breathe, striving to draw out the moment, which always ended too soon.

"Timing will be everything, Mr. dea'Gauss," he had said at their last meeting, where Er Thom and Daav signed the papers that made Er Thom *Korval-pernard'i*—holding the Ring and the Clan in trust for Val Con.

"I understand, your lordship. It shall be done appropriately."

"Of course it will, sir. You have never failed us."

Mr. dea'Gauss had inclined his head, and said nothing.

The last meeting had also established that Kareen had been offered the Ring in trust, and had refused it. The Ring should pass entirely, *she* argued; since there was an adult in the Line Direct to take it up.

There was, of course, precedent for this claim, Kareen being expert in such close readings of the Code.

It was all done now, though, and at last, saving one more thing.

Val Con held his hand tightly as they walked down Jelaza Kazone's public hall to the Delm's Hall.

The lights came up as they crossed the threshold, each portrait illuminated individually.

He and Val Con walked slowly, down the long line of Korval's delms. Most frames were inhabited by one face, often stern, rarely by two.

Like the one at the very end.

Daav yos'Phelium and Aelliana Caylon, the Eighty-Fifth Delm of Korval, the inscription ran, and there they were—a good likeness, as the phrase went. He, piratical and sardonic; she, open-faced and intelligent. They were holding hands, Korval's Ring and the Jump pilot's cluster side by side.

Val Con sniffled, and Daav dropped to one knee beside him.

"I miss her," the boy said.

"I miss her, too," he answered—and caught the child close as Val Con threw himself 'round his neck.

"And I'll miss you. Father—don't go!"

"I must, child. I endanger all if I stay."

"But if you go, the clan can't protect you!" Val Con cried, which was closely reasoned, for one so young.

"Sometimes, it is the clan that requires protection," Daav said slowly. He closed his eyes, holding his son tight. "The clan is people, *denubia*; never forget that. We can only protect each other. Sometimes, in order to protect those others who are the clan, a person must do something that is very hard. The clan asks much because it gives much."

His mother had used to say that. He had often

boon of the opinion that the clan took more than it gave—and yet...

"When will you come back?" Val Con demanded.

Gods.

"When I can," he said carefully. "It may not be for a very long time. You'll have Shan and Nova and Uncle Er Thom and Aunt Anne, and so very much to learn. There will hardly be any time to miss me."

Val Con sniffled again, clearly indicating an opposing view.

Daav picked him up.

"Look again," he urged.

"All right," Val Con said after a few moments.

"Good. Now, come with me, of your kindness, Val Con-son. We must make an entry into the Delm's Diaries."

FORTY

· · · · · · · · · · ·

To be outside of the clan is to be dead to the clan.
—Excerpted from the Liaden
Code of Proper Conduct

DAAV YOS'PHELIUM, ONCE-DELM OF KORVAL, WAS DEAD—
a matter of an error in the unrevised edition of the
ven'Tura Tables, which, once embraced, had sent his
ship tumbling into a sun.

Jen Sar Kiladi heard the news, but really, it was
of but passing interest. More pressing was the need
to find a position for himself—and that right quickly.

He had written letters, to colleagues, to former
students, to rivals, begging their condescension and
pointing them to his applications. He had fortunately
gained a place for the coming term as an Expert
Lecturer on Cultural Genetics at Searston University,
thanks to the very kind office of a former student,
now an influential alumnus.

He was bound there now, and how fortunate that
he had indulged his whim, back when he was a graduate student and had time for such things as whims!
A first class pilot's license was a useful tool, and if

the good ship *L'il Orbit* was not as posh as some, it was everything that a research scholar who had lately taken the decision to bring his insights to the classroom could need—or afford.

He finished his last packet and queued it to send. He had one more to compile, then he could quit the wayroom and return to *L'il Orbit*. Time had gotten a bit tighter than he had wished and he was going to have to fly hard in order to reach his Expert Seminar by the date and time stated in his contract.

Kiladi reached to the keyboard, his fingers fumbling enough so that he botched his command. He sighed. He was very tired, but he dared not make use of the thin bunk provided. There was...only... this one...more...

He couldn't have been...absent long—the screen was still live when he blinked into consciousness once more.

Relief that he hadn't lost his search was quickly replaced in quick succession by puzzlement and joy.

A string of dense math filled the screen, both familiar and all but incomprehensible.

"Aelliana?" He scarcely knew he spoke, his heart was beating so that he thought a rib might break. "Aelliana, is it really you?"

You are not, her voice said so strongly that it echoed inside his head, *going mad, and I wish you will listen to me. We are lifemates, and I will never leave you, Daav. I swore it.*

"So you did."

He looked again at the screen. Almost, he could understand the premise, but the argument, while elegant, left him baffled. Clearly, it would require study—and if he were able to produce this sort of work while he was unconscious, then madness was the least of his troubles.

It is not a perfect bonding, I think, she said. *At first—van'chela, it must have seemed to you that I had truly gone. Everything was so strange, and you were so ill... When I learned how to make my voice heard...*

"I denied you," he whispered. "Aelliana, how has this—the Tree."

It would seem so, she said. *Daav?*

"Yes?"

You must sleep before you fly, van'chela. *Please.*

Kiladi, he would risk, but—Aelliana? Not a second time.

"I will," he murmured. "I promise."

EPILOGUE

· · · · · · · · · · · · · · · · ·

THIS IS MORE TEDIOUS THAN RECEIVING THE GUESTS AT *your sister's Festival Eve ball*, the voice only he could hear commented.

It was fairly said, he allowed, bowing yet again, this time to a sandy-haired woman with trembling hands. As much as he might otherwise deplore her, even he acknowledged that his sister possessed impeccable taste.

The sleeves of the sandy haired woman's blue robe were innocent of braid, which marked her as junior faculty. Her name, which she offered in a trembling whisper, was "Irthyn Jonis, Comparative Mythology."

"Scholar Jonis," he murmured, and she smiled nervously, dipped her head and made an escape.

He straightened, one hand resting lightly on the head of his stick. A very good stick it was, black ironwood, collared in silver; the grip bound in leather, so that it would not easily escape inattentive fingers. Simple though it was, it signaled his status to others of the community, and was otherwise useful.

Do you think, asked the voice inside his head, *that's everyone?*

It might, he thought, glancing about him, very well be everyone. He hadn't counted, though he supposed someone might have. Dean Zorminsen was in deep conversation with First Director Verlin at some remove from the reviewing station where he and his auditor stood. Likewise, there were clumps of scholars all about, none seeming particularly interested in the new tenant of the prestigious—no, he was wrong.

Two junior scholars were coming toward him, arm in arm. Lovers, he thought, or at the least old and comfortable friends, one dark and rounded, the other angular, her hair a wispy, middling brown. They approached with firm steps, heads high, the dark-haired one allowing a pinch of cynicism to be seen, her friend openly curious.

Ah, said the voice inside his head.

The dark-haired scholar slipped her arm free and stepped forward first, showing him the palms opened like a book, which was the style here.

"Ella ben Suzan," she said, in a fine, no-nonsense voice, "History of Education."

He bowed the bow between equals.

"Scholar ben Suzan," he murmured, committing name and face to memory.

She gave him a firm nod and stepped aside, tarrying a half-dozen steps out to await her friend.

"Kamele Waitley," said the friend, bringing pale hands together to form the open book. "History of Education."

Ella ben Suzan's voice had been fine, but to hear

Kamele Waitley speak was to wish for her to speak
again, perhaps to recite some poetry or—

"You are a singer, Scholar Waitley?" he asked.

Blue eyes widened, a flush stained her pale cheeks,
and her shoulders stiffened beneath her robe. For
an instant, he thought that he had overstepped the
bounds of custom, but she recovered herself with a
slight smile.

"I'm a member of a chorale," she acknowledged.
"Recreational only, of course. My studies are my life's
work."

"Certainly," he said carefully, "study illuminates the
lives of all scholars. Yet there must be room for rec-
reation as well, and joy in those things which are not
study. I myself find a certain pleasure in ... outdoor
pursuits." The smile he offered was a mirror of her own.

"Outdoor?" She looked at him doubtfully. "Outside
the Wall?"

He raised an eyebrow. "There is a whole planet outside the Wall," he murmured. "Surely you were aware?"

Blue eyes sparkled, though her demeanor remained
grave. "I've heard it said," she replied. "But tell
me—what manner of pleasure may be had outside
of the Wall?"

"Why, all manner!" he declared, pleased with her.
"Gardening, fishing, walking among the trees and growing things, watching the sun set, or the stars rise ..."

"Watching the sun set?" Another doubtful look.
"That seems a very ... fleeting pleasure."

"I have heard it argued that the highest pleasures
are ephemeral, and best enjoyed in retrospect," he
said, the voice inside his head crying out, *Not so!*
"Though there are those of us who disagree."

Kamele Waitley glanced to one side. Following her gaze, he saw that her friend had left them, moving away in the company of a tall, bluff scholar, the braid on his sleeve gleaming new, and felt a pang for her own loss of pleasure.

"Forgive me," he began, but she shook quick fingers at him—a meaningless gesture, though for a split second he thought...

"I think we must have been the last faculty to introduce ourselves," she said seriously. "Would you like a glass of the Dean's sherry?"

As it happened, he had previously had a glass of the Dean's sherry and found it execrable, though he could hardly say so—and besides, Kamele Waitley was still talking.

"I'd like to learn more about the pleasures of watching the sun set, if you'd be kind enough to teach me."

It was, still, easier in the dark. In the dark, he could imagine that she was lying beside him, her voice a murmur accessible to the outer ears. Sometimes, in the dark, for whole minutes at a time, he could imagine her head on his shoulder, a silken leg thrown over his...

"Aelliana," he said now, staring up into the darkness. "What are you planning?"

Planning, van'chela?

He snorted lightly. "No, *that* will not do, minx. Tell me—what necessity drives us to escort Scholar Waitley to a local sunset?"

She asked so nicely, his dead lifemate said. *Besides, I like her. Don't you like her, Daav?*

"She's well enough."

Oh, clench-fisted, van'chela! she chided him *How has the scholar offended you?*

He sighed, and closed his eyes against the darkness.

"The scholar is blameless," he admitted, ashamed of his churlishness. "Indeed, I enjoyed our discussion, and would, I feel, enjoy another. She has a ready wit and seems not so bound by local culture as . . . others of my colleagues."

"In fact," Aelliana murmured, "she might well be someone who could become a good friend."

"I did not," he said tiredly, "come here to make friends."

Indeed you did not. I only ask you to pity poor Professor Kiladi, separated from clan and kin, wholly unsupported in a strange and cloistered environment. A man in such circumstances might have need of a friend—or even two.

"Professor Kiladi is a fabrication, my lady . . ."

Professor Kiladi has published widely, his scholarship is noteworthy, and his achievements undeniable, Aelliana said tartly. *He is a work of art,* van'chela; *a work of art with a heart and a soul, sorrows and joys. You owe him at the least a brother's care, yet you drive him and make demands of him and allow him not a single joy or pleasure. I never knew you to be so meager, Daav. It troubles me. Indeed, it troubles me deeply.*

Tears pricked his eyes—his or hers, it scarcely mattered. Nor did it matter that the fabrication of Jen Sar Kiladi had begun as a game; twenty years, three degrees, and dozens of scholarly papers, hundreds of students . . . Surely, Jen Sar Kiladi was every bit as alive as—as Daav yos'Phelium.

...or perhaps more.

Daav?

"Aelliana..." he gasped, the slow tears suddenly fast and hot. "Aelliana..."

He twisted, burying his face in the flat pillow, sobbing, and seeing it all, all again—the street, the flash, her hair swirling as she leapt to shield him, the blood, the blood...

Some time later, as he lay shivering and exhausted, he felt her stroke his hair, then slip close and put her arms around him. And so at last he fell asleep, imagining that she held him.

PARTIAL LIADEN LEXICON

· · · · · · · · · · · · · · ·

a'nadelm	Heir to the nadelm.
a'thodelm	Heir to the thodelm.
a'trezla	Lifemates.
al'bresh venat'i	Formal phrase of sorrow for another Clan's loss, as when someone dies.
binjali	Excellent.
cantra	Liaden unit of currency, named for Cantra yos'Phelium.
cha'leket	Heartkin; a person for whom one feels a sibling's affection.
cha'dramliza	A Healer. PLURAL: cha'dramliz.
chernubia	Confected delicacy.
chiat'a bei kruzon	Dream sweetly.
coab minshak'a	"Necessity exists."
delm	Head of clan.
delmae	Lifemate of a delm.

denubia Darling.

dramliza A wizard. PLURAL: dramliz (The dramliz...).

eklykt'i Unreturned.

Eldema First Speaker (most times, the delm).

Eldema-pernard'i First-Speaker-In-Trust.

Flaran Cha'menthi "I(/We) Dare," Korval's motto.

ge'shada Mazel tov; congratulations.

Glavda Empri yo'Lanna's house.

indra Uncle.

Jelaza Kazone The Tree, also Korval's Own House. Approx. "Jela's Fulfillment."

Korval-pernard'i See "Eldema-pernard'i."

Megelaar The Dragon on Korval's shield.

melant'i Who one is in relation to current circumstances. ALSO who one is in sum, encompassing all possible persons one might be.

menfri'at Liaden karate.

mirada Father.

misravot Altanian wine; blue in color.

nadelm Heir to the delm.

nubiath'a Gift given to end an affair of pleasure.

prena'ma	Storyteller.
prethliu	Rumorbroker.
qe'andra	Person of business, i.e. an accountant.
relumma	Division of a Liaden year, equaling 96 Standard Days. Four relumma equal one year.
thawla	Mother.
thawlana	Grandmother.
thodelm	Head of Line.
tra'sia volecta	Good morning.
Trealla Fantrol	The yos'Galan house.
Tree-and-Dragon	Korval; a reference to their clan sign of a winged dragon over a tree.
Valcon Berant'a	Dragon's Price or Dragon Hoard, the name of Korval's valley.
Valcon Melad'a	*Dragon's Way*, the Delm's Own ship.
van'chela	Beloved friend.
va'netra	Charity case, lame puppy.

STANDARD YEAR

8 Standard Days in One Standard Week

32 Standard Days in One Standard Month

384 Standard Days in One Standard Year

LIADEN YEAR

96 Standard Days in One Relumma

12 Standard Months in One Standard Year

One Relumma = Eight 12-day weeks

Four Relumma = One Standard Year

ABOUT THE AUTHORS

SHARON LEE AND STEVE MILLER live in the rolling hills of Central Maine with three insistent muses in the form of cats and a large cast of characters. The husband-and-wife team's collaborative work in science fiction and fantasy include seventeen novels and numerous short stories in their award-winning Liaden Universe®. In addition to their collaborative work, Steve has seen short stories, nonfiction, and reviews published under his name, while Sharon has seen published short stories, newspaper pieces, two mystery novels, and *Carousel Tides*.

Steve was the founding curator of the University of Maryland's Kuhn Library Science Fiction Research Collection and a former Nebula juror. For five years, Sharon served the Science Fiction and Fantasy Writers of America, consecutively as Executive Director, Vice President and President. Sharon's interests include music, seashores and pine cones. Steve also enjoys music, plays tournament chess, and collects cat whiskers.

The following is an excerpt from:

GHOST SHIP

SHARON LEE & STEVE MILLER

Available from Baen Books
August 2011
hardcover

ONE

· · · · · · ·

Bechimo

THE GALAXY WAS UNDERGOING CHANGE.

This was empirical. *Bechimo* was not one for flights of fancy; nor for humor. Sadness, yes; and yearning. Those had been close companions; comrades of long standing—gone now to brilliant ash as a new and vivid emotion flared into being.

Its name...

Bechimo consulted archives, cross-referencing psych and legend, which search matrix had yielded insight during past periods of disruption. Nor did it fail this time.

The burning new emotion was called...

Hope.

The emotion that had prompted the opening of the hatch, admitting a man who was not on the Approved List—*that* had been despair. Despair had found the berth, nestled in among the Old Ones. Those who were able had taken note of *Bechimo*'s arrival, sharing such data and comfort as they might. In time, they failed, their voices going silent, their signatures fading out of the aether.

Others placed themselves into slumber, in order to conserve what was left to them.

Still others raved, on and on. *Bechimo* filtered those frequencies, and sat at berth, listening to silence, within, and without.

Deliberately, *Bechimo* began to shut down systems.

There was no need to move on. There was nowhere to go. No crew to serve. No captain with whom to bond. There were those others who from time to time invited communication, but they were New, not on the Approved List.

Dangerous.

Bechimo was alone. It was best to sleep, here among the others not precisely of one's kind, but near enough.

Near enough.

Sleep, *Bechimo* did.

Until—*Bechimo*'s safeguards registered the arrival of a ship—nothing more than metal and programs, less aware than the slumbering Old Ones.

The man, though...the *pilot*. Not on the Approved List, no. In all the time since...since...

In more than five hundred Standard Years, no one on the Approved List had requested entry.

Bechimo entertained the theory that the Approved List might be incomplete.

The man—the pilot—put his hand, respectfully, against the plate.

Bechimo took the reading, accessed archives; ascertained that this person was not on the *Dis*approved List, and—

Opened the hatch.

The pilot came aboard. He toured, monitored closely by *Bechimo*. He comported himself well, inspecting without taking liberties, and came at last to the Heart, where he sat in the second seat.

Having achieved this much, however, it seemed that the pilot lost purpose. For long seconds, he sat, unmoving, possibly reviewing an internal logic-tree. He might have reason to assess his situation, were *Bechimo* as much of a surprise to him as he had been to *Bechimo*.

And yet—a pilot aboard, for the first time in…in…

Perhaps he was merely uncertain of his next proper move, *Bechimo* thought. That might well be so.

A prompt was therefore sent to the B screen.

Please insert command key.

The pilot accepted the prompt, looking about him and taking up a key from among the objects on the catch-bench between the two seats. Perhaps he hesitated, holding the key in his hand. *Bechimo* registered increased heart rate, deeper breathing, a slight dampness of the palm cradling the key, and felt a thrill of what might have been fear, that the pilot would rise without completing the sequence.

In the moment that *Bechimo* thought he would rise and depart, the pilot instead sat sharply forward and placed the key properly in the board.

Bechimo—that flash of heat, of *hope*—*Bechimo* accepted him.

Samples were taken, and archived; systems were introduced to this, their Less Pilot. *Bechimo* stood by to receive orders.

The pilot, though—Win Ton yo'Vala was his designation. The pilot abruptly turned the command key to the off position. It was no matter, though it would not do for him to leave it behind, were he to exit the ship. *Bechimo* sent a prompt, reminding the pilot to remove the key.

This he did, appearing suddenly agitated. *Bechimo* considered administering a calmative, but the pilot's stress levels were somewhat below those readings necessitating such action.

The pilot Win Ton yo'Vala took the other command key from its place on the bench, stood, returned to the hatch—and exited.

Bechimo puzzled over this, coming at last to understand that process was at work, and rightly so. First came the Less Pilot, to inspect, and to declare himself. Once satisfied that all was in order, the Less Pilot would report to the Captain-candidate, and present the Over Pilot's key. Did the key accept, then properly would Pilot yo'Vala escort the Captain to *Bechimo*, and the Builders Promise would be fulfilled.

The keys retained contact, as was their function, and thus *Bechimo* knew when the Captain's key left the Less Pilot and entered the keeping of another. That other, however, did not propose themselves. It would seem that the key had become cargo.

Systems alert—even feverish, were such a thing possible—*Bechimo* stirred in the berth among the Old. Stirred, but did not disengage.

The key could be recalled, If necessary. Yet *Bechimo* chose to believe that the Less Pilot had acted with what he considered to be honor. Perhaps, indeed, the Less Pilot had sent the Overkey away while he decoyed enemies of the ship.

Such things had happened before.

It was that memory that impelled *Bechimo*'s careful disengagement from berth, the rippleless slide between the fabric of space. Best, perhaps, to be near when the key found the Captain. Enemies were no light matter.

Bechimo followed the Captain's key, and thus knew the instant that the Captain-candidate received it, and was found fitting. Hope flared ever brighter. *Bechimo* drew nearer yet, slipped fully into space...

But the Captain did not divert the course of her dumb vessel, nor order *Bechimo* to stand for boarding.

Slipping away, *Bechimo* monitored the situation. It would appear that the Captain, also, was in a state of flux. On consideration, *Bechimo* again withdrew to the berth among the Old Ones, trusting that the Captain would come, when it was safe to do so.

Time passed.

The Captain did not come.

Others came, as others had before, not on the Approved List and lacking that quality which had moved *Bechimo* to open for Pilot yo'Vala. These *others* behaved as pirates, and thus *Bechimo* issued a warning that even pirates might comprehend. They withdrew—and returned in force, wielding weapons, hull-cutters, overrides.

The answer to this was well known. *Bechimo* did what was required, in defense, as the Builders had taught.

And still the Captain did not come.

Worse, Less Pilot yo'Vala fell into the hands of another band of pirates, who introduced programming in opposition to his native environment. *Bechimo*, no longer safe among the Old, informed by the key, slipped closer, though hidden still. From a prudent proximity, those things that could be done were, including influencing to Pilot yo'Vala's cause those of the Old which were enslaved by the pilot's captors. An escape was effected, but not before the pilot had experienced file corruption on a catastrophic level. The key wavered, then, and would have withdrawn. *Bechimo* overrode its impulse; it was for the Captain to say who of the crew was worthy. Thus the key remained with the damaged pilot.

Until it reported itself in proximity, yet physically estranged from the Less Pilot.

Bechimo understood this to be process. The pilot's compatriots would of course work to restore him to precorruption conditions. It was understood that such restoration might consume some time. It was understood that, sometimes, such processes failed of restoring...all. And yet, it was the Builders Law: the Captain alone decided, for the crew, for the cargo— and for the Less Pilot.

Prior to the Less Pilot's estrangement, both keys had been in the same place. *Bechimo* had moved then, slipping between the layers of space, certain that, now, at last—but the keys separated.

Bechimo translated to a less chancy location, and entered normal space, simultaneously noting an anomaly in this well-known quarter. Cautious sampling was performed. Recordings were made. Data, in a word, was gathered, analyzed and filed.

Bechimo slipped away between the layers of space, to another location, and so remained, listening to the keys, harvesting that data which came across the common bands, the while musing upon the alteration of the galaxy, and the fragile durability of hope.

—end excerpt—

from *Ghost Ship*
available in hardcover,
August 2011, from Baen Books